David M Henley has worked in Australian trade publishing for many years and grown a successful design and publishing studio, written and illustrated two esoteric novellas (*The Museum of Unnatural History* and *Bumbly Goes Forth*) and one love poem (*The Story So Far*), has featured in multiple exhibitions and is the art director and co-founder of *Seizure*, a magazine for new writing. He is based in Sydney, Australia, but can be found on the Weave.

pierrejnr.com
Twitter @DavidMHenley
facebook.com/TerenceBumbly

# THE HUNT FOR
# PIERRE JNR

## DAVID M HENLEY

HARPER
Voyager

**Harper*Voyager***
An imprint of HarperCollins*Publishers*

First published in Australia in 2013
by HarperCollins*Publishers* Australia Pty Limited
ABN 36 009 913 517
harpercollins.com.au

**HarperCollins*Publishers***
Level 13, 201 Elizabeth Street, Sydney NSW 2000, Australia
31 View Road, Glenfield, Auckland 0627, New Zealand
A 53, Sector 57, Noida, UP, India
77–85 Fulham Palace Road, London W6 8JB, United Kingdom
2 Bloor Street East, 20th floor, Toronto, Ontario M4W 1A8, Canada
10 East 53rd Street, New York NY 10022, USA

National Library of Australia Cataloguing-in-Publication entry:

Henley, David M.
  The hunt for Pierre Jnr / David M. Henley.
  ISBN: 978 0 7322 9560 8 (pbk.)
A823.4

Cover design by Matt Stanton, HarperCollins Design Studio
Cover images by shutterstock.com
Typeset in Sabon by Kirby Jones
Printed and bound in Australia by Griffin Press
The papers used by HarperCollins in the manufacture of this book are a natural,
recyclable product made from wood grown in sustainable plantation forests. The fibre
source and manufacturing processes meet recognised international environmental
standards, and carry certification.

5 4 3 2 1     13 14 15 16

*For Alice, my light and love*

# Pierre Jnr is eight years old

Newton Pembroke was happy to be home. He'd flown back from his prospecting in the midlands with a buoyant heart and an appreciation for everything that met his eye. He landed his squib outside his house and, grabbing his aluminium attaché, sauntered inside.

'Darlin'?' he called.

A woman with overlapping curls of short blonde hair came out from the kitchen. There was flour on her hands, forearms and the navy dress she was wearing. Gail was obviously experimenting with manual cooking again. Normally when Newton saw the ridiculous occupations his wife employed to pass the time he would sigh; today, he smiled.

'What is it, Newton? I'm in the middle of some scones.'

'So it would appear.' He grinned, and came close enough to give her a small kiss on the cheek.

'Despite appearances, I did not mean that literally.' She liked it when he was nice to her. Not that he was ever *mean* to her; it was just that life hadn't turned out for him as he had planned and he was sometimes a bit dour. She turned back to the kitchen and spoke over her shoulder, 'How was your day then? Something has put you in a good mood.'

'Yes. I do seem to be in a good mood, don't I?' Newton's search for reasons was short and ended with a shrug. 'Nothing in particular, except I did come across this remarkable family today.'

'Remarkable how?' Gail was bent over a bowl of wet off-white mixture, brow furrowed and not really listening.

'Well, it's hard to explain really. I was out in the midlands looking for acquisitions and I stopped at this farmhouse where a family was outside, playing.'

'Uh huh ...' Gail nudged the story along while trying to understand the instructions in the recipe book beside her. She couldn't tell if the mixture before her matched the description of what it was supposed to look like. Were her circles 'short'?

'Anyway, the thing is, the entire family was focused on the little boy. I can't quite explain it, as it took me a moment to realise what was happening, but they orbited him like planets, bringing him food, water, or wiping his chin. He just sat on the grass as the others moved around him and he didn't say a word the whole time I was there.'

'Maybe he was shy.'

'Maybe, but it was almost unnerving the way he watched me. He seemed a very strange little boy — intense, murky — but he left me with a good feeling about him. You should meet him.'

'Me?' Gail squawked. Newt sometimes had odd ideas. *Why in the world would I want to go to the midlands to meet some creepy child?*

'He wants to learn to read. Didn't you say you wanted to help people? Now's your chance.'

4

'I never said I wanted to teach midland lumps.'

'They're not lumps. Their farm is functional, and their house is quaint and clean. You'd love it.'

'I would?' Gail was beginning to wonder what had got into her husband. Did he really expect her to squib out to the midlands to teach a lump the alphabet? 'Really, dear, I'm not sure.'

'Trust me. Tell me you'll go. What if I went with you?'

'Well, maybe.'

He nodded with pleasure, so glad that he had made her agree. Gail looked down at her hands and began scraping the mixture off her fingers. She had lost the impetus to cook.

It was, as they say, only 'a hop and a squib' to get to the midlands. The Pembrokes lived in old Tennessee, just on the edge of the metropolitan area, and the squib needed a quick recharging to make the distance. The midlands were the unprotected zones between the two weather-controlled areas of the east and west coasts, where the big farms used to be. Now, any farms that still existed struggled with temperamental grazing lands and scattered herds. Making a living out here was a risky — some might say unnecessary — pursuit for throwbacks and reclusives.

Husband and wife spoke very little during the journey; she had become used to him having notions and found that the best way to deal with them was simply to let him tire himself out. Why it had to involve her, she had no idea, but she was happy when they began descending toward a double-storey whiteboard house. At least now her husband's fascination might be explained.

They landed on a patch of previously flattened dry grass. The squib doors opened and Gail stepped outside. *It's often hot in the midlands*, she thought, and she raised her hand to protect her eyes. When it wasn't hot, it was typically raining and being decimated by twisters. The midlands took the brunt of the weather's extremes.

'Come on, Newt, let's get this over with. Newt?' She turned around to find him slumped over the dashboard. 'What are you doing?' She leant in and shook his shoulder. 'Newt?' In alarm she clambered back inside and felt for his pulse. He was alive, but unwakeable. She pushed him back into his seat and ordered, 'Computer, patch me into Services, quickly.'

There was no response. All the power seemed to have drained from the vehicle. Gail screamed in frustration and panic. After a final ineffective shake of her husband, she rushed into the house, calling for help, but received no answer.

Her eyes adjusted slowly to the darkness inside, diminished only by the dry light pushing through the brown curtains into the haze. The place was like a museum, one dedicated to the poverty of a previous century, and she sniffed at the baked air and the smell of degrading synthetics.

Her next call for help caught in her throat as she recognised shapes in the room: a man lying on the floor, a pair of children folded over the arms of a giant settee, a woman slumped in the doorway to the dining room as if she'd become exhausted trying to push the doors closed. They were alive, breathing dully, like Newton, but flopped carelessly about like dirty laundry.

'I am glad you came.'

A voice from behind made Gail jump. It was a boy about eight years old, obviously the one her husband had spoken of. 'What's wrong with everyone?' she asked.

'Nothing is wrong. Do not be afraid.'

Newton never mentioned the size of the boy's head. She was surprised he could stand up straight. 'My husband has collapsed. I need help.'

'It is okay. I understand.' He didn't speak like a little boy. His diction was immaculate with a confidence bordering on arrogance. 'They are just asleep. It is good to let them sleep when you are not using them.'

Though she looked at him from above, it seemed that he was beginning to tower over her. She was in his shadow and he tilted his eyes down upon her. His lips pulled back as if smiling. She was terrified and then her fear was slipping from her as though a drug was calming her, stripping her emotions while keeping her conscious, and she knew that it was because of him, and it was good that it was him. He was inside her head, where she wanted her darling little boy to be.

She reached down and he reached up, their hands meeting with a friendly squeeze. 'Am I your mother now?' Gail asked.

'Yes. You shall take care of me and show me the world.'

'I love you, Pierre.'

'I love you too, Mother.'

# His whereabouts are unknown

Peter Lazarus checked into a sweetheart motel with a minimum stay of fifteen minutes. The room was a polyplastic reformable, a self-contained unit of pull-out benches, bed and bathroom, washed down and sterilised after every visit.

He folded his legs beneath him on the bed and calmed his thoughts. He was used to such places and, as voyeuristic as they may have seemed to other telepaths, the good thing about sweetheart motels was that people kept to themselves and didn't ask questions. It was one of the only places a man like him could hide.

The walls might block out the sounds in the other rooms, but nothing could protect him from the mental gyrations in the sex lives of others. In the cube of his room he couldn't help but read the thoughts of the people around him.

On the floor above there were three couples within his range, plus another man who was sitting alone. On either side of him was a *ménage à trois* and a room being cleaned. Below, a woman slept while her lover spoke with his wife. The trysts of the masses were enacted time and again in these boxes, the saga of the ages, the ebb and flow of lust. Pete sighed and thought how nice it would be to sit in this room without picking up the thoughts around him. It was built for silence, but not the silence he needed.

n up in this area until he was thirteen; a bay
negapolis. He'd taken the north-south tracks
 his last day of freedom to be by the seaside.
were the former Serviceman route that was opened
to the public when the weather went haywire a century ago, an
underground series of moving walkways that could take you
across the city in as much, or as little, time as you wanted it to
take.

Pete liked the tracks. They were dimly lit, surrounded by
subterranean piping and pulsing with a steady stream of
bouncing walkers. The articulated path clicked regularly
over certain joins … thck thck thck thck. Fading closer, then
diminishing as he overtook them and moved on. The passing
murmur of thoughts lapped over him, too quickly for him to
discern clearly. Pete was happy.

On his way out from the motel, Pete swiped his carte
through the auto-clerk, paying forward for the whole night.
He was spending big and had chosen this particular sweetheart
motel for being across the road from the beach and just a short
walk from the expensive French restaurant that had become his
traditional place for last meals.

This was his third visit to La Nouvelle Maison. From the
outside it was a small peach-walled block in the shadow of
the window-dotted towers that built up like a mountain range
behind. The owners had furnished the inside with any wooden
furniture they could get their hands on. The slab walls were
covered in flocked wallpaper, divided with heavy curtains that
implied there were windows behind them. The hum and slur of
the city were successfully blocked and replaced with the tinker

of plates and cutlery and wisps of discreet conversation. Pete chose the duck and a carménère vintage that was distinctly outside his normal budget.

His first visit had been when he was thirteen, before they took him to the psi-camps. His father wasn't a bad man, he continued to remind himself; they had both known Pete would be taken the next day. His father because he had arranged it and Pete because … well, because of what he was. It was an odd repetition of events for him, actively leading himself through the same steps that would result in his renewed incarceration.

The wine had depth and the duck was luscious with flavour. The gratin potatoes were made with convincing butter.

All his life he'd shunned the thoughts of others, overwhelmed by the range and breadth of what was truly on people's minds. The alcohol played its part, but he was unusually tranquil and let the pandemonium walk and dance around him, seeing but not looking, hearing but not listening. He knew it was unfair, the way things were for psis, but, on the other hand, being a telepath made it easy for him to understand what Services had to worry about; if he was more malicious than he was, they would be right to impose their strictures.

There was an estimated population of ten thousand psis worldwide, although it was unclear to him what data this was based on. Of these, some were cured and the others were sent to the islands. A very few found the cracks and escaped the prescribed fates.

For dessert he had a selection of cheeses. It was all rather delicious, which was as it should be for a last meal.

Pete stared at the empty chair across from him. It seemed as though a barrier was coming down in his mind. Now that he had decided to turn himself in, the closer the moment came the more it seemed his life of hiding was someone else's life, and another him was now returning ... the world he knew as a boy, before it changed so suddenly.

Then he thought of his sister. He had seen her born. Had held her that very first night and they'd known each other. Instantly.

He had only seen her two times after that. Once when she needed him and once when he found her too late. The memory made him angry. The first time he knew her. The second time he knew it wasn't her. The last morsels of his meal lost their flavour.

He thought momentarily about finding a partner for the night, but he wasn't very good at ignoring another's thoughts mid-coitus and it was all rather unappealing. Instead he returned to his room, took a double dose of dreamers and lay back. Thoughts, emotions and dilemmas swallowed him whole and he fell asleep.

The next morning Pete Lazarus woke and walked to the beach for one last swim before turning himself in.

The water was too cold for most swimmers, and only a few women dotted the beach to catch the early sun. They were sleepy under the warmth so their thoughts were peaceful to him, except for one lady with overlarge sunglasses who watched him approach the waves, her thoughts too tawdry for his liking.

The day was bright, the million reflections brighter. In the shallows small waves wet and re-wet the sand, sucking the ground from under his feet and sinking him centimetre by centimetre into the beach. It had been a while since he had last swum, and the sight of a pontoon in the middle of the bay called to him. It wasn't too far.

The waves pushed back at him. Crisp coolness and the potent sunlight energised his muscles. He clambered onto the old planks and air-dried while watching the horizon move up and down with the swell.

The ocean glittered. The sun and wind were hitting the waves, creating a shimmer that blinded if stared at for too long. Pete closed his eyes and lay back, letting the waves roll him up and down and the light imprint striking red patterns through his eyelids.

He could hardly hear the people on the beach now, nor their thoughts, for which he was grateful. This could well be the last moment of peace he would ever know.

The first problem was proving his Citizenship, which Pete refused to do. That would trigger a lockdown before he could get out the words he needed them to hear.

'I would like to see Lieutenant Baumer, at his convenience,' was all he would say.

'On what business?'

'For now I will keep that private.'

'As you wish,' the ugly man sneered.

Pete was more familiar with small minds than most, and this man was a typical example. Typical to Services and typical to humanity at large.

It was his right as a Citizen to request an audience with the commanding officer, in this case Senior Lieutenant Baumer.

The choice of offices for his surrender was not an arbitrary affair and he'd settled on this particular bureau after probing half the Servicemen of the city. The last thing he wanted was a hothead; what he wanted was a man like the Lieutenant.

Nobody but a telepath could know that Baumer had unspoken sympathies for psis — his mother had been persecuted for some minor talent — but he was also a rigid officer who followed regulations and that was precisely what Pete was counting on.

There was, of course, no privacy possible in this building. Services offices were permanently under surveillance, as were all public areas, and refusing to reveal his business as he had done was one sure way of flagging himself for closer attention, thus the officer's sneer.

Behind him a younger man, straight of back, uniform buttoned and wired to regulation, opened a door and invited Pete through to a closed room. Baumer had a casual and confident manner, despite beginning an interview that had instant complications. They sat across an empty table, wondering about the other.

People like Baumer were essential to Services. Without men and women who could relate to the public, resentment would quickly build against the institution. Pete suspected the Lieutenant had some of his mother's empathy and might be able to sense that he had come in peace. Or so he hoped.

'I am obliged to tell you this interview is being actively monitored.'

'I understand. Thank you, Lieutenant Baumer.'

The young man raised an eyebrow at the use of his name without any formal introduction. 'We are having some trouble with your records, sir. Can you explain why this might be, and please begin by stating your name for the record.'

'What's in a name?' Pete teased. The Lieutenant put on a professional not-amused expression, though Pete knew he was a little entertained by the answer. 'I have many names.'

'You are a Citizen?'

'I have been.'

'But one who won't reveal his identity. You understand that I must treat you as a non-Citizen?'

'Of course.' Pete paused to read over Baumer's mind; the Lieutenant was listening to the remote communications of his superiors while keeping his eyes locked onto Pete's. He was being ordered to gather more information and advised that the status of the interview had been raised another level. 'Before I begin, I have a request.'

'A man with no clear identity does not have the rights of a Citizen, sir.'

'It is a small request, in light of the fact that I have come to you of my own free will, am not hostile and, if required, will freely accept any restraints you deem necessary. I also understand that any rights I have as a Citizen will be revoked once I reveal myself.'

'This interview has been regraded.' Baumer repeated the words as if wired straight to his lips. This meant more people were watching the interview. Underneath he was becoming worried and was pondering the need to order a facility lockdown. 'You are offering yourself into custody? For what crimes?'

'No crimes.' Pete swallowed. 'I have committed no harmful acts. I am here to offer my services.'

17

'What is your name, sir?' the Lieutenant demanded.

Pete for a moment didn't answer. The small room suddenly felt smaller as it hermetically sealed itself and the air-conditioning closed off. They were preparing to gas him and the Lieutenant both; they were simply waiting for confirmation of their computed suspicions.

'My name is Peter Lazarus, Citizen W4 3358Q AG210385 of Los Angeles.' He heard the disapproving hiss of venting gas. 'I have come to help in the hunt for —' He looked at Baumer's alarmed and rapidly drooping eyes. His voice became wet, lips nearly too heavy to release the words, 'Pierre Jnr.'

The Lieutenant slumped in his chair as if his soul had oozed out through his feet. Pete imagined he must look the same before his head fell back and he passed out.


Pierre stood on a stool to be measured and let the tailor waiting at his feet see the real him. He didn't often reveal himself, instead keeping an image in watchers' minds of a normal eight-year-old boy. It was what they expected to see, so it was quite easy for him to do. Now he stood bared, not naked by literal definitions, but naked for him, reflected in the tall mirrors that stood *en garde* around the walls.

He tipped his head towards the balding tailor at his feet, who looked up at him with the stiffness of awe and fear, mesmerised by the monstrous head and the tatty hair that was unable to cover the lively streaks around Pierre's skull. *Am I such a fearsome sight?*

Pierre put a soft hand on the man's pate and placatingly stroked the surviving white hair. 'You may start.' He smiled.

# Many believe he does not exist

Pete awoke under a mask. He knew what it was, though he'd never been under one before. Masks were used to keep prisoners and patients unconscious and obedient. He blinked under the opaque face-plate as it depressurised from his face with a stiff sigh.

One by one his senses slowly returned to him. His ears told him he was in a large open space. They also told him it sounded dark, but he put this down to a minor synaesthesia caused by the fading intoxications.

Sight was the last sense to return to him. Blinking to clear his eyes, Pete saw an old man in uniform snoring softly in a leather armchair across from him. An enormous moustache of white and ginger rose and fell with the dry snores, matched in magnificence only by an equally daring pair of eyebrows.

Attempting to move, Pete found himself bound to his chair, which was secured to the floor. Around him a line of servitors lit up at his struggle, tracking his every move with ominously steady weapons. He was square in the middle of an empty pre-slab hangar, the floor and walls composed entirely of reconstituted stone hexagons that tiled out forty paces in each direction. The space echoed with the tracking adjustments of the robot *gendarmes* that lined each wall. He wondered if they had built this prison just for him.

*Oh, well, it was to be expected.* Pete forced himself to relax. He was, after all, a wanted fugitive, a dreaded psi; he could hardly blame them for their precautions.

He coughed politely and the snores ceased. Silently the origami of the Serviceman's eyelids folded in and watery eyes peered through the eyebrow canopy.

'Yes?' the old man said.

'Where am I?' Pete asked, finding himself too drowsy to tap into the man's thoughts.

'I could ask you the same thing,' the old man objected, straightening in his seat and looking around him. Slowly he nodded and stroked his facial hair as if it was a pet that required comforting. 'Ah, yes, I remember now. We're in isolation.'

'I can see that. Who are you?'

'No point getting tetchy with me, boy.'

Pete was at last confused. Nobody had called him 'boy' for thirty years. This wasn't exactly how he thought Services would react to his submission.

'I am Colonel Abercrombie Pinter, and the Will has assigned me as your intermediary. Aren't you meant to be a mind-reader?'

'I'm still a little drugged,' Pete defended himself. Now he understood. They were putting a retired inconsequential in charge of him, so as not to risk the mind of anyone important. Damn it. It would have been better to have had a remote as his case-worker. 'What do they intend to do with me?'

'I am quite sure you would know more than I do. The request only came through last night, and most of that time I've spent asleep. I haven't even had any breakfast yet. Are you hungry?'

'Yes,' Pete responded, his stomach momentarily taking over his priorities. 'Thank you.'

The Colonel stood and walked to the farthest wall, where a servitor stepped forward with two trays. It was curious that they had chosen this method. *Why an old man? And why is he only half-wired? Is he too old, or is it another precaution?*

They ate a typical Serviceman breakfast: rashers of bacon, an orange mash of some sort and an eggy goo spiced with extra nutrition.

'Tell me more about yourself. What do you do as a psi? To make a living, I mean.'

'I work as an investigator mostly.'

'Do your clients know what you are?'

Pete declined to answer. Of course they didn't; he wasn't that kind of person. It was well known that only Advocates and casinos made overt use of telepaths, siphoning the thoughts of others for their own exploitation. 'I'm not what you think.'

'Well, you would know.'

Pete tried again to feel the other man's thoughts, but he was still foggy. The Colonel looked friendly but presented himself as standoffish, and everything he said seemed tinged with something else. *Humour? Sadism?* Pete was so reliant on being able to probe people's minds, body language and tone were almost a mystery to him.

'Tell me, Mister Lazarus. What is it about this Pierre Jnr that has made you change sides?'

'There are no "sides", Colonel. Only the non-psis have created this opposition.'

23

'If you say so, my boy.'

'I do.' He bristled at the amusement the old man hid beneath his moustache, but Pete hadn't come here to talk about the psi problem. He wouldn't let that distract him.

'You were saying …?' Pinter motioned with the chunk of bread he was using to garner the last of the goo from his plate.

'Colonel, do you realise what Pierre Jnr has become to a lot of psis?'

'I'm sure I don't.'

'What exactly are your qualifications? Why did they choose you?'

'Until last night I was retired. At the moment, I am the limit of what Services will risk on your offer.'

'How does that make you feel?'

'Son, when you're in Services you serve. This isn't the worst tack I've been assigned.' Pete could tell when the Colonel was being remotely instructed; his ripostes trickled out more slowly to cover his distraction. 'Go on. Tell me more about Pierre and the psis.'

'Psis are an oppressed people — you'd agree with that, wouldn't you? It's illegal to exercise our capabilities. Suspect children are sent to camps to make sure they are "clean".'

'Facts,' the Colonel agreed, paying more interest to a cigar he had taken from his pocket.

'Well, when a psychic of Pierre's capabilities escapes the authorities and goes into hiding, what do you think happens? He's become mythic. The psis are looking for a leader and he's the prime candidate.'

'So why are you here and not with him?'

'Because he's not a saviour. He's just a boy who uses people like toys. He doesn't know what he's doing. I've seen what he does to people.'

'What do you mean? You've had contact with him?' The Colonel's rushed question came straight from the hierarchy.

'Not directly. I've just seen the results.'

'Explain.'

'It may be hard for a norm to understand, and I myself might have missed it if I wasn't already familiar with her mind before, but somehow she was … rewired. She didn't think in the same way, and parts of her memory had been deleted.'

'You use the machine analogy then?'

'Sometimes. Sometimes it is like that. Each person has recognisable patterns you can learn. Consciousness is sometimes like a point, a moving beacon. Sometimes there are multiple points of consciousness or it can be like electricity in clouds. I knew this person well, and she was changed. It was a lobotomy, Colonel.'

'Hmm. So who was this person?'

'My sister.'

'Your sister … There is no record of a sister in your files.'

'No. I had the information redacted. She only died two months ago.'

'She was like you?'

'In some ways, yes.'

'How did you manage to erase all record of her?'

'There are ways.'

'Do we have any way of verifying your claim?'

'I hope not,' Pete answered.

The Colonel smoked his cigar for a moment. Amused. 'So, what happened to her?'

'She killed herself.'

'That's not unusual with you people, is it?'

'No.' Pete swallowed that one. 'This was murder.'

'Murder by suicide?'

'That's the kind of thing Pierre Jnr is. He's not a part of humanity; he grew too fast. We are like toys to him and he is the greatest threat to our civilisation there has ever been.' Pete stared straight across; the old man stared back calmly. Underneath he was sceptical. 'Can they hear me direct?'

Pinter nodded. 'They are listening.'

'Well, why don't you and they have a moment to yourselves? I'll walk over here, the guns can point at me, and you can reach a decision.'

'That's not necessary, Mister Lazarus.'

'Damn it, Pinter, I came in of my own free will. What more can I do?'

'If you can calm yourself a moment longer, please,' the Colonel admonished gently, the corners of his lips tilting toward humour. 'What I was soon to say was that the decision of what to do with you was made long before I even arrived. You and I are merely having a conversation, getting to know each other as we await a delivery. It shouldn't be long.'

Pete looked across the table at the faded flecky eyes and peered into what was about to happen. *A symbiot lock.* He felt the old man's pity, though he could see no reflection of it on the outside.

'Okay.' Pete swallowed.

'Spoken as if you have a choice.' The smile that had been so long waiting on the dried-out lips broke open. 'In the meantime, we could practise ending our sentences with "Colonel".'

'I apologise. Colonel. I am not used to respecting Serviceman ranks.'

'Something you should master.'

'May I ask who the man in your head is? The one coming with the bot.'

'I've never met him. He's a weaver, and will be part of your team.'

'That much I know. Services' best.'

'We're not going to get along very well if you can't have a conversation like a normal person.'

Pete blinked. 'I apologise. I'm nervous.'

'I can see that.' The Colonel nodded. 'Is it the bot?'

'A bit of that. I've also got thirty death sentences aimed at my head.'

Pinter shrugged. 'They can't trust you. The botlock is the simplest fix.'

'They can trust me.'

'As you trust them?' The white eyebrows rose once more. 'Services doesn't work on trust, Mister Lazarus. Let's pause for a moment and look at these recent events from the establishment side. The problem is that we don't know why you're doing this. You say it is revenge, but we have no evidence of the crime you say has been committed. You claim a sense of duty, to protect a society that excludes you and your kind. You can speak as openly and honestly as you like, but either way you are untrusted and, so, we need some insurance.'

27

'Then I guess there are no choices for either of us.'

The Colonel laughed. 'Yes, well done.'

Pete looked above the old man's epaulets to see the large metal doors easing open for a tall, well-shouldered silhouette with a suitcase.

A table was brought and placed before Peter and the tall bearded man. Geof Ozenbach, Pete tapped from the Colonel. Services bred. A sequence baby that even a DNA test couldn't match to a mother. Surprisingly, for a man whose life was so prescribed, he seemed good-humoured and unconcerned about his current assignment.

Geof set down the anodised box and held his thumb to the locking plate until it recognised him and clicked open. The top of the case divided and receded to reveal what looked at first to be a sleeping black-skinned lizard.

The weaver reached in and gently lifted the thing out with both hands. It looked heavy, gravity dragging its shape over his fingers. He had to keep moving it from hand to hand to stop it gaining a grip.

'Hold out your arm.' Pete hesitated and the big man smiled gently. 'It's not as bad as you think. He's friendly, see? Really, there is nothing to be afraid of.'

'Get it over with and we can proceed,' Colonel Pinter drilled placidly.

'Once it's on me —' Pete cut himself off. It would crawl inside him and Services would be able to track him forever, know everything he did or said. He had been free so long ... Once it was on him, it was final; he wouldn't be able to remove it without killing himself. 'No, you're right. I made this choice already.' Slowly he lowered his arm to the table and rolled back his sleeve. Geof laid the machine down on his skin like a chef handling a fine cut of meat. It felt cool and smooth. A snake on his arm. Even as Geof moved his hands away, it slumped down, adding so much weight that Pete wasn't sure he could lift his arm.

'He's sleepy now, but he'll warm up as he goes. Just relax and let him do his thing,' Geof said in a soothing tone. 'Symbiots work with you and they'll never go deeper than you're able.'

Pete had never had a symbiot, but he knew all about them — that's why he feared them. Having a symbiot was like having a second brain, one permanently connected to the Weave, and everyone of age wore one, but it also meant Services would always know where he was and could use the symbiot against him. The one he was being fitted with was specially designed for suspects like him and could torture or kill if instructed to do so. He shivered as the scales spread, reinforcing his bondage a millimetre at a time.

Symbiots absorb energy from the bodies they are attached to: from the warmth, the beat of the pulse and the nutrients in the bloodstream. By this time tomorrow Pete's would have settled in, a new skin encasing his arm and shoulder. And gradually, as Geof explained, it would begin working with Pete's brain, tuning itself to the subtle signals until it could read it and then communicate with it. If Pete wondered what the time was, his symbiot would know and could present it screened on his wrist or in overlay on his vision. If Pete needed to calculate the volume of a swimming pool or count the people on a street, the symbiot would know, and then he would know. Apparently, or at least, as advertised, it would become a true extension of the mind, so that the bearer could perceive no distinction.

Pete was somewhat comforted by the obvious affection the big man had for the thing. He was the type who had been connected to a symbiot all his life. For him it was as natural as breathing, or growing a beard.

Pale red numbers were displayed along the skin of the bot, and Pete realised it was giving him the time: 10.13 a.m.

'Right.' Geof clapped his hands. 'Have you two eaten already?'

Geof refused the Serviceman's breakfast and insisted they find a real meal. Now that Pete was locked to a symbiot, there was nowhere in the world he could go without Services knowing about it. After a meander in a squib, they ended up at a franchise Geof was fond of for its paisley decor and generous helpings.

'Pete, when it comes to keeping your energy up for your new beast, think flapjacks and syrup. You can always tell a weaver from what they eat for breakfast.' The man had a likeable manner, and Pete relaxed. The situation wasn't as oppressive as it had seemed.

Geof ordered not only a triple serve of pancakes but also a steady stream of side-orders that soon dammed up on the tabletop. Though Pete's new colleague was built like a nineteenth-century lumberjack, the amount of food he'd consumed and the amount still on the table before him was intimidating. Pete could only lift one arm, and the constant reminder of the crawling bot took away his appetite. 'How can you eat that much?'

'I'm eating for two,' Geof laughed, tapping the crust of the symbiot that reached up from the neck of his shirt. 'You'll find you need to eat more as well, though yours is a fair bit smaller than mine.'

Stuffing one last forkful of pancakes into his mouth, he stood up and lifted his shirt to reveal his back. It was all bot. A two-inch layer of matt black lamella disappeared into his trousers and stretched over his shoulders, triceps and the rear hemisphere of his head.

*Can you hear me?* Geof thought to himself.

Pete nodded.

*But you can't project?*

*If there is need.*

'So you're not just a tapper then. Still ...' Geof hesitated, thinking in the way that weavers do, their thoughts travelling along the world's information channels before returning to the brain. 'I'm not quite sure why you're considered to be so dangerous.'

Pete watched Geof finish his second plate of pancakes, folding syrupy loads into his mouth and wiping the dish clean with his finger before leaning back and dabbing at the syrup on his beard with a napkin.

'Well, let's get this over with then. You dive in while I digest a moment.'

'I'm sorry?'

'Come on. We're going to work together, aren't we? You're going to tap my brain sooner or later, I imagine, so let's make you sure that I'm not keeping any secrets from you. We need to trust each other.'

31

Geof reclined, catching the sunlight across his face and relaxing himself for Pete to explore his mind. Pete had never encountered someone so *blasé* about having his or her brain tapped. It was unsettling, but he leant forward and concentrated on the buzz of the big man's mind.

'Where were you born?' A question that usually took someone back to their childhood. The earliest memory Pete could see was of a simple white building, tucked into a foothill covered in conifer trees; similar housing was scattered nearby.

'I don't know. I grew up in Yellowstone. I wasn't born there, but I don't remember anywhere before then.' The white building was part of a Services cluster, hothousing weavers in a competitive environment. 'Science was my mother and the Services my father. That's what we were taught.'

'But you still had a mother and father?'

'No, not really. The zygote I once was would have been generations beyond the original sperm and egg, and each step would have been resequenced. If you go by genetics alone, I don't have any relatives.'

'One of a kind then?'

'Probably not that either.'

Geof Ozenbach had been working in the data for the last thirteen years, seeking and developing ways to interpret the mountains of information that circulated the Weave, especially investigating methods to detect psis and other off-gridders. He was currently the most qualified weaver to work with Pete on finding Earth's most wanted child.

'How can you detect a psi through the Weave?' Pete prompted. Even though Geof's mind was extremely well

32

ordered, it always helped when tapping to usher people to think about what you needed them to. Otherwise you would have to become actively invasive, which was painful for the victim and somewhat risky for the interrogator.

Terms and concepts floated up that Pete couldn't understand. *Anomalies, breaches, greys, patches, black holes … direct detection.*

'I might have to get you to explain those better for me.'

'Another time. These aren't exact sciences, mere theory. But the World Union is always pushing for Parity and one of their reasons is to get rid of the places psis can hide.' Geof smirked. *It would do no good. There may be gaps in the Weave for people to hide, but that also means we know where to look. Parity would get rid of the grey areas, maybe scoop up the lesser psis, but the big fish would go into deeper hiding. Real threats always find a way, and the strongest psis could just use surrogates to avoid directly using the Weave. Pushing them to extremes will only make them more powerful.*

'You're an interesting man.'

'I'm glad you think so.'

In a strange parallel to Pete's probing, Geof was mining the available data on his new colleague, scanning the official and unofficial records regarding the non-Citizen Peter Lazarus. Pete observed this process with some fascination, not only a little shocked at the speed with which Geof processed the stream, but also at the content. He'd never known how close Services had come to capturing him.

Geof broke his concentration. 'I still can't see why you're ranked at the threat level you are, Pete. No offence, but you're just a reader who hasn't even attempted any manipulation for personal ...' Geof's voice trailed off as he figured it out. Pete was tagged as an alpha-type, a born leader.

'I have no intention —'

'Of course not.'

Pete smiled. 'Isn't there a contradiction at work when we don't wish our enemies to share the very traits we deem valuable?'

*You're not my enemy.* Geof thought these words three times to make sure Pete received the message. Out loud, he covered, 'Let me show you what I've been working on.'

Geof's vision went in and out of focus as he concentrated; whenever he was immersed in the Weave, he glazed over as if probing an old memory. When talking to Pete, he flicked between watching what was before him and visualising the data flowing from his symbiot. Of course, he could still see what was before his eyes, but it was peripheral. As his gaze focused and defocused, datastreams bounced to Pete's symb, crowding into a reading pile.

'You see, in the Weave there are anomalies and then there are abnormalities. Anomalies we get used to, they're patterns we see again and again. Some we can identify, others not, but we're used to them. Abnormalities, though, are more kinky. They are sporadic and spiky. You understand me?'

'I'm trying to.' Pete floated over Geof's inner eye, but only saw images of digital sunsets and wire-frame landscapes. 'I don't understand what I'm seeing.'

'I'm showing you some common visualisations. You can do anything with data. Most of our information is number-based, or we can attribute values along any parameters we like and in this way create an image that we can then adjust with filters and tweaking until patterns emerge. There's too much data to search the Weave by hand, so we have to use different techniques to get overviews that react usefully to the flow of information. You with me yet?'

The look on Pete's face was enough for him to continue.

'Okay, graphs are a simplistic data visualisation, and that's where it starts — ways to compare data that work with our innate bias toward visual stimuli. Like we use the analogy of the Weave for the combined Earth networks because we can only understand it that way. Strands of information that go from one point to another. They overlap. They interact. But it's not *woven* — that implies a neatness that doesn't exist on any level. When we add in *all* available information, it becomes a visual mess we can't possibly interpret, but by using abstractions we can turn the data into something we *can* see. We set conditions to limit the data and calibrate different patterns into focus. That's only part one. After you've found a pattern, then you have to figure out what it is that's going on, whether it's spending patterns, weather impacts or an amusing joke that's being passed around. A lot of the time the patterns are unidentifiable.'

'You've lost me.'

'It's not important. This is what I do. It'd help you to understand, but, then again, I don't understand what you do.'

'I feel there may be some similarities.'

'Let's talk about you,' Geof suggested, while ordering milkshakes for them both. 'Natural-born psionic, son of a

Services Sergeant ... lived without confirmed suspicion until the age of thirteen. When did *you* start questioning?'

'When I was eight. I kept hearing others' suspicions about me, in my head. Eventually I had to wonder if they were right.'

'So you were in limbo for over four years?'

'What do you mean?'

'That's what we call the time between when Services suspect a Citizen and when the subjects themselves suspect. You were on your own there for a fair while.' *What changed between you and the world in that time?*

'How long do most last?'

'Hours mostly. They start giving themselves away pretty quickly.'

'Are we ...?' Pete paused, a little reluctant to ask. 'Are we talking about what I think we're talking about?'

'You're the psychic.'

Pete leafed through the pages of Geof's mind, watching story after story of boys and girls caught out receiving extra desserts without asking, and beneficial, sometimes harmless, accidents befalling those around them. 'This is how you catch us? Hunt us down? I don't know how you live with yourself.'

*You know exactly how I live with myself.* 'I'm not the one who brings them in at least. You can look forward to that one.' *She's a humdinger.*

'Great.'

'Who did you think they'd send, Pete? If you thought you'd get the Flies With Honey Brigade, you should have thought harder. Services is amuck, my friend. Normally you'd be botbolted and dropped on the islands. The fact that you're not says they're willing to accept help, even from you.'

Of their third team member, who was finishing up her current assignment in Omskya, STOC, Pete gathered little information. His symb revealed no record of her, Pinter knew her only as *the* top anti-psi operative and Geof had only ever worked with her by proxy.

'I've run for her a few times. She's the best on the ground I've been teamed with.' What Geof didn't say aloud was that he found her cold and abrupt. 'If you need any more reassurance that Services consider Pierre Jnr a threat, putting her on the job carries some weight.' *She's ruthless, Pete. She hunts you guys down for sport.*

A week passed with Geof and Pete working in close consultation for the majority of their waking hours. They discussed at length the problem of finding and tracking their target, and Geof trained Pete to work with his symbiot, beginning with the most basic call and response exercises.

Geof: Pete. Pete. Pete.

'I think I'm hearing that. It's not like hearing it though.'

'I know the difference, Pete. Try responding.'

'Did that work?'

Geof: No.

'No?'

'No,' Geof confirmed. 'I wouldn't lie to you. Any setback would be more annoying for me than for you.' Pete had already felt the mild frustration Geof felt, but suppressed, with those of lesser tech proficiency. 'Let's try a little call and response. I'll send "tick", to which you respond "tock". Okay?'

'I'm ready.'

Geof: Tick ... Tick.

'I'm trying.'

Geof: Tick.

Pete: Tock.

Geof: Tick.

Pete: Tock.

'At last! Let's eat to celebrate.'


Tamsin Grey arrived on a Sunday and the hunt began in earnest.

There were few other patrons in their usual diner that day. A pair of youths sat at the window, plugged in and blind. They barely moved, aside from lifting squeeze-pack drinks to their lips. Two servitors rolled back and forth from the prep room. There was an older man at the back, and a woman of thirty whose table Pete, Geof and Pinter had sat near. She wore all darks with a strapped-in corset and was quite fetching. Geof had subconsciously chosen to sit where he could idly view her eating. The Colonel and Pete sat opposite and watched the entrance. Pete still found the symb cumbersome and he had to use his other arm to lift it up to the table and rest it there.

'Don't worry, Pete. It'll feel just like normal soon. Just give it another week for your body to adjust. You hungry? No? You've got to learn to eat. These things take a lot out of you, even when you're not using them.'

'Order me a caf, Ozenbach.'

'Certainly, Colonel. Pete, you should try and order for yourself. Perhaps some Pavlovian conditioning will help you get the hang of it.'

'Tock.'

Conversation quickly turned back to Pierre Jnr. It seemed the more they talked about him, the more of a mystery he became.

'We must try to understand him. What is he like? What is he after?' Pete questioned Geof. Pinter usually nodded off at this point in the discussions.

'For a start, I think we have to stop thinking of him as a child. From a learning standpoint he isn't like us. Humans learn one piece of data at a time, one thing connected to another. This kid, from what I understand, is an information sponge. He takes on data like the Weave does: linearly, yes, but so quickly it is effectively instantaneous. If he walks past someone, he can know what they know, right?'

'But can he take on skills?' Pete asked.

'Maybe, but he doesn't need to. This kid controls. If he needs a squib, he controls the driver.'

'Of course. But he still must have the development level of an eight-year-old boy. The same level of processing.'

'Why? Nothing about Pierre is normal. Not how he was born, not how he was raised, and not how he's developing.'

'You're right. You're right.' Pete threw up his hands. 'We should talk to his mother.'

'Colonel, can that be arranged? Colonel?' Geof raised his voice to rouse the snoring man.

'What? Yes, of course.' He blew out through his moustache. Colonel Pinter kept a constant link with Services decision-makers and within minutes an answer was always supplied. He didn't really need to be awake, so he wasn't. 'Interviews have been arranged with the surviving facility staff. We are to wait until Tamsin Grey joins us.'

'Where are they now? His parents, I mean.'

'The islands,' Pinter answered. 'Where else?'

A long silence condensed in the paused conversation — a typical reaction to any mention of the facility or the project. Two decades ago it had seemed like the first step to destigmatising psis, or people with psionic tendencies. In the Psionic Development Program, Doctor Yeon Rhee had created a place where psis could gather and be open about their abilities, a place for study or even to investigate ways to enhance their skills, and then for the researchers to see if it was possible to spark the talent in all humans.

Over time it became something else. The participants were restricted like prisoners 'for their own protection'. The world turned fearful of the risks psis posed. Tests became experiments, looking for 'cures' and controls. It was turning ugly long before Pierre was born.

'How do we know he even exists?' The woman from the nearby table was standing behind him. Pete had forgotten she was there, which was strange for him; he couldn't feel her mind at all …

'I'm sorry?' Pete asked as he turned to face her.

'I mean, you're going to all this trouble, gathering a little team together, pulling the great Pinter out of retirement. All based on the testimony of a non-Citizen.'

'So you would like to join us now, Grey?' Pinter invited dryly, awake for the moment.

'No, Colonel, I wouldn't. But since I've been ordered to, I shall obey.' She pulled her chair into the ring around their little table.

Pete and Geof reacted to Tamsin the way men inclined toward females always did. Sexual advantage was too much for Tamsin to pass on, and she dressed to best accentuate it. Though Geof's reaction was as she expected, she was annoyed as Pete immediately clamped down on his sexual interest. For Pete to ignore her attractions was slightly offensive, especially since it was caused by a weakness that any grown telepath should have overcome. *The poor fellow*, she thought to herself and smiled.

'Let's get the show started then. The sooner we blow the lid off this charade, the sooner I can get back to work. Colonel.' She saluted cleanly.

Pinter declined to return the antiquated gesture. 'Tamsin Grey, I'd like you to meet Peter Lazarus, volunteer, and Geof Ozenbach, who'll be running data on this operation.'

'Ozenbach. I'm glad to be able to thank you in the flesh for keeping me alive.' Tamsin reached for his hand and shook it, smiling.

Geof smiled back. 'I don't remember you needing much help.'

'A good weaver keeps it that way.' She now turned to Pete and sized him up. 'So you're the man who has the ups jumping at shadows? Why did you come in from the cold? Nobody would have cared if you had stayed there.'

Pete was still stunned by her blocked mind. *Are you real? Are you human?* Only bots and rocks were silent to a telepath.

*Real enough and more human than you want me to be*, a voice licked into his mind.

*I can't see your thoughts.*

*Fancy that. Now, answer the question. Everyone is watching.* 'Why, Mister Lazarus? For the attention? Trying to get on the inside?'

Pete slowly found his voice. 'Some things are more important. And who's jumping at shadows?'

'You are. You've got them hopped up on stories of Pierre Jnr, as if there weren't enough myths about him already.'

'I think his existence is well documented.'

'It hasn't been for the past eight years. And if this Pierre is as bad as you've got everyone thinking, then there's no way he could have — or would have — been hiding this long.'

'I have evidence. That's why I'm here.'

'What you found was a blanked mind, nothing more. You just leapt to the conclusion that it was an all-powerful, psychic eight-year-old, who no one has seen since he was born.'

'Clearly there are some people who take this more seriously than you.'

'Or, the point of this exercise is to dispel the myth once and for all.' She smiled at him with closed teeth.

'Why would Services care so much if they didn't believe he was alive?' Geof asked.

'*Because* of the myth, Ozenbach. He's keeping the flame alive for all the psis out there waiting for the day when their saviour comes to free them.'

*How can you be so callous?* Pete thought to her.

*I'm just asking the questions you haven't.* Her retort left him stunned. She was one of them, a psi like him, but so very different. Her eyebrow arched, waiting for his response.

*… You hunt your own kind.*

*My kind? Psionics is a skill. Being able to dress yourself doesn't make you my brother. Understand?*

'Tamsin,' the Colonel said. 'The order is clearly stated that we are to bring him in. The command is the command.'

'Of course, Colonel. There must be something that Command isn't sharing if they've already reached the conclusion that Pierre is still alive. And furthermore, why now? Can you get me an answer to that?'

The Colonel swallowed. 'No answer is forthcoming.'

'So, just because a second-rate telepath volunteers himself, two of Services' best are seconded to dig out a myth?' *No offence, Pete. I'm just trying to see what I can get out of them.*

Her mind was amazing to him. On the outside she was a closed, calculating woman, but underneath she was like a gleeful child throwing stones at windows.

The Colonel tapped his head and smiled at Tamsin as a torrent of data began streaming into Geof's and Pete's symbiots.

The data was a backlog of evidence gathered on, or regarding, Pierre since his disappearance. An archive of 'sightings', blackouts and abnormalities that bore no actual evidence of Pierre Jnr's involvement but were connected by the fact that Pierre was a possible cause. A wealth of junk information.

43

*You see that, Pete? Ask and ye shall receive.*

'So, you're our weapon?' Pete concluded.

'I guess I am.' She smiled benignly. 'Where do we start?'

'The islands,' Pinter answered. 'Interviews have been arranged.'

Tamsin shuddered. 'I hate the islands. I think I'll take a bath.' *You want to scrub my back for me, Pete?*

Pete stared at her incredulously until she shrugged and walked toward the diner doors. Geof was the only one not watching her stalk away, too busy sorting through the datastream.

'The midlands,' Geof concluded out loud, eyes gazing elsewhere. 'We have to go to the midlands.'

'How's that?' Pete asked, still gazing in the direction of Tamsin's exit.

'From the pattern I'm seeing, if he isn't there, then something just as bad is.'

'Keep looking,' Pinter added. 'They don't think you have it yet. The data may point at the midlands but nothing narrower. We need more specifics.'

When they returned to the hangar, Tamsin was nowhere in sight.

Geof sat in the makeshift lounge to digest data. The Colonel had a servitor carry his leather armchair to join him and was soon asleep. Pete went to his own room and lay down, letting his mind amble outward around the complex. As far as he could see, there was only the Colonel, Geof, Tamsin and himself — no other sentience within reach. Beyond the walls was only a soft susurrus of sound passing by, with few distinguishable thoughts.

*Pete?*

He didn't respond.

*Peter? I know you're there. You can't hide from me, so you may as well talk to me.*

He sighed.

*Do you want to know what I'm doing, Pete?*

*Not really.*

*I'm having a bath. Just like I said I would.*

*That's nice.*

*It is nice. I like the water on my skin, just like you.*

*I like the ocean.*

*Would you like to go swimming with me, Pete? I'm not a very good swimmer, but you could teach me.*

*How can you be how you are?*

*That's very philosophical, Pete. I thought we were just playing. Nobody knows that we're talking. I'm having a long bath, as I'm known to do, and you're having some quiet time. We've already shown them that we don't get on, so nobody will suspect that we are having a conversation.*

*You've been acting this way intentionally?*

*What way? I am what I am and you are what you are. Was there ever a possibility we could be other than how we are?*

*Now who's being philosophical?*

*I'm trying to make you understand, Peter. I know more than you about how Services works. You've spent your life running, but I've been in it. Don't think you know about choices. You chose to turn yourself in. You know what I call you?*

*What?*

*An idiot.*

*Well, that's your opinion.*

*You escaped in the early days, after the project was shut down. Services has improved since then. Earlier spotting. Mechanical traps. Weavers. Conditioning.*

*That's good to hear.*

*You need to know that the advantages that psis have are not as big as they often think. Telepathy doesn't make you smart; it just gives you inside information. And using that information for your own benefit is the biggest giveaway that leads us to awakening psis. We often know before they do if they're about to go psionic.*

*You must be so proud.*

*Why should I be? I got picked up in the first sweep, but I wasn't smart enough to get free.*

*Maybe you didn't want to.*

*Well, I'll let you wonder about that.*

*I don't understand you.*

*Tell me something, Pete. How long is your reach?*

*What do you mean?*

*How far away do people have to be until you can't, you know, give them a tickle?*

He thought it before he could stop it. It was something he always counted, every time someone walked away. How many steps until he couldn't peek in? His record was ninety paces.

*I will be telling them that, Pete. So they know they can trust me. For security we're going to have to isolate the compound a bit more. You won't be getting any traffic noise from now on, if you know what I'm saying. What can I do to gain your trust?*

*Nothing I can think of.*

*Okay. Let me know if you do. My bath is getting cold now, so I'm going to dry myself with a big fluffy towel and slip under some sheets. Goodnight, Peter Lazarus.*

Since 2134, all registered psis were housed in semi-voluntary imprisonment on artificial islands — plastic bergs with a fair stretch of ocean between them and the mainland and only a passive connection to the Weave, which meant they could watch but not contribute. They were segregated completely.

The squib to the islands took only an hour. Geof and the Colonel remained at the warehouse trawling data while Tamsin and Pete went to interview Pierre's parents. They were alone in their squib, remotely guided and prowled on either side by two escort vehicles packed with servitors. Pete tried to study Tamsin surreptitiously, but when occasionally, accidentally, he made eye contact, she grinned at him proudly.

While she repulsed him with her manner, the fact that she could shield her mind from him was fascinating, and he could do little but stare at her, hearing only the sound of the air rushing around the squib. No thoughts, no emotions.

*Are there more like you?*

She didn't answer. She looked at him but responded neither out loud nor in projection.

*Did you learn this somewhere? Have you taught this to anyone else?*

She raised an eyebrow. *This is what it is like for normals.*

Pete relaxed somewhat and kept watching her.

All psis on the islands were tagged and trackable, their actions passively monitored. The conditions weren't too bad, better than the penitentiaries, partly because the residents were not criminals requiring punishment, and partly because Services knew if they didn't treat them well it might ignite an uprising, which was the last thing they wanted. Actually, the last thing they wanted was another Pierre Jnr, and so the residents also had to agree to be rendered infertile.

Their first appointment was with Pierre Sandro Snr, the father. It was organised so that he would meet with them in a holding room on the mainland side of the island, away from the other inmates and under full Services monitoring. All the islands had such a room. Tamsin was in an annex behind a one-way mirror, to observe the both of them no doubt. Pete waited in a chair, feeling watched. He tried not to let a thought cross his mind.

A diode above the doorway lit up and a man older than his years shuffled in. He obviously wasn't one to shave regularly and, to Pete at least, his thoughts were as wild as his eyes.

Pete stood and held out his hand. 'Mister Sandro. My name is Peter Lazarus.'

Pierre Snr looked warily at the hand and then shook his head in declaration.

*Mister Sandro, I am one of you*, Pete thought to himself.

Pierre Snr didn't react; his file was seemingly correct that he had no telepathic ability and was skilled mainly as a bender. As if in demonstration, the empty chair in front of him pulled backward of its own accord and Mister Sandro sat down. His posture sagged and his eyes fell low, moving side to side rapidly.

As he took his own seat, Pete's arm thudded down hard on the table, alarming them both. 'Sorry, I'm still not used to the weight of this thing.'

48

Pete pulled back his sleeve to show Pierre Snr the symbiot. It flashed a hello at him and Pierre recoiled. 'I hate those things.'

'Have you ever had to wear one? This is my first time.'

'I've got a passive on my ankle.'

'Oh. Of course.' Pete watched the man slouched across from him. His mind was all over the place, a bit like a child's, a drugged child's. 'Do you know why I'm here?'

'It's about Junior, I assume.'

'That's right. I'm part of a Services team trying to find him.'

'Good luck to you.'

Pete couldn't deconstruct Pierre's stain of emotions that came at the thought of his son. He decided to leave the probing to Tamsin and concentrate on the interview; it was too tiring doing both.

'I've told them everything I know a thousand times.'

'I've read your testimonies. I'm more here to get a sense of what you're like. I'm hoping if I can get to know a little about the parents, it may give us a picture of Pierre Jnr.'

'Yeah?' Sandro scoffed. 'I don't know whether to be insulted by that or not.'

At first he was. His reaction to being linked with Junior was strong, then it grew vague and his eyes wandered more slowly as if he'd forgotten where he was.

'I guess it makes sense,' he mumbled.

'Tell me, Mister Sandro, what is it like here? You've been on the islands nearly seven years now.'

Sandro nodded. 'Yes. After the project, they left us on the islands. I've only been on this one for eight months. They like to rotate us.'

'Sounds like they're trying to stop you getting so bored.'

'Oh, nothing can stop the boredom, mister.' Sandro smiled miserably and looked downward again. 'But you're right, it keeps life moving along.'

Pete waited for him to speak again; he was determined to get Pierre to open up.

'You know they're talking about sending us into space?' Pierre Snr commented at last. 'We hear it on the Weave.'

'I've heard that too.'

'Some of us wouldn't be against it. Maybe we could set up a new society someplace. You know anything about this?' He was assuming Pete was higher up than he was.

'I'm afraid not, Mister Sandro. I'm really just assigned to your son's case.'

Pierre grunted and stretched his neck. 'Yeah, I wish I could help you more. I've had no contact with him since he left.'

The man's mind was uncomfortable; the memory was like a dream that refused to fade away, leaving forever a moment of unreality inside him.

'I understand that, Mister Sandro. I just wondered if you could give me any impression of Pierre Jnr from the time you spent with him.'

'He ruined me. He ruined all of us.'

'As an infant?' Pete asked.

'He was never that. He was a monster born whole.'

'When did you first become, let's say, *aware* of him?'

'I never did. Not like that. I'm just a bender, you see?' The table playfully floated up and down.

'When did you first know that your son was different?'

'Well, we knew what he was about six months into the pregnancy. Mary knew before then. We didn't tell anyone. We were excited. My partner, Sullivan, was even more excited, even though … you know.'

'He was your partner at the time?'

'Yeah. Yeah. But our partnership was annulled. A lot of partnerships were annulled during the project. We all thought we were being accepted, you see, that the laws would be lifted …'

He drifted off again. These memories made him mopey and he obviously expended a lot of effort trying to ignore them.

'Please go on, Mister Sandro. I need to know as much as I can.'

'Okay.' A glass of water floated to his lips and he drank in big gulps. 'As I was saying, my partner, Sullivan, loved communicating with Junior. We'd already named him by then. It was sort of a nickname we never explained to the researchers. Sullivan stuck with Mary through the whole thing, more than I did. I spent my days competing against the other psis. Even at the birth Sullivan made sure to be there, and he had already explained to Junior what was going to happen so he wouldn't be frightened.'

Pete sat forward and let the man talk it out.

'I'd never seen a surgical before, not even a real birth, but I know there's supposed to be crying. It had to be a surgical because we knew about Junior's head already. There was no way he was going to fit through. When Mary was opened up, it was dead silent in the room. Even the operating team was silent. I watched from the viewing room and nobody spoke, only the machines moved ... and then they lifted him out. There wasn't a sound from him ...

'And they were right about that head. It was big. He couldn't turn it. I know most babies can't, but the doctor holding him took him around the room, stopping so the baby could have a look at everybody present. I didn't even think they could really see at that stage, no?'

'I don't know. I could check.' Pete began to interface with the symbiot.

'It doesn't matter. It's just how things were I'm trying to tell. That's what you wanted. Junior didn't cry. Ever. But we all did for him. If he was cold, we wrapped him in a blanket. If he was hungry, he got fed. If he wanted to look out the window or cross the room, the nearest person would pick him up and take him. Do you understand? We knew what we were doing, but we weren't the ones doing it. It was incredible. Like a dream where things happen and you just watch. Do you understand?'

'I think I follow, but I've never experienced it.'

'Good.' Sandro's blue eyes stared wildly into Pete's. 'I hope you never do.'

'What happened to the mother after the birth? Miz ... Kastonovich?'

'She was worst off. Mary had been under his control for the longest. When he left, she just dropped to the floor.' His eyes lost their edge, and dropped back to an obsessive study of the tabletop. 'They had her on intravenous right up until she had the strength to kill herself.'

'I didn't know she died,' Pete said, and he ran a query through the symbiot. It confirmed his prior information that

Mary Kastonovich was alive and living on a nearby estate. 'I have an appointment with her later today.'

'That woman — that *thing* — is an abomination, a clone so the researchers could continue their studies.'

It was clear that Sandro believed what he was saying, but the Weave said otherwise. Pete sent a missive to Geof to check it out. 'Tell me, Mister Sandro ... didn't anyone in the project, one of the readers, sense that she was going to kill herself? Couldn't somebody have stopped her?'

'Stopped her? Perhaps, if we weren't all thinking the same thing. Those were bad days. The project was over. Everyone knew it. Even the docs were wasted. You don't know what it was like.'

'I'm sorry to bring back such memories for you.'

'It's okay. I know you're under instruction. But you've got to know what he took from us, Mister Lazarus. He ruined any chance we psis had. Mary was the best of us. She was a beautiful lady, and she had the most amazing abilities. I don't want you confusing that clone with her. That thing never went through what she went through.'

'I understand.' Pete thanked Pierre Snr for his time, watched from his chair as the man exited, and waited for the diode above the door to flick to safe before looking toward the mirror. *Are you there?*

He stared at his reflection, waiting for a response. It would be just like her to sit there and not respond. And just as likely for her to have left and not told him.

*I'm here.*

*What were your impressions of Pierre Snr?*

*The same as yours. He's of no use to us.*

*Where's Sullivan? He and Junior seemed close.*

*Missing.*

*Missing?*

*Would you prefer 'in the grey'?*

*Is Mary a clone?*

*There is no basis for that claim. Pierre Snr must have created that delusion.*

*I'd believe it. Then again, I'd believe almost anything.* Pete sighed and stood up, stretching his back. 'I can neither see you nor sense you.'

Tamsin chose to respond over the intercom. 'Does that frustrate you, Pete?'

'It certainly does. I'm not used to it. It's like you only half-exist.'

'Oh, I exist, Pete. You can be sure of that.'

'How?' he asked the mirror.

Silence was the only response.

*How?* he asked again.

'We spent our days training.'

'Training? How did you train?'

'Oh, you know, party tricks mostly, at first. Card reading, putting out matches from across the room. Later it became a real gymnasium, lifting tables up and down, talking over distances.'

'Was it hard?'

'For some.' She shrugged. It was to her the plain truth; she couldn't help that she was skilled. According to the records,

54

she had once managed to communicate a coded sequence over five hundred metres. 'They worked on developing stimulants.'

'Did any of them work?'

'They seemed to, but it could have just been placebo.'

'And now, can you still ... do some of those things?'

She hummed to herself and rolled her head. 'On good days. The islands are covered in the black noise, which makes it annoying. Not debilitating, just annoying. And they lace the water too, you know. It's hard to focus, but it keeps us happy.'

A miniature breeze evaporated on Pete's cheek. 'Was that you?' he asked.

She nodded. 'After eight years, even that was hard.'

Pete looked Mary over again. She was still a beautiful woman, dark-haired and athletic, a dancer out of training. He couldn't quite credit Pierre Snr's statement; her sadness was embedded deep. 'What was it like when you were pregnant?' Her eyes and mind glazed over at the question. 'Do you remem—'

'Sleep,' she answered. 'It was like sleeping.'

'Like a dream?'

'Sort of. But with no real dreaming. It's hard to remember.'

Pete could see she really didn't recall much from those months, just a vague sense of existence. Maybe Pierre Snr was right, though the memory gap could be explained just as easily by contact with Junior.

'Do you think memory is tied to consciousness?' Mary asked quietly.

'I'm sorry, I don't follow.'

'I just wonder if the reason I can't remember is because I wasn't really aware. I can't remember much from the time he controlled me.'

'That's an interesting thought.'

'Is it? I don't know.' She smiled and looked blankly at him.

'You aren't resentful at all? He used you, Miz Kastonovich.'

'He didn't create himself, Mister Lazarus. I did that. Me, Pierre and that whole institution.' Her gaze quickened as she spoke. 'Are you going to try and stop him?' Her dull lips rounded in amusement. 'Peter?' He looked at her without answering. His symbiot informed him that no answer was permitted. 'You can't, you know? He's a force of nature. I gave birth to a god.' Her face was bright with excitement. 'He will save us.'

'I doubt that.'

'Doubt? I have doubted a great many things that have come to pass.' Now she looked straight at him and stretched: *I notice you haven't touched your water.* But then she was gone again, pupils dilating and energy fading away.

'If you find him, you'll just disappear like I did … Can I go now?'

The halls were floored with synthetic panels of grey-blue and white. There was a murmur from each door they passed: children learning, out of sight.

'I'm sure you'll be happy here, Pierre,' piped the Matron touring them. Pierre said nothing and the woman took this for shyness. He seemed such a lovely boy. She chose to speak to his mother. 'We use only the most contemporary techniques:

56

mixed classes, no symbiots until sixteen — but that's a while away for you, Pierre.' The boy's placid smile flickered.

'That sounds fine,' Gail answered.

*The boy has no bot. A boy his age should have a bot. Maybe it's small, hidden in his pocket perhaps. Or, the mother might hold with some more traditional beliefs. Unless he is wired already ... it has been known to happen.* The Matron shuddered with thoughts until her worries disappeared and she looked down at the most darling child she had ever seen.

'Can we see the lower grades, please?' Gail asked. 'Just to see.'

'Of course. They are just down this way.'


As they took off from the islands, Geof reported a mass collapse at a school in the Dakotas, and they were redirected toward the midlands.

Pete: What's the connection? He was only just getting comfortable with querying through his bot.

Geof: Gail Pembroke is recorded as being a visitor at the time of the syncopation, but there is no record of her leaving. She and her husband, Newton, disappeared from the Weave nearly two weeks ago; no recordings of children.

Pete: So where are you sending us?

Geof: We have the squib Mistress Pembroke was travelling in, and from its log we can deduce her itinerary over the last fortnight. Services are covering each drop, but you're going to a farm, out past the brushes. That's where I think Pierre has been hiding all this time.

Tamsin: Okay, send us what you know — who owns the place, who should be there, and any other missing people who might be involved.

Geof: Already compiled and streaming.

Tamsin: A step ahead as usual.

Pete: Have you seen the interviews?

Geof: Most of them.

Pete: What do you think?

Geof: I think we need to find this kid before he starts up again.

Pete: And Mary? About what Pierre Snr said, is she a clone?

Geof: I have nothing that says she is.

Pete: Okay.

Tamsin deigned to raise an eyebrow at him. 'Why does it bother you so much if she's a clone or not?'

'It would be interesting if it was true.'

'I don't see the relevance.'

'How do you hide your mind from me like that?'

'That would take time to explain, and I don't think you could stand me for that long.'

*It is unfortunate that I can't hide my mind from you.*

'What? You don't like it? I imagine this must feel pretty uncomfortable for you.'

...

'Yep. Not used to playing without the advantage, are you?'

...

'What's my body language saying to you? Do you know how to read body language, Pete?'

...

'What are you gleaning from the timbre of my voice?'

...

'Why, Peter. Those are quite mixed emotions. I don't know how you stand the conflict.'

...

'Would you like a peek?'

...

Below them, the mottle of the landscape cascaded into shapes and lines. Old fields, scratched with the torn and toppled structures of bankrupt endeavours, divided by weather breakers of all sorts and quality. Barns, farmhouses, the spinal remnants of long fences, wrecked turbines and a generation of people beyond repair.

Few properties were managing to establish their prescribed micro-climates, but those that did dotted the land with their productive greens and golds.

Pete and Tamsin's squib banked south, momentarily tipping their view toward the gigantic black funnels of a windeater — flexible piping that transduced wind to electricity. They worked to serve two purposes, but they didn't work enough.

The midlands was a waste. Only evangelists and recidivists stuck it out for long. A great place for Pierre to hide out — one of Geof's grey areas — but not the ideal environment for a growing mind.

'You shouldn't think of him that way,' Tamsin told Pete.

'Why not?'

'He chose it.'

'He was an infant. He fled without direction.'

'You don't know that. And besides, he stayed.'

Pete left it alone. She was right, but she didn't know for certain either. He saw her smirk. *I hate telepaths*, he thought, and she laughed.

Beneath them a sepia yard wavered in the wind. Farming tools lay collapsed and overcome by the patchy crab grass. Window shutters shifted slowly back and forth. All the buildings were covered in the same faded dust.

The squibs settled facing the farmhouse. Pete watched through the screen, looking for any sign of life. The escorts unpacked their servitors, who then arrayed themselves on either side of the vehicle, waiting for Pete and Tamsin to lead them in.

'What a great place to grow up.'

'Exactly what I was going to say.' Tamsin grinned. 'Shall we?'

'Do you think he's in there?' asked Pete.

'No. It's quiet. If he was in there, I'd be able to tell by now, and so would you.'

'Unless he knows your trick. There's something in there.'

'Don't be so nervous.' Tamsin popped the hatch. 'He's long gone, Pete — if he was ever here in the first place.'

Pete took a deep breath and climbed out after her, keeping a watch on the homestead. 'Your power for doubt is incredible. You saw his parents.'

'All I saw were two unreliable witnesses.'

Geof: Any time you two feel like heading in ... We're all waiting here.

Pete nodded and looked at Tamsin. 'Ladies first.'

'I'll watch your back.'

'I'm not sure I'm comfortable with that.'

'It'll keep you on your toes then.'

Geof: Pete! Just go in. I've got your back too.

There was no more excuse to delay, and Pete approached the creaking house. The path was dry under his feet, and the wood of the steps bowed under his weight.

'Hello?' he called out as he climbed the stairs, and then once more when he got to the porch. 'Hello? Is anyone at home?'

'Try knocking,' Tamsin suggested.

Begrudgingly, he hammered his fist on the door frame and called out again.

They waited for something to happen. The shutters swept back and forth, and the structure whimpered under the growing wind.

Pete: Let's send a servitor in.

'Coward,' Tamsin accused.

Geof: He's right. Move aside so I can send a bot through.

'Forget that.' Tamsin pushed the door open and stepped inside. 'Hello, householders. Services are entering your premises. Do not even attempt to resist.'

Pete followed her in, a grey sort of darkness thickening a few steps from the doorway.

'Lazarus, get in here,' Tamsin called, more emotionless than ever.

He found her in a lounging room, nearly full of dilapidated couches and armchairs, everything covered in dusty crochet and piles of discarded clothing.

'Not clothes, Pete. They're breathing.'

He looked closer and recognised them as bodies. There were four of them, two on chairs and two on the floor. 'What's wrong with them?'

'I'm not sure. Is this what your sister was like?'

Pete shook his head. 'No, it wasn't this blatant.'

Tamsin knelt beside the closest of the crumpled forms. 'I'm not reading anything from them. You?'

'Something, but it's odd. Stray thoughts. Incomplete —'

Arms shot up and suddenly fingers were clawing at Tamsin's neck, dragging her down.

'You shouldn't have come here,' the body rasped. 'You shouldn't have come here.'

Before Pete could help her, two more of the bodies had awakened and grabbed at him from behind. In his mind he heard one thought, *you shouldn't have come here*, echoed by four dry voices repeating the mantra as one.

'You shouldn't have come here.'

Pete: Geof!

It was less than a minute of desiccated fingers trying to pull off their skin and dusty bodies holding them down before the servitors swarmed into the room and tore their attackers away.

'You shouldn't have come here. You shouldn't have come here. You shouldn't have come here. You shouldn't have come here,' they repeated, rasping continuously as they were dragged outside.

Try as he might, Pete couldn't read their thoughts. Pierre had reworked their minds into a composite, so that the first disturbed was a tripwire for the others. They all went crazy. Though he was sweating on the outside, fear had dried out his throat. 'I've never seen anything like this. He's … I don't know what he's doing.'

'Hakking,' Tamsin supplied. 'He took four people and fused them together.'

'You've seen this before?' Pete was alarmed.

'Of course not. I'm just hypothesising.'

'You admire him?'

Tamsin looked at him with her grin-smirk. 'Don't you? This is unprecedented.'

'He's demented,' Pete protested. *Look what he's done to these people.* 'This is inhuman.'

'Is it? I think we'll find before this is over that he is actually very human. More human than any single person should ever be.' *I am looking, Pete, and I'm impressed.*

*Impressed? A moment ago you didn't even believe in him.*

*A little evidence can go a long way*, she thought back to him while watching the servitors drag the husks into the squib. Tamsin turned to him with a smile, her thoughts fading from his reach. 'We should go. I have a lot to think about.'

Tamsin maintained her block in the squib, staring fixedly through the window at the ground passing below, not letting Pete see her thoughts or her face.

Pete kept taciturn, spending his time sending data back and forth with Geof, selecting images from his symbiot and flicking them across without commentary. Geof in turn fed him background information on the midlanders they'd found, mostly irrelevant details of their lives before they disappeared from the Weave.

Every now and then Tamsin or Pete would glance at the horizon toward the approaching weather front that now covered the skyline; the warning gauge amped up from dull amber to a piqued red until at last Colonel Pinter patched through and projected on the screen. 'Mister Lazarus, Miz Grey, it looks like we've got some weather ahead and we're going to have to land you quite soon.'

'We can't divert?' Tamsin asked.

'Only by turning back. We've been given clearance to land a few miles to the south, behind some brushes, and sit it through.'

'Is that standard practice?' Pete asked.

Pinter shrugged. 'Oftentimes. This is quite a front coming on, so perhaps they think it's better to bunk down than try to outpace it. Don't worry, the squibs can take it. It may just get a little rocky.'

'Okay, Colonel.'

'When you're down, please do not leave the safety of your vehicle.'

'As you say, Colonel.'

'It's coming in fast so this should be over in a matter of hours, and the escorts will be about fifty feet away in case there's an emergency. Even if the comms cut out through the worst of it, we'll be able to keep you in sight.'

*For our safety*, Tamsin projected ironically.

Pete assented once more to the Colonel and caught Tamsin looking at him as he switched off the screen. *What?*

*You're trapped with me, Pete. No avoiding it for either of us.*

*No avoiding what?*

*Don't be scared. You've got me all wrong.*

They angled down steeply and Pete swallowed through the shaky descent. The mood of the landscape around them had changed remarkably in the last minutes. Clouds had blocked the sun, and what had been a golden hodgepodge of light and shadow was now discoloured to purple and grey. Shadow had disappeared and one could see the quick dimming toward black. The lights of the squibs pushed out as they neared the ground and curved in behind a dense brush wall. The brushes were tall artificial trees of plastic designed to cut and slow the wind. They would give some protection, though nothing could withstand the big storms.

Static washed over the speakers as they landed, the wind rolling the rounded hulls back and forth. A gust shoved them side to side and Pete put his arms out to steady himself, accidentally pressing his hand on Tamsin's thigh. He jerked around to catch her grinning at him.

'Really, Pete, at least turn the comms off,' and she reached over to do just that.

'No, I didn't mean —'

'Don't be afraid.'

'We should keep the comms on.'

'That would be indiscreet, Peter,' she said, running her fingers into his hair. As if to match her words, the squib jumped and rolled, pushing them into each other somewhat uncomfortably. *Somewhat.* Tamsin laughed. 'This *is* going to be fun.' And then her lips were on his and her hands were under his shirt as the wind dragged the squib through the dirt like a plough.

'No, Tamsin. I can't.'

'You can with me.'

'No. It's too much. I can't.' He'd stopped enjoying sex a long time ago. Knowing every thought that ran through his partners' heads left him with the mixed emotions of anger, sorrow and disgust.

*I know, Pete. But I'm different. I can block you out. You can be free with me. See?*

Her block came back up, which was more of a disappearance for him, and he was left staring at her face. Just a face. Lips and skin, eyes and eyebrows. Eyelashes and fine wrinkles. The glint and glimmer on the iris as her eyes kept moving to capture his own. He couldn't remember when he'd last seen *just* a face. Her dark hair blocked the overhead lighting, a corona of white flaring around the edges. Her eyes were black and steady, holding him to them, drawing him into their silence.

With a hunger he'd long suppressed, he pushed himself atop her and began seeking out buttons and skin.

The now familiar corrugated walls of the hangar were a relief after the tumultuous day Pete had gone through. Colonel Pinter was waiting for them at the gate, a dressing gown over his uniform and a tin cup in his hand.

'You've been having a rough time of it, I hear.'

'You don't know the half of it, Colonel.' Tamsin laughed and dabbed a quick kiss on Pete's cheek as she passed. 'See you inside, Pete. I need a shower.'

Pete sighed and answered the Colonel's raised eyebrows. 'It's not what you think.'

'Your comms were down for nearly an hour.'

'It's not exactly what you think.'

'Just watch yourself with that one. I've met men like her, but not so many women. If I wasn't under orders to do so, I wouldn't trust her.'

Pete nodded. 'I don't.'

'Well, you've got some time to clean yourself up, then the three of you debrief. The ups want a plan from you by tomorrow.'

'I wouldn't mind one myself. After the homestead, I'm more lost than before.'


'How do you want us to proceed, Colonel?'

Pinter raised his hands. 'Sorry, Mister Lazarus, I really am just here as a functionary. You three go on as you wish. I'll interject if the ups have something to add.'

Pete nodded, taking a moment to gather his thoughts. 'Well, I guess, at best, that we discovered where Pierre Jnr has been hiding for the last eight years. Beyond that I'm not sure what we gained from our visit.'

'If it helps, I'm taking him a bit more seriously than I was before. I apologise that I didn't believe what you said about him,' Tamsin offered to Pete. 'I've never seen minds like that, so reworked and mashed. That was one of the most troubling elements of today.'

'From my side this was a very productive encounter,' Geof added. 'Short of actually stumbling upon our target, we now have two footprints of symptomatic phenomena that indicate where Pierre might be or has been. He's on the move now and we've just found a way to track him.'

'So do you know where he is?'

'Not yet, but give me until tomorrow.'

'Tomorrow?' Pete was shocked and somewhat disbelieving.

'That's right,' Geof said, winking. *There's nowhere to run from people like me, Pete. Just remember that.* N E W T O N P E M B R O K E, Geof queried through the symbiot. The link was almost telepathic. 'Last seen thirteen days ago ... Wife missing from the same time. She wasn't in the house. She was with Pierre Jnr, visiting a school ... So we're thirteen days behind. A lot better than eight years, and we've only been on the case for under a few weeks.'

'Do you think he's with this woman? Gail Pembroke?'

'What use could she be?' Tamsin asked.

'Cover. Camouflage,' Geof answered.

'Maybe,' Pete considered. *Maybe he is still a child needing a parent.*

'I don't think so,' Tamsin scoffed.

'Why not?'

'The farmers?'

'And? We're just objects to him. He doesn't even see what he does as bad.'

'If he can read minds, he knows right from wrong.'

'That's pretty simplistic. I don't even know that sometimes.'

'Okay, people, focus. This is getting off track.' Pinter stood up and stretched, pushing his hands to his back as if holding his spine together.

'Geof, can you show me how you'll find him?' Pete asked.

'I can try. If you look at the streams here ... Pete, open up.' Pete had to allow overlay access through his symbiot. Lines, diagrams and other data threw themselves over his eyesight, mostly transparent but concentrating on them made the world around him disappear. 'What you see here is a flat globe and a mapping of anomaly patterns. I'll block them out for you.'

'They're everywhere.'

'Well, yes and no. This is why we call it the grey. But, I can clear up most of these, based on what we saw at the farmstead and the school ...' — Geof counted them on his fingers — '... loss of linkups, uninterpretable behavioural fluctuations, unrecorded characteristics, lowered reporting and contact with the Weave. This could just be a natural anomaly, but when we scale the pattern to the rate of incidents, we home in on the places with the highest cumulative symptoms.' Geof blinked, and Pete watched the clumps of data change colour and shrink down, leaving four grey patches of significant size. 'Only three if you disregard the midlands.'

'The Dome, Asia and the middle of the Pacific. What could be in the middle of the ocean?' Pete asked.

'Don't worry about that one. That's not him.'

'How do you know?'

'He can't answer that,' the Colonel cut in. 'You now have two target zones, but how can you be sure of them?'

'We can't be *sure*. What is "sure" when it comes to data? I can only identify the grey areas,' Geof parried.

'We can debate data theory all night, or some of us can,' Tamsin said, smirking at Pete and Geof, 'but let's assume there's something to these two grey areas. If Pierre has gone to Asia, then he's hiding. If he's gone to the Dome, then he's heading for the elevator.'

'Why do you say that?'

'Because that's what I'd do. I'd get off Earth. It's hostile to him. We're hostile to him.'

'Does he know about us?'

'Pete, we don't know what he knows,' Tamsin growled. 'For all we know, he could have come into contact with a Ministry man and know more than we do.'

'Colonel?'

'Well, I won't say it's not possible, but it is unlikely.'

'Why unlikely?' Tamsin asked. 'We don't know where he is. It only takes five hours to blast around the globe, so tell me why it's unlikely.'

'No.' Pinter's watery eyes froze on her.

'Why not?'

'Because you are making demands again and you should know that won't work with me.'

'Colonel —' she protested.

'Tamsin Grey,' Pinter cut her short. 'Your status has been reclassified.'

'That's a little unnecessary, isn't it?' Geof spoke up. 'Aren't you just saying it is unlikely because the odds are against it? And secondly,' Geof turned to face Pete and Tamsin, 'the higher up you go, the more you are monitored. Anomalous behaviour would be noticed.'

Geof was trying to calm the room down; neither he nor Pete knew what the Colonel's game was. Or Tamsin's.

'Colonel, Tamsin, with all due deference, this is wasting time,' Pete said. 'Geof, explain to me the grey patches again. How do we derive these?'

'Okay, but this is the last time. You could just trust me, but never mind. This is a two-level patterning filter I'm showing. If you go back a step to the raw data, you see nothing much. I'll keep this geographic for you to save confusion.' As the overlays changed with Geof's explanation, Tamsin and the Colonel dropped their staring match and she stalked out. 'To this data we apply certain structural patterns. In this case, I've gone with established behaviourals, which is a data-set built up over time that tracks an individual's behaviour. By knocking out what we expect, we are left with unexplained variations and unpredicteds. This is normal, don't forget — we can't predict everything people do — but based on a large enough survey, even a shift of one per cent is significant.'

'Alright, you two. You've made your point.' Pinter grinned. 'I certainly don't need to hear this again. It's like basic training over and over.' He stood up to go. 'Let's have a direction by morning. And, Pete, come by my rooms when you're done here.'

'Yes, Colonel.'

When he was gone, Geof expelled the air from his lungs and stood up. 'Pete, my friend,' he said as he headed for the kitchenette and gathered some snacks. 'Do you ever feel that you're in over your head?'

'Just in this lifetime.'

'I know what it's like for outsiders. You see Services as a giant unfathomable system, but you never see how true that is.'

'I'm not sure what you mean.'

'I was bred for this game. I wasn't given a choice.'

Pete was too slow with a response.

'You see? Bigger and more unfathomable than you think.'

'I just handed myself over.'

'I know,' Geof laughed. 'You still think one psi child is worth it?'

Pete shrugged. 'Yes. I think so. You saw what he did to those people. He doesn't see us. We're just clay in his hands. Have you ever seen anything like that?'

Geof hesitated before answering, but Pete caught remembered visions flickering through: fields of reanimated bodies, grey and jerky; a battle of cyborgs where human bodies were used for shields; a ship deck sloshing with blood and a bearded woman enjoying a cigarette. 'Well, not exactly the same, but just as bad.'

They said nothing for a moment. Geof ate pickled eggs, cheese and dried fruit, thinking as little as possible. It struck Pete that they still weren't taking Pierre as seriously as he was; to them he was just one threat amongst many.

'For what it's worth,' Geof went on, 'I think Tamsin is right. But there is an easy way to settle this: we wait. I'll keep tracking the grey overnight. A natural anomaly probably won't have direction, it will stay in one place. If there is a clear vector for one, then that's the one we follow. If it goes well, you could be face to face with Pierre by midday tomorrow.'

'Why midday?'

'Let's at least keep it until after breakfast.'

'Excellent,' Pete replied, chuckling. 'Let's call that a plan. Now I'd better go see what the Colonel wants with me. Perhaps I'm being reclassified too.'

The Colonel welcomed him with surprising cheer. 'Ah, there you are, Lazarus. I was hoping you'd join me for a drink.'

Pete noticed the Colonel's lodgings were very different to his own, with many touches that added to the comfort: recliners with blankets and cushions, a sideboard littered with trinkets, the leather armchair he had carried to him whenever he would be sitting somewhere long, and a thick rug that almost entirely covered the slab floor. The central light above was dimmed by a lampshade that looked to be made of animal skin. Something about the eclecticism implied that every piece was a memento of some sort.

'Real Scotch? I'm not sure what there is to celebrate, but a good drink is cause enough for me.'

'I'm not sure what there is to celebrate either,' the Colonel grumbled as he broke the seal of the bottle and fumbled about for a matching pair of glasses.

'Oh,' Pete responded emptily, trawling through what was on his superior's mind.

'Don't read ahead, Pete. Talking may be redundant to you people, but I still require the outlet.'

'Of course. If I may ask, how did you know?'

'You're too obvious. Despite the assumption that a telepath is always reading your mind, you struggle to do two things at once.'

'I'll try to remember that.'

'A good thing to practise in your line of work.'

The Colonel poured two-finger measures into the crystal, watching the light playing through the caramel-gold liquid. 'I was once stationed on the Skye Isle, some time ago, and became quite close with a young couple who had inherited a distillery. Every year they send me a bottle.' There was more behind the story he didn't speak of, but he had no intention of taking it further than the twitch of a smile he couldn't control. 'And every year,' the Colonel continued, passing one of the glasses to Pete, 'my wife and I would have the first drink together. It is a little tradition we have continued since we were married. This year, of course, we can't be together and she has sent the bottle on.'

'I'm sorry.'

'It's not *all* your fault.' The old man raised the glass to his nose and swirled the liquid about. His soft eyes melted a little more. 'She's chosen to be rejuvenated. Do you know what that means?'

'Yes.' Pete decided he wouldn't take a sip until the Colonel did. It was important for him to talk this through.

'It means when I go back to her, she will effectively be forty years younger than me.'

'Perhaps that's not all bad?'

'No, no ... of course not. She was a beautiful woman at that age. A most beautiful woman.' He sighed deeply. 'She insists that nothing will change between us, that she will still be my wife, but ...'

'She is going to suddenly be a young woman with her life ahead of her.'

'And I will be an old man with a life behind him.'

'You could rejuvenate.'

'I don't think so.' He shook his aged heavy head. 'I don't think I have it in me to be young again.'

Pete was silent. He found older minds harder to read, memories overlapped so much and the consciousness switched

74

between them almost without connection. The Colonel's thoughts circled his options: divorcing his wife, or staying with her and growing older until he died, not being able to satisfy her. He could hardly blame her for wanting to live longer — most people wanted that. If only he did. Mixed with the present was his Serviceman life with all the horrors and victories he had been a part of.

'You're right. There really isn't much to say.' The Colonel bobbed his head until the thoughts passed, then lifted his glass slightly to meet with Pete's own. 'Here's to a good drink then.'

For a long time they were silent, each appreciating the fire of the drink and the associations brought by its taste. Pete had rarely experienced actual Scotch. The traditional distillery and fermentation drinks had been long ago replaced with synthetic reproductions that replaced the intoxicating effect of alcohol with a weak psychogenic or chemical manipulation. For him the taste was historical, like a museum or photographs, and he reflected on humanity's past.

Pete couldn't make sense of the Colonel's past. 'You think a lot like my father,' he commented, perhaps to share an intimacy, the way the Colonel had with him.

'I thought I told you to keep out of here,' the old man said, tapping at his temple in mock reprimand.

'I can't help it. It's like sound to me. I can't close my ears either.'

The Colonel chuckled. *I know, boy. I'm only teasing.*

'Hah! H—'

*Don't give the game away*, the Colonel thought with alarm. *I can't project or anything, but I'm smart enough to assume you're listening. That gives us one-way communication at least.*

Pete retracted and corrected, 'You are a *lot* like my father.'

'We would be of an age, I believe.' Pete nodded to this. 'Services man, was he?'

'Yes. All his life.'

'How did he feel about you turning out atypical?'

'He wasn't too happy.'

'And your sister. Doris, wasn't it? Did he know about her?'

'I won't tell you her name and no, he passed before she showed any sign.'

'Does my asking bother you?' the Colonel inquired, somewhat gently though slightly rebuking. *You know we still have no information on her. Are you sure you didn't make her up?*

'Didn't you get everything from my file?'

The Colonel nodded. 'Of course, but I've never been one to think I know a man because I've read about him. Especially when the person in question has himself told me how easy it is to rewrite history.'

Pete could see the wisdom in this and submitted to the discussion. The Colonel doled out another finger for each of them.

'Don't get me wrong. I respect my father for what he was, and I understand what he did for me.'

'Didn't he have you taken to be tested?'

'Yes.'

'A good Services man.'

'Yes, he was. I understand that he had no choice. In his mind, it was my duty to keep it from him, so I'm the one who failed.'

'You can't blame people for what they are. Their beliefs and reasoning are subject to the situation.'

'Exactly,' Pete agreed, 'but before they took me, he told me that if I could get through the testing, then I could get through life. He thought it would challenge me.'

'Yes, fly or fall,' the Colonel said, stating the obvious, one of the clever adages Services were indoctrinated with.

'I don't hold with that principle.'

The Colonel shrugged. 'There are twenty billion people on greater Earth. What philosophy do you follow?'

'I haven't figured that out yet,' Pete admitted.

'Your problem isn't with the fight, it's with the kill.' The Colonel looked deeply at him, the calm watery pools inviting him in. It became clear to Pete now that the Colonel's need for a drinking companion was attached to other motives. 'In basic training they teach us that our fear of killing is greatly linked to our own fear of dying.'

'What right have we to take another life?'

'Rights are the constructs of our civilisation, lad. They come and go.'

'And we should respect them, or we are just animals.'

'Aye, as far as we can. What about the matter at hand though? Have you thought about what you will do if you succeed in tracking down this boy?' *Unless you're planning on joining with him.*

'I haven't thought about that yet. Or I have, but I don't want killing him to be the only answer.'

'It so often is though. Much as we like to deny it — with these clothes, and rights, and tech — we are only animals, and sometimes animals have to be put down.'

'That's a harsh way of looking at it.'

'It's a harsh world.'

'We don't even know what he is.'

'True enough, but we know some of what he is capable of.'

'Capability is not a crime.'

'I think I see where you stand, Pete. Thank you, I needed to know.'

'You did, or Services did?'

'There is no difference.'

'And now we find ourselves returned to where we started.' Pete stared hard at the Colonel, who stared only into his glass, thinking about the past. 'Anyway, I had presumed Tamsin will take over once we have found him.'

'Yes. She will hide and then provoke him. Our first move against an unfamiliar opponent is always a push, to see how he responds.'

'You see, we start in opposition.'

'Peter, what are you hoping for?' Pinter put down his glass. 'You saw what he did at the school and the farm ... to his parents. Are you hoping to reason with him?'

'No, I just — I don't understand him.'

The Colonel had no answer that would help, and Pete sat there limply. 'I think it is time we called it a night,' Pinter suggested.

Pete could see the Colonel wasn't as bothered by the discussion as he was, and this only angered him more. 'Yes. Alright. Goodnight, Colonel.'

'Goodnight, Pete.' *And think about what I said.*

When pollution and climate change deformed the planet to a state where humans could hardly breathe without apparatus and the weather turned vicious, giant arches and cupolas of translucent plastic were hastily erected over buildings, communities and cities, and eventually grew into the greater domes that covered a continuous portion of the Eurasia continent, extending as close as is feasible to the Siberian Terminus and south toward the equator, to where the elevator rose into the stratosphere, a taut cable taking the intrepid and the desperate to the first staging point of their journeys.

Civilisation builds on the past, and this was especially true for the Dome. Now, as the world was becoming breathable again, the tops of the domes were becoming the new fashionable locales for people to experience a natural breeze, with fine-weather cafés and eateries appearing in the more sheltered crevices and nooks, following the pattern of the resilient and adventurous flora that had also begun to colonise this new level.

Squib traffic was kept to a minimum under the Dome, to protect the preservation area; just Services vehicles and the odd exception. Most transport was conducted by train, sky-rail and ground vehicles. It was never entirely dark in the Dome. The light of the cities below was bent and reflected so there was always a dulling of complete dark.

They'd left the west coast at dawn and been in the air for about an hour when, all of a sudden, the cabin bristled with alert silence. The armsmen in the rear paused their chatting and weapons checks and straightened their backs. The Colonel and Geof closed their eyes while Tamsin stared straight ahead at nothing.

'Geof, what is happening?' Pete whispered.

'We're getting orders, Pete. We have movement on a possible target.'

'Pierre?'

'It looks like it. We're tracking a siphon slow-cruising through trad-Paris. We have surveillance gaps and people breaking off from the Weave.'

'So soon.' Pete breathed out. 'What's he doing here?'

'We don't know it's him yet, Pete. It could be a hakka.'

*Maybe he's just after information*, Tamsin thought.

*What sort?*

*It doesn't matter. Don't you see? Pierre has been travelling the world brain-tapping in a pattern we can't identify. It could be he's just scouting.*

*Learning?* Pete suggested.

*Exactly. We have been telling ourselves not to think of him as a kid, even though he is. Not like any other, of course, and we can learn little from matching childlike behaviour to him. But doesn't it seem that he's simply finding his way around?*

'Black limousine, matched to the siphon pattern. Check your symbs for visual,' Geof reported.

Geof routed the available surveillance, and Pete and Tamsin watched an innocent-looking limo-style hover float through the metropolitan streets silently like a shadow, windows dark and impenetrable.

'Nothing else, Geof?' the Colonel asked.

'This is my best guess.' *Take it or leave it.*

Pinter chuckled slightly. 'Okay, let's not change the surveillance pattern. We don't want to tip him off, but if you can keep it monitored that'd be great. Let's get a little closer, shall we?'

Tamsin took a stern breath, sucking strength into herself. *I'll go under now. Is there anything else before we go in?*

*What are you going to do?*

*I'll do what I have to, Pete.*

The rest of the squib was filled with clicks and twists of preparation. Pete and Tamsin just stared at each other, fathoming silently.

*I wish I'd learnt that trick of yours by now.*

*It's hard to teach an old dog, Pete. Luck to us.*

Pete looked directly into her eyes as Tamsin's mind disappeared from him. Visually nothing altered — her eyes glistened and her smile kooked at the side — but he felt the disconnect as if a canyon now ran between them.

'Colonel, what are the orders?' she asked, just a voice and a face again.

'Trap and subdue. We'll try taking him alive first. Ozenbach, you're on co-ord. The strat-mat will be piping to you when it's complete. Pete, you and … Pete?'

'Colonel?'

'You and Tamsin are up first. Get close, look him over. Do not let him have any warning and do not try to stop him yourself. Tamsin knows the drill, so let her work. Your job is to watch and let us know when to jump in. Do you understand?'

'Yes, Colonel.'

'When do we jump in?'

'When I say to,' Pete replied.

'At what point will you give the order?'

'I don't know.'

'Then you don't understand. Don't say you do. Tamsin has sixty seconds to cripple him. We go in at precisely sixty-one seconds, or earlier if you tell us.'

Pete stretched his mind out toward the sharp-eyed woman opposite. *What are you going to do to him?*

She didn't answer. Tamsin was closed, mask up. She smiled at him like a mannequin. White, clinical, a refined expression.

Pete: This happened faster than I thought.

Geof: What did? The operation? How long did you think it would take to find him?

Pete: I don't know.

*What happens to me after this? They won't let me go.*

Tamsin turned to focus on him. *You become like me, or you go to the islands.*

They landed an estimated ten minutes ahead of the target. Pete and Tamsin separated, keeping their locations and plans secret in case one of them was compromised. Tamsin had hidden herself in mind and body, but he presumed she was close, ready to strike.

Pete stood by a light pole near the kerb and gazed down the street until he saw the silver and black nose come into view. He watched an overhead view of the approaching vehicle and a numerical countdown of disappearing metres.

A silence surrounded it. The pedestrians paused as it passed, their steps hovering until they were out of reach. The closer it came, the more he could hear that interruption to the buzz of activity. It drifted closer and closer, pausing the pedestrian flow like a blood clot.

It was an expensive model, stretched and elegant, with chrome edging and grilles wrapping beneath. It was raised a foot from the ground, gliding, it seemed, like a cloud. The windows were in a classic two-part halving, tinted and opaque. Pete could hardly believe that the boy might be inside.

*Pierre ...*

Pierre felt the call just before an invisible force squeezed the car inward on each side. He reacted immediately by pushing back and keeping the metal walls from crushing him. He tilted his head to look at his mother. She was broken and leaking fluid.

Gail Pembroke gasped at the pain. The boy beside her floated away from the seat while she tumbled to the floor as it folded and opened. She could hardly react as the metal and plastic masticated her toes and the pain crushed her from above.

Pete saw the limousine lurch into the air and compact inward; Tamsin's attack, he presumed. The movement stopped just as suddenly, and the limo tilted forward until it stood on its nose.

Everything in sight lurched. Plate-glass windows bulged and exploded onto the street, announcing the cacophony that followed. Parked vehicles juddered toward the limo as if tugged by strings, then crumpled and lifted to create a wall around it.

Pete didn't know if this was part of the attack or not, but ran forward, probing with his mind for any sign of Pierre or Tamsin. Around him the ground simmered before cracking and lifting skyward. Light posts and street furniture twisted and dismembered themselves, adding to the growing mass of the manifestation.

For a moment the hillock cringed before stretching into a vague anthropomorphic form. It grew and grew, compounding itself with everything in range of its suck. The monster spawned tentacles that careened through the surrounding buildings, creating more debris to feed itself until it stood tall above the rooftops.

Like a cyclone the golem grew. Walls, squibs, bots and humans. Everything was pulled into the skin, still clutching and writhing with reflex.

The maelstrom kicked forward, swinging its heavy legs out, knocking the walls of the Tuileries as it came straight toward him.

Pete: Geof?

From the moment the limousine came in sight of the team, a data hole erupted in the centre of metropolitan Europe. Services was blind. Geof kicked the table he was at, scattering his snacks to the ground. 'One minute until satellite, Colonel.' In the meantime Geof scanned for any feed coming from the zone.

The satellite image came on, showing an explosion of dust rising upward from the ground.

'What is that?'

'I have no idea, Colonel.'

'It looks like a volcano.'

'Colonel, what's the reaction strategy for this sequence?'

Pinter had been monitoring the operation through wall screens that were now black and static. The view from above showed the roof of the Dome and a growing brown mist spreading along the Rue de Rivoli.

'That is not a resolution you will be happy with, Geof. We need to know what is happening down there and fast.'

'The satellite image is no good, Colonel. They're under the domes. We need something in there with working optics.'

'Find something, Geof.'

*Pete*, he thought to himself. *You are on your own.*

As the monster trampled and assimilated everything in its path, Pete wondered if this was the sort of reaction the Colonel had expected. The body of the limousine was sucked upward and inside, shielded under the growing layers of flattened debris. Even the paving stones flew up to add themselves to the mass of the golem rushing forward, sand and grit falling in ragged flows.

Pete felt a hand around his neck that transformed quickly into a shackle of unbreakable air lifting him up. He choked and gagged under the hold. Attempts to grab at his invisible noose resulted only in his arms flamboyantly flailing about, finding no purchase on the grip Pierre had on him. His body felt hot and was covered with a tingle of small pains as blood vessels popped in his cheeks and eyes.

Floating and struggling, a peace encased him, gravity relinquished his weight and silence wrapped around him like wool. Even the alarmed heartbeat in his ears faded to nothing.

He stared forward, his last vision the ill-constructed torso of aggressive collage that was the golem. Pete was intoxicated by a calm he couldn't explain.

The vision changed. The golem's shell cracked and opened up, petal by petal as a flower to the sun, until he was staring at the unnaturally intelligent face of a young boy. He felt his mind absorbed by a wave passing through him.

It was a strange face for so many reasons. The visage was serene and nonplussed, the eyes dark and shadowed as if the child hadn't slept for his entire life. He'd never seen such understanding in the face of a boy so young. The skull was too big, with only a light scattering of wispy mouse-brown hair that couldn't cover the tiger lines of his stretch marks.

The child made no move and Pete could only stare, held in place to the millimetre, enraptured. He knew he wasn't dead when the pain began.

*The eyes.*

*The eyes are staring into me … They do not blink.*

*He is not one like the rest of us. He goes on and reaches beyond the one.*

*Unblinking hazel eyes. Not unkind. Not curious.*

*The infinite through the one. The parasite has taken hold in this boy.*

*How long have I been in this darkness? I wonder if I've even been born yet. Yet … I must have lived to know such terms. There is only that staring darkness. The unblinking void.*

He dissolved.

For a moment he was floating in the ocean. A tugging of blue and piercing reflections.

He was a different man than he had been before the blackout. He didn't know how he even came to be this way. Piece by piece he remembered who he had been. This memory connected to that one. Some experiences were lost to him. Or were as unsortable as sand. Smells and sounds just couldn't be placed. He had visions of places he couldn't remember visiting. These illusions were left to disappear.

As he lazed in half-consciousness, unsure if he existed or not, Pete had many nightmares.

He stared up into the eyes of the woman straddling him. *Why do you want to destroy everything?*

*Things have to change. I want things to change.*

*There will be a war. A war like we haven't seen before.*

*Yes. But we'll win, Pete. We have to. How long can we go on living like this?*

'Oh, let me go, let me go.' He moaned and tried to push her off him. She tightened her legs and beat back his hands.

*You want this too.*

*I don't.*

*Don't forget I can see inside your head.*

Pete woke up feeling chewed and as if he was staring out from the dark inside of some creature's mouth. His eyelids forced themselves up, the light cutting shafts through his lashes. He wanted to cling to the shafts, drag his way free through them, but they were ethereal and he even more so.

This dream version of reality reluctantly popped, and he was able to open his eyes fully and twist his head to look at the window that was administering the light. Thin curtains hung

87

open, waiting for something to happen. Pete suddenly longed for the touch of a breeze, cool water on his skin.

He laughed a single syllable, a gulp of humour before his rickety chest complained about the movement. He really hadn't expected to ever wake up again, and his worldview had to adjust to the idea.

There were two things he became aware of first: the light filtering through his eyelids and the persistent call of the symb on his arm. It gently repeated his name to him until he acknowledged it.

Pete: I'm here. I'm okay …

Then he fell under once more.

He woke to the trim of an air razor skimming over his cheek, each revealed strip colder at the touch of fresh air. His mind leapt up, a painful throb that nearly made him fall back under, but he stretched enough to find it was just a nurse doing her job efficiently, grooming the coma patient again.

Light spilt into his eyes as he forced them open, a cathedral almost too bright to behold.

She seemed a woman efficient in every area of her life.

*Hello.*

Her eyes flicked to his.

*Don't be frightened. And please, continue. In fact, cut it all off. Please.*

She squeezed the razor back to speed and released her gaze. *There's no need for that, Mister Lazarus. You have friends around you here. And you'll have to tell me out loud.*

'Can you please cut it all off?'

'Are you sure?'

'Yes.'

She proceeded to trim around his scalp until it was only pale unripe skin.

*Friends?*

*Friends they don't know about.*

*Thank you. How long have I been sleeping?*

*Two days.*

She completed the job and rested his head back onto the pillow. 'A doctor will be with you soon.'

She faded from his reach at fifteen paces and he faded too.

He knew they were there, the symb had warned him, and he peeked through its sensors. Colonel Pinter and Geof had taken seats on either side of his bed, waiting patiently. Geof was, of course, fiddling with data, and the Colonel, well, the Colonel seemed distracted.

'I'm awake.'

They both stood.

'How are you feeling?' Geof asked.

'I can hardly feel anything.'

'You're being medicated heavily. Maximums all the way.'

'Am I that bad?'

'Well,' said Geof, peering down at him, 'from the little I can see through your bandages, I'd have to say yes. But the prognosis is positive.'

Pete nodded and felt woozy. The Colonel hadn't said anything yet. 'So, what happened? What went wrong?' *How am I still alive?*

'We're piecing it together,' Geof answered. 'By the time we arrived, he was gone. There was just a crater of rubble and twitching bodies like yours.'

Though it hurt his skull, Pete stretched toward Geof's mind and caught a glimpse of the scene — road torn through to the catacombs below, buildings caved in or flattened, the random jerk of a bloodied limb.

'He just left?'

'We didn't find him.'

'And you couldn't track him?'

'All we had left was a satellite that was peering through the Dome. Services was blind for a bit there.'

'What do you remember?' the Colonel asked gently. 'Obviously we're going to need your full account when you're rested and off the medication, but for now anything you can relate would be helpful.'

'Did Tamsin make it?'

'She's well. Bruised and scraped but alive,' Geof answered.

'What happened to her attack?'

'Why don't you tell us what you saw first?'

'Okay.' Pete took a deeper breath, closed his eyes and pushed back to when he was standing on the street corner. 'I remember the limousine had just come into sight and then ... I was lifted up.' His head protested, as if the memories were sharp grains scraping at his brain. 'I can't remember after that.'

'We lost comms at about the same time. Every eye we had on the scene went dead.' Geof was making an effort to make his thoughts obvious, repeating over and over that Pete and Tamsin were both under suspicion of tipping Pierre off.

90

Pete groaned. *That's ridiculous.*

'Do you remember anything else, Mister Lazarus?' Pinter spoke up, prompted from above.

'I saw him.' Pete's head throbbed. 'He held me up and — ahhrr!' He lifted his hands to his temples. Inside all he saw were those pale hazel eyes boring into him. He blacked out.


'Look at you. More bruise than man.'

'Hello, Tamsin.' *You're not looking that much better yourself.* Her exposed skin was raked red with lines.

'Mister Lazarus.' *Pete.*

'What happened to you? You were meant to strike.'

'I did, but he was too fast … As soon as it began, I got knocked out and was sucked into the mess.'

*And yet somehow you lived.* 'So, do you believe in him now?'

'I guess I have to.' *Do you? We witnessed the manifestation of Pierre Jnr, and the world will be changed by it.* 'Well, at the least, we can say that we gained one useful piece of knowledge from this assignment.'

Pete itched all over and his own pulse sent missives of pain throughout his body. He hadn't as yet discovered any positives to the situation. 'That is?'

'Pierre may now know everything you do, which means he might adjust his plans to whatever was in your head. Even knowing what he knows gives you something.'

Pete grunted. *Which means he knows about you.*

*Yes.* 'Hey, it may not be much, but it's more than we had to go on before.' *I'm leaving.*

'True.' *I'm not surprised.*

'Don't be like that, Pete. It's not all bad.' *Please don't think of me like that.* 'You're still alive. You've seen the face of the enemy now.' *That's what you wanted.*

'Yes.'

*Did he scare you off?*

*Clearly I'm not the only one.*

*If we have a chance, Pete, our only chance is to split up. I can't know what you're doing, and I can't have you knowing what I'm up to.*

*Is that really your reason?*

*You still don't trust me?* She leant close to him, her hair falling forward to encircle his face, and she placed her lips on his. He was surprised at their warmth. Breaking off, Tamsin straightened and looked down at him. 'I'll come by and see you again tomorrow. If they'll let me.' *Goodbye, Pete.*

'I'll be here.'


As Tamsin walked down the corridor, watching the repetitive tiles of linoleum passing beneath her stride, a young boy took her hand and began walking beside her. *Who is this boy?*

She smiled at him, and he smiled back at her. 'Am I your mother now?'

'Yes, and now we must hide, until it is time.'

'I love you, Pierre.'

'I love you too, Mother.'

# Pierre Jnr is confirmed alive on April Seventh, 2159

To the outside world, it looked like an explosion. Even as the ground still vibrated, the streams of nearly two hundred thousand people flooded the Weave with recordings as they ran for their lives. Walls cracked and blocks fell from above. Many didn't reach safety and their avatars froze on the last messages they projected.

Around the world, daily life halted. In the hours following there was nothing else worth thinking about. The Weave was dominated by the events in the Dome. Along with thousands of surveillance flies, a terrified world watched as the cloud lost momentum then slowly spread out into a fog.

The surrounding area was evacuated as soon as it began, Citizens fleeing north and south in a rush of squibs and jets. Soldiers and other personnel took control quickly, processing witnesses in a battalion of medic tents. Even when the threat seemed to have passed the exodus continued.

Services cordoned off the assaulted area and none protested. Teams of transports landed and armoured soldiers rapidly spread out, checking every street and building. At the cordon, Servicemen formed a two-deep human perimeter, one facing into the hot zone, back to back with a soldier facing out at the crowd and the swarm of remote cameras.

The natural airflow took an hour to dispel the cloud, by which time Services had erected a wall that blocked intervention from non-Services personnel. No cameras or sensors were allowed through. Nothing was allowed to fly overhead. Not until they knew what had happened.

Every kind of check was performed. Team after team of scientists and experts were let behind the fence to perform their tests: radiation, explosives, distortion, chemical and bacterial, but nothing was out of its ordinary range for the area. At least that was what they reported into the Weave.

Most of the Citizenry of 2159 hadn't been alive for the most recent Dark Age. It was fifty years since the Örjian blitz and, as educated as the older generation could make them, the majority had grown up surrounded by the authority of Services and the security of the World Union.

That this event in the Dome went unexplained was unacceptable. Though nobody knew exactly what had happened, opinions and suspicions were quick to build. Some pundits speculated it was the actions of an anarchist group, but none were known to have such destructive capabilities or inclinations, and none claimed responsibility.

Around the world people stopped what they were doing to watch and rewatch the scant evidence that had been captured. A minute of satellite grabs, looping like a slideshow, showed the Paris street from above, obscured through the Dome roof, as the dust cloud appeared, twisted like a tornado then stopped as suddenly as it started.

Most people in the twenty-second century liked to believe that violence was something the world was evolving away from and this disturbance was a significant breach. A smaller population, mostly Services enrolled, knew the world wasn't as peaceful as it seemed, and presumed it was either another eruption of tensions or a criminal syndicate with aggressive factions that needed quelling. Most Citizens didn't like to observe this aspect of the world too closely; after all, that was what Services was for.

Witness reports were collected. People outside the radius who saw their neighbourhood collapse and rise in a wave of debris were asked to repeat their experiences for a multitude of interviewers and forums. These joined the mix of footage that was growing around the mystery of the blackout, catalogued and discussed by every chat and media blast to build a comprehensive picture of what had taken place.

A number of Citizens attempted to draw what they had seen over their shoulders as they fled from the confusion. The streets lifting up like a wave; buildings breaking into shards and clouds of dirty fury chasing them from their homes. Some artist sketches depicted a figure, squat and thick-limbed, standing up amongst the fray. It was fanciful enough to capture the mind of the Weave even before someone concocted the glowing eyes, or the figure rearing back to the sky and bellowing like a titan. Most spectators felt this was just a natural inclination to anthropomorphise an inexplicable event. Those who had run from it could not dismiss it so easily.

Penelope Renaud arrived on foot and was blocked by the wall of armoured Servicemen. She could barely see through the phalanx of marauder units to her zone. Above them — the soldiers and crowd — a swarm of observation drones spiralled over the area, unable to pass the cordon. Up close they were as big as your hand with wings of solar panels that made only an insect's worth of sound, though the swarm of them produced a tense hum that was increasingly annoying.

Services couldn't hold back the spectators forever. Public pressure was too great and the media teams, politicians and the curious wanted to see for themselves what was beyond. When the area was declared safe, the soldiers stood down and made room for the people to pass through.

They were told not to go too far and not to touch anything. What Penelope saw was not the home she had lived in, nor the streets she knew. It was wreckage. Some foundation walls stubbornly held up their edges to mark the route of the streets, but Rue de Rivoli was now only a midden twenty feet high.

The group that went through first were silent. Their cameras floated around the scene, pushing their footage out to an equally breathless audience on the Weave.

Penelope had been the mayor of this quartier for seven years, and had lived there all her life. She crouched down and touched the pebbles, struggling to compose herself under the tears that had instantly risen in her eyes. There was so much pale dust; it stuck to her fingers. Then she realised the white limbs she saw in the rubble were not the appendages of statues but the dusted limbs of her constituency.

The new evidence was digested and disseminated. Every dialogue and account was soon accompanied by graphics showing the area before the event, the satellite snapshots of the dust cloud, and then afterwards with the buildings erased and only a hill of detritus in their place.

With all the replaying, and dissipation into new thought vectors, there was a tectonic shift in the civic structure of the World Union. The Will of the people was changing. Penelope Renaud, the mayor of the quartier, was one of the first victims of the civic fallout. With a large portion of her local supporters deceased and the remainder desperate for answers, her status plunged. It would not be long before the Primacy was brought into question and the global governance was reordered.

The Will of the people could change in an instant, theoretically. It only took a significant proportion of the Citizenry to recast their opinions for the hierarchy of society to shift, but there were some unfaltering factors that slowed the pace of change. Firstly, the world being round with half the population awake while the other half slept meant the fastest possible transition from one governing Primacy to another could be twelve hours. The other significant factor in the rate of change was that sixteen billion people had to independently make up their minds. This was not like in the mad old days when people voted for a particular person or faction; choices were not limited to yea or nay or personally vouching for a candidate they would never meet or speak with. Despite the disruption it caused, many people liked to take their time and understand any new choices presented to them.

Citizens contributed the influence of their streams at the detail-level they preferred. For less engaged Citizens the question was always a simple vote of confidence: do you want to keep the current Primacy? And if they didn't want to decide that for themselves, due to apathy or a humble recognition that others might know better, they could abstain or assign their vote to another person, interest group or voting bloc. Other portions of the population were also accounted for, despite their inability to participate, such as the young and infirm. The Will determined who spoke for the silent proportion, be it teachers or a medical board. Children's votes were determined by the parent or guardian until the child voiced that they wanted to control their own influence.

Even so, the first influence wave after the manifestation was quick; the fastest change of government since the founding of the civic system. Within a day of the incident, global confidence shifted, determining that the current Primacy were not in control of events and not speaking openly about what had caused the devastation was impeachable. Of course, the standing Primacy *could* have revealed what they knew, but they were still guided by the Will that had placed them in power; that Will felt the information was best kept restricted and until the Will had selected new representatives this would not change.

The second wave of change came via the passive Will. This wave was bigger and would take longer to flow through. Every mundane decision, from the local pool temperature to arbitrating flight paths, was determined by those who participated, and how much influence they each had. The value of companies and groups rose and fell as people used their services or bought their products. For example, the decision to raise the temperature of the pool affected the support for whatever energy system was in place, which was determined by the ethical and sustainable inclinations of those who took an interest. This gave these collectives a stronger vote to contribute upward in the decision-making tree, forming interest groups for distribution of resources, land rights, research and development; everything.

This hierarchy formed a pyramid of influence that was constantly fluctuating but stable, and accurately reflected the opinions and motivations of the world's population, or at least the eighty per cent that chose to participate. Since the collapse, or more precisely, since the beginning of the Weave and the spread of the World Union, the focus of the Will had been on rebuilding, bringing the weather under control, health improvements and schooling. Many now felt the threat of the unknown, and perceived that the peaceful tenor of the current decision-making tree was not suitable for confronting an unknown and destructive enemy.

In school assemblies, where students met between classes, they buzzed with expletives while sipping at boosted drinks and swapping notes.

'Ya all see that?'

'Cryppy.'

'Hectic cryppy.'

In the communal halls that stretched their tunnels through the big cities, thousands met with friends and colleagues to pass on the insights they had to offer.

'My partner's father said that he has never seen anything like it. And he's been around a long time; this old guy is pushing one-thirty, though you wouldn't know it to look at him,' said a woman to an old friend.

'And they don't know who did it?' her friend asked.

'Anarchists most likely.'

Even the dymo-gyms with their energeneration machines were filled with people talking as they added juice to the grid.

'Did you watch the manifestation last night?' one man asked another man who had a visor over his face.

'I'm watching it now. I was operating all day and didn't get out until six.'

'I didn't even go to work today. No one did.'

On the open Weave the riot of words never paused. Chatter, blame and hypothesis mixing with rant and rave turned almost every platform into an uncontrollable storm of unfounded propositions.

'We have to start asking the questions. Who did this? Who is responsible for these deaths? And how are we going to stop this happening again?'

It was deep in the night when Ryu Shima first saw the event. He was tall, thin, shaven and patient. On a floating dock, he looked out at a sampan bobbing in the lagoon and the red seconds dropping by in his overlay as his squad approached for collection.

His scheduling was precise. Five seconds until they were in position, fifteen until disarmament, seventeen until the snatch. It was an unusual collection tonight as the small boat was no bigger than one of their armoured suits and they had to approach from underwater. He carefully monitored their heart rates and ceregrams and made notes on their overall performance.

The squad had an agent with them that Ryu had recently processed to solve some behavioural issues. He didn't approve of using agents — no psi should ever be fully trusted — but when he had to use them, there was a simple maxim to follow in the capturing of psis: use tappers on benders and bots on tappers.

The agent in question had shown hesitation in recent months and, now that he had been reoriented, if he didn't perform he would be restricted to the islands. Ryu waited and watched the dot that represented Okonta as it approached the boat. For two seconds his cerebral activity flared, normal, but his pulse barely shifted.

'Clear,' the agent reported.

The offensive team jumped at the signal and Ryu heard a crack and splash echo across the canals. A moment later the team leader confirmed the target as masked and inert.

'Well done, Ten. Bring the psi to me and send Okonta back to his capsule.'

'Yes, sir.'

He opened a private line to the agent. 'You did well, Okonta. Your behaviour is much improved.'

'Thank you, Master Shima.'

'There shall be a reward waiting for you at home.'

'Thank you, Master Shima.'

At the edge of the dock the water swirled as the armoured units rose up and scrambled onto the landing, forcing the platform to rock back and forth as the new weight settled. One of the soldiers carried a narrow box, like a coffin, on his shoulder and placed it before Ryu.

'We haven't done an underwater job since training. That was more fun than I remember,' the man commented.

'It isn't meant to be fun, Three,' Ryu answered and made a note in his report. 'That will be all.'

The soldier huddled with the other men and they chattered amongst themselves as Ryu bent over the box to confirm the target's identity and check her vitals were stable for transportation. He noticed a mark on her arm and with a gloved finger pushed her sleeve back to reveal heavy bruising on her shoulders.

'Ten, come here. Can you explain these marks?'

The soldier came and looked over Ryu's shoulder. 'No, sir. I did not see that. She probably had it before collection.'

'No. This is fresh. And about the size of a marauder gauntlet, wouldn't you agree? Who did the collection?'

'Three, sir.'

'Have him reprimanded.'

'But, sir. It was on water —'

'Thank you, Ten. That will be all.'

Before the man could protest again, an alert came over both their symbiots. Ryu held up a hand to stop the other men speaking. Something was happening in the Dome and he switched his overlay to the incoming scenes.

The squad kept silent, themselves tapping into the Paris footage to watch a dust storm shred the Louvre and the whole quartier become consumed by billows of pale dirt.

Ryu thumbed the verification tab and closed the lid of the box. 'Process this one and get straight back to base.'

'Yes, sir.'

'Stay alert in case I need you.'

'Sir, yes, sir.'

There is a rhyme taught to children that is intended to help them learn the basic cause and effect of civic value and Ryu mumbled it to himself as he watched the ebb and tide of the global stream of consciousness.

> *Jack and Jill went up the hill*
> *To see who was the faster*
> *When Jack broke his crown*
> *His vote went down*
> *And Jill became the master.*

Like most, Ryu Shima watched the footage on the Weave with great interest, but his interest was perhaps greater because his value was rising because of the event. As the local enforcer of the Will for the last five years, he had a proven record of effective psi collection and community administration.

Every person in the World Union has what is known as a stream, which logs all their activity on the Weave. Everything they view, endorse or connect to, as well as what is recorded from physical life. Civic status is partially tied to how many other Citizens took an interest in a person's stream, and to what level.

As more people on the Weave became aware of Ryu's history and his way of thinking, his vote began to lead the way on a number of categories and issues. He made sure his supporters knew that he was taking an active interest and was attentive to the situation and there was no suppressing it now; the Primacy had seriously erred. He found the clip from the Dome satellite feed particularly riveting. Overlays calculated the measurements and readings as the dust stretched down Rue de Rivoli. A tornado of unknown force that reached over five hundred metres. Such a demonstration of power was unprecedented.

He had his suspicions about what had taken place. The lack of forensic evidence left only one possibility: a psionic attack. As his position elevated, his permission level rose and his stream could now access the reports and minutes from the undisciplined Pierre Jnr hunt which, as far as he could tell, had provoked this violent eruption in one of the Dome's most venerated areas.

The psi's file made light, but interesting, reading. One capture and one escape, then managing to stay off Services' radar for two decades. Despite his alpha-type, Peter Lazarus had remained hidden and inactive until he was thirty-five. Everything about this case was feeling wrong.

For the first time in decades there was no recorded evidence of an attack. No pictures, no sound, no footage … nothing that revealed the source. No direct recording of history. There was one satellite view that showed little more than a smudge on a screen, and there were erratic testimonies from witnesses who were on the edge of the event; all of those closer were dead or incoherent.

Had this group really found the mythical boy? Or was this the psi rebellion Ryu had been expecting his whole life? It seemed an odd coincidence that within weeks of a psi fugitive volunteering himself they managed to locate Pierre Jnr. After the boy had been eight years in hiding, they drew him out almost instantly? It was more likely that this Peter Lazarus had led them into a trap.

It was as piecemeal an operation as he'd ever seen and he knew that there was really only one person suitable for the job of stopping Pierre Jnr, and that was himself. He was divided between the need for rest and the need to study. The decision was made for him as more and more information became unrestricted for him. He experienced repeated satori as his world was widened a jump at a time.

The Shimas were an old family, well established, able to trace their heritage back to before the collapse. Even before the Dark Age passed, the family was flourishing and Shima Palace was the biggest single structure in Yantz.

There were eight levels to the palace. The top two floors were reserved for the Alpha of House Shima, Yoshiko Shima, and her partner and Regent, Hachiro; Ryu's mother and father. Ryu occupied the third floor from the top, followed by his sister Sato and then his brother Takashi on the fifth level down. The next two levels were for the extended family who had more shifting statuses, and two more siblings who were yet to come of age.

At 3.14 a.m., Yantz time, Ryu's value rose enough to trigger his family's civic insurance and a guard team stationed themselves around the palace and outside his door. He hailed them through his symbiot and verified their identifications. It was then he started calling people.

He knew his brother would be awake already — Takashi never really slept. He took naps between functions, for data to compile and render, or to digest information in his brain. The Shima brothers had trained together as boys, and Ryu often relied on Takashi to run data and even access information that neither of them were officially privy to.

Ryu connected through to his younger brother and was glad he hadn't visited in person. There were many ways in which the two were not alike, hygiene and lifestyle amongst them.

Cannabis was not the only flora bent into new species over the last century of do-it-yourself genetic farming, but it was the most popular one for bio-inventors and it now existed in such diversity that everything descended from the original plant was referred to as mesh. Chew it, smoke it or let it dry in a canister under your nose; each method had a different effect. Takashi was hooked on it and the only time he left his room was when the family forced him to be involved or when his horniness drove him to expand his harem and go doll shopping.

He was totally high when Ryu buzzed him.

'Reeeyuuu! You're up. Did you see that?'

'I saw it.'

'That was cryppy. That was amazing.'

'Yes, it was, but what was it? I need a picture of what's happening, Takashi. I need to know what happened and how we can push it.'

'Nobody is saying — or rather everybody is.'

'Takashi, I'm on the rise,' Ryu cut in.

'Yeah? I haven't been watching any of that.' There was a pause. 'Wooa, Reeeyuuu, check yourself. The vox is speaking. They must be thinking it's psis, to put you ahead like that.'

'I'm pretty certain it was, Takashi. My access just increased and from what I'm seeing this was a botched collection.'

'Hectic. So what did they do to blow an area that big? Crash an air-carrier?'

'No, Takashi. That was the psi.'

Takashi paused. He didn't repeat his favourite expletive; he turned in his chair, his chameleon oculars peering closer to check how serious Ryu was being. He still held out hope his brother might learn to jest. Tonight was not the night and he swivelled away to concentrate on the feeds. He commentated out loud as he made his way through the data. Ryu was used to this and didn't even try to keep up.

'Taka …?'

'Ryu san?' When Ryu went familiar, Takashi went formal. Only his parents got away with the nickname.

'I want to stir the pot. How hard would it be for you to encourage a particular meme?'

'Oh hoo, brother mine. Nothing is easier. A little tagging, anonymous drops in the thought stream … What did you have in mind?'

'All it needs is a little push, Takashi, and I could be in the Primacy.'

'Is the world ready for you, Ryu san? Have they read the fine print?'

'Takashi. Do you support me or not?'

'Of course I do. Go, House Shima! Tell me what you need.'

'I only want the truth to come out. That is all. Services went into Paris thinking they were chasing a potential Pierre Jnr. It might be interesting to know what the world thought about that.'

This excited Takashi and he rubbed his hands together. 'I like it. Let the manifestation of Pierre Jnr begin.'

One of the great paradoxes of the Weave, of having an information and communication network that spanned the globe, where all data could be corroborated or dispelled instantly, is that people still did not know what they should believe. Events were recorded and indisputable, but the explanation of them, the interpretation, was always diverse.

Like a flipped switch, the tune and topic focused on the potential of psi involvement. There had been incidents in the past. Benders lashing out before Services rendered them unconscious, grand frauds that only a telepath could execute, but nothing like this had ever been recorded. Nothing even a tenth of the scale.

The only psi who had ever shown such strength was the semi-mythical Pierre Jnr. It was only eight years ago that Doctor Yeon Rhee had had his experiments shut down. Most of the psis and academics from the project were reallocated to either the restricted islands or hidden from public view and only a part of the world stratum was aware of the Psionic Development Program even when it was going on. Of those who took it seriously, the majority took the stories of a three-month-old baby overcoming staff and security before levitating to freedom with a natural degree of scepticism.

This incident brought all that old bunk to light once more. As soon as the figure in the witness sketches was tagged as 'Pierre Jnr', the name stuck and the records were dusted off.

Takashi and Ryu egged each other on into the late hours. With only the slightest of suggestions and the most innocent

110

of questions on a forum, the Will began to coalesce around the notion that what had happened was caused by Pierre Jnr.

As the night progressed, the civic hierarchy collapsed further and new members vied for position. Sentiment swung toward people who had strong backgrounds in social order and psi security. Retired Servicemen such as Admiral Luciel Shreet and Blair Butler were obvious candidates, having been active in the last great period of social unrest, but they also had many detractors. Janette Orielo the pro-restriction speaker also came to the fore, for the fifth time in her life, but just as there is always a section of people who turn to discipline in times of crisis, there were just as many who turned against it and abhorred any sort of conflict. Ryu dubbed them the 'tolerance vector'. Those people thought that psis should be engaged in the discussion of how they could fit into society.

Ryu Shima was young for a candidate, but he was one of a few showing success in managing the psi problem, and he was, after all, a Shima. Others like Ryu were also rising in rank. People who were from a Services background, or who had been vocal about psis in recent years. There were men and women who had experienced psi conflicts before, like General Zim, whose heavy-handed factions were pushing a policy of total restriction and that the 'manifestation' was a direct result of letting psis run free in our world.

The Shima brothers were both tired by dawn, no longer interacting with the Weave, simply watching the fall of the Primacy and the steep ascendancy of Ryu's influence.

'The Elders have called a breakfast,' Takashi reported.

'Then they must think we have a chance too. The Shimas may be in the Primacy for the first time in forty years.'

'I wonder how Mother will feel about this.'

Father and Regent, Hachiro, stood at the foyer door as each of the children entered. This particular ritual involved a quick inspection of each guest's attire, physical and mental state, and, if necessary, a briefing to make sure they were acquainted with the subject matter that might be discussed. Each member had a few moments alone with the Regent before being allowed entry to the dining room, where the Alpha waited.

At this meeting only the inner circle of the family were in attendance. Sato arrived first, dashing in steps before Ryu. She was younger than him by two years and into freaking her appearance, though today she was restrained and hadn't worn her tail.

Ryu could not hear what Sato and his father said to each other. The Regent simply straightened her kimono and made her pull her hair back from her face before admitting her.

At a gesture from his father he stepped forward. Ryu was immaculately dressed as usual. He'd been preparing as soon as the breakfast agenda came through and he had showered, shaved and groomed while maintaining his link with Takashi and monitoring the pulse of the Weave.

'Good morning, Ryu.'

'Good morning, Father.'

'My son, soon to be my superior.'

'Perhaps, Father.'

Hachiro embraced his son in a bold hug that was very unprofessional and was withdrawn after a moment.

'Can you forgive an old man for his display?' Hachiro asked.

'It is welcomed, Father.'

'It is earnt.' They bowed to each other.

'How is the Alpha receiving the news?'

'She has some questions.'

'But is she happy for me?'

'As a mother I am sure she is, but she is Alpha Shima first. You must reassure her.'

'What is her concern?' Ryu asked, tilting his head slightly.

'The Alpha will need to know your intentions toward the family.'

'My intentions are only the best. Surely she does not question that?'

'No, of course not. But she wonders if you will also be requiring leadership of the house.' Hachiro raised his eyebrow to show the question.

'I see. I had not considered it. I am a servant of the Will.'

'As are we all.'

'Thank you, Father.'

Yoshiko, his mother, was not born a Shima, but after bonding with Hachiro had risen quickly in the family and into the Primacy. It was not an overnight jump like Ryu's, but still impressive. Her influence faded within a year, but her position as the leader of the house was affirmed.

The Alpha sat at the head of the table and then rank position dictated the seating position for the rest of the family. The Regent sat to her right, with Ryu on her left, leaving Sato and the youngest member at the foot. His mother sat peacefully, cross-legged. She acknowledged his entry with a bend of her neck and torso then returned her watch to the doorway. Yoshiko would sit this way until everyone was present. No discussion was allowed to commence until the family was together. Sato similarly sat without moving, her expression more amused than Mother's.

Most high family meetings were planned for evenings, to accommodate all members, as Takashi wouldn't normally be available at this time of day. In the mornings, he would still be in his chambers, nibbling sweet crisps and wrapped in a large quilted bedspread. And in this state of dress, he arrived.

Hachiro rejected him. 'Taka, go put on some pants.'

'I'm covered, Father,' he protested, as if taking the reprimand for genuine concern. By 'covered', he meant the blanket around his shoulders and the symbiot that coated over eighty per cent of his body.

'Taka, we are at table and you are a Shima. This is a special occasion for your brother. Please show appropriate respect.'

Takashi bowed abruptly, bumping a side table and a vase. 'For Ryu san, I shall get pants, even though it discomforts me to do so.' He bowed again and shuffled backward from the room.

The rest of the Shimas remained in their places, and this too was often part of the ritual. Taka's rebellion against the strictures of the family he was born into was a constant amusement, and the bane of his parents.

Ryu and Sato exchanged looks. Through her make-up and cosmetic tweaks he found her expression difficult to gauge. Her eyelashes were as long as his fingers, shadowing blue bone-shaped irises. He was nearly sure the shape of her teeth had been altered, but her mouth wasn't open enough to be certain.

'It seems my children have spent the night awake again,' Yoshiko said.

'This is why we don't have morning meetings,' Sato responded.

'Patience is divine, Sato. Hachiro, please order some tea while we wait for Taka.'

Each Shima wore the chameleon sigil of their family at all times. Even to bed. At the meeting table, and in public, it was expected that they wore it proudly, as a commissioned brooch of rubies as in the case of Sato, or embroidered into their robes as per the Alpha and Regent. Ryu wore a long jacket with a climbing chameleon e-ttooed on the lapels.

Takashi returned after a few minutes wearing a dress-robe to the thigh and a pleated skirt. Hachiro turned to the Alpha, who nodded acquiescence. With his full-body symbiot and the oculars on his head, Takashi seemed to be dressed in a full chameleon costume, though he also had the house sigil printed across the back of his robe.

'Thank you, Taka. And thank you for helping your brother last night.'

The tea arrived and breakfast was ordered without pause. When the servants left the room, they closed it from outside sensors.

'Takashi, is a wall in place?' Yoshiko asked.

'Yes, Alpha. None but I could get through.'

'Good. Let me first thank you for your time this morning. It is only under extraordinary circumstances that I have upset the schedule.' Everyone replied that it was an unnecessary apology.

115

'Sato san, how did your liaison with the Alderson boy advance your position?'

'Mother, I confess it did not. I had hoped it would bring me into contact with his friend Earl Grimshaw, but this Dome fiasco kept most of the scene home last night.'

'I am sorry to hear that. Grimshaw has great potential, though you may be overstating his future position.'

'Isn't love worth the risk?' Sato's favourite gambit was met with a wry stare-off with her mother.

'Something to consider in your rooms with your maids. It may depend on what you are willing to risk, daughter.'

'Yes, Mother.'

'Taka.'

'Uh-oh.'

'Your level has not been properly cleaned in two months.'

'I don't like to be disturbed. Are they not my chambers for private use?'

'Of course, but if you don't organise it within the week, we will have the servitors go through and who knows what will become of your toys. Are we clear?'

'Yes, Mother.'

The meal began with an amuse-bouche of pickled caviar in rice cream. The Shimas preferred the tastes of a human chef over the sensors and calculations of a bot, and it was also considered much more civilised to employ humans where one could.

As they ate, other standard items of business were cursorily discussed. Hachiro's health was reviewed and it was agreed that his diet would be adjusted. The spring weather would mean the opening of the ground floor to the public markets, and each member of the family was to be seen at least once a week purchasing from the locals. The Shimas lived by the principle of supporting those who supported you.

Sato was at last frustrated. 'Aren't we going to talk about what happened last night?'

'It has happened, what more is there to say? Would you like to discuss the footage?'

'This is crazy. The Weave is hectic.'

'Hectic!' Takashi repeated like a child, hearing his favourite word.

'Taka, please. Sato, what is it that you need?' The Regent leant forward.

'She needs to understand what it is that has taken place.' Ryu looked at his sister. 'Isn't that right, Sato? The lack of information leaves the majority unable to even know how important the incident was.'

'Ryu, what do you think is happening?' Hachiro asked. 'Tell us what you can.'

Ryu paused a moment, filtering what he knew from his increased access and what each member of his family knew. He and the Alpha knew as much as each other, and Takashi knew all through him. How much Yoshiko had shared with her Regent was unknown, but he could guarantee that Sato was privileged to very little.

'Yesterday in the Dome an unknown force destroyed a large area of a populated region. We do not know who did it or why. Without answers the Will of the people has reacted by deposing the existing hierarchy and is replacing it with one that is more defensive in nature.'

'So was it important? Is this a war? Should we be bringing in the guards?'

'Yes, Sato, it is important. The guards we have in place will be sufficient. This is why your boyfriends stayed home last night. In our lifetime there has never been a more important event.'

'So who did it?'

'There is only speculation. I cannot share any more.' Ryu put his palms flat to the table.

'Don't be a donkey, Ryu. The room is closed.'

'I am aware, but it will open again and I do not believe you have the restraint to remain silent on any information I share.'

'Go —'

'Sato, enough,' Hachiro commanded. 'Ryu san, please speak with respect to your sister.'

'Yes, Father. I apologise, Sato san. I have been up all night. I let my emotions get the best of me.'

'Ryu,' Yoshiko raised her voice. 'Are you convinced this was a psionic manifestation?'

'I can see no other explanation.'

'And do you believe the rumours that it was caused by Pierre Jnr?'

Ryu and Takashi looked at each other. They could never be sure how much Mother knew. He took the safe road. 'I am not convinced. It seems more likely the act of a group.'

Both parents seemed to sag. Hachiro reached out and took one of Yoshiko's hands.

'I am not sure which is more worrying,' Mother admitted.

'I know you have long predicted an uprising in the psi population, so it comes as less of a surprise for you.'

'If you knew it was going to happen, then why didn't you do anything?' Sato asked.

'What do you think I have been doing the last five years?' Ryu asked.

'Sato, your brother has developed ways of finding and capturing psionic threats for a long time now. He has had much success,' their father explained.

'In provoking them maybe.'

'Sato, I think that is enough. If the Will didn't want Ryu to continue, his team would have been disbanded.'

'What if the Will is wrong?'

Only Sato would ever ask such a question. 'Now that really is enough. We will hear no more from you today.'

Takashi bounced in his seat. 'It's happening, Ryu. It's happening now.'

Together they turned their attention to their symbiot feeds, their information streams watching as Ryu's civic value rose until it joined the 0.00062 per cent that made up the World Union's council of one hundred. A member of the Shima was once again part of the Primacy.

'Takashi, Sato. We must speak with your brother alone for a moment. Please return to your rooms and have your staff double-check to make sure there is nothing in your recent activities or history that might negatively impact on the family. Alpha, do you have more to say?' Hachiro turned to his wife.

'We must all do what we can for Ryu, but no Shima must be seen at this time as hungry for power or to be taking advantage of the situation. The chameleon must tread silently for a time.'

'Yes, Alpha.' Sato bowed to their mother and father, and then after a moment to Ryu. 'Do well, brother.'

With Sato and Takashi out of the room, the walls reconfigured, forming a much smaller box. Mother Shima slowly finished her breakfast, delicately plucking at morsels and keeping her nails clean. She would continue this way until Father had had his say.

Ryu knew they would have consulted beforehand. His father always followed instructions and was respectful about it. There had been a struggle for the Alpha Shima position when Yoshiko first became anointed as his wife; he was blood-born, after all, and hadn't been raised to come second. But over the years he had learnt to enjoy his position as sidekick to the matriarch.

'You have brought great honour on the house of Shima, Ryu san.'

'Thank you, Father.'

'You are poised for greatness. But even now you will need the support of your family to reach the position of Prime.'

'Do you think I have a chance of reaching Prime?'

'Only with our help,' Hachiro spoke carefully.

'Have I displeased you, Father? Mother?' His mother did not look at him; she ate as if she was alone.

'No, Ryu. It is nothing you have done. It is what you could do, if you attain your ambition.' The Regent looked at him questioningly.

'I do not understand.'

'Being a member of the Primacy is both an honour and a most heavy burden. It is not a role all people are suited for.'

'I have been preparing for this all my life,' Ryu argued.

'This is not something one can ever train for. The Prime is the Will, and the Will is the Prime. Do you understand that the Prime is nothing but the peak? That it is not a position of power, but a position of weakness? Which way will you choose to go, I wonder?'

'Father, I am not following you.'

'Have I taught you so poorly?' Hachiro asked.

'No, Father. You have taught me well. Everything I am is because of you and Mother.'

'Listen to me now. When one reaches a high position in our society, it is because many people have faith in your history and your character.'

'I know this —'

Hachiro raised his palm, then waited in silence until the conversation had come to a complete stop.

'Often when people are honoured this way they begin to change. They begin to think that they have power, but this is not the case. The Will is the Will, and it has power over you.'

*I know what this is,* Ryu thought. *Mother is afraid I will take over the Shima as well and use the Primacy in concordance. It would be a natural power base.*

He bowed low to the table. 'Mother. My duty is to the Will. I cannot let my familial ties prevent me from executing its command.'

Mother patted her lips dry. At last prepared to talk, to reveal her prepared judgement. 'We will support you, Ryu. You will be made Prime, but only if you stand separate from Shima.'

'Are you saying I must leave the palace?' he asked.

'If you fail, we must not also be brought down.'

'I will not fail, Mother. I promise.'

'And if you succeed, your method of success must not bring shame upon you or the family. You have received this attention honourably, through your work. Remember why you have been chosen.'

'I understand.'

'Look at me, Ryu san. You must learn to look at me as an equal now.' He straightened and turned to face her. 'The world is spinning on a knife's edge, Ryu, my son. And it has chosen you to lead it to safety. Already you must see the way a Prime must submit to the Will. Count on nothing. I have never seen a change in the Will this fast before. It is a cause for alarm. This change has come so fast, it could happen again while the first dust is still to settle.'

'Surely the cause for this reaction is what we should be alarmed by.'

She nodded. 'Yes. Yes. You see clearly, that is why you have been chosen.'

The old man told his stories as he drove. He used to be a commercial pilot. Sixteen years ago he was on his way to becoming a hauler on the Belt run for the Kuiper mining outfits when the girl he was with said she wanted to become pregnant.

'As soon as she told me, I no longer wanted to go. Who'd want to spend all that time in cold space when there are warm arms for you at home, eh?' He looked over at his passenger with a wink, but found the seat empty.

Who had he been talking to …?

'Anyway,' he smiled and turned back to his piloting, 'we've had our two since then. A boy and girl.'

He tabbed some photos to appear on the dash.

'That one is Mindy. She's nine now and dancing. Floyd is fifteen and about to become a Citizen.'

The driver looked over at the empty seat. Wasn't he talking to someone?

'It's funny. Every time I look at these old photos, I think about going into space. It would have been so empty.'

The fervour of the Weave continued to escalate as a new Primacy rose and new measures for restricting psis came into place. Ryu Shima went from monitoring his local precinct to command of the entire prefecture. Quickly he imposed his procedure for psi collection and shifted ineffectual — possibly sympathising — sheriffs to administration roles. He personally monitored every collection and trusted House Shima and his own growing staff to spread the message that while others were talking, Ryu was doing.

There was no stopping the reports of people being taken from their homes by Services marauders, never to be heard from again. Message to message, hub to hub. Forum rooms were crowded with voices as more and more people windowed on the discussions, hoping the expert panels might be able to explain the whole mess.

'I think we can conclude that this psi problem is more widespread than anyone ever thought,' one panellist speculated to another. 'It seems that Ryu Shima is the only person out there making a difference.'

'I couldn't agree more. What is Zim doing with his Services influence? What is holding him back?'

'I think this is just a new kind of conflict we are seeing and General Zim is simply not equipped to deal with it.'

The pundits continued to cluck and chuckle together. At the fixit shop where Stefan was working they'd had the common screens on all week, spreading their attention across the spectrum of opinions.

He had given up caring, and given up watching, pretty quickly. Big deal. Services would clean it up.

Stefan bent closer to the glider-bike he was reworking and pushed his music up until the world was blocked out.

The machine he was fixing was a fixer-upper from the mech repair shop. It was an antique: part-motorcycle, part-hover. They'd only ever released a few thousand of these before the first squibs entered the market and the line was ended. It was as close to unique as you could get and he liked that.

He'd been working on the thing for months now, before classes and after, and he had had to custom every nut and bolt. But today was the day it was done. The fuel had been waiting in the freezer all that time, because he'd bought it just after the owner said he could keep the bike if he fixed it. He set a sylus to double-check his work and while everyone else was watching the screens he carried the canister over to the tank with a large pair of tongs.

On start-up, its first purr was quiet. He felt it under his hand and he stroked over the frame, feeling for heat like his boss had taught him. There was nothing. It was cool, and shivering like a skittish horse; though he'd never touched one of those, of course, it was just an expression. His boss, Romeo, was behind him, watching him check over the machine. With an approving slap and a short laugh, he told the bot to release the locks and they both took a quick step back as it lurched up to waist-height.

'Now that's a nice machine.'

'It sure is. They don't build things like this now.'

'No, everything's much safer. If this wasn't an antique, it would be illegal.'

Stefan mounted and pumped the motor of the glider-bike, feeling it push and pull between thrust and brake.

Romeo keyed the double doors to open, giving him plenty of room. 'History is unfolding and you are going for a joy ride?'

'You can tell me what happens when I get back.' And he was gone, perhaps a little faster than intended.

He knew it was a bit over the top, and loud at full throttle. It didn't even touch the speeds of a squib, but tearing through the streets below the official flight level, with the wind in his hair as he twisted between avenues of high-rises, Stefan was the most excited he'd ever felt.

He spied two girls from his grade waiting at a bus stop. Tiffani and Myfanwy. They made quite a pair. He looped round and drew up in front of them.

'What is that thing?' Tiffani asked.

'I restored it. I'm going to the deserts. Wanna come?'

'Get lost, Stefan. I'm not getting on that thing.'

'What about you, Myf? You want to burn up some miles with me?'

'Yeah, why not?'

'Myf, what are you doing? I thought we were going to study?' Tiffani protested.

'It's just some fun, Tiff!' she yelled back, hopping on the bike behind Stefan.

'I'm telling your parents.'

'Okay. Let them know I'll be home late.'

Stefan kicked the hover to green and they leapt forward. She had to grab at his jacket and huddle in close to hold on. The machine was working perfectly; he banked and rolled, making Myf squeeze him tighter each time.

It wasn't a real desert they ended up in. The deserts was just what the kids called the old city because nothing much grew there; only stunted trees and bushes were sprouting out of the collapsed buildings and weeds through the cracking tarmac.

'Cryppy. What a ...' Myf looked around.

'Yeah, isn't it great? Nobody comes here.'

'I can see why. Is it safe?'

'So long as we don't go under any roofs, or over any basements.'

'I mean, is it radioactive or anything?'

'Nah, it's fine. I've checked it.'

'So why don't people live here any more?' She started walking up the central avenue he had parked on and he

126

sauntered behind. With a cooperative breeze her skirt was showing enough skin to keep him happy.

'Too hard, I guess. It's pretty busted.'

'What happened to it?'

Stefan shrugged. 'Nothing, I don't think. It's just what happens when no one takes care of things.' She laughed at him for that.

'I'm starting to see a pattern. You like fixing old broken-down things that nobody wants.'

He shrugged again. It wasn't *not* true.

'Hey, I didn't mean it in a bad way.'

'It's okay.'

'I think it's cute.' She was staring at him earnestly, standing close to him, big eyes alive and sweet. He tipped his head down — for sure she wanted him to kiss her — then the glider gave out a loud smoky belch that made them both jump.

'Was that meant to happen?' she asked, following him as he ran back to the bike. He began sliding his hands over the engine, feeling for heat. He swore.

'I forgot to park it right. I've blown one of the cells. You're meant to cool them down when you stop. I knew that.' He started irritatedly flicking switches.

'Will it still fly?'

'Yeah, slowly,' he answered. 'I'm sorry.'

'What for? You didn't mean to do it, did you?'

'No, but I won't be able to get you home any time soon.' This made her laugh again.

'That's okay, Stefan. I like it out here. With you.' Myf placed her hand on his shoulder.

'You do?' This time when he turned to her, ready again, she was embarrassed, red, and spun away from him.

'Let's walk around a bit more.'

They walked back down the main way and then decided to turn right and then left, and then up a street that had tree stumps lining each side of the road. They took turns looking at the other.

'Thanks for coming out here with me.'

'You don't need to thank me. I said it was alright.'

'We just don't even know each other really.'

'I suppose that's true. Why did you ask if you didn't think I'd come?'

He didn't have an answer for that one, or not one he wouldn't be embarrassed to give.

'What? You thought I wasn't hack enough for you?' she asked.

'Something like that.'

'Hey. Don't judge what you don't know.'

'I'm not judging,' he replied quickly. She was running circles around him. 'You're just always so good.'

'I just do what I'm supposed to do.'

'Yeah? So why did you say yes?'

This time, she didn't have an answer.

'Is something wrong?' he asked. Myf shook her head. 'So why do you always do "what you are supposed to do"?'

She shrugged uncomfortably. 'That's how you get somewhere, I suppose.'

'My parents want me to enrol for Services placement,' he said.

'Is that bad? I've been enrolled since I could speak.'

'No. It's not bad.' Stefan rolled his head around. 'I just —
not that I'm against Services or anything, I get it — I'm just not
sure I think that way.'

'What way?'

'Oh, you know … I don't know.'

'Did you watch the feeds last week?'

'Yeah, I watched it as it happened. We were at the shop late.
When it started, we just dropped tools and sat in front of the
screens.'

His phrases were odd to her. 'You talk funny.'

'You talk funny,' he weakly countered.

They smiled and then looked down to the safety of the
ground.

'What do you think it was?' Myf asked.

'Who knows? Probably just anarcs. Or some nation holdout
with a grouse about something.'

'Stefan, you don't get a blackout like that from a bomb. Not
even a big bomb. It was a total data drop-out. For fifteen minutes.'

'I don't even know what that means. Who cares if people
couldn't fritter with their friends for a little bit? I'm like that
all day.'

'No satellite, no camera coverage, no witnesses? Thousands
of people died and no one knows how.'

'Yeah, yeah … You're right.' Stefan swallowed and thought
for a moment. 'I'd forgotten that bit.'

'How could you forget *that* bit? That's the main bit.'

'I don't know. The Weave just goes on repeat about the
drop-out.'

'Yeah, but that's what makes it so huge.'

'It's hectic. Thanks. I see it. What the hack happened?'

They wandered around until sunset, which this far north meant until 4 p.m. He didn't want it to end, but it was getting dark and he hadn't fixed the lights on the hover.

'You know, you're a lot more fun out here, out of classes.'

'Perhaps if you came to classes you might know me better.' Her smile was small, but he liked it. He thought that smiles on girls were like flowers first stretching their petals. They grew broader and brighter with age, until they started to wrinkle, like his mum.

'Huh?' He felt a light finger of pressure on his lips. 'What?!' he repeated, more alarmed and swatting at his face.

Myf pulled back quickly, hugging her knees in front of her and peeking at him over the top. 'I'm sorry.'

'What? What are you sorry for? I just thought I felt something on me.' He could see she was shaking a little. 'It's okay, Myf, it was nothing. It's stopped.'

'I'm sorry.'

'Don't be, it … was that you?'

Myf's breathing was becoming fast and shallow, skin paling like rainfall. Her eyes were large and unblinking.

He put his hand out slowly, resting his fingers on her arm. 'It's okay, Myf. It really is. It's cool.'

'Are you …?'

'Me? No. But that doesn't mean you have to worry.'

'You won't turn me in?'

'No. Of course I won't.'

She managed to exhale, dabbed her sleeve around her eyes

and regained a bit of control. She stayed as she was though, knees up to her chest.

'Can you read my mind?'

Myf shook her head. 'No, I can just push stuff a bit. Look.' She pointed down at the sand.

At his feet a pebble was sliding in a curve. At snail-pace it completed an unsteady circle and he looked up at her. 'That's pretty cool. I can see how that would come in handy.' He thought of small screws in places where his fingers couldn't fit.

From directly above, a spotlight hit the block they were sitting on and a ring of bulky figures dropped down around them. Myf screamed.

'Glue 'em,' one ordered and instantly three of the soldiers pumped their guns, hurtling gloop-shots that hit their legs and arms, sticking them to each other and where they sat.

'Drop her and mask her, Seven.'

One of the soldiers took another step forward, holding a different gun that shot a smaller blob of white adhesive at Myf's face. His head jerked backward as if struck and the goggles cracked on his helmet, but the soldier didn't pause and in one more step he was lifting a white mask to her face.

Stefan felt once more a softness against his lips and saw Myf's frightened eyes before they were blocked from view. As the mask went on, her touch faded.

'Lights.' Shoulder lights flared up on each of the squad. They were tall, around twelve feet, and encased in battle suits. These guys were heavy duty — 'marauders' was the Services term and Stefan was puny beneath them.

'What about this one, Ten?'

The one they called Ten must be their commander, though whichever one it was, he was physically indistinguishable from the others ... and Stefan didn't have the right clearance to see the strategic overlay in his visuals.

'You got enough ice in your tank to get you home, Citizen?'

Stefan nodded mutely.

'Then go home.'

Ryu Shima marked the collection as closed and successful, logging it to his record for all to see. The target's stream was confiscated and her connections were marked for higher monitoring, so he sent a motion to increase training and acceleration of the remote operators program.

Ryu Shima was not the only one to be thrust into the limelight by the political shifts. When Charlotte Betts's door rang early one morning, she couldn't believe who it was.

His face brought back a lot of memories. She had built a new life since she last saw him, a spiritual life, and Charlotte only referred to that earlier period, when pushed, as the time when she was her mother's daughter.

'Hello, Charlotte.'

In her shock at seeing him, one of her cats rushed to escape through her legs and the man bent down to grab it before it could get too far.

'Come inside, quick, before they all try to get out and Miz Robertson has something to say about it.' In thirty years, Maximillian had become grey and paunchy. 'Max ... what are you doing here?'

'What am I doing here? What do you think I'm doing here? Are you not plugged in?'

'No, I haven't today. I was up late.'

'And you still didn't hear?'

The truth was she had hosted a gathering of the Lingua Pax. They were a rather benign group, deconstructing languages to identify word-concepts, or lexemes, that had potentially negative impacts on the human mind. It was a fun group that spent many evenings in idle speculation over the harmful effects of such terms as 'perfection', 'entitlement' and 'fate'. They wasted the whole night determined to remain inconsequential.

'I can't believe you are still into that wabi sabi nonsense.'

'Max, if you came here to insult me —'

'I didn't. I promise.'

'Well, whatever you came here for, please, just make it quick.'

'You've got to listen to me, Charlotte. This is big, and you're going to need someone you can trust.'

'I have thousands of people I trust, Max. You are not one of them.'

'Well, now just listen to what I have to say and plug yourself into the Weave. The world is shifting and your name is on the rise.'

'Me? But I hate all that stuff.'

At Max's urging she pulled on a visor, warmed with bright crochet from a long-forgotten guest. He sat watching the bottom half of her face react to the news of the disturbance that caused the dissolution of the Primacy and how she, Charlotte Betts, had become a person of interest in the civic hierarchy.

'How did this happen?' she wondered aloud, plaintively.

'There is a void in the new structure and it's looking for people to fill it. Let me break it down for you,' Max began, counting points on his fingers. 'An explosion has damaged a part of the Dome and the majority believes it was a psionic attack. There are two ways people are reacting to this: one is with a reinstatement of authoritarian rule, and the other is ... looking for another way.'

'And that other way is what? Why should they think I can help?' *To go from writing a few columns about psi tolerance to entering the Primacy race overnight, the world must be upside-down*, she thought.

Max clasped his hands and spoke to the sky. 'Oh, why could I never get you to read any of my books?'

'Have you read any of mine?' she asked back.

'I've read them all, but that doesn't matter. And you know why? Because there's a bunch of people out there who agree with you. They don't think that locking up every psionic on the planet is a good thing. There are people who don't even think psionics are a threat.'

'Yes, I'm one of them.'

'I know that, Charlie. That's why I'm here.' Max's face was redder with frustration than when he had come in, very excited, a moment ago.

'Did I always annoy you this easily?' she asked.

'I don't know, but my heart isn't what it used to be.'

'Oh, Max. Is whatever it is worth all this arguing?'

'It's the world, Charlie. It's humanity. It's everything you care about.'

'But why me, Max?'

134

'Because there aren't many out there saying what you've been saying.'

'Max ... as I said, I really hate this stuff. I hate civics. It does terrible things to people.'

Max twisted in his seat, biting his lip. 'Are you trying to insult me now?'

'Oh, sorry, no. I forgot.'

Max was a civics professional. He taught, and also consulted, on civic matters. He was a politician for hire and exactly the kind of person she swore she would no longer abide.

'No, you didn't, but let me not lie to you. I know you've had experiences with people manipulating you to enhance their own influence, but that is how it is in this world. Civics doesn't make people bad: selfish people can find a way to manipulate any system. When one person has power, another wants it. You think your new friends aren't interested in you for what you can do for them? That's what friendship is ... it's allegiance, it's helping. You can look at it with your soft-glow light if you want, but when it comes down to it, it is people who are useful to you.'

'Max! Get out. Get out now.'

'No, Charlotte. You wanted honesty. Don't reward me by throwing me out.'

Silence fumed between them.

'Can I get you a cup of tea then? I find it very relaxing.'

'What kind of tea?' Max asked.

'Just normal tea. Unless you wanted something more experiential?'

'Normal is fine for me.' He followed her to the kitchen. Charlotte didn't keep a servitor to cook and clean, and the

135

collected porcelain, mostly teacups and saucers, were in disorder in the sink. She ran a tap and gave a few of them a quick rinse.

'I apologise for what I said.'

'I'm sorry too,' Charlotte replied.

'I don't know why I frustrate you so,' he said.

'Oh, for the same reason I frustrate you. One of us always wants something the other doesn't want to give. Which by your definition makes us not friends.'

'Let's not go backward, Charlotte.'

'Ah, but seeing you *is* going backward. You are the stepping stone between my two worlds.'

'You don't have to go back to that world.'

'Isn't that what you're trying to get me to do?'

'Not in the way you think. You're a Citizen, aren't you?'

'Yes, otherwise we wouldn't be having this conversation.'

'Bear with me. When you're a Citizen, you're always a part of the world. In your head you've divided it up into your mother's world versus this island of spiritual fulfilment you've created. But they are still part of the same world.'

'They are very different.'

'Yes, they are. But multiplicity is what the World Union is founded on. There is a plurality to the system that makes you one of many voices, even when you choose to be silent. The only thing that has changed is that more people are listening to you now. The question is, do you want this? Do you believe in what you've been saying all these years, or is it just made up?'

'No, Max, you're being cruel again.'

'Look around you. This room contains your whole life, but the world is asking you to speak. And if you do nothing, it will pass.'

'Why does it have to be now?'

'Because now is an extraordinary opportunity. You have a following who are curious as to your perspective on recent events. This may come as a surprise to you, but there are very few voices advocating tolerance for a class of people who can control our thoughts.'

'That is scaremongering, and there are many ways our thoughts are controlled.'

'Th-that's good,' he stuttered. 'That's what we need to get ahead of this. I want to make you the face and voice for tolerance. But you have to act quickly to keep them interested in you.'

'Don't pressure me. I can't decide like that. I only awoke a few minutes ago to find my opinion suddenly mattered.'

'Then do nothing, just let it go.' He threw his hands up. 'I just thought ...'

'What? It's infuriating when you don't finish your sentences.'

'I thought that you might like to have your say.'

'You mean *your* say,' she said.

'No.' Max hesitated. 'Perhaps,' he confessed and sat down at the junktique kitchen table.

'We're old, Max.' She put a cup of tea in front of him and patted his hand.

'Yes. This could be our last chance to make a difference.'

'We are *old*.'

'You said that already.'

'It just crept up on me is all. The last time we had this argument was after my first book. Do you remember? We were young; you wanted to agent for me.'

'I wanted to sleep with you.'

'Well,' she patted his hand again, 'it wasn't bad for me either.' She stroked the skin of his fingers, drier, thicker and more creased than in the days of their dalliance. 'You can tell them I'm going active. For now, you speak for me. I can't handle all that direct contact. Bring me your best candidates and let's build a team.' Resolve settled in her belly. 'Imagine what it would have been like if I'd listened to you last time.'

As soon as she announced her acceptance of candidacy, Charlotte's life changed, like a pot of water leaping to boiling point.

With Max and her new assistant, Amy Watson, a younger woman Max had worked with previously — and she wondered how closely — advising her, she worked through the influx of writing commissions, guest speaker invitations and right of responses that were clamouring for her attention. Most had to be declined for strategic reasons or due to time constraints.

She had never written so much in her life, nor given so many interviews. It was hard to stay on top of everything that followed on from the events. The day before last she had been cornered by a questioner about a psi hate group that she had never heard of and now she was about to appear in front of a bunch of irate avatars to explain her position.

Max and Amy waited by the immersion couch for her to be ready. Though her physical form wouldn't be seen, for her own peace of mind she had dressed as if it would be. Respectable, professional, representative.

'What are you smiling at, Max?' she asked.

'Don't take this the wrong way, but you have never looked so much like your mother than you do right now.'

'I should slap you for that. She would never wear this much colour.'

'Okay, you two. Enough silver-haired flirting. I just want to do a little prep before you go in,' Amy said.

'If you must.' Charlotte loosened her shoulders and lay down on the long black lounge.

Amy sat on a rolling stool and wheeled close to her. 'Okay, they call themselves the Anti Psi League and their leader is a man called Nigel Westgate. Formerly involved with the Sapien Brethren and Minors' Rights. He's built his career on being a troublemaker.'

'He looks like a wet berry too.' Charlotte was flicking through snaps of his career.

'Oh, he is. Now, Miz Betts, I need you to remember one thing and one thing only.'

'Yes?'

'He is smaller than you. In terms of influence, in terms of civic ranking, he isn't in your class.'

'Really?'

'He's not even breathing the same atmosphere as you. So just remember that when he starts shouting at you.'

'He's small and I'm big,' Charlotte repeated, nodding.

'You got it. You've got to dive in three minutes. Are you ready?'

'I think so.'

'You've had some water? Gone to the bathroom?'

'Okay, Amy. Let's give Representative Betts some space.'

Amy smiled and moved to her desk, instantly clicking back into the stream that was growing around Charlotte's campaign.

'She is very efficient.'

'She is. Sorry if she's a little overzealous,' Max said.

'And she talks strangely. Young people!'

'You should hear her son.'

'She has a son?'

'A ten-year-old. His slang is incomprehensible.' Max put a professional hand on her shoulder. He knew she was nervous. 'Now, focus for a minute. There's something I picked up that I think you should be ready for.'

'What is it?'

'This Westgate guy has been making accusations that your sudden rise is an act of psi manipulation.'

'How can he suggest such a thing? Just because there are more people in the world who think like I do than he does ...'

'Of course. But it's the kind of seed that might spread.'

'Really?'

'It happens.' Max smiled his award-winning smile at her. 'Charlotte, you have to relax now. Don't react, stay calm. And remember what Amy said: no matter what happens in there, more people will be replaying your words than his. Understand?'

'Okay. Give me the goggles.'

'I'll be right beside you the whole time.'

\* \* \*

The Anti Psi League held their meetings in avatar spaces. The rooms replicated real-life public spaces, and the speakers appeared on a raised platform at one end and viewers in the larger open area before it. When there were more avatars attending than visual space allowed, a count was registered of how many people were watching and a generic amalgam of crowd demographics was shown. This meeting had close to ten thousand and their overall mood was interpreted through an algorithm that combined their reactive expressions, so the speakers could gauge how they were faring.

The rules of the meeting were clear, and more easily enforced in avatar spaces than in the real world where anyone could shout out at any time. The panel of speakers would speak; in this case it was the leader of the mob, Nigel Westgate, and Charlotte. If someone in the audience had a question, they could post it at any time, or wait for the opening address to be completed and the floor opened. Once the floor was opened the questioning proceeded in the order of who put their hand up first and also a little by who had the greater influence. The APL had a strict policy of no moderation, which meant it could not be held accountable for any views expressed by the crowd, no matter how rude or ignorant. Charlotte did not expect a warm welcome. In the last twenty-four hours she had watched selected highlights from its previous meetings and if this meeting was being held in the physical world she would have felt afraid for her life. Here, on the Weave, it was only her civic life under threat.

But it was a chance she had to take. She had to come out strong and show she could stand up to the opposition view. At least that was how Max had convinced her. It was time to show some backbone after a life of slinging her opinions from a safe distance.

Amy, the assistant, or consultant or whatever she was meant to be, had made alterations to Charlotte's regular avatar. 'I don't care where they are or what they're angry about, a good bosom can remind men what is most important to them.' Max had shrugged and left the room to avoid laughing and Charlotte had given in. If only it was so easy.

The other person on the podium was the self-appointed president of the Anti Psi League. Nigel Westgate was young and abrupt, short with hair cropped to the scalp. He dressed in a fashion that seemed referential to Services' dress uniform, but in browns rather than blues. The tactic did give him the look of authority he hoped it would.

'Miz Charlotte Betts. I was surprised you accepted our invitation. You are the de facto voice for psi tolerance, but as yet have no official position. How should I refer to you?'

Charlotte was ready for this one. Max had suggested she may as well not hold her tongue with this demographic. 'As I understand it, in your meetings I am most commonly referred to as "that woman". Perhaps to avoid confusing yourself you should stick with that.'

'Miz Betts would be more appropriate, I think. Thank you for taking time out from your busy schedule of spreading psionic propaganda.'

'I appreciate you asking me here to help cure your ignorance.'

'Are you a telepath, Miz Betts?'

'I am not.'

'Then are you under the influence of a telepath?'

'No.'

'How can you be so sure?'

'My cat would have told me.'

'Miz Betts, are you not taking this seriously? Our way of life is under threat.'

'Is it? I think your phobias are causing more harm to our way of life. We have lived with psis amongst us for a very long time ... in peace.'

'Until last week. Can you deny that a psionic entity took thousands of innocent lives?'

'Do you pretend that if you were attacked you would not protect yourself? Besides which, not even the Primacy can confirm what caused the incident under the Dome.'

'How can you be so foolish? We all know what it was.'

'No. You don't. You have a fear of what it could be and without adequate proof you have decided that your superstition is fact.'

'I am reassured that you speak only for a small minority, Miz Betts.'

'Large enough that you felt the need to invite me here.'

'The APL welcomes all honest opinions and points of view.'

'Then may I speak?' Nigel indicated that she could. 'Thank you all for attending this gathering and listening to a voice you know already that you disagree with. I think it is extremely important for our society to have groups like yours who can come together to discuss common fears that affect our lives. It is the very foundation of our civic structure.

'I knew, coming here, that my standpoint would not be commonly shared, but there is a growing portion of the World

Union who are questioning whether psionics are a threat to our society. We have known of the existence of psionic powers in humans for ninety years, and we can safely assume that the potential has always been there.

'Humans always have fear. There has never been a time when we have not found something to be afraid of. But why do we always let fear guide us? Are our imaginations so limited that we cannot be guided by hope?

'I believe that, in the absence of any other major threat, we have found something that we don't fully understand and we are working hard to make it our enemy. And by making it our enemy, by persecuting these people, they will make us their enemy. They are human too. They love just like the rest of us. They hurt just like we do. Why do you feel they should be punished for their gifts? Why do we let fear haunt us?

'When I first heard of telepaths, when I was a girl, I thought to myself, "How wonderful that someone might now understand me." When I first heard about telekinesis, I thought of the amazing things one could do with that ability. I choose to meet this unknown with wonder. I have been greatly saddened to discover that others meet this concept with fear. Can you not imagine the great things that could be done in teaching, in therapeutic medicine, in entertainment, in simply understanding each other better? Could we not, for once, try a different approach than aggression and domination?'

'Miz Betts, you are either hopelessly naive or you are working for the psis,' Westgate's avatar sneered, one of two expressions it seemed to be programmed with.

'Did you hear nothing I said?'

'Oh, I heard. I heard your fear. Your fear is so great that you think we should simply roll over and let them do what they want to us.'

'Why is it, Mister Westgate, that you feel more afraid of a psionic than you do of a person with a gun? Both can cause harm. Both can force you to do what you don't want to do.'

'Because I can get a gun of my own and level the playing field.'

'And once again, violence is met with violence. How many times must humanity follow the same path to destruction? Are you too young to understand what was lost in the collapse? Have you not viewed the horrors of that time? Would you really want us to go through a war like that again?'

'And your answer is to submit?'

'To understand.'

'I think we do understand. I think you are a puppet of Pierre Jnr and I can no longer tolerate you spreading your lies.'

In a blink, Charlotte was staring at the inside of her goggles. The little bastard had ejected her. Before question time.

She sighed and pulled the helmet off. Max was sitting nearby grinning and Amy was bringing a fresh pot of tea to her side table, with a biscuit.

'That didn't end well.'

'Quite the contrary, Charlie. Your performance and his reaction at the end have put us over. You're being quoted all over the Weave. You've done it.'

* * *

145

The incubator room was tranquil. The babies were too young to roll. They could only move their arms and legs and peer about at the fuzziness of their surroundings.

A boy of eight years stood amongst them. He kept them calm and made them coo with happiness.

He leant over the plastic cot of the latest newborn. It was only an hour old, still red from its exciting entry to the world. It stared at him with big fresh eyes. It was too young to see anything but the blur of the older boy looking down on him, but it could hear him.

*Hello.*

Of course it was too small to understand even the concept of hello. Pierre watched its immature brain rabidly networking, making sense and constructing patterns as quickly as it could.

Pierre put his finger in its hand and it clamped down automatically. *Learn, little one.*

A nurse came in through the sliding doors. He didn't seem to see Pierre amongst the cots; he just walked to the side and lay down upon the floor.

*You see, little one? It is that easy.*

After Tamsin's disappearance, the team originally assigned to the capture of Pierre Jnr was removed to a semi-permanent compound for isolation. Peter Lazarus was kept under guard in a hospital tent, while Geof Ozenbach and Colonel Pinter found themselves roomed in the officers' barracks. It was normal procedure to put a hold on operations while a change of command was underway and the team and mission under review, so their segregation was reinforced by a complete disconnect from the world's data channels.

For two days they sat together, confined in a stark barracks room with a dozen generic publications and a trio of viewers, their information filtered to grunt level. They were shown again and again the footage — and testimony from every possible source — of the events that were reshaping their world.

It had been a long while since Geof had had so little knowledge at his fingertips. A lifetime, in fact. He had no more contact with the outside world than the Colonel did with his Services-issued plastics spread before him on the table. Geof felt twitchy at not being able to dive into the raw data and see what was really happening.

His symbiot had never felt so heavy.

The Colonel slid one of the sheets from his pile and nudged it toward him. It was quite a nostalgic feeling for him to lift it closer and watch the animated lines and text, remembering his days in preparatory before he was botted for the first time. Geof had to remind himself that the information it presented was current rather than historical.

The article the Colonel thought would be of interest to him was tracking the influence of the Primacy, the group of people who held most sway in the world and were the top of the civics hierarchy. Since the manifestation, and disclosure of the damage, an unprecedented swell of opinion was sweeping the population.

The balance of authority and power was sliding into oblivion. People had to decide what to believe, which meant taking sides if they hadn't before and changing sides given the new circumstances. Only about one per cent would have the level of access to know what had really happened, and what led up to it. Within twenty-four hours the entire Primacy would change and those who had reigned would now become subjects.

The Colonel removed the thread from his ear that fed him communications from his Services superiors and sat back in his chair.

'Tell me, Geof, have you ever played Criticality?'

'The card game?' he asked. 'Only in the mandatory classes.'

'It's a trench game. When I was active, in my early days, we played it all the time. It's a good way to pass the hours when you're waiting for something to happen.'

They ordered food, Serviceman meals only, and Pinter took a box of palm-sized cards from his kit and brought them to the table.

Geof laughed. 'We're not using those, are we?'

'Of course we are. Don't mock. We're not *all* wired to the cerebrum, are we?'

'No, sir.'

'Now, do you remember the basic rules of the game? You can pick up as many cards from the draw deck as are already in your hand and you can lay out as many as you choose. Stacks can only go as high as there are piles and when a stack peaks it falls down and goes into your prize pile. If that has a knock-on effect and more stacks are toppled, they also become yours. To go out, you must trigger a collapse and empty your hand. Clear?' He began dealing the cards, ten to each of them. 'Remember, the point of any game is to play. It's not life or death.'

'I find it a bit abstract, to be honest.'

'It is intended to be analogous.'

'Of civics.'

'That is one example. Should I go first?' They began playing slowly, while Geof found his feet in the game. 'It struck me, Ozenbach, that we don't exactly know each other that well. Do we?'

'I guess that's true.'

'We met Pete before we met each other.'

'Yes. Is that important?'

'I don't know. Is it?' The Colonel only briefly flashed his eyes from the game to look at Geof. 'You're an incubator baby, aren't you?'

'Yes, sir.'

'And what's that like?'

'It's all I know, sir.'

'Well, that's a dull answer. I was hoping for more.'

Geof sat back, not sure how to respond. There wasn't much more to tell. He was born (which he couldn't remember), he'd gone to a weaver ranch for his training and since he was fifteen he'd been running assignments for Services. All of which the Colonel knew already.

'You can't read minds, can you, Ozenbach?'

'No, sir. I cannot.'

'Pity. It would make things an awful lot easier, wouldn't you think?'

'I can see how it might be useful sometimes.'

'You found Peter Lazarus pretty easy to talk to, didn't you?'

'What is with all these questions, Colonel? Am I on trial?'

Pinter stopped in the middle of laying down his cards. 'Of course you are. We all are. That's why we're in the middle of the desert. You understand that, don't you?'

'You're right. I don't know why it didn't occur to me. I've never been on trial.'

'Nor would you ever expect to be.'

Was the Colonel back to this again? Why were norms so fascinated by the bred? Geof knew the mantra, because it had been drilled into him since birth: born to be better, born to do good. It was written on the wall of every nursery and every ranch, always reminding them that they were genetically compelled to do what they were meant to do and be what they were meant to be. It wasn't something they had to accept as it was impossible for them to challenge.

'Does my asking make you uncomfortable?' the Colonel asked.

'I simply don't know what answer will satisfy you.'

'I ask because you have more experience in being controlled than I do. I wondered what it felt like. If there was a way to recognise it.'

'You're suspicious of Peter? You may as well be suspicious of all of us.'

'Oh, I agree. One can't doubt everything. That way leads to madness. And yet ...' The Colonel let the 'yet' hang in the air. 'Geof, a little bird has whispered in my ear.'

Geof's gaze stopped straying and focused on the faint blue irises of the older man.

'I too found him very good to talk to,' the Colonel said. 'And now I ask myself if I would normally have been as open as I was with a non-telepathic stranger.'

'Are you suggesting Pete was manipulating us the whole time?'

'Somebody has suggested it to me. I am now asking if you think the idea has merit.'

Geof clenched his teeth, dimpling the skin under his lip. 'It would be denial to say that it wasn't possible.'

'Did you ever dig out how he escaped the camp he was taken to? When he was fourteen?'

'No, the records are restricted.'

'Oh, come on, Geof. I know how weavers work. It's only restricted if you can't get to it. Why didn't you look it up?'

'I assumed others would have already.'

'That's not like you, is it?' Pinter turned back to the game and laid down three cards on separate piles. 'It's not a remarkable story. He just walked out. And nobody tried to stop him.'

'Why would they let him do that? Did he supposedly control them to let him go? He's not strong enough for that.'

'You'd have to ask him. The hypothesis is that continued exposure to a telepath increases their understanding of you and their ability to control you, to a certain extent. Inserting thoughts, triggering emotions. Who knows where that sort of thing would end?'

'Look, I can't say that it's not a good theory, but it doesn't feel right to me.'

'Because you liked him? I liked him too, and I'm a seventy-year-old man who doesn't like people on principle. But then again, when you know the person you're talking to can read your mind, it might just be a natural reaction to be more open. One may as well submit to it, so to speak.' Pinter smiled wanly at the end of his point, and then brightened as the food and alcohol arrived.

They continued to play Criticality as they ate, and sipped at the aniseedy liquor that was provided. It was a good game for their current situation, since it had no end when playing with an infinite deck.

'I'm not used to waiting around like this,' Geof complained.

'Most of a soldier's life is waiting. At least we can't be in too much trouble.' Pinter raised his cup of liquor. 'If you were Peter —'

'I refuse to believe it, Colonel.'

'No, different topic. If you were Peter, I wouldn't have to tell you this, so this is the first time I'll be saying it out loud. My wife and I are now parted.'

Geof put down the fork he was holding. 'And you are telling me this why?'

'Because if you weren't cut off from the data right now, you'd already know. I believe the restrictions on us will be lifted. I didn't want you to think later that it was why I've decided to reactivate.'

'Reactivate?' Geof stumbled over the thought. Pinter was an old man who hadn't seen action in decades. 'So why are you?'

'Didn't you see what happened in the Dome? Are you not watching the same screens I am? A single child destroyed a kilometre of a city. Thousands of people were killed. By one boy.'

'We don't know for sure that is what happened.'

'But we both believe that it was. Peter said he saw him.'

Geof nodded agreement. 'But didn't you just say we shouldn't trust him?'

'I was just passing on what someone told me. It's always wise to question one's assumptions.'

'Okay, so what if he and Pierre were working together?'

'And Tamsin.'

'Is there any word on her?'

'Not that I have been told.'

'Now there's something I could be doing. She wouldn't be able to just slip away if they let me track her.'

'But we are all on trial for now. Ah.' Pinter emptied his hold of cards onto the table, collapsing seven tall piles and sweeping them into his prize count. 'Would you like to play through or restart?'

'Restart. I think I know where I went wrong.'

'Every game is different.' The Colonel gathered the cards into one pile and began shuffling them for a new game. In this way they passed the hours. Reading, talking and Geof losing hand after hand of Criticality.

Geof looked over the news sheets. 'Are you familiar with this Ryu Shima, Colonel?'

'I can't say that I am.'

'Things will change if the Shima family makes it into the Primacy,' Geof said. 'I reviewed his case studies before we started the hunt. The man is efficient. He has developed a good formula for psi collection.'

'Some efficiency might be what this team needs if the hunt is to continue.'

'Surely it must. Catching Pierre is more a priority now than ever. We've seen what he is capable of.'

'You are missing the bigger picture, Geof. It won't just be about Pierre now. There is already a suggestion that this is the first sign of a psi rebellion. Of which we can only assume that Pierre Jnr and possibly Tamsin Grey are a part. Maybe even Peter. The appointment of a man with Shima's record might be a response to an act of war.'

'So what should we do?'

'We wait for the command. As we always do.'

'And until then we play games and talk?'

'A soldier's life for me.' Pinter smiled and dealt ten new cards to each of them. 'You start this time,' he said.

'There's something I've been meaning to ask.'

'Go ahead, Ozenbach. I think I know what it is.'

'Well, I know who you are of course. I know your history.'

'Not really any secrets there, are there?'

'I was wondering what you would do to beat Pierre. Now that we've seen what he is capable of.'

'Ah, well, now you're in my area.' He doubled his hand and laid down no cards. 'For a start we might not have seen what he is really capable of. We've seen one instance. We need to know more about his weaknesses. We don't even know if a simple missile strike might be effective.'

'Collateral damage be damned?'

'I think I can guess which way the majority would swing.'

'That means the first place we think we found him becomes a death sentence for the surrounding Citizens,' Geof said.

Their conversation was interrupted as a sergeant knocked at their door and entered with a cursory air salute.

'Colonel, your presence has been requested by the Primacy.'

'More debriefing?'

'I have passed on the entirety of my missive. If you'll come this way, we have a jet waiting for you.'

The Colonel looked at Geof. He turned his cards around to show what he was holding. 'I was about to get twenty points in one turn.'

Geof followed Pinter to the opposite end of the compound. A two-seater Services cone waited on its haunches in the cleared area slightly away from the squibs.

'It's time for the reprimand or the medal, I'd say.' Pinter winked at Geof as they shook hands.

'Let me know which it is.'

'I will if I am able. So long, Geof.'

'Goodbye, Colonel.'

Geof stood and watched as the jet flung itself into the sky, a hiccup-explosion, then pulled swiftly up as if towed by a line.

Before returning to his quarters, Geof strayed over to the fence to look beyond. The compound lights pushed full dark back for a hundred feet, revealing a red sandy waste. He craved data. His near-useless symbiot fed him what its sensors could gather, but it wasn't enough. Temperature: six degrees and dropping. Wind speed: eleven kilometres per hour. There were one hundred and fifteen bio-signatures within the compound — though he couldn't access their files to find out more about them.

He'd read that people in olden times could predict the weather by the smell on the wind. It didn't seem to work for him.

Nobody stopped him entering the hospital tent. Only one nurse was allowed near the patient while he was conscious;

other Servicemen were kept away. The tent was guarded by a single rank of servitors standing at attention with lasers and tranquillisers.

He sat in the only chair and watched Pete's chest rise and fall. Geof had only known Peter for a few weeks now and wasn't sure why he felt as close to him as he did. Just liked him, he guessed. And what difference did it make whether or not Peter influenced him? Geof's whole life was like that …

'It amazes me … that you don't resent them,' Pete croaked through a scratchy throat.

'You're awake.'

'It's hard to sleep. It's also hard to stay awake.'

'You're on a lot of stuff. No, don't move,' he said as Pete tried to sit up.

'What's happening out there, Geof?'

Pete seemed different. Not simply because of his injuries or because his hair had been removed. *Is it the calm of defeat or the extent of his injuries? Or has Pierre Jnr shaken the sense out of him?* Geof remembered that Pete was probably reading his thoughts and he looked up to catch his eye.

'The Colonel has been called before the Primacy,' he said.

'Is that bad?'

'It could be. Though it's the Primacy itself you should worry about.'

Pete must know everything that had passed between him and the Colonel. That the suspicion had caught hold.

*I want you to trust me*, Peter projected to his friend.

*It's hard to, Peter. I want to, I do, but the thought has been planted now.*

*I understand. You're right. I can show you what you want to see though. Then you can decide whether you can trust me or not.*

*What are you going to do?*

*I'm going to show you how I escaped.*

'Can you give me some water?' Pete asked. Geof raised the sipper to his lips and waited until Pete nodded that he'd had enough. He sat back in his chair and waited for something to happen.

'You see, Geof,' Pete said, his voice back to normal after a drink, 'it is not that I am strong, but that I am good.' He shuffled in the pallet to focus more directly on where Geof was sitting. Abruptly Pete swung his legs off the bed and began detaching the splints from his arms and chest.

'Should you really be doing that?'

'I'm fine, Geof, don't worry. They're just being cautious with me, trying to keep me in here longer. See?' Pete jumped agilely off the bed and stood feeling the floor with his toes.

Geof helped him get dressed and then held the tent flap up for him to duck through. A few metres down the canvas corridor Pete stopped and turned to Geof. 'This is as far as I can go.'

'What do you mean?'

'I haven't seen what is down the corridor and you didn't pay enough attention. If I extend the illusion, it will be too thin a version of reality. We're also getting too far from your body. Your senses will protest soon.'

'I don't understand.'

'You're still sitting in the chair by my bed, Geof. My bones are too weak to stand like this.'

'You're putting all this in my head?'

'Yes.'

Geof looked around him, pressed his fingers to the grain of the canvas, then pushed at the flesh of his own arm. 'How long can you maintain it?'

'We're in it together. You have to stay convinced. If you want out, it'll end.'

'You can't hold me here?'

'I could try, but you would become nauseous.' Geof sensed this was indeed starting to happen; as soon as he was told it wasn't real his stomach became unsettled. 'Close your eyes,' Pete suggested.

'But —'

'Just do it. It stops the sensory conflict. Good. Now, you are in my room, you are sitting in a chair facing my bed … Open your eyes.'

Geof blinked and looked around him, at the reality. It looked the same. He looked at Pete, bandaged and bruised in his bed.

*That's what I can do.*

'Why didn't Pierre kill you?' Geof asked.

'I don't know. He didn't kill Tamsin either.'

'You know she's gone, don't you?'

'Gone? Where?'

'She disappeared when you were in the hospital. Hasn't anyone told you?'

*I knew, Geof. But I couldn't let them know I knew. The suspicion on me would be even worse.*

'No one speaks to me in here, Geof. How did she get away?'

'I don't know and I can't find out.' He patted his symbiot. 'I'm cut off for now too.'

'What are you doing in here?' a voice screeched from behind him. The nurse entered the tent with a tray of food.

'I was just leaving.' Geof stood. 'Goodnight, Pete.'

*Goodnight, Geof.*

At the end of the corridor a squad of armed Servicemen was waiting for him. Geof held up his hands.

'If this is about —'

'Please come with us, sir.' The leader indicated the direction with his weapon and Geof was marched out, three soldiers in front and three behind.

They led him back toward the launching area where an open squib waited for him. 'Where am I going?' he asked.

'Sorry, sir. That information is privileged above my level.'

The squib windowed shut and lifted into the sky. All he knew was that he was heading north and east. The squib was on autopilot and closed off to him. If he wasn't on trial already, he would be tempted to override it.

This thought was interrupted when a connection tapped in from Ryu Shima, the man the Weave was pushing to be the new Prime.

Geof: Ryu Shima, this is an unexpected honour. Congratulations on your escalation.

Ryu: My humble thanks to you. I hope my call is not entirely unexpected.

Geof: I suppose it shouldn't be, but I have been out of contact.

Ryu: Your access must remain limited while your trial proceeds. I expect it to end soon.

Geof: What am I on trial for?

Ryu: Your entire team is under suspicion after the Dome event. With the unexplained departure of Tamsin Grey, we must examine all the evidence thoroughly. I hope you understand.

Geof: We have done nothing wrong.

Ryu: That really depends on how we interpret 'wrong'. The operation was a debacle, you must appreciate that.

Geof: We did the best that we could.

Ryu: I certainly hope that isn't true. If this hunt is to continue, I will expect a lot more from you.

Geof: So we are to continue?

Ryu: Of course. The apparent threat has not dissipated. Now we must start over so it can be expunged.

Geof: And may I ask about Peter Lazarus?

Ryu: I fear his trial will be more prolonged than yours. He is a known telepath and was in the zone when the event took place.

Geof: I cannot believe he had anything to do with it.

Ryu: Your support for Mister Lazarus has been noted.

**Geof realised that everything he said would become part of the trials: his, Pete's and probably the Colonel's. He refused to believe that Pete had been complicit with Pierre ... Then again, after Pete's demonstration, perhaps he could have been.**

Geof: I acknowledge that you have grounds for suspicion.

Ryu: An excellent choice, Mister Ozenbach. I am glad you have the rational mind I surmised you had. As part of my inquiries, I must ask what you think happened on the day and where it went wrong. This is not a debrief, I simply want your opinions.

Geof: As you wish. It is hard to say, for me, what went wrong. We were simply tracking a possible target that we had pinpointed due to a pattern established from earlier evidence. We landed Tamsin and Pete, who were to attempt an intercept. Very quickly we lost the data connection with Pete and Tamsin, as well as with our drones and the neighbourhood passives. You must know the rest.

Ryu: Would it be fair to say that the threat was underestimated?

Geof: Yes. By myself at least. I admit I had no conception of what we were tracing. I've never encountered anything like it.

Ryu: And what would you do differently, knowing what you know now?

Geof: I think the evidence we had of the farm, and from the school, should have heightened our precautions, but I don't see how we could have approached the Paris target differently.

Ryu: I concur. There was insufficient data regarding the threat and while the operation seems clumsy in hindsight, it followed all standard procedures. Do you think it was possible that one of the psis could have warned the target?

Geof: Everything is possible. The limousine was more than two hundred metres from Pete's location, which is outside of his known reach.

Ryu: Known reach?

Geof: If the information we received from Tamsin Grey was correct.

Ryu: Which would be hard to verify.

**Geof peered out the window. The vegetation below looked like a museum model.**

Geof: What happens now?

Ryu: Your trial will be resolved, then the hunt will begin again under my supervision.

Geof: You have an impeccable record.

Ryu: That is true, but I am not so filled with hubris to think that this incident is similar to the collections my squads make. Do you know that the Weave has dubbed this incident the manifestation of Pierre Jnr?

Geof: I did not.

Ryu: Do you think that is what it was?

Now that the question was asked he wasn't so sure. A day before he had only thought of it as Pierre Jnr, but all he had actually seen was a data drop-out, a dust cloud and the aftermath.

He related these thoughts and in return Ryu Shima fed him some of the new evidence, visuals and forensics from the site.

Geof nearly gagged.

Ryu: Do you still think this was the work of an individual?

Geof: I couldn't be sure.

Ryu: Concur. That is an excellent starting point, Mister Ozenbach.

Geof: So what do we do now?

Ryu: We start over. Clearly this operation was misconceived from the start so we must begin again.

Geof: No presumptions.

Ryu: Exactly. What is the nature of the enemy we face?

Geof: I no longer know. How do we know it is our enemy?

It was Ryu's turn to pause. In a conversation of symbiot messages, any lag in response time allowed the receiver to re-notice the outside world. Geof felt the glide of the flight, the constant tuning of his senses as the gravity became lighter then heavier as the squib rose and fell. He looked down at the desert pixellating into farmland and the edge territory of what could only be Seaboard.

Ryu: The results of its passing can only be interpreted as a destructive force. Your question is whether it is conscious or not. Vindictive or ignorant?

Geof: Concur.

Ryu: We shall make that part of your task. You will find new evidence, you will examine old evidence. You will determine the nature of the threat and follow it to its source. Then we will disable it.

Geof: How will we do that?

Ryu: There are many people already working on that problem. The Will is behind you now. A way will be found. You will assemble a new team, of your choosing. You will have full access to my squads, they hold the most experience, but half will be needed for training programs.

Geof: What about Colonel Pinter? And Pete?

Ryu: We will see what happens with their trials. If they are released, you may approach them for your team.

Geof: How should I start?

Ryu: You are a capable man. Your record is faultless, which I admire and respect.

Geof: Shouldn't I be part of the hunt?

Ryu: Geof, have I not made myself clear? You are the hunt.

*Merde*, Geof cursed.

Geof: Yes, I understand. I thank you, Shima san.

Ryu: Start at the beginning. I have little doubt that the threat we know as 'Pierre' will manifest itself again whether we pursue it or not.

Geof: Understood. I won't let you down, sir.

Ryu: I will expect daily progress reports. Out.

Geof: Out.

As a reward for his cooperation, Shima opened up Geof to a select but plentiful flow of raw data from the Dome investigation, and reconnected him to the Weave. The ability to immediately check and verify information felt like an ecstatic release and he plugged in deep to catch up on what he had missed.

The sun was just beginning to come up and the water of the harbour was scraped with dawn light. Geof was deposited in a Services tower block that was raised above the megapolis of Seaboard, the city that got higher and higher. It had never experienced the ravages of the wars on the larger continents. If anything, it became a safe haven for many during the collapse, and had built on top of itself multiple times to manage the influx.

It was good to be connected again. It was like waking up. He took a long shower, staying on the Weave the whole time, water and data washing over him.

Then Geof sat on the end of the bed in his damp towel and worked backward, skipping swiftly over the horrors of the explosion, into the data drop-out and back to the moment when Pete and Tamsin first had visual contact with the limousine.

He tried not to think it, but watching it again, knowing what came after, he couldn't help but wonder who pulled the trigger. Was it Pete? Tamsin? Or whatever was in that limousine?

* * *

Ryu reviewed his conversation with the weaver and was pleased. If there had been any manipulation from the psi in the first team, he would be able to erode its influence quickly. Next he would have to tackle the telepath, but for now he had a full day ahead.

The farewell ceremony began at dawn and in the afternoon he had to jet to Den Haag for the first sitting of the Primacy. His ascendancy had doubled his collection load as well as requiring him to make public statements and allow interviews.

He sat impatiently in the palanquin with his mother and father, Alpha and Regent of Shima, as the sun rose on the green web of Yantz and the overwhelming enthusiasm of the local residents.

The procession from the palace to the newly renovated needle he had been assigned was two kilometres long, but the pace of the parade would make it take at least an hour. Time the Prime could barely afford, but his mother had insisted. 'Give the people their moments, Ryu,' she said.

Many Citizens and denizens had turned out for the event. A Shima was moving from the family palace and it was none other than the newly exalted Prime. As eldest son of this de facto royal family, Ryu was well known. Many of the people waving chameleon flags had supported him becoming the local enforcer of the Will, never thinking he would rise to the ultimate station.

Still, even as he sat, waving side to side, he could work through his symbiot on organising the next collections. His area of influence had increased exponentially. To reach Prime, he had taken the validation of more than a thousand precincts, each more poorly run than the last and doing their best to ignore all but the most obvious psis. *But*, he thought to himself, *it's the ones who hide that you have to worry about the most.*

While they proceeded through the throngs of supporters, he was watching in overlay as his best team surrounded one of those strange Scando schools for a collection. One more success to add to his record.

Each successful collection brought more validation and more work and the world was in short supply of competence. While the civics structure encouraged a natural meritocracy, there were times when its priorities were confused. Not today though.

Ryu smiled at the thought and twisted to wave more enthusiastically at the people. They knew it too. They knew he was the one. The streets were mixed with those full of pride in the Shimas and, of course, those who wanted to be seen showing support: the business types and the young women of age.

Roll call was taken automatically, and class began when Moreau trailed in, last as always. 'Now that we're all here ...' Miz Rose Lia was a good teacher, a nice woman who encouraged her students to ask the questions on their minds.

First-year synthesis began at the average age of twelve. In her current class Rose Lia's youngest member was eleven and her oldest sixteen. It was one of the subjects that most teachers avoided due to the chaos it often brought out in the children's behaviour. But that was the aim after all.

Understanding the basics of synthesis was judged by many parents to be the key to success in a multiplex society and they duly encouraged their children to take the course. But synthesis was not a basic subject like mathematics, geography or computing; this class was not based on facts, it was based on connections. The full name for what Miz Lia taught to introductory students was 'Synthesis, analysis and history' and it gave her scope to let the students exercise their ability to make broad and unexpected connections across a range of topics.

It was bedlam and Miz Lia loved that. It was exciting to watch and participate with the children as they discovered unique combinations of knowledge and theory. The second part of the process was to help them analyse and discover which of their brilliant ideas were reasonable and which were simply patterns without foundation.

'Okay, Sulci, you may sit down now. You are right. The list of events is in the correct chronological order, but a list does not always convey the meaning or implications of what took place. Can anyone tell me why we study history? Anyone?'

'So we can learn from the past?'

'Yes, thank you, Vincenzo. I've heard that one before too. If only wishing made it so. Mostly people trying to learn from the past end up justifying the uniqueness of their own situation, thus enabling them to ignore the past. Tådler?' Tådler was the youngest one, a little too bright for his own good.

'A study of the past can help us understand the trajectory of event vectors, giving us the ability to deflect or predict future events.'

'Spoken like a true overachiever, thank you, Tådler. Could you perhaps rephrase so the rest of us might understand?' He shook his head: no, he couldn't paraphrase it.

Tådler was a great admirer of Miz Lia's technique. She knew the answers, had a hidden symbiot at the small of her back so she could cheat, if she needed to, all the while protesting her own mental limitations so she could get students of different grading levels to discuss and parse together.

She had spent most of her life aiming at becoming a synthesist herself, but in the end found her daily joy in teaching — it was, after all, a synthesising of sorts, helping others see the patterns of human thought year after year. Her studies had been necessarily broad and made her such a delightful sophist. She could help any child discover their own path.

'What Tådler has introduced to the discussion is the concept of reaction chains, the cause-and-effect pathways that flow backward through our history. Every action seems to be the offspring of earlier actions, with a resultant effect. Which is what makes last week's events so significant because they are, as yet, unexplained. Since the second Dark Age, the World Union has been on a steady path toward the ideal of Parity —'

Sally leapt from her chair and responded unbidden, 'Why do we study ideals if they are unachievable?' Sally was one of the most impetuous and demanding of Tådler's classmates. Her mind seemed to froth with thoughts, with the occasional flare that spat up to become vocalised. While Tådler could clearly see her thoughts, he still found it hard to predict what she would come out with.

'Because we must strive. Being a Citizen comes with responsibilities and duties, but mainly it is the ideal of equality that binds us together.'

Tådler had known for two weeks now that he was a telepath. It had crept up on him until he was struck with a moment of certainty. Knowing the thoughts of your family was one thing — that can blend with empathy — but watching strangers in the park and tapping into their most private considerations was disturbing. Tådler had quietly stopped being a little boy.

Miz Lia's symb communicated with her and the blood drained from her face as she stopped speaking and looked at Tådler. A message had come through her symbiot that Services were here to collect him. She was beset with fears of wired-up fusers bursting through the doors and yanking him bodily from the room. This was overlaid by her fear of being labelled as a sympathiser.

'Though justice is the ideal of the legal system, laws themselves do not fully nullify the injustices of the world. Laws are to justice as bricks are to buildings.' She was speaking to him, Tådler realised. He wondered when she had first known, and then saw that she had identified him some time back as a possible. Almost a year ago, when he began completing her lessons ahead of the class.

He raised his hand.

'Yes, Tåd. You have a question?'

'May I be excused to visit the bathroom?'

'Of course you can,' she answered, her mind flooding with relief. She wouldn't have to watch him be taken.

'Thank you, Miz Lia,' he replied formally. He hoped she understood that he didn't blame her.

Tåd left the classroom and followed the corridor two turns until he reached the elevators. One of them was rising to his floor and he waited patiently. The doors opened, revealing a small posse of Services Blacks. The man at their front knelt upon seeing the boy standing there, bringing himself to eye level.

Even though he knew who the boy was, out of courtesy he confirmed, 'Are you Tådler Moore?'

'Yes.'

'You have to come with us now.'

'Yes, I understand.' He understood an awful lot.

Ryu filed his report and focused again on his waving.

The architectural template of the needle was developed to enable protection, or confinement, of special individuals and families by keeping them isolated from the population below. It looked like an upright toothpick with an olive on top; it was under constant surveillance and the neck could be blocked at the first signs of betrayal or endangerment for protection. City skylines around the world were now dominated by these minarets that housed a revolving parade of dignitaries and civil servants.

He was actually looking forward to staying in the needle. His rapidly expanding retinue would live and operate from the base and he alone would live in the head, away from everyone. He didn't like having people near him. It was unsettling and risky. Since his candidacy, he had become surrounded by too many, and only since Gladys Schuster had accepted his appointment as his senior secretary had he been able to withdraw from the daily onslaught and concentrate on his duties.

Ryu had admired her work for a long time as the co-ordinator of the Scandinavian resortment and she was as good as he'd hoped. Now a whole day could pass by and he need only communicate with her through symb. He blocked out the thought, smiled and waved through the petals that were being thrown over them as they passed.

The Prime passed quickly through the lower levels to the elevator, now waving and smiling to the welcoming committee of his staff and major supporters.

With a sigh of relief the elevator closed around him.

The first room he stepped into was an open panorama of the surrounding city. He was five thousand feet high and Yantz unfurled before him in a polka-dot pattern of raised white fortifications that looked like lily pads rising above the green level of canals, walls hanging with vines and shanties. The desperate squabble of civilisation spread out below him, with Shima Palace squarely in view.

Amongst the presents that were taking up a significant amount of living room was a large metal crate.

'What is it?' he wired down to Gladys.

'A present from an admirer,' she responded, ready for his inquiry.

'What is it?'

'A surprise.'

'Who is it from?'

'You wouldn't prefer the surprise?' she asked.

'I don't find that surprise ever improves the quality of a gift.'

'Alright. It is from Boris Arkady in Atlantic.'

'Atlantic? Why would he be sending me anything? You've checked it, I presume?'

'Yes, Prime. It is safe to open. It is an historical piece from his private collection.'

'And he wants my favour for something ...' Ryu wondered as he slid his hands over the surface. He pressed the release button and the crate retracted down into its flatbed.

Inside was a glass case with an old droid lying on its back. Ryu bent down to peer closer. It was severely damaged, at one time completely dismembered but now held together with small pins. He let his symb run a search and found out it was from the Örjian guard, which meant, yes, there was the outlet in the abdomen where the ruisbuss would have been plugged in.

'You recognise this, of course, Miz Schuster?' he asked.

'I do. I have seen many of them.'

'Does it offend you?'

'Humanity has much darkness in its past.'

'Yes, well put. But why would a man from the Cape send me something like this? Find out what you can for me about Boris Arkady.'

Tamsin awoke lying on her back. Above her a float of surgical lights radiated down. Behind that there was only darkness. She could hear breathing and shuffling nearby, but she couldn't move to see who was there.

'I can't move.'

'You are under paralysis,' a male voice answered from her feet. 'You fell asleep.'

'How long have I been here?'

'Oh, only three hours. The first stage is nearly finished.'

'First stage?'

A man walked up into her view. He was small and craggy,

an old freaker whose augments hadn't kept pace with age. His hair was tufty and silver. Metal, actually, for each strand was a soft coil of wire; implants, of course.

She didn't know how she got here. She remembered a dream with Peter lying in a hospital, and before that looking out a window in Paris ...

'Where is he?'

'Who?' the man asked.

Her mind reached out for the answer. The doctor's memory showed her coming alone. She grabbed for more: her entering his offices, the discussion about the procedure.

Otis Plunkett was an off-Weave doctor who performed illegal surgeries in Joberg. His own past was a mire of casual missteps that had led him to become extremely non-judgemental and non-inquisitive about the clients he attracted.

'Miz Grey, could you stop that, please? I'm trying to concentrate.'

Stage one was the preparation of her body. Nerve stimulation and systemic foundation.

Stage two would be the skin transference: a neural-less symbiot would cover her in a soft shell, thinning as it spread. By the time it was finished she would be two inches taller, twenty pounds heavier and appear to be a lightskin from the Cape.

Not only did the symbiot disguise her body, it weighted her muscles differently and affected her gait and mannerisms, thus preventing detection by kinetic patterns. It would also dive deeper to tweak her vocal cords and tongue in order to change her voice. And, of course, her eye colour would change to blue.

The process of becoming unrecognisable took twenty-four hours, most of which she wasn't allowed to move for. When the doctor was satisfied with the first stage and had begun the skin transference, he sat by her side and helped her drink juice through a straw.

'Now, Miz Grey, what were you talking about before? It was sounding like a spot of amnesia.'

'It was. It passed.'

'Nothing unusual then. Happens all the time with the anaesthetic. You'd be amused by the things people say when they start waking up. I once had a man insisting I was his father, and he became so upset when I said I wasn't that he couldn't stop crying. I had to pretend he was my son for four hours.'

The third stage was the slow install of her new symbiot with the backstory of her new identity. It was best to go slow so her own brain could take on some of the information. It was loaded linearly from childhood until the present.

There were no memories, of course; none of the data was more than fabrication. The evidence was all counterfeit: photos, footage, interactions that had been implanted into the Weave years ago; an off-the-shelf identity that was pre-made for clients such as Tamsin. An identity grown over years so as to infiltrate the omnipresent Weave with corresponding evidence.

In this new life she was born of Joberg parents who managed a herbarium and was named Maria, after her grandmother, Maria Steyn. Her parents were Johan and Anna Steyn. They were real people who had rebelled against the population controls and had had four offspring. Maria, their third, was raised with her sisters in a shed in the gardens. This background was good for its plausibility and because it didn't require much recorded evidence.

There were photos of her as a child: birthday parties in the gardens; planting and harvesting; rescuing their meagre possessions when a burst water pipe flooded them that one time. Despite the ramshackle squalor, it was a place filled with life, and the games she and her sisters made up.

Maria played catch and kiss with the local boys. The Steyns were not the only family to break the child ban. Her first boyfriend was Adam Roux and though she thought he was a tad big-featured, he brought flowers to where she lived every day until she agreed to be his girlfriend.

It was all fake, every detail made up or copied from another similar life. The more of the timeline that was soaked into her symbiot, the more Tamsin felt the loss of this life she never lived. In *her* childhood, after she had been collected, she never saw other children. Her daily life had been testings and punishments. She didn't even remember her parents. She didn't even know if Tamsin was the name they had given her or whether Services had created it.

'Saudade,' she whispered, though where the word came from she didn't know. From herself, from Maria. Or Pierre?

Tamsin next awoke in another room. There was space for a bed and just enough standing room to disrobe. There was a faux window on one wall with a default forest vista, a blank viewscreen on another, a door on the third and the fourth was all mirror.

She watched herself undress before the mirror. The disconnect was like watching a film, or immersing in a sensorium, seeing some other person strip while feeling every sensation. She touched the cloth under her fingers, felt it slide over her skin. But now her skin was paler, heavily freckled, hair a heavy blonde. Turning around, she could see the arch of her back and the shape of her legs had rounded. Nothing about her was the same.

It was hard to feel like her.

She leant in closer to look this stranger in the eyes.

'Hello,' she said, though it sounded more like 'healyo'. She must learn to control that. 'My name is Tamsin Grey ...' That certainly felt odd; a naked stranger was standing before her claiming she had her name. 'My name is Maria.'

Tamsin closed her eyes. *Pierre? Are you there?*

She waited for no answer. She knew why he had made her do this. So she could hide in plain sight. So she could act. But he had never told her what she was meant to do.

*Pierre? Where are you?*

Otis let her rest in the room and practise with her new body until the next morning. She did not see him again, only heard his voice through a hidden speaker telling her when it was time to leave. Her path out from the building led her on a long and twisted trail, down stairways and along tunnels. He was well hidden and she admired his precautions. Many of his clients would be tempted to remove the sole witness to their transformation. She wondered how he had learnt that lesson.

Tamsin felt as though she was walking in a dream. A body not her own, walking through unrecognisable tunnels. When a doorway led onto the street, she stopped and stared, taken aback by the sunlight and noise.

She had never spent any time in Joberg. It was crowded, but organised like all the megapolises in the WU. The groundways were slower-moving and colourful, varied as a parade. People walked the streets in loose clothing of dense patterns, carrying baskets, pushing prams, leading animals or bots, riding on camels, hovers, even bicycles. Overhead, lines of squibs zipped across the sky.

As Maria Steyn, Tamsin was free. There was no Services botlock on her arm, no squad following her around and nobody knew where she was.

*Thank you, Pierre.*

She knew so little of this outside world or what and how the people thought. Tamsin had not had the opportunity to simply stand and wait and figure out her choices in living memory. She didn't know what to do. At first she just stood to the side of the busy thoroughfare and let the million minds go past her. It was a jumble, but there were patterns to their thoughts.

There was only one way to get information that she knew of and it wasn't by asking for it. As the people rushed by, she dipped in and out of their heads, looking for clues. A lot of them were just thinking about their own lives, their next task or meeting, but quite a few were still troubled by the recent manifestation. She concentrated on those. Very quickly she was up to speed on what was recorded from that day, and the civic fallout that had taken place.

Tamsin was certain now that Pierre must have been controlling her. It was too much of a coincidence that the last thing she could remember was waiting to confront him, and then she was in a strange city unable to recall what had happened since.

She felt edited.

*Why did he take me in the first place if only to leave me now?*

The Weave was pushing for stricter enforcement, more psi control. That much was clear. There would be a clampdown across the globe. And she couldn't have that. They were her future army.

She had to get more data. The clampdown was starting, and she needed to know where and when if she was to do anything about it. She also needed help.

Ryu Shima's first act was to call a meeting of the highest council and to broadcast a public speech to the Weave from the steps of the Adjudicators Ministry.

Randstad was one of the most intact historical areas under the Dome. When the Örjian menace ploughed the lands, they luckily tilled east rather than south and everything below the trajectory line was untouched.

For Ryu it was a strange grey land. Hard. Yantz was verdant like new growth, but places like this were like older woody branches. The age of the cultures was aptly captured in their architecture.

The World Union had no permanent seat, but Ryu had nominated Den Haag so it would look to the world as though the authority was coming from an old and established part of civilisation, counteracting his unfortunate youth. It was also as close to the manifestation site as he wanted to go.

That word twisted around his mind like a worm. Wriggling with a life of its own. That word had got him where he was now, squibbing a slow descent toward the crowd of pedestrians who wanted to 'be there' when the Primacy council met in person for the first time in nearly thirty years.

'Citizens, Servicemen and denizens of Earth. Whether you consider yourself a part of the World Union or not, this message is intended for all.

'An unknown force has attacked us. Without reason or provocation one of our proudest cultural centres has been decimated. What has been lost cannot be rebuilt or retrieved. The thousands of men, women and children who lost their lives are lost to us forever.

'I, Ryu Shima, of House Shima in the Yantz precinct, have been chosen by the Will to confront this threat. My position is clear, and as the Will has selected me for Prime I must surmise that the majority also believes this manifestation was of psionic origin. Whether it was the actions of an individual or a group, I will root out this threat and, together, we will pacify it.

'With regard to those who have come before us, whose inaction may have led us into this turmoil: I remind you that they governed based on the circumstances of the time and the information they had at hand. In the light of this new day, we could present criticism, but it is only hindsight that makes today's choices any stronger than yesterday's. I urge you all not to prosecute members of the previous Primacy. They have spoken for us through fifty years of peace. There is no cause for reprimand.

'Despite the horror of this recent act of violence, our way of life remains sacrosanct and secure and it must remain so. Though we are strong, a weakness exists. But let me tell you, we can and we will defend ourselves and our society from this growing threat.

'All Citizens can take comfort that preparations have been put in place to cleanse our union of the psionic threat. The defensive actions we can take have commenced and I hope that soon we will be able to report to you that my job is done and we can again live our lives as normal.

'For the World Union, the Will, peace and prosperity.'

Takashi: Well done, Ryu. Now for the real thing.

Ryu: Don't listen in. If you are discovered, you'll get us both in trouble.

Takashi: I don't expect you'll be saying anything interesting anyway. I think I might order me a new doll in your honour.

Ryu: Enjoy yourself.

Takashi: You too, brother.


The Adjudicators Ministry was one of the few places in the world with sanctioned privacy. Citizens could find unmonitored, unrecorded privacy anywhere at any time by disconnecting temporarily from the Weave or reducing to passive observation. But it was always recorded when people dipped into anonymity, which bred speculation.

It was recognised that some discussions, of sensitive issues, required discretion. Conflicts and negotiations happened in adjudicator facilities around the globe, but the ministry that

180

founded the practice began with this one building, to plan the end of the Örjian ordeal and co-ordinate the fledgling World Union.

The outer wall, the first ring of silence, was built of old stone, collected as a symbol of unification from buildings destroyed in the collapse. At this first checkpoint Ryu changed from his own clothes into a suit that had been pre-checked for electronic equipment. It was simple black.

Before leaving the ring, official attendants confirmed that his symbiot was disabled and a discharge lock was fixed in place. If the lock detected any electrical activity, its small light would turn from green to red and release a powerful shock that would kill the symbiot and cause grievous harm to the wearer.

The second ring of silence was a lively garden despite its name. It was a large cultivated indoor forest, inhabited noisily with chirruping birds and the tones of insects. The attendant led Ryu along an artificial creek that took him to the doorway of what looked like a mausoleum, built of heavy cream marble with a double doorway of reinforced oak.

The attendant pulled open the heavy doors and left Ryu in an antechamber that led to a waiting room. Designed for occupants who weren't allowed directly into the inner sanctum, the room held a long bench for sitting or lying down, and some paper reading material about the founding of the World Union and catalogues of precedent adjudications. Each member of the Primacy would arrive in this way.

The inner building of the original ministry was religious in character. A rounded steeple of authority atop a central chamber. Before it was turned over for public use, it held the first ministry forum, was witness to the birth of the World Union and Services, and the trial of Örj.

Here the forum sat, a ring of tiered stone seats, almost a Greek agora in design, now filling up with the world's most influential people. Ryu stood on the open circle that was the focus of the arena. He had studied the people in the room beforehand. Many he had been watching and supporting his whole civic life. They knew who he had endorsed, past or present, and he knew the same about them.

There were six in the room who had been members of the first ministry. The changing of the guard had brought some of the old soldiers back into focus. General Zim, Admiral Shreet, Blair Butler, Chayton Miller, Mona Vigg and Mary Blessing. He bowed to each of them in turn.

There weren't many in the Primacy who were happy to have such a young man at their head, but they knew how the system worked. They could angle all they liked to change the hierarchy, but for now, the Will lay with him.

Ryu already had the unerring support of at least two members, one a manufacturer and one who was heavily involved in the upkeep of the psi islands. He had his work cut out with the rest to get their support.

If he understood the military-minded correctly, they would reserve judgement until he succeeded or failed, unless of course he proposed something they deemed utterly crazy.

He called the meeting to order and they all took their seats. The room was closed.

'Honoured council. I thank you for agreeing to meet in

person. It may seem like an extraordinary measure, but I think you will agree, a necessary one.

'You have all heard my public sentiments. Let me assure you that they were sincere. An unexpected event has occurred. Its origin is suspected but unexplained. It has capsized the civil balance and brought an all-new council into being — excepting Senator Demos, who has survived the transition.' Ryu indicated the larger than standard man with spiky black hair and the jowls of a hound dog. Demos was the only legacy member of yesterday's Primacy, a feat largely due to the ongoing faith of his constituency that he would always act in their own interests. Ryu wondered if self-interest would drive him also.

'This is the total of what we know. At 5.58 a.m. on April Seventh a psionic individual or group of psionics destroyed an historic area of a populated metropolis. This not only shows a callous disregard for human life, but for our history and all that we have been trying to rebuild since the collapse.

'If the recent events, as the evidence leads us to believe, were the result of a psionic manifestation, and if we carry this realisation to its logical conclusion, then our entire civil structure could be at risk.'

'Surely you are exaggerating?' Charlotte Betts interrupted, even though he held the floor.

'I hope so, Representative, but who knows if you or I are under the influence of a telepath?' Ryu glanced at each member in turn. 'Any of us could be. We may have been affected in the past, or we might be in the future. In fact, who is to say that the voters that have brought us here were not themselves affected?'

'You are taking this to an absurd level to introduce irrational fear.'

'Perhaps I am. I confess, Miz Betts, I do not know. But I would like us all to consider the point and question how safe our minds can be. And how large an effect a stray telepath or two could possibly have.' Ryu focused on Charlotte once more. 'Can you tell me for certain?'

'Of course I can't.'

'Many of you, like me, are new to the Primacy, and we must be vigilant of misusing this new-found power. We must be sure not to take any misstep. We work for the Will of the people. Don't be too alarmed, my suggestions are nothing unreasonable, but it is simply that we must be sure. I recommend that each of us shelter our minds from possible interference. However you interacted with the world before, you must change it. We must begin to limit outside contact.'

'Are you mad? What will the people think?'

'People will think we are doing what we need to do. The world feels it is under threat. I will do my utmost to remove that fear. I will find the cause or reveal the fraud. I entreat you to work with me. The Will has brought us together. We may be here a day or a year, but as long as I am here I will remain steadfast to the principles that have brought me to my position. Because I believe in them, and the majority believes in them.

'Do we have suspects? Yes. Do we have all the information we need? No. Do not be fooled into thinking that this is simply an issue with psis. This is an issue of stability and trust in our fellow Citizens. Without the ability to trust that another's thoughts are their own and their actions are the act of free will, our society cannot continue to operate.

'We must close the net. To protect our way of life and maintain the balance of our civil structures. This World Union was built around the sanctity of knowledge and the only cure available to us will come in the form of perfect data.'

After the opening speeches, the council had a short break and mingled. Charlotte found herself ignored by the rest of the Primacy and so stood as proudly as she could and sought tranquillity through memories of perfect cups of tea and sun-touched moments by a window. She stood by what she said and no amount of cold shouldering would change her position. Strangely, an old phrase of her mother's drifted up to help her: 'The burden of the minority is the weight of the majority.' As if her mother had ever been in the minority.

Her repose was not allowed to last long.

'Representative Betts. You are perhaps the odd one out of this group. Placed here as a balance for our positions. May I compliment you on your speech?'

'Only if you do so sincerely.'

'Of course I do. I am here by the call of the Will, just as you are. May I ask your intentions? You know mine already.'

With Ryu standing before her, she was reminded of the vitality young men could wield and how it once took her breath away. Now it reminded her of the many follies she had witnessed in her life and been party to. 'Prime, I am here to do my duty as appointed by the Will.'

'But you are a sympathiser, are you not?'

She didn't like that word. 'I, like all humans, have the capacity for sympathy, empathy and kindness. Is that what you mean?'

'I think you understand my question. Your writings are clear: you think psionics should not be outlawed.'

'Correct.'

'I think you will find your place here most uncomfortable.'

'I thank you for your concern, Prime. I can only hope my views will be heard and I have the ability to present alternative actions to the council.'

Ryu stared at her a moment longer. 'As you wish.'

'Excuse me, Shima san.' Senator Demos licked his lips nervously as he managed to divert the Prime's attention from Charlotte.

'Yes, Senator. You have a question for me?'

'I do, Prime, yes. Am I right that, at the end of your speech, you were alluding to Parity?'

'That word has gained a taint recently,' Ryu answered.

'Yes, well, it can only be promised so many times before the public builds a resistance. But that is what you were implying, yes?'

'Only with complete knowledge will we be able to root out the cancers that continue to plague our society.'

'Indeed, of course. So it is not just the psi resistants that you will be hoping to dig out.'

'I am Prime of the whole World Union, Senator Demos. I work for the Will.'

'The Will is not always unanimous. There are, in fact, a great many who would prefer to … I'm not sure how best to phrase it so I will quote Miz Betts here: "harbour their freedoms rather than chase utopia". Am I getting that right, Representative Betts?' Demos asked Charlotte, who was still standing nearby.

'You quote correctly, but I wrote that thirty or so years ago. I'm not sure I still —'

'I understand that many will resist.' Ryu ignored her in his reply to Demos. 'Humanity does not have a history of accepting what is best for it, but with the Will behind me I will leave no harbours unchecked. Now if you'll excuse me.'

Ryu Shima bowed and moved away to speak with one of the other members of the council. Any would do.

Charlotte breathed out; her memory of a perfect cup of tea had turned bitter.

'A most competent young man, don't you think, Representative Betts? The council will certainly be safe in his hands.' The tiniest of smiles rested on the pucker of the Senator's lips.

'The whole time I felt like everything he or I said was being interpreted on three levels. I couldn't understand half of what passed between you two.'

'It was about boats, Miz Betts. My boats in particular.'

'Oh.' She wondered if he had also read what she had written about the floating Greeks and the voting bloc of the selfish. Sometimes she just wrote what sprang to mind; it had never occurred to her she might end up in the same room as the highest branches of society. 'Was he threatening you?'

'In a fashion. More threatening to threaten. Have you not heard that Shimas are like onions?'

'I hadn't heard of them at all until this week.'

'Ah, well. Consider it more a piece of advice then. Cut a Shima and they will make you cry.'

He snickered at his own joke and she smiled. 'I will remember that.'

The next item on the schedule was a revision of recent events, beginning with a review of the relevant data and then an interview with one of the co-ordinators. There weren't many who were considered directly responsible for the operation. One problem with the civic structure was that sometimes there was no single person to blame.

This left them with only one constant intermediary, who had been put in the position mainly for being available and redundant with age.

'Is this *Pinter* Pinter?' Charlotte leant toward Demos. 'As in, of the Terminus?'

'Only one of his many exploits, I believe.'

The dossier on the man had a list of engagements that went for eleven screens; he was extremely accomplished. The 360° showed a proud man, detailed with age. Not many men let the years show like that any more.

'I bet you this man knows my mother,' she said. Demos probably wouldn't be Max's ideal choice of ally, but at least he was speaking with her.

'And how is your dear mother? It has been months since I have seen her.'

'It has been years for me.' The Senator showed no surprise. 'But you knew that already.'

'Of course, Representative Betts. I know your mother well. I know about you and everyone in this room does too.'

'Am I that interesting?'

'Anyone who makes it into the Primacy is "that interesting". You may have fallen from the sky, but the rest of us crawled our way up here.'

'I meant no offence ...'

'Oh, but I did. My point being that you won't be staying here long unless you begin working for it.'

His comment left her speechless. Maybe he wasn't going to be her ally after all. She wished she could contact Max for his interpretation.

'Aren't I just here as a voice for the people whose beliefs I represent?'

He chuckled deeply in his torso. 'Of course. That is how you got here; staying here is a different job altogether. But you are in here now and you have as much influence as the rest of us.'

'My people are outside this room.'

'Yes. So are mine. But I at least know who is who in the room.'

'Point taken.' She stiffened her posture.

'Now that's more how your mother raised you.'

That was one step too far. Charlotte turned to retort, but the doors opened and the Primacy silenced. She settled for sliding a little further away from him.

It was unusual for the Primacy to be cloistered, or indeed to be meeting in the same physical space. It was unusual for the Primacy to ever work in co-ordination either. Such tactics were reserved for more nefarious activities, but in this case Pinter approved. It meant the new council had some appreciation of the threat before them. It also sent a clear message to the Weave that they felt the need to protect themselves from possible interference.

As Colonel Pinter passed through the first ring into the garden, an old acquaintance approached him, which was strictly against protocol.

'Abercrombie?' he called and Pinter recognised him instantly. What hair Rupert lacked on his scalp was more than made up for by his sideburns.

'Rupert.' The two men shook hands. 'I thought you had already left. Fleeing the ship, I understand.'

'The writing is on the wall, old chap.'

'Yes? And what does it say?'

'It says, run while you still can!' Rupert joked.

'When did they call it closed?'

'When Shima arrived. Almost two hours ago. They are just fussing about now ... I should have known you were involved in all this.'

'I had presumed you had made sure I was.' Pinter smiled. Rupert waved the accusation away in such a fashion it was clear he thought that the Colonel was responsible for all that had happened and no amount of arguing or evidence could change that.

Their banter slowed to a stop and Rupert heaved up a big sigh. 'Old friend, wouldn't it have been nice to spend our twilight years in quietude?'

'One of us already was — and now you're the one exiting the stage.'

'Yes. I do apologise. My star has faded though. Nothing I could do.'

'How is the room?'

'Interesting. Brimming with testosterone.'

'And the new Prime? How do you measure him?'

'He made it to the top, didn't he? He is a Shima and he knows what he is about.'

'Brash?'

Rupert so-soed with his hands. 'Under the circumstances, who couldn't be forgiven a little brash action.'

'Excuse me, Colonel Pinter?' the attendant politely interrupted and indicated that it was time for him to enter the council chamber.

'Duty calls.'

'Not for me, Abe. Anyway, I just wanted to say good luck.' They parted as they met, with a warm handshake and a light pat on the shoulder.

The room beyond held one hundred people, seated in a tiered half-circle around a stage. Behind was a large wall that acted as a common screen and was scattered with images of the manifestation. Nothing that the Colonel hadn't seen.

At the centre of the crescent was the young man in question, already confident in his position as the speaker for the Primacy. His hair was clipped short at the front and left in a shiny black curtain at the back. Ryu Shima stood as the Colonel arrived before them and made an impeccable salute, the infantry air fist, as though he had lived and breathed the life of a Serviceman. He probably meant it as a sign of respect. Pinter returned the gesture.

'The council welcomes Colonel Abercrombie Pinter. Colonel, thank you for coming so promptly. These are extraordinary circumstances.'

'They are indeed. It pleases me that you are taking such great precautions.'

'I am glad you approve. Now, Colonel, we have all read your testimony regarding your part in the recent events. Do you swear that to be a true and accurate account?'

'I do.'

'Then I suggest we skip over an interrogation. We are, after all, not interested in finding anyone to blame. Time would be better served discussing what is to be done.'

Pinter raised his hands and clapped once. The sharp sound resounded around the room, focusing their attention upon him. 'Your eminences, I believe that we are at a juncture here, and how we meet this challenge, how we go about what follows, will define the kind of people we are and what kind we will become. The kind of people we are.

'Now, here's what I suggest we do ...'

Days on the islands passed interminably slowly. Only the daily ministrations kept the residents phlegmatic and calm.

Their access to the Weave was limited to viewing and only that through the communal handscreens and larger monitors in the entertainment rooms.

Every day since the manifestation someone would rewatch the collected footage, staring open-mouthed at the smudge that destroyed a street. Others flicked through the forums and began to think that the islands were the safest place for them right now.

Pierre Sandro Snr was shunned by all but a small group who would play cards with him.

'We should expect some freshies soon,' one commented.

'Yup.' The circle nodded in agreement.

'Hey, Pierre. When is that son of yours going to bust us out of here?' another joked. Pierre Snr ignored him. He ignored everything to do with that boy.

Then he smiled, perhaps at the cards in his hand or at a pleasing thought. 'He will come. And he will set us free when the world is ready for us.'

'Senior, have you gone toxic? I thought you said he was a monster?'

'Yeah, yeah, I did say that ...' Sandro hesitated. That *was* what he said because it was what he thought. He hated that aberration for what it had done to them, especially Mary — no, Mary was fine. She had recovered. Pierre was out there making the world open for the return of psionics. 'He is a monster, but at least he is on our side.'

The boy that nobody saw stepped away from the card players. He made a resident change the viewer to show the new Primacy council gathering at Den Haag and the reprised composition of his manifestation.

They watched the common screens in awe, silent with amazement. Some wept, tears drawing paths down their cheeks. Again and again they watched in rapture, never noticing that there was one spare chair in their circle where a small boy had joined them.

Pierre could hear their emotions. Any who felt a twinge of fear he turned. Any who wondered if it was really Pierre Jnr who had caused the destruction, he made certain. He left them without a doubt that what they were watching was the manifestation of their long-awaited god. He had come to save them.

# He can control
# people like puppets

Not all psis allowed themselves to be taken peacefully.

Seven: 24601 is on infra.

Nine: Odds are in place, Ten. Ready on your signal.

Ten: We have a go order.

He'd seen the speeches. He knew what it meant. Alone in his room he packed his things, taking what he needed from his wardrobe and the house pantry. Pierre had shown them the way. Simon Adderton would hide no longer, would pretend no longer.

He would join Pierre and fight.

His wife didn't know about him. She would still love him, he was sure, but he wanted to leave before she came home. She would always be able to make him stay.

At the moment he was about to step out the door, the roof of his house disintegrated and five burly shadows dropped around him.

'Nooo!' Simon screamed, slashing out in a blind sweep. Three bodies fell to the floor, deep cuts through their armour.

Simon had never seen so much blood.

The door to his room blew off its hinges, heading toward him like a battering ram. He deflected and threw himself to the side as two more of the soldiers bashed their way through the frame, raising complicated weapons at him.

He pushed them to their knees and smashed their heads nose-first into the floor. He was about to crush their throats when he stopped. He didn't know why. He wanted to kill the Services scum for attacking him. He wanted to lash out at something and they had come at the perfect time. His anger was pure and righteous, but first he needed to lie down. He lowered himself to the floor, his anger battling with this urge to curl up on the rug.

A man in black stepped through his bedroom door and knelt beside him, pushing a white oval toward his face.

'No, please no!' Simon shouted, but it was no use.

Okonta fixed the mask on 24601 and stood up to leave. The second half of his ten would arrive soon and could complete the collection. Something was wrong though and he couldn't tell what.

He probed and found no one else in the vicinity. Where were the other MUs?

Okonta to Services: My team has gone silent. What is the command?

Services: Second and third squads inbound. Stay in position.

Okonta: Cut that, I'm going defensive.

Services: Concur. You may take unrestricted precaution.

Outside the bedroom, the lights of the house faulted suddenly. Beyond the bedroom doorway he couldn't see through the black. Okonta listened for movement, pushed his mind out for sentience, but found no one there. That meant it could be bots out there waiting for him. But who could have organised a bot hit on his team? The target didn't have that kind of influence and only Services ups should have known they were going to be here.

He bent down to one of the MUs and pulled the stumpy weapon away from the loosened fists. It was an ungainly, thick disc, with a handle on the flat side and six barrels attached to the front to point toward the target.

Okonta: Can you unlock this weapon for me? If it's bots out there, I'm defenceless.

Services: Access granted. Use only as a last measure. Backup in minus four minutes.

The weapon hummed and clocked the readings to green. His symbiot accessed the operational embed of the gatling hand cannon and Okonta held it pointed at the open doorway.

'Hello, assassin,' a woman's voice called from above.

Okonta splayed his legs and released the gatling on full throttle. Most of the energy went straight up into the sky through the hole in the roof. Only a small crumble of dust and prefab fell down.

'Tsk, tsk. That's no way to treat a friend.'

'Who are you?'

'I'll give you a choice, Okonta. Join me or die.'

*Tamsin?*

*Now you're getting it. Quickly. Which side would you be on if you had the choice?*

*You can't.*

*Haven't you ever thought about freedom?*

*Of course.*

*It's wonderful, Okonta. You could never dream it …*

Services: Agent, report. What is happening there?

*Time to choose.*

*Yes, I want to be free.*

*Brace yourself.*

Okonta's symbiot shook on his arm, and was instantly striped with cuts as Tamsin shredded it as quickly as she could. The botlock reacted, releasing toxins into his blood and heating ready to explode. Tamsin continued the lacerations until the shell was destroyed.

He had nearly blacked out by the time she dropped from the hole in the roof. She was a blonde freckled woman he didn't recognise. He felt upward through her face.

'Tamsin?'

'Hold on, Okonta. All you have to do now is not die.' She pulled a brace of syringes from her pocket and began stabbing them into his shoulder and chest.

*Is that really you, Tamsin?*

*Sure it's me. Don't let the disguise fool you.*

The injections kicked in, counteracting the poisons and enlivening his body with artificial enthusiasm. He stood up.

*Quickly now, we have to get you transfused before these wear off.*

*What about him?* he asked, nodding at the body lying unconscious on the floor. Okonta bent down to remove the man's mask.

*Wait.* Tamsin touched his arm. *I have a better idea.*

It had been a week since the incident, three days since he had said goodbye to Geof Ozenbach. Peter Lazarus remained isolated in the medic tent of the remote Services compound. He waited as his body healed and his memories trickled together.

He woke and passed out many times, and his sentience was continuously impaired from medication.

Sometimes he'd waken with a blank mind and it took him time to remember who he was and where. Sometimes he passed out with an image of eyes looking deep inside him.

His healing was rushed as much as it could be. With such extensive damage though, it became a hierarchy of priorities that had to be fixed one at a time.

Anchali fed him six times a day with a variety of protein fluids and chewing paste. She would ask him standard questions that nurses ask their patients, such as, 'How are you feeling today?' and he would try to answer with a nod. 'Does it hurt when I do this?' Nodding made his head swim and he would groan.

'Don't push yourself, Mister Lazarus.' She smiled.

It was as she held straws to his lips or sponged his body clean that they hurried through as much real conversation as they could. She couldn't linger at her duties without raising suspicion.

*What is happening in the world?*

*Officially I am cloistered, as are most of the soldiers here, but from what I've heard there still isn't any official statement for what happened under the Dome yet.*

*That is odd, isn't it?*

*Yes and no. The Primacy is shifting, so those who were responsible are not commenting until the next council is in place. There is a lot of speculation.*

*And I bet none of it is close to what really happened. They'll want to keep it secret.*

*We won't let them.*

*How can you stop them?*

*Whispers, Pete. As soon as I get relieved, I'll spread the truth.*

*The truth ...?*

The visions beset him again and he went into a fit. The last thing he heard was the alarm of his bedside machines and Anchali calling for the doctor.

Each time he awoke, the pieces slid into place, though not always in the same way. Those staring eyes that held him in thrall; the squeezing pain and the moment before, when he was waiting on an everyday street.

As time went by, his telepathic reach slowly came back to him. They kept the building clear to one hundred paces so mostly he could sense nothing until the nurse came to visit and he would count her steps as she approached: seventy-nine, seventy-eight, seventy-six ...

*Anchali*, he would call. She was a good nurse and the kind of woman who liked everything to be kept neat and tidy. Especially herself.

Twenty-two, twenty-one ...

Without even passive Weave access, Nurse Anchali Risun was the only person he had any contact with. He tried communicating with Geof through his symbiot, but received no response. He could not even be sure his messages were received. He wondered what could be happening. Was Geof alive? Had Services blocked them? Was he choosing not to respond?

Peter and Nurse Anchali had many long, silent conversations while he was unable to move. Twice a day she would gently dab his body with a soft cloth and massage the muscles that weren't too bruised to touch. He had never been so pampered in his life.

'How are we feeling today, Mister Lazarus?'

'Please, call me Peter.' *Why are you the only person in this hospital?*

*This is only a temporary building. Just for you.* 'That wouldn't be protocol, I'm afraid.' She smiled as she said this, professional-friendly.

*With only one nurse?*

*No. Just the only one you're allowed contact with. I'm a sacrificial lamb, which they think I don't know. The others only come when they put you under. Let me reassure you, there is a team of doctors rushing your recovery along.*

Pete found it incredibly difficult to be alone since the incident. As soon as the nurse faded from him, ninety, ninety-one, ninety-two ... his heart rate elevated. Panic would set in and trigger a chemical dose from the machines around him. When he recognised that he panicked whenever he lost mental contact, he began to wonder about himself. He recalled being more of a private person. He'd spent his life drifting from place to place, using travel to hide, making no lasting contacts. That was a psi's life, wasn't it?

It was only a month ago that he had been in that life. There didn't seem to be that many scenes from before that he could recollect. He remembered a lot of empty hotel rooms, sitting on the edge of a bed watching viewscreens. He was over thirty years old, surely he should remember more than that? He couldn't even recall the faces of his parents. He did have one vision in which he sat in a Francophile restaurant eating an expensive meal, with his father he thought, but then he was eating alone. It was more dream to him than memory.

What had those eyes done to him? Was his mind this empty before?

Anchali tried to console him, and to help him put the pieces together from what she could see in his mind and what she could learn from the outside world.

*From what I can gather from the two men who visited you, you were part of a team that was in Paris during the manifestation.*

*What happened?*

*You were in an operation to find Pierre Jnr, but when you did you couldn't control him.*

*Those eyes I see? Is that the boy?*

*That is him.*

*Why didn't he kill me?*

*That is something everyone would like to know. I must go, this sponge bath is taking longer than normal.*

'I'll be back with your afternoon snack in a little while. Alright, Mister Lazarus?'

'And some ice?' he croaked.

'I should be able to manage some ice, but not too much. It's not good for your throat.'

*Anchali? You didn't know me before, did you?*

*No, Peter. We've never met. How much of your memory do you think you have lost?*

*I don't know. Most of it. I can't remember anything. I remember the last week and then ... Only scattered images that aren't making sense to me.*

*We'll work on it, Peter. Every day, one bit at a time. I'll help you. Don't be frightened.*

*I'm not. I'm angry. I've never felt such hate — well, that I know of. My mind feels like my body does.* He pushed to her a sense of the pain he was in.

*I'll get you more painkillers.*

*No ... just, visit more often.*

*As often as I can, Peter.*

He let her go at ninety paces. In truth, he was growing stronger, psionically. He found that if he followed his awareness of Anchali as she left, he could stretch far beyond his previous limits. He wasn't going to tell her though. He'd trusted Tamsin; he couldn't bring himself to trust another psi again, not one that had been introduced to him by Services.

One hundred and ten, one hundred and eleven, one hundred and twelve ... He found someone else as Anchali left the hospital corridor, a guard sitting at a desk in a prefab capsule. He was scanning data surveillance of activity surrounding the enclosure; Pete watched it somewhat distantly, as he'd never stretched so far before. He could see that the compound they were keeping him in was set in a desert of ruddy-orange sand, surrounded for miles by sharp clumpy grass; he saw his quarantine area isolated from the nest of tents and capsules that huddled on the far side of the fenced-in portion of the desert; an annex held an airstrip with three large transports and a half-dozen squibs.

The man Pete had made contact with turned in his chair and spoke to a woman sitting at a similar desk across the room. The man fantasised about the woman but betrayed no sign of it in his manner. 'Private, monitor the dust front from the north while I step out, will you?'

'Yes, Sergeant.'

The man stood and exited the room. Pete's connection followed, one hundred twenty-seven, one hundred twenty-eight. Just as the man pushed open the door that would lead to the outside, Pete's bond with him slipped away.

Nearly one hundred and thirty paces. Was this a gift from Pierre? What else could it be?

He felt her dabbing him with cold water. His body was in pain. It shrieked at him.

*I'm alive then.*

*You must be more careful.*

*Must I? What's the point?*

*Peter, calm yourself. Every time you black out like that you ruin your healing. They will sedate you completely, if you don't settle down.*

He opened his eyes.

*Where are my team? Why haven't I seen them?*

*Please don't be angry with me. I don't know where they are.*

*I'm sorry. I don't know what it is. I don't mean to be so frustrated …*

For no reason he bounced between emotions, all just reactions. Anger fear anger fear.

*I'm going to sedate you, Peter. Your pulse is rising again.*

Each moment of consciousness was like a day to him, and he would wake and pass out perhaps ten times a cycle. Each time he opened his eyes he was in a new mood — he couldn't seem to control it.

Nurse Anchali tried to explain it to him, but he was suspicious.

*You've been through a traumatic event. This is natural and the only cure is time. You must be patient.*

*How do I know he didn't do this to me?*

*Because you are still you. Trust me, I'm a nurse.*

*How can I trust you? You could be like her.*

*Tamsin Grey? How dare you say a thing like that? People like her are monsters.*

*I can't trust anyone. Not Geof, not her, not you. I shouldn't even trust myself. I've been tampered with like a computer.*

*Perhaps you have, but there's no point letting it eat you up. Look, I have to go. I'll be back in an hour, try to stay positive.*

She gathered the remains of the meal back onto the tray and dabbed around his mouth.

*You're right not to trust though. It hurts me that you don't trust me, but it is better than you trusting anyone from Services.*

Without thinking about it she wiped the tears away from his face, letting her hand rest on his cheek for comfort.

'Why are you crying, Mister Lazarus? Are you in pain?'

*They'll never let me go. I'm stuck here, in this bed, in a room like this —*

*STOP!* she demanded before his paranoia managed to creep into her own mind.

Anchali stood up. 'I'll consult the physician and see if he can help you rest. I'll bring you something to drink in an hour. Until then, just relax as much as you can.'

She walked away, trying not to appear hurried. They watched everything. It was probably already too late for her and Pete might soon have her life on his conscience too.

There is always the kind of person who will do anything for money and Gock was one such person. His full name was Gock Meyon Cshirasu from the Yantz region. He was onto his third life partner and had two children. None of them liked him. Pete knew the man inside and out before he entered his room and already he felt discomforted by his presence.

Gock was a proxy. A person who lived out the actions of the highest bidder. Those who could afford proxies saw through their eyes and heard through their ears. Controllers often used proxies for anonymity or, as in this case, to protect themselves in dangerous situations. Gock spoke what he was told to speak and did what they bid him. He was Gock and he was at somebody's service.

It was this second person that Pete was most interested in. Pete knew all he needed to know about Gock without having to lay eyes on him, but the person who commanded him was an unknown.

The man did not know where he was or why, only that his next instruction would be received at the end of the canvas tunnel. He was surprised to see only a man in a healing pallet.

For a moment Peter thought that if he never opened his eyes he could avoid meeting the man, but Gock shuffled as he sat in the chair, thinking of his family back in Yantz. He was irritated by how happy they were that he had been indefinitely repositioned and would be out of contact with them for the foreseeable future. He was also jet-lagged and ready to sleep as soon as the opportunity presented itself. Pete pondered a moment the term 'foreseeable future'. He could foresee very little of his own future at this point, or his past. He'd given up his freedom and was now at the mercy of Services.

When he did eventually open his eyes, the squat little man stood up. 'You may call me Gock. I speak for the honourable Ryu Shima, Prime of the World Union.'

Until he spoke the words, Gock himself didn't know who had hired him. Ryu Shima, the young man of Yantz who had risen nearly overnight to the position of Prime. This made Gock smile. This was a powerful man. This was a man with pull. This man could change Gock's life.

For Peter Lazarus it was as though the Prime himself had walked into his room. The most influential individual in the world, and he had sent a proxy so he was safe from the telepath.

He didn't know how long it took him to raise a reply. 'I am not sure how to address you.'

Ryu was quick to respond, then Gock repeated the words in his own slippery voice. 'You will address me as Prime. I can tell it is painful for you to talk right now, so please keep your answers short. You can nod to indicate you understand.' Peter nodded. 'Are you aware that you are under suspicion of treason and sabotage?'

'I knew I was under suspicion for something.'

'Your trial is taking place now and everything you say or do will contribute to the determination. Do you understand?' Pete nodded. 'If at any time you wish to confess and spare Services the time and resources burden, your crime will be looked upon more favourably. Do you wish to confess?'

Pete remained silent and did not nod.

'As you wish. I have appointed Gock to shadow you for the length of your reorientation. You may contact me through him, but I will not always be available to you. I will work on your case as I can.'

It was difficult to keep up. Pete had to remind himself that it was Ryu Shima who was speaking, not the sweating proxy who was just a relay. It was extremely disorienting to hold a conversation with someone who was thinking things contrary to what they were saying. 'What's reorientation?' he asked.

'Reorientation, Mister Lazarus, is when a Citizen is found unable to perform or has become confused about their civic duties and requires correction.'

'What does that mean?'

'It means you will continue your investigation. For now.'

'But what about the others? Geof and Colonel Pinter?'

'Mister Lazarus, Gock and I have put strain on you enough. If time wasn't of the essence, we would have waited for your full recovery. Please accept my apologies.'

'Okay ...'

'A ten squad will collect you at dawn. Do you understand?' Pete nodded. 'Good. It will be hard for you at first. I have found that few have the discipline I demand, but most eventually learn to try. I also understand that this way of life is not what you intended and it is outside of your belief system, but you must prepare for reorientation. The only advice I can give you is not to resist. Allow us to help you and you will learn faster.'

Gock bowed, reluctantly, but he was under duress. Pete did not know what to think about his new situation.

* * *

Pete awoke with Anchali gently shaking him. 'Mister Lazarus? Mister Lazarus? We must dress you.' *Wake up, Peter. Some men are here to take you away.*

*Is it time already?*

*Where are you going?*

*I haven't been told.*

'Do you think you can stand? That's good. Gently now. That's good.' Slowly they managed to get him out of bed and dressed. He swayed on his own two feet; the ground under him felt like a raft at sea.

*Will you be okay?* Anchali asked.

*I think so. It has just been a long time since I was last vertical. What will you do now?*

*I'll be reassigned. Back to a more normal hospital.*

*Will you contact your people? Tell them what happened?*

*I will. As soon as they find me. Good luck, Peter Lazarus. I hope we meet again.*

*Thank you for nursing me.*

*Be strong.*

*Don't look sad, Anchali. They are watching.*

*Yes.* She sniffed back her emotions. *They are always watching.*

She helped him all the way to the landing area, acting as a crutch until he found his balance. She left orders with Gock that he should eat as soon as possible and then she left.

Pete held onto their connection as she walked back to the hospital tent. They said nothing, only sharing the emotions that were going through them both.

Thirty-one, thirty-two …

Pete had seen marauders before. On parade. Even out of their armour the team were of impressive size. Biceps as big as a regular man's head, with shoulders that could pull a plough across a field.

'This is the marauder team,' Gock introduced them. 'They'll be your ten squad.'

Pete didn't need clearance to know the ranking of the small team. There were ten men, numbered for clear hierarchy. He reached into their minds as they saluted the air in front of them with metal-bound fists.

Pete stood shakily before one of the soldiers, a swarthy man with a black stubble of hair. 'You must be Ten,' he said, though he knew the man's real name was Clarence Daveraux.

'Yes, sir.'

Seventy-nine, eighty …

'And what are your orders?'

'To take you to Yantz, sir.'

'And then?'

'To help train you into proper physical condition.'

Pete's body did not like the sound of that.

They helped him aboard a transport squib, one of the big berths that could hold twenty armoured Servicemen. As soon as they had him buckled in, they were in the air.

One hundred and five, one hundred and six — the squib pulled him out of range.

*Goodbye, Anchali. It seems I can't hold onto anyone.*

\* \* \*

Busan was on the southern edge of the traditional territories of Korea, on a belt of coastline where the city existed half in the water and half on land. Stacks of buildings crept up the hillsides, their roots branching out over the bay in such density that a pedestrian could cross the bobbing expanse merely by stepping from platform to platform; a practice the older generation were trying to discourage in their adolescents.

It was a place of crowds and people packed into small rooms. There were two worlds here: where half spent its hours plugged into the Weave, the other half ignored it as best they could and spent their time engaging in energetic outdoor activities. The majority were Citizens, but non-participation was common.

Geof technically could have spoken to Li over a safe connection, but Shen no longer answered outside calls. He kept himself locked in a subterranean basement and hadn't been heard from in two years. At the least it would be good to let the world know that one of its gods of tech was not dead. Or was.

To gain entry, he had to go through two sets of sterilisation showers. First shower, then through a hermetic partition, and then repeated a second time, followed by a long elevator ride downward. If Geof plotted it correctly in his head, Shen's hermitage was like the inversion of a needle, underground and pointing toward the centre of Earth. It consisted of a five-hundred-metre elevator shaft ending in a chamber of prefab rooms at the bottom. Things were made down here so that they would never see the light of day.

The elevator opened into a holding area and Geof stepped through. He pushed at the grille door and sparks flew off. He leapt back, stuck inside the electrified cage.

'Sensei Li. It is me, Geof Ozenbach,' he called out. Beyond the fence, from the other side of the cage, he could see the glints of camera eyes peering at him. A man approached. His eyes were hidden behind a pair of flat oculars and he turned his head from side to side, viewing him from different angles.

'Ozey?' The cage clicked off and Geof opened the gate.

Shen had always liked his whiskers. Over the years they had just gotten longer. Twin moustaches hung down to his chest, complemented by long plaited twines from his temples, forehead and chin, like the barbels of a catfish. His face was dominated by large circular spectacles thick with enhancements. Shen was as Geof remembered him, though older and with more details about the eyes — but as alive as ever.

The 'gods of tech' were interchangeable, like the Primacy, though for the last few years there were only three who had been named so. All the gods were synthesists of the highest order, at the peak of their prowess. They made connections between human wants and desires, and created technological innovations and new paradigms for civilisation, time and again unleashing a string of code or production advance that changed the nature of possible human existence.

It was an unofficial primacy in the data world and every action of the gods was watched, interpreted and reacted to. The gods themselves responded in their own ways to the effect of that ever-watchful gaze.

Two of the gods had become rivals of sorts, taking great pleasure in their game of one-upmanship. Egon Shelley and Morritz Kay were both pioneers of the Weave age. In a constant search for serendipity, now the paths of their influence created connectivity wherever they went and it would be impossible for them not to be gods even if they wanted to stop. Shelley and Morritz disagreed on many things, from basic production methods to life philosophy.

Neither could agree on, nor had they signed, the Digital Rights of Humankind, though both had been consulted on the treatise. The question that currently divided them was over the right to self-controlled evolution. Thus were the problems of the gods. They were called 'gods' because their actions were so sweeping and the problems they seemed to dwell on so abstract as to be meaningless to most.

The longest-standing member, Shen Li, chose to live in seclusion and had barely left his grotto under Busan in two years. Sixty-three years ago he had fathered the early symbiots, the nearly animal wearable computers that were no more than a simple mollusc, and his position amongst the gods was assured.

'Thank you for seeing me, Sensei Li.'

'Ozey, please call me Shen. You know I don't like protocol.' Geof nodded assent. He did know this, but he liked paying his respects. 'What brings you down here?'

'I have come seeking your help with an urgent problem.'

'Uh huh,' Shen grunted and crossed the room to take a seat at a workbench set up with a forest of tools and mini-floodlights. The room itself held ten workbenches of similar disarray and small piles of scrapped projects and parts. Geof hadn't seen anything like it: a giant, squat egg-shaped room, made entirely of a poly-metal he didn't recognise, perhaps a Dark Age design ... some sort of mass-produced bunker. Shen must have been delighted when he found it; the perfect home. He probably only used the one room, but the dark oval orifices on the walls must lead to sleeping areas and amenities. One of the portals was closed and ostentatiously secured with locks.

'What are you working on?' Geof asked.

'Oh, many things.' Shen waved his arms to indicate the workbenches covered in his thoughts taking form. 'And you, Geof? Please, have a seat. Tell me about this problem of yours.'

Geof found a stool and pulled it over to sit near Shen as he turned back to whatever he was tinkering with. He told him about Pierre Jnr, the rising psi rebellion and the task he had been set by the Prime.

'Well, it sounds like you are doing very well for yourself,' Shen murmured.

'Thank you, sensei, but I didn't come here to update you on my life. I wanted your help.'

'With what?'

'With everything I just explained. Weren't you listening to me?'

'Yes, yes. I heard. There is a new and unstoppable threat to the world. What do you want me to do about it? These things happen.'

'But people have lost their lives, and more will if he is not stopped.'

Shen waved that away. 'People are always dying. Nothing to be done about that either.'

'I don't like to think that way.'

His old master turned his head and grinned. 'Of course you don't, Ozey. You weren't bred for it.'

'Oh, not you too?' Geof stood and paced away. Shen didn't respond; he just continued to fiddle with the metal bauble he held in his tweezers. Geof found himself standing in front of the bolted hatch, reading the label that hung from the pin lock.

'What is Kronos?'

An arc sprang up between Shen's tools and the metal sphere. He swore. 'Now look what you made me do.'

'My apologies, sensei. I was only curious.'

'Well, don't be. What's behind that door is my failure and nobody else needs to see it.'

'Yes, sensei.'

Shen sighed, put his tools down and flicked the power off to the bench. 'Alright. You can set up over there. Move everything from that table into one of the spare rooms, but don't get it out of order. Don't talk to me while I'm working and don't mention the door. Agree?'

Most of Geof's internship with Li had been spent in the opposite corner of the room with the instruction to not interrupt.

'Just like old times, sensei?' Geof grinned.

Shen grunted.


For the next two days Geof worked behind Shen. While Li fused and fussed with his widgets, or fed and drained new symbiotic materials, or probed and tweaked the metal ball, Geof sat in near stillness, immersed in the data. He had to go back to scratch.

Since the first hunt had only followed a few leads before discovering Pierre's location, there wasn't much left to pursue.

Geof started a new file and tapped in what they really knew about Pierre Jnr. After removing as much speculation and supposition as he could, it amounted to very little.

*Pierre Jnr was born from a breeding and development program for psionics.*

*Pierre Jnr was born to Registered Psionic Pierre Sandro Snr, and Registered Psionic Mary Kastonovich.*

*Three months after his birth Pierre Jnr escaped and was lost to surveillance an hour later.*

*Pierre Jnr is eight years old.*

*He can make people forget.*

*He can control people like puppets.*

*He is a kinetic of unprecedented strength.*

*Pierre Jnr is confirmed alive on April Seventh, 2159.*

Geof closed off these earlier strands as dry.

One question leapt up at him. If it was Pierre — and he had been in hiding for eight years — why was it so easy to find him? Was it luck or had Pierre wanted to be found? Was it coincidence or circumstance? Or was it due to Peter Lazarus? The idea of a group entity as the threat quickly became the more elegant solution.

Left to his own devices, he began approaching his task like a research assignment. A routine collsyn, or collect and synthesise, as they had been taught on the ranch.

Most of the data about Pierre Jnr was old. *No*, he corrected himself. *Data has no age.* 'You can never step into the same data twice,' he mumbled to himself.

'What was that?' Shen asked from across the room, where he was tending his slime jellies.

'You taught me that one can never step into the same data twice,' Geof began.

'Why do you always forget the second part of that adage? You can never step into the same data twice, and you will never get the same answers if you try. *Id est*, Ozey, information theory isn't an exact science. Empirical method doesn't always work with data.'

'That always seemed like madness to me.'

'I know.' Shen smiled at him. 'But if you only follow the paths of logic, you will only discover logical things.'

'You do love your adages, don't you?'

'They keep me on the winding path. Who knows what you'll discover when you stray from the road of what everyone else knows? Take Kronos for example.' Shen indicated the reinforced steel door that occasionally ticked as though a large grasshopper was fluttering against the other side of the hatch.

'Are you sure you can't tell me what's in there?'

'No, I honestly can't. I don't know what it is. A failed experiment, but I'm keeping him. I think there is something to learn in that unhappy accident. I just don't know what it is. I feel sorry for it, of course. A part of me is in that thing.'

'Another digitalis experiment?' Geof asked. 'Is it dangerous?'

'Yes. I think it would be. But I'm not going to open the door again to find out.'

'Why do you still pursue digitalis? What need is there?'

'Don't you see, Ozey? No matter what we try to do with civilisation it fails. The problem lies in the base animal.'

'It's not so bad. There has been peace for over fifty years.'

'Yes, peace, but at what cost? Look what we've done to humanity. We make it easier and easier to live. Every job has an auto-generated procedure. All the human has to do is push a button. Our machines are better than us.' Shen put down his watering can and looked over at Geof. 'Cracking biological machines released a torrent of developments, leading to symbiots, weavers like yourself and independent mechalogical inventions. But the barriers between man and machine are still there — if the interface differences can be reduced close to the null point, then the difference will be irrelevant.'

'Won't that just compound the problem?'

'I don't think so. We can't go backward, so we have to go forward. We have built machines to replace us in every facet of life, now we must become the machine. It's the only way for us to regain our agency.'

They returned to their respective projects and the room succumbed again to silence.

Geof took a quill from the side table and began scrawling on a thought board, each question writ in fat black lines. *What questions can I ask and how can I answer them?*

*Manifestation = Pierre Jnr or another.*
*If Pierre Jnr: Was he found by the team or was he waiting*
*    for us?*
*If not Pierre Jnr: Who? + Why?*

*If Pierre Jnr: Why?*
*If found: How to find again?*
*If ambush: Why?*

Every question and assumption had to be challenged. The dominant logic was that it *had* been Pierre Jnr and it was an intentional attack, provoked or not. What motivation could there be?

*Effects of the manifestation = Global civic turnover. The hunt disrupted. Lazarus under trial. Tamsin Grey disappeared. Large area of land decimated.*
*Were these effects desired, accidental or incidental?*
*Reactive or proactive?*

This was getting nowhere.

*If not Pierre = Entity X.*
*Group or individual?*
*Psionic or technically advanced?*

*If Lazarus can be trusted = Pierre.*
*If Lazarus cannot be trusted = Unknown.*

*Conclusion = ?*

*I know nothing.*
He tossed that aside and started over.

In the centre of a blank field he placed an icon that represented Pierre, which he interlinked with the material gathered so far. In a ring around that he placed icons for Mary Kastonovich, Pierre Snr, Tamsin Grey and Peter Lazarus. After a moment's thought, he added in the family from the midlands house, the Pembroke couple, the students from the school Pierre had visited in the Dakotas, and everyone from the PDP. This circle included everyone who was known, with certainty, to have come into direct contact with Pierre Jnr. It numbered one thousand, three hundred and forty-five individuals. Geof then set his symbiot to compile a second circle of people who had interacted with those in the first circle.

The growth was exponential, growing to over one hundred thousand. A third ring, representing the people that the second ring had come into contact with, brought the count over three million. A fourth enlargement included most of the twenty billion souls upon the planet.

It proved nothing. He was just making an infection model as if Pierre was a contagious disease. He shuddered at the thought, but at least it showed quite clearly that if that *was* the case the world would have been overrun long ago. Geof shrugged but flowed his schematic to Shen's stream, then sat patiently as his mentor looked it over.

'Where is time, Ozey? You always forget time. This measure is from when?' Shen was standing by the board, pointing at the first event.

'This is just confirmed contacts.'

'Ah, this is useless then. What about the eight years you didn't know where Pierre was?'

'Yes, you're right.' Geof felt foolish. 'If I add a chronology to the points of contact, there's a chance that some change vectors might be patterned.' He could have kicked himself. Without including the incidence of contact he was only getting half the information.

'Then you could cross-reference external data to track a path of movement. Then you'd have something.'

Geof nodded to himself. In his head he tried to see where this method might fall down. 'We need more data.'

Shen turned back to his own work and spoke offhand, 'Of course, the challenge you and the Prime are facing is no longer about whether it is Pierre Jnr or not. Now it is about what the Will believes happened.'

'What do you mean?' Geof stood and stretched. He archived the infection chart and started looking around for something to eat.

'Well, let's put Pierre aside for now and say that what you are patterning is the beginning of a psi revolution. The Prime and psis must be aware that the emergent narrative of history will affect the future Will of the people and each side must try to frame the story to suit them. Will it be the long-suffering psis seeking freedom from oppression? Or the innocent majority under threat by fanatical mind-raping telepaths? If support for the psis continues to build, and the restrictions on their activities are cast in a more sympathetic light, guilt for past actions may persuade the Will to shift to a more open position. If the swing goes far enough, say to a point akin to four decades ago when psionics were more fascination than threat, then everything that is being done now will be undone.'

'And that is the true nature of the threat?' said Geof.

Shen shrugged. He went into one of the antechambers and Geof followed. It was a kitchen only a scientist would build. 'It is the political threat. The Will controls everything. If the Will wants to believe it is Pierre, then it is Pierre. If the Will wants to allow psis equality in society, then that is what will happen. It is a battle for minds now.'

Geof took this in while Shen built a pile of ready-made foods on the bench and began heating Serviceman trays.

'Are you too young to remember the resistance that tried to block cybernetics? Or gene-selective breeding before that?'

'I knew some people didn't like it, but I didn't know it was opposed.'

'Oh yes. Violently. It was much like cloning is considered now, verboten. But still some do it. Eventually both sides in a conflict run out of ammunition, the leaders driving the emotions die off, or get replaced by more dogmatic successors.'

'But what was the problem with cybernetics? Humans have been technologically enabled all through history.'

'Come, come, Geof. No need to get defensive. At some point even clothes were technology, but eventually the technology becomes part of the animal. When cyberism became more than just replacement body parts and people like you, wired to a symbiot half your size, then cyborgs had an unfair advantage and others didn't like that.'

'So what happened?'

'The numbers changed. When cyborgs became the majority, it became the norm.'

'I don't really think of myself as a cyborg.'

'Of course not. You came after the time when there was a difference. But as an incubator baby, your links to cyberism began before you were even born.'

Geof filed all this away and began scooping mash and repro from his tray. 'So is there a precedent for this kind of conflict?' he asked.

'The weapons always change, but there may be something in the annals of religious oppression, or media wars for mental domination ... though that's unrec history, so the information is highly questionable.' Before the latest Dark Age, very little of human events was recorded for replay. Nearly everything before the twentieth century was only verbally recounted or written retrospectively, so objectivity was non-existent. Most of human history was unrec. 'I will say this though: it is natural for a group to defend what it thinks makes it a group.'

'And what distinguishes the group in this case?' Geof asked.

'Well, for a start one group can read and control other people's thoughts and push things without touching them. The boundaries of the individual are under threat. The majority — the World Union and all that they comprise — are a group of individuals. Groups of individuals that form a super-group, yes, but a psi society on the other hand may be something entirely different.'

'Are you suggesting that individuality is under threat?'

'Not precisely, but yes, in a way. If the sanctity of one's own mind and the sanctity of one's neighbour's mind cannot be guaranteed, then where does one individual end and another begin?'

'You could make an argument that people have always been under one another's control.'

225

'Influence perhaps. But that isn't the same as disempowering one person to the status of a bot. A machine you can turn on and off and program to do what you want. To do that to a human is subjugation.'

'And the threat of Pierre Jnr is the same as that from every psi. Only magnified.'

'A thousand per cent.' Shen nodded. 'To be honest, I haven't thought about the psi problem in a long time. It used to interest me but,' he paused to hand Geof a second and third tray that had finished heating, 'we just don't understand psionics very well, scientifically speaking. We know what can happen and what can be done, but the mechanics behind it are still a mystery.'

'Do you think the PD experiments contributed to Pierre being what he is?'

'I wouldn't discount it. If I understand Doctor Rhee at all, he was the sort of scientist who didn't miss an opportunity.'

'You don't like him?' Geof asked, peering around the kitchen.

'There is little to like in that man. What *are* you looking for?'

'I was just wondering if you had any chocolate.'

Shen sighed and retrieved a block of foil-wrapped dark from the upper shelf. 'Don't eat it all. I only get an order once a month.'

'You're right,' Geof said, breaking off a thick chunk with a knife. 'Rhee performed every experiment he could think of to find a result. Diets, hormones, stimulants, gene surgery ... meditation. But they never found any concrete evidence and were shut down after Pierre's escape.'

Shen chuckled. 'Shut down? Oh no, they wouldn't do that. The PDP was appropriated by Services.'

'If that was true, I would know about it.'

'You can see behind every wall now, can you, Ozey? How do you think they train and control their psi operatives?' Geof said nothing. 'Embarrassing though it may have been, the origination of Pierre Jnr was a breakthrough. They found the hereditary link.'

'No.' Geof shook his head. 'I don't want to believe that.'

'And that is your choice.' Shen leant forward and flipped his oculars back. 'Look at my eyes, Geof.'

He did as he was told and looked eye to eye with his mentor. Shen's pupils were contracted and the capillaries were etched in red. Too much close-up staring was making him look feverish.

'Always question the data. Then question yourself. Then question the question.'

'What is that one supposed to mean?'

'There is always another level. There is always another wall to get through.'

Geof stared into the focused pinheads of his mentor's eyes, trying to see what he saw; to catch the hint he was being offered.

Shen broke off and sat up straight again, snapping his oculars back over his eyes. 'You should go. That is more talk than I've had to sustain in months. You wear me out.'

'Yes, sensei.' Geof stood and returned to the main chamber to collect his things. It was not the first time he had been booted out of Shen's presence. The old man often waned into a mood after too much conversation. 'May I return to discuss any developments?' he asked.

'Yes, yes. You can always come back.' Shen was tired and seemed shorter now. He moped behind Geof as he went to the gate. 'Did I help you, Geof?' Shen asked.

'Yes, sensei. Very much so.'

The old man nodded to himself. 'Good. Perhaps you will forgive me for the rest of it then.'

'"There is always a lesson to be learned",' Geof quoted.

'And some to unlearn,' Shen replied.

The doors of the elevator shut and Geof returned to the world above.

That night Geof was dozing when a message came in from an unexpected source.

Pinter: I've been keeping up with your progress.

Geof: Colonel! It is a welcome surprise to hear from you. Where are you? I don't have a visual of you.

Pinter: My location is classified, Geof. I'm being rejuved.

Geof: I am in shock and disbelief. You?

Pinter: It is hard to believe, I know. I'd sworn against it, but I didn't feel I could perform my duty with what I had left in me.

Geof: What is it like? Is it painful?

Pinter: There are moments.

Geof had read widely on the subject. Rejuving was still fairly new; rebirth, some people called it, or internal cosmetics. There were reports that suggested one should proceed with caution. Some psychological side effects had been reported, but without a control group they were unverifiable and most likely the natural result of a second youth and a doubled lifespan.

Geof: How young will you be when I see you next?

Pinter: I'm going back a long way. I think I looked my best at thirty.

Geof: So I guess this is getting serious then.

Pinter: Do not tell Peter Lazarus. He is not to know about me.

Geof: As you command, sir.

Pinter: I'm contacting you about your report.

Geof: You've seen it?

Pinter: Let's not waste time on redundant questions, shall we?

Geof: No, sir.

Pinter: Tell me your reasoning for the infection graph.

Geof: I was following a hunch, sir. I am not sure what I was aiming for.

Pinter: I want you to do something for me. Take the approximate psi population density and apply that to your connectivity spread.

Geof: And in the centre?

Pinter: It doesn't matter. Like Li said, it's the idea that counts.

Geof: Yes, sir.

**Geof duplicated the diagram and ran it again based on the Colonel's instructions.**

Pinter: I want to know how many telepaths would be needed to forcefully bend the Will in their favour.

Geof: I can tell you that without a run, sir. Anywhere between one and ten billion.

Pinter: That's a big fluctuation, Geof. Can't you do any better than that?

Geof: Colonel, it depends on what the average abilities of a telepath is. If they can only control one other person, then only half the population is needed. But if they can control ten, then only two billion. Etc.

Pinter: And if you include existing influence vectors?

Geof: Impossible to predict. The environment of the Will is as reliable as the weather. It could be as few as one.

Pinter: One.

Geof waited while Pinter processed this information. One telepath. In other words: Pierre Jnr.

Pinter: Okay. Thank you for your help, Ozenbach.

Geof: Will you be coming back, Colonel?

Pinter: Only if it gets to the worst case scenario. Until then, you have to step it up.

Geof: I will. Out.

Pinter: Out.

*He seemed like such a nice old man* … Geof reflected. But in his younger days, in more desperate times, he knew that Abercrombie Pinter had been a man of action and that many of those actions were still brought into question fifty years on. A hundred-year-old man whose glory days involved ending the Örjian assault with a single act of devastating violence.

One of Geof's proclivities was history. Of most interest were the periods before all the global wars. He was fascinated by the great loom of cause and effect that eventually crashed under its own weight; the cresting wave of causality. This wasn't the first time he'd asked himself the question, but each time it felt heavier and heavier: was this one of those moments?

As was his routine, Geof closed off his working files, typed in his last thoughts and lightly scanned over what had been happening on the Weave. One item caught his eye. At the site of the manifestation people had begun to lay flowers. He wondered if they were flowers of mourning or tribute.

# He can make us forget

Pete passed out during the journey to Yantz and woke as he was lifted up by one of the marauders. His symbiot warned him the weather was about to break and the soldier — *Five*, he thought — broke into a run before the clouds turned over and dumped their waterfalls.

The bombs of the first drops built to a roar just before the automatic doors closed it out. They had only got a little sodden, Gock somewhat more so.

They were in a small lobby with a single lift waiting, open. Five set him down in the elevator and saluted his way clear. There were no buttons inside, nor a command console for their symbs to interface. It simply rose at speed and broke into daylight — or what was left of it under the storm — before quickly arriving at their destination.

Yantz was probably the greenest place Pete had ever seen. Set on a delta of narrow canals, it was painfully luminescent with algal blooms. It was only broken up by the whites and browns of the raised islands and the hovels of timber and fibro that encircled them.

There were dozens of needles, just like the one he was now looking out from. The giant window in the main room looked squarely at Shima Palace. He only knew it as Shima Palace via

Gock. It covered five hectares and rose three times higher than everything around it. It was big enough to act as a crossing point, allowing pedestrian traffic to flow in the tunnels beneath. In typhoon season the Shimas allowed the food markets to be housed in the open area on the ground floor. Their residence was held metres above by decorated pylons.

Gock looked east. His home was out of sight, beyond the second kink in the river. He wondered what they'd make of him being up in a needle. Most likely, they wouldn't believe him.

The next morning Pete was able to walk without aid. He ate heartily, more than he had since the attack. Ten arrived early and immediately began working on his physical improvement regime.

Pete's training would be as accelerated as his healing. On the first day Ten made him complete three hundred circuits of the main room. This was more movement than he was ready for, but Ten made him suck on a strip of the dry chew that Servicemen often used in the field to boost their energy levels. Sugar and stimulants.

'I need to rest. I'm not fully healed yet,' he protested at the seventieth lap.

'Physically you are. The aches and pains you feel are the new muscles in your body. They just haven't been broken in yet. You need to use them or the pain will get worse.' And so they continued until Ten declared it to be enough.

Pete washed, trimmed his hair down to skin and scalp, ate a Serviceman's dinner and slept through the night.

Ten was right, the pain from the new parts was fading away; they had just needed to be used. He hadn't known until now how they had healed him so fast, with grafts and implants. Anchali certainly hadn't known.

The next day he didn't hurt at all and his exercise circuit trebled while Ten introduced weight carrying and light aerobics.

On the third day he was taken outside and Ten stepped him through a long course that took him in a ring around the needle before returning him home.

'Ten, this is all very good.' Pete panted around his words. 'But what is this training for?'

'You are asking me? My rank doesn't tell me anything except what I'm meant to do. But from a soldier's point of view it's never a bad idea to be able to run a little further.'

The canal water, stippled with surface insects and clouds of midges, clung to the shadowy overhang of the wooden sidewalks. Most people travelled on foot, carrying their goods in netted sacks, or paddled in narrow canoes. Few could afford to squib, and few of the structures would be able to support any sort of landing.

The richer families of Yantz had more permanent docks by their walls, with long staircases Pete had to climb. These artificial plateaus raised the communal areas and affluent families safely above the water level and held orchards of citrus trees and stone fruit, or pens for animals and market areas. The largest of these artificial islands held up the most established families, such as the Shimas. Other islands were the size of small towns. Such was the nature of Yantz; a million pockets of people that made up the megapolis.

On the fourth day, Ten began teaching him how to use his symbiot better, how to think during an attack and how to act, assess and plan at the one time. Well, those were the instructions that Ten had been given. What it amounted to was increasingly hard circuits that Ten dotted with squad members who would leap out and attempt to push him in the canal.

The water had a potent chlorophyll smell he quickly became familiar with. Each member of the squad managed to dunk him that first day.

'The brain is a muscle,' Ten lectured. 'You train it until actions become reactions: just repeat and repeat. Every time you run down a street, before you turn a corner, or if you can't see behind some hard cover, check your sensors. Both of them for you, telepath. If we do this for a few weeks, it will become automatic. We'll take care of your conditioning, don't you worry about that.'

'Where are the rest of the squad?'

'Always nearby. When you need us, we'll be in range.' By that he meant they would always be close enough to ambush Pete on one of his runs. Ten made sure he worked hard. He was a great believer in the mind-body connection.

Ten was right, Pete did get better. He quickly made it his practice to use the sensors of his symbiot and any data it could access, as well as reaching out psionically to see who was coming at him and from where. It was tiring at first. He was used to tapping particular people, stationary ones who were in the same room as him, not running through a crowded city where the opportunity for steady contact could be counted in seconds. Keeping a cursory eye out like this was a huge strain.

Each night he made it home exhausted. The high-speed lift nearly brought him to his knees. He often only had an hour to rest and eat before Gock was hounding him to review footage and case studies of psi collection missions.

Once a week he had to report on his progress to the Prime, like a child to his parents after classes. *Yes, sir, my heart rate has improved. No, I have not managed to stop the squad pushing me into the canals.*

Ryu's prosecution, as part of Pete's trial, was unrelenting. Every time they talked, through Gock, he would try to corner Peter with the same trap of questions: 'What is the nature of the enemy we face? Is it one boy or a multitude? Or both?'

'I don't know,' was Pete's most common answer.

'Are you under the control of Pierre Jnr?'

'No. I am not a puppet.'

'The trial will determine that. Tell me the difference between Pierre and other psis.'

'What do you mean? Pierre is vastly more powerful.'

'But all telepaths have the ability to subjugate others. Is that correct?' During the questioning Gock would often drift into his own reveries and merely repeat what was spoken to him while looking out the window and cultivating pornographic fantasies.

'To some extent,' Pete had to answer and try not to hear Gock's mind at work. 'But not all psis act like Pierre.'

'But you see why they must be considered one and the same threat?'

'You won't convince me to hunt my own kind.'

Gock could not accurately replicate the laugh that came from his speaking master, and Pete could hear both: Ryu's amusement and his proxy's vulgar schadenfreude. 'The thing about you, Mister Lazarus, is that I know exactly how you will react to every situation. I know you may be frustrated by the process, but your reorientation is on schedule.'

'What kind of monster are you?' Pete asked, himself not sure if he meant the Prime or the proxy.

'Me? I wouldn't have to manipulate you if you were more willing to help with the conflict.'

'It's you who is keeping me away from the hunt.'

'You are weak. You would be no match for Pierre Jnr, or any psi.' Then, abruptly, Ryu would disconnect from his proxy and Pete was left with no chance to reply.

Between the talks with the Prime-Gock and the constant instruction from Ten, Pete began to learn the collection procedure that Ryu Shima was enforcing across the WU.

'The trouble with fighting benders is that anything we bring against them might be turned into a weapon against us. Same with telepaths: you may carry a gun, but they might pull the trigger. You know what I'm saying?' Ten asked.

'Of course I know what you're saying.'

'Yeah, right. Of course you do.'

'So what do you do?' Pete inquired.

'Luckily most of the psis we go up against are young and have barely realised their powers. Intimidation is often enough, so we go in hard and loud. Stun, confuse, disable. Drop some flash, try to glue them in place and then try to get the mask on them. Once the mask is on we're safe. If the first team doesn't get it done, we send in a second, which gases the area and we all fall down.'

'Why don't you just start with the gas?'

Ten shook his head. 'The Will doesn't like that. There can be unnecessary injuries.'

Over a period of weeks Pete developed quickly. There was always something new that Ten or Ryu would add, and there was always something he thought of himself to try as well. His reach was now above one hundred and fifty paces and he was working on a more open way of tapping. Not targeting specific people, just opening himself up, sampling whatever he could as he went past.

Pete felt sidelined though, excluded from what was happening in the investigation. Or in the world. He only managed to piece together bits and pieces from the passers-by during his training. It was not a good time to be psionic.

Despite himself, he grew to like Ten, even with his daily administrations of forced exercise and Services catch-alls: 'Pain is noise. Emotion is noise. Filter and focus.'

Clarence had been in Services for a decade. He had one more tour before he could become an operator and run a team of remotes. Five years training, five years to get from ranks One to Ten. Most of that time was spent in soldier games, with only the rare disciplinary action. Until Ryu had taken over and set them to work.

Marauders liked being the biggest guys around. Amongst the crowds they swaggered as only twelve-foot-high armoured men can. Disciplined and rough. Cut stone. The point of making

239

men like this was so they would be there to do anything. Physically and mentally prepared for anything that was asked of them.

The squad trained hard. After running the morning circuit with Pete, Ten spent the day putting his men through spread-and-sweep manoeuvres, which involved them dispersing as fast and far as they could, circling a set target and then coming together in perfect co-ordination.

Pete couldn't keep up. Eventually he had to give in. He was too tired to do otherwise. He did what Ten told him to do, and he did what the Prime told him to do.

'Why can't I just get synaptic training like the rest of you?' Pete asked, doubled over, gasping for air.

Ten laughed. 'Chum, nobody gets syned until after their first year. They like you to do it the hard way first.'

One day he returned to the needle, soggy with sweat and canal water, to find two teenage girls waiting on the crescent settee in the centre of the main room.

Pete could sense no sentience from the two figures and as he got closer he found out why. They weren't people at all, merely skinbots with the cursory dressing of humans. They wore flexible athletics clothing with their hair tied up in an array of tiny pigtails. They had exaggerated eyes and giggled like the schoolgirls they looked to be — if not for the hefty pistols on their belts.

'May I introduce you to two new members of your team, Aiko and Endo.' Gock indicated which was which, though they were too similar for Pete to distinguish between them.

'Aiko and Endo are our most successful collectors in the Yantz province. They have been working with me for years and have an impeccable track record.'

'Only thanks to me,' one of them said.

'Aiko?' Pete guessed.

'Endo.'

'Sorry.'

'You're wet.'

'And green,' Aiko added.

*Well done, Prime,* Pete thought. *More non-people around the telepath.*

'What's wrong? Doesn't he like us?' one asked the other.

'Don't you like us, psi-man?'

'He hasn't even looked at us, Aiko. I don't think he's into girls.' The two skinbots giggled.

'Let's get started,' one of them moaned.

'I'm bored,' the other added.

'Today we are collecting a psi who has just entered the precinct,' Gock announced.

'Yeah, he's in this room. Get him!'

'No, not him. File 378.'

'Oh, right.'

'How have you detected him?' Pete asked.

'Target 378 is shopping. By that I mean he is not paying for anything, which is incredibly stupid.'

'Yeah, stupid psi. If I had powers, I wouldn't be so dumb about it.'

'Yeah. Psis are so stupid. Pete, we're going to show you how to take down one of your own. You can pretend it's you if you like.'

'But don't get in the way.'

'Watch and learn, psi-man.' They both giggled.

He had time to change before he took a squib north and landed on a small open area that branched out on all sides into the green lattice of canals. The only things on this particular island clearing were an old man with a muddy taxi and a single Serviceman. Like everywhere in Yantz, it was hot. Hot, humid and green. Pete had to frequently skim the sweat off his scalp.

Aiko and Endo leapt out of the squib and sprang around the landing area before running off. 'It's on foot from here, tapperman.' The twins were quickly out of sight, but they pinged his symb and sent teasing messages about being slow, old and, of course, being a psi.

'We're going to catch your friend. Tee hee,' they laughed and skipped ahead. Pete didn't even bother correcting them. He trudged forward and Gock trailed behind. Gock's family was to the east and he looked habitually in that direction. Their target pulled them west.

'You can consider this a demonstration, Mister Lazarus,' Gock sneered. 'This is how we catch psis in my province. You won't have to do anything. This time.'

Two weeks ago Gock had been a vendor of refurnished tech, and would be again when he returned to his less-than-reputable business. He knew what Pete was now and he didn't like that he had to be the one escorting him around Yantz. He didn't want them to be seen together.

'This way. He is on the move.' One of the twins jumped forward.

242

'Can you tell me more about how you discovered this psi?' Pete asked Gock.

'Firstly, we monitored a number of ambiguous interactions with some members of the opposite sex,' Gock sneered, the kind of thing he would do if he could control minds.

'And he wasn't simply charming them?' The proxy snorted in response.

Endo: Psi-man, hurry up or you'll miss the whole thing.

Aiko: Uh-oh, 378 is about to squib it. Let's go.

Endo: I call that perfect timing, sis. We can pluck him from the air.

Aiko: I bet I can jump higher than you can.

Endo: No chance. This one will be on my count.

Aiko: I thought we promised not to fight over men any more?

Endo: Yeah, but that's no fun. Let this one be the first exception.

Pete and Gock had just crossed a bridge and climbed the side wall of a larger island. Well-dressed people milled around or sat in the open piazza. The twins were waiting perched on rooftops on either side of the square, watching the exit of the squib outlet.

Pete: How do we know he's inside?

Aiko: He was painted days ago, silly. He hasn't left our watchful eyes that whole time.

Endo: We know what he's been up to. We suspect he's been playing the area for weeks.

The showroom doors parted and a clean new squib floated out and began curving its ascent.

Aiko: That's him. Go, Endo.

With a shout the twins leapt, Endo then Aiko. Endo landed on the nose of the squib and slashed her arm into the membrane, gouging a handhold for herself. Aiko's jump just missed and she dropped gracefully down to the piazza. Two huge guns arose from her arms.

'Oh no you don't, 378.' With her spare arm Endo drew a pistol from her holster and blasted smoking holes into the side of the vehicle until it began to flare and wobble. The power fluxed and the squib quickly succumbed to gravity. 'See you on the ground, mister.' Endo leapt off to land safely away from the crash site.

The squib slammed down on some tables, smashing them to sticks, before flipping end over end to land on its broken back. The crowd in the piazza ran for cover. By the time the squib had stopped sliding around, the square was clear bar the camera drones that forever circled. After the manifestation, no one was taking any chances with spontaneous outbreaks of violence. The Weave was watching.

'That's another one for me, Aiko.' Endo laughed.

'Let's make sure he's down first before we start counting.'

Gock pushed Pete in the back, urging him toward the splatted squib and its pilot, who was trying to untangle himself. 'Go, they might need you.'

Pete let himself be prodded forward, and was near enough to hear the target shouting as he clambered from the wreckage. 'You little bitch, I am going to melt your brain.'

'Wait,' Pete called out. The man was really just a boy, only sixteen or so. Pete felt his mind and read that his name was Risom Cawthorne and he wasn't just telepathic but also a kinetic. Services had their information wrong.

'I doubt that, mister!' Endo shouted back at Risom. 'You can't mess with wires.' With that the two sisters glooped him: from their hips two slim tubes slid out and fired blue gunk at his feet, sticking him down. 'Now, don't move. I'm going to fix your ugly face.' Endo pulled a mask from her shell and moved toward him.

'You!' Risom shouted at Pete. 'Help me. Why are you letting them do this?'

*I can't stop them.*

*You could try.*

*They would just do the same to me. Or blow my bot. There's no point fighting when we can't win.*

*That's when we need to fight the most.*

Gock lurched at Pete, throwing his hands at his throat.

'What are you doing?' Pete shouted. 'Get off me.'

'I can't. I can't!' Gock screamed and clawed at him. Pete pushed him off, but he came again. Then another passer-by jumped toward him in clumsy attack. Risom was controlling them like marionettes.

*Don't do this, Risom.*

*Traitor!*

Pete kicked his attackers away and sent an SOS to Ten. Wasn't the squad meant to always be in range?

*They can't help you, traitor. I've taken care of them.* Pete probed and saw that Risom had tinkered with the marauders, triggering their interference protocols and locking them in position. *You're next.*

A street pole twisted and snapped near Pete, swinging at him with tremendous force. He leapt out of the way, only just avoiding it. Gock grabbed at his legs and pulled him down.

'It's not me. It's not me!' he screamed.

Pete's chin hit the ground and his vision went from blur to white to black. Inside him he saw the staring eyes and then he reached out. He pushed across the square and … changed Risom's intentions. The pole dropped from the air and the human puppets fell stunned to the ground.

*You bastard. You've turned on your own kind.*

By now Endo was close enough to shove the mask at Risom's face, but he thrashed his head back and forth. 'You're a fucking coward! Peter Lazarus is a coward!' Risom bit at Endo's hand and she took the opportunity to land a punch square to his cheek. He was dazed and she pushed the mask on. The nearly opaque shell softened over his face and then after a heartbeat or two, the body of the psi relaxed; legs deflexed and slumped, his rapid breathing calmed.

'378 is secure. One point, Endo.'

That night Peter stayed awake. The only time the Prime had for him was at the end of his scheduled day. He couldn't sleep anyway. He heard the boy screaming out his name again and again. Calling him a traitor.

Something wasn't right about the whole situation, but he didn't think on it long. What he had done to Risom was irritating him and he worried at it like a loose tooth. He could ignore it, but now that he'd done it he knew he could do it again.

He looked at Gock, snoring, head back, mouth open to show less than a full set of teeth. He thought how easy it would be to suggest he go to his room and leave Pete in peace. He resisted

246

the temptation and returned to staring out over the megapolis of Yantz.

The view through the lounge window showed the weather rolling in, dusting up the stars until they disappeared beneath the grey. *This is how it is to be now*, Pete thought to himself. In an isolated tower, high enough from the ground level to be unable to sense the pedestrians. All human contact filtered from above through a snoring proxy, two teenage remotes and a squad of sacrificial soldiers. He was better off in hospital with Nurse Anchali visiting him every two hours. He missed Anchali. He wondered if she had been able to get word out about what had really happened under the Dome.

Ryu came online after midnight. Gock's loud breathing snorted to a halt and he turned his weary head toward Peter and announced that the Prime could speak with him now.

'You did very well today, Mister Lazarus,' Ryu-Gock began.

'Please don't congratulate me.'

'But why not? You managed to defuse the situation quickly enough. Just think how it might have ended if you hadn't stepped in. Innocent people might have been harmed.'

'Your information was wrong. You didn't know he was a kinetic too.'

'Was it? I shall look into that.'

'So this is what you want of me? I am to hunt psis?' Pete seethed. 'I won't do it. I am only here to stop Pierre Jnr.'

'Yes, Mister Lazarus. You have said that plenty of times already. But after your recent failure under the Dome, surely you can see that you need some sort of practice.' Gock blinked, waiting for Pete to respond or for more instructions from above. 'It is this or the islands — but what good could you do there?'

'What about the rest of the team? Where is Geof? And Colonel Pinter? What have you done with them?'

'There is no need for paranoia. Both Geof Ozenbach and Colonel Pinter are still part of the hunt.'

'Can I see them? Can I talk to them?'

'Perhaps in time. When your trial is over, your request will be reassessed.'

'So I'm to be isolated from everyone else? No contact with anyone, but your proxies and remotes?'

'We are nearly ready to move forward. We are just securing one more member to bring your new team up to a full fifteen.'

'Who is that?'

'No one you know.'

'And once the team is assembled, what will you have us do then?'

'You will do what needs to be done, Mister Lazarus. There are some new directions to follow up. Geof Ozenbach is working diligently on the problem as we speak. Please don't bother asking for more information now. None shall be provided.'

Pete bit his lip. 'There's nothing I can do to make you trust me, is there?'

'If I think of anything, I will be sure to let Gock inform you.'

'Do you think I'm guilty?'

'Guilty of what? Being a psi? Yes. Did you conspire with Pierre Jnr? Perhaps, perhaps not, or perhaps unwittingly.'

'Then how can you trust me to be part of the hunt?' he asked.

'I'm not trusting you at all. You're botlocked and watched every minute of the day. Not to mention that my proxy is with you as a constant reminder of my presence.' Gock smiled. 'The way I see it, we may as well make use of your skills and presume that the truth about you will reveal itself in due course. My main problem is that your skills don't amount to very much.'

Pete knew the Prime was right. He had always been able to read anyone who came within his range, but he'd never been aggressive with it. Instead of taking hold of a mind and drilling for the information he was after, he preferred to ask leading questions. Aggression had never been his way. If he encountered Pierre again now, he would do no better than he did last time. He did need to become used to his powers, to command them better.

He closed his eyes and tried not to see the eyes that always seemed to wait for him in the darkness. It was only a small step from reading someone's mind to writing something inside.

'Tell me, Prime, you've shown me how you track down and disable telepaths and benders. How would you approach a psi like Pierre Jnr?'

'It is good that you are now asking this question. It shows me that you are willing to learn.' Gock paused, slack lips ready to repeat what was said to him. 'I think, if he is fully manifested, as he was, it would be beyond us to stop him. We must try to strike before he is ready. This is presuming, of course, that your Pierre Jnr is a single entity rather than an organised group.'

'A group of psis? Is that your other possibility?'

'One of them.'

'Is that what I am on trial for?'

'Yes,' Gock confirmed. 'It is conjectured that you are a plant by a psi group.'

'That could be a hard thing to prove either way.'

'Yes.'

'And the trial will continue forever?'

'Indefinitely.'

'How am I meant to find Pierre Jnr like this?'

'You should know by now that your team is not leading the investigation. Geof Ozenbach is in charge of finding Pierre. Your team, and others, are training as response units. If there is a Pierre Jnr, and we locate him again, we must have a way of defeating him.'

'I was never really leading the investigation before, was I?' Pete wondered aloud.

'No. Did you think that you were?'

'Then who was? The Colonel?'

'Services, of course.'

'Yes, but who in Services?'

'You really are a simpleton, aren't you? I didn't think there could be that many left in the world. Services is never one person. Every command goes through a decision-making tree. Many minds voting at many levels with different authorities and the combined result is the directive. "The command is the command", as the soldiers say.'

Pete had heard that refrain reverberating in the mind of every Serviceman he'd ever encountered. Something learnt by rote and a lifetime of reinforcement.

'Services really is something I never fully understood,' Pete admitted. 'I didn't realise that the people within it believed in it. It makes sense to you.' By you he meant Ryu Shima. Gock's grasp of the system-based governance of the WU was as loose as Pete's own. His only interest was how he could use the system to benefit himself.

'It is better than the alternatives.' As was taught in schools, all the old systems failed: capitalism, communism, democracy, psycho-socialism, cooperativism. The Services system did not segment the population into positions of governed and governing. It was a system that made every Citizen a working component.

'I must go. You must rest,' Gock ordered.

*Yes, rest for more training tomorrow.* Pete wondered if the twins would now be involved in his reorientation program.

'I will leave you with these thoughts, Mister Lazarus. For now, I am at the front of this challenge. This threat, be it Pierre Jnr, or a psi rebellion, must be met one way or another. But finding an enemy you can't see is like catching the wind. It is a great challenge and we must be patient and prepare for the day when the enemy finds us. You did well today.'

'Thank you, Prime.' The words slipped out before he could stop them.


'Without further ado, I would like to invite Charlotte Betts to the stage.'

The room applauded as she came out from between the curtains and took her place at the podium. There were close to three hundred students attending, aged from eleven to seventeen, each of whom had declared their rights as a Citizen of the World Union.

Charlotte smiled warmly as their clapping eased and began her speech. 'If I recall correctly, when I was sitting where you are now, the speaker made a comment that they felt like it was only yesterday that they had taken their own vows of Citizenship. It would be nice to reiterate that, but I can tell you that for me it feels like a very long time ago.

'I have been asked to speak to you today about the new period of your lives you are entering. But if any of you know anything about my past, I may seem like an odd choice for promoting social responsibility. Most of my life has been spent *not* being a good Citizen. I didn't contribute and for twenty years I didn't vote.

'When I was sitting where you are now, I didn't really know what it was all about and whatever the speaker tried to tell us just went out my spare ear. I knew that I was meant to use my opinions wisely and I understood that my actions counted toward something, and in the vast machine of the Weave those who were in the Primacy were there because they had the support of the Will.

'I knew all that, but it was only recently that I understood where it all came from, and how causality made it all fit together. I realise now that it's all about history and history takes time to focus. Much like the events of your own lives will only seem clear once they are long past. Viewed too closely an event's significance and implications are often hard to determine. Only time brings the necessary distance to events to make their meanings, and the reactions to them, clear. The more distance one can have from events, the more clearly one can see how they are connected. And thus is history born.'

Charlotte paused for a sip of water. The auditorium was silent but for shuffling. That was part one done, now for the push.

'There are academics who suggest that the great collapse was unavoidable, that the foundations of society were unable to bear the burden of the swollen population and the imbalances within the social ecosystem. But I think it was more than that.

'The climate is often described as the tipping point. As it became more and more erratic and farms began to fail, the hunger of the population could no longer be sated. But one can only blame the weather for so much.

'It was an apocalypse. A true ending of an age. Infrastructure broke down, the weather and rising seas provoked mass, emergency migrations. Much of civilisation was destroyed. Over fifty years, the population dropped from thirteen and a half billion to five. There is no end to the horrors that people visited upon each other in those bleak decades.

'It was only when a pact was made between the Asiatic peoples to resist the Örjian threat that the spiral was reversed. They welcomed all comers, and the new World Union spread across the globe until there are now only a few small areas that are not included.

'You know this. You have read and seen records from that darkest of times in human history. You have seen how the people of the time thought they were doing right. They thought they were doing what was best for their survival, and their way of life. You have seen what can become normal in the mind of a human being.

253

'There are some today who say that we are in extraordinary times. That we are living now and should not worry about how history will record us, but the truth is that we stand facing the past with our backs to the future.

'The future is the past we will see once it has happened. It is not history that will judge us. It will be ourselves. Every action you take in your lifetime will be with you forever. It takes no special talent to fear the future, but it takes a wise person to fear the history they are making.

'You have taken your vows at a time when we need you the most. There are big changes taking place in our world. Some are obvious, but others are so subtle we won't see their effects for many years. I ask you, as a reborn Citizen myself, to be aware. And be active.

'Please rise. You are now part of the World Union. You are Citizens and you are the Will. Be wise.'

After listening to Charlotte Betts's Citizenship address, Ryu Shima was not in his best frame of mind when his mother called him to share tea with her.

'How are you, my son?' his mother asked.

'I am well.'

'Do you sleep enough?'

'As much as I can.'

'And are you still trying to reconcile the world?'

Ryu didn't have time for this. Not only was he trying to tame the rising fervour of the Weave and its constant demands for him to deliver details of his progress and strategy —

— but that ridiculous woman was growing in popularity, largely in reaction to the measures he was taking to protect them. For doing what he was elected to do …

No, Ryu Shima did not need to be called before his mother this day to discuss how he was sleeping.

'Ryu Shima, I asked you a question.'

But he could not deny the request because she was the Alpha of the house and he could not afford to be out of her favour.

'Ryu? You can hear me, can't you?'

He looked down. She had placed a hand on his knee. She looked at him with such worry.

'I'm sorry, Mother. I have much on my mind.'

'What troubles you, my son?'

'Easier to ask what does not trouble me. For the burdens of the world are the burdens of the Prime.' She smiled at him, patient, indulgent. 'I see my weariness pleases you somehow.'

'First comes the weariness and then comes wisdom.'

'I have not heard that one before. I fear it may be true.'

'Can I lighten your burden in any way?'

'Are you asking as my mother, or as the Alpha of House Shima?'

'Can I not be both? You will return to the house in time, Ryu san.'

'But for now my house is bigger than that.'

'It is. Perhaps you can share the essence of your problem without sharing the details?'

'Is not the essence of every problem the same? A demand meeting an insufficiency.'

'I shall get your father to talk with you if you want to speak philosophically. Where is the insufficiency? In you?'

'Of course, but also in everything. We have insufficient information.'

'And the demand?'

'There is a demand to act.'

'I see the problem.' His mother nodded. 'Let us enjoy the tea. It will give me time to think.'

She rang a bell and the tea service was presented. He knew that this was deliberate stalling on her part. Making him take his time. Time to sift through the build-up of unfinished notions that accumulate when one is too hectic to think.

'As Prime I must appear active, or I will lose my position.'

'And if you lost the position?'

He could not answer.

'What is it you fear would happen if you were no longer Prime?'

He could not say that he thought the threat to the world would overtake them. He couldn't speak his fear that without him there would be no one who could marshal the World Union to do what needed to be done.

The fine lines around her mouth deepened as she tightened her lips. He was just like everyone else. The only fear was that he would no longer be Prime.

'Your father gave me one piece of advice when I rose to the Primacy. Perhaps it may serve you now. No matter what happens, no matter how much is happening, no matter how

256

they push you: don't react. If your actions are reactions, that means someone else has control. Respond. Never react.'

'I understand. Thank you.'

'I won't keep you any longer. Your wellbeing is of great importance to me.'

'I am looking after myself,' Ryu insisted.

'You are not. You are isolated and carrying too much of this burden by yourself.'

'Who else is there?'

'There is a whole world of people, my son.'

'No, Mother. There is only me.'

'You trust Takashi, don't you? You seem to share everything with him.'

'I already rely on him too much.'

'Perhaps you would consider taking him to live with you. He would be a good companion as well as a comrade.'

Ryu smiled. 'Are you asking this for my benefit or for yours?'

'Well,' she spread her hands in mock innocence, 'there is a charm to striking two birds with one stone. He needs to move out, experience more of the world, break some of his bad habits.'

'He enjoys himself.'

'I mention it only for your consideration.'


Bidding his mother goodbye, Ryu took the elevator to Takashi's floor.

Takashi's room stank, as always. Ryu's brother lay sprawled on the floor with a mesh evaporator thrumming by his side. There were more dolls than chairs. They draped themselves over the two large day beds and over each other. A tangle of delectable limbs.

'How was Mother?' He wasn't sure Takashi had noticed him until he spoke. His eyes were concealed behind the oculars he wore to immerse in the Weave.

'She wants you to move in with me,' Ryu replied.

'In the needle? There isn't enough room for my friends.'

'No. There isn't. What are you doing?'

'Our sister is about to pact with Alderson.'

'Mother didn't mention it.'

'She doesn't know yet. I'm watching it now.'

Ryu didn't want to know any more. Takashi had no boundaries. It was a point of pride for him. Ryu could see that his brother was aroused and he looked away. There wasn't anywhere safe to look in Takashi's chambers though.

'You have something for me?' Ryu asked.

'What do you need?'

'Information. You said you had something and — can you turn that thing off? It's giving me a headache.' Takashi instead turned the evaporator to a higher and louder setting. 'Takashi, please.'

His brother sat up and tapped his ears. They might be listening, he meant. 'Relax, brother. Breathe in and learn to relax.'

'I can't have the Weave thinking I'm getting high in your den.'

'My den. I like that. Lucinda? Come here, would you?' One of the dolls activated and crossed the room to kneel by her master. 'Open your mouth.'

'Takashi, that's enough. I have to go.'

'Wait, you've got to see what she can do with her tongue.' Takashi fingered under her lip and took a tiny disk from the doll's mouth and passed it to Ryu.

'Takashi, what —'

'Okay. Go. Don't play with me. Some things *are* better kept private.'

'I'm going. Let me know if you find anything useful.'

Ryu left, feeling the effects of the steam, and fumbling his normal stride as he took the outer walk up to the roof to clear his head. What could be so important that Takashi felt the need for this sort of charade? It must be too dangerous to transmit, even behind his walls.

Since he had become Prime, Ryu's immediate circle of contact had shrunk dramatically. Besides the shifts of anonymous bodyguards, there were only four people he had regular face-to-face contact with: his mother and father, Takashi and his secretary, Gladys.

Most of his day was spent in his null office. It was a semi-circle that had two entrances, one to his bedroom and the other to the corridor that lead to the lounge area. He could sit at his desk and see the whole of northern Yantz stretching its blocky islands to the horizon, dotted with needles and the looming Shima Palace.

Or he could have the whole window opaque to work on. He liked to have the option of being able to pace before a giant screen of data and inputs.

To make his day manageable, he broke it up into six blocks of four hours, to be flexible to the needs of the Primacy. Around the globe he was co-ordinating with the other members of the council, briefing and debriefing the teams in the field, pushing for progress in tech development, holding closed sessions with other world leaders, as well as monitoring and working through the material required to keep the hunt for Pierre Jnr on track.

Ten minutes later Ryu sealed the needle and took an unconnected handscreen into his bedroom. The window darkened and a lightshield rolled down; in this configuration, his room was a black box, though without recording abilities. He touched the disk from his brother to the screen, hesitated, then climbed into his bed and pulled the blanket over his head.

The data played automatically, beginning with a tap from Takashi.

*Ryu, this was out there, accessible, but no one has compiled it yet. I've deleted what I could. You don't want this getting into the wrong hands.*

The first footage was from Kyushu.

The markets were a press of skin and a mob of sound. Everyone had to shove their way from vendor to vendor. Everything was for sale in a place like this, but there was never enough everything to go around and people yelled to get what they needed, and sellers shouted about their bargains and shouted at their helpers.

A boy of thigh-height in a neat suit of ivory linen walked slowly through the lanes, the crowd parting unthinkingly to clear him a path.

As he passed, people handed items from the tables to him without looking. In this way the boy wandered the busy avenues, grazing on apricots and pastries before leaving the area and disappearing from the passive surveillance.

Ryu watched it twice.

The next was from a private home. There was no indication as to why there was a recording. It may have been for a religious sharing.

A balding man prostrated himself before a painting he had mounted on a side table. It was one of those artist sketches of the Pierre Jnr manifestation.

The same boy from the Kyushu market sat on a junktique footstool, chewing grapes one at a time and watching the man bow to the picture. A woman came into view and gave the boy a glass of water before joining the man in supplication before the picture.

Neither adult seemed to really see the child in their room.

The third clip was taken from a STOC Services post. The boy stepped in through the automatic doors and the woman at the desk didn't look up. He wandered behind the bench and waited as she came to open the door for him.

She walked in front of him the whole time as he ambled through the corridors and back rooms as if inspecting for a report.

There were dozens of clips just the same. Everyday people going about their daily activities with the boy watching them.

Takashi's present disturbed him greatly. Pierre Jnr was real.

Each recording made him feel sicker and sicker. His stomach melted. His own heartbeat made him jumpy. He watched Pierre Jnr walking through city streets ... listening to presentations in boardrooms … sitting with a co-ord in a 720° watching the trajectories of thousands of inbound vehicles … attending classes and raising his hand to answer and ask questions …

He did not hide, but none saw him. He seemed to be doing no harm, but people fetched and carried, stepped out of his way and even held their umbrellas over him when it rained. All without any communication or recognition of their own actions.

Ryu couldn't move.

He sat under his cover for half an hour until there was a knock at the door. His heart paused. Nobody should be able to gain access to the needle, let alone his bedroom. The needle was locked down. His symb should have warned him. The door handle of his room shook once, then silently it clicked to unlock.

'Ryu?'

'Taka?' he replied quietly.

'Yes, Ryu. It's only me.'

The Prime pulled the blanket slowly from his head, expecting to see the melon-headed boy standing in the doorway. But it looked like Takashi. Pallid, covered in symbiot and sweating, hastily dressed in a woman's kimono. 'Is it really you?'

'Yes, Ryu.'

'How do I know?'

'Have you flipped? Ryu, it's me.'

'Takashi never leaves his rooms.'

'I do when my brother needs me.' He sat down on the bed beside him, his bulk making it lean toward him.

'But how did you know?'

'My simulation did not react well to the new data. I ran it three times and twice resulted in full catatonia.'

'You have a simulation of me?'

'Of course. I have simulations of all the family.'

'Takashi, why would you do that?'

'To test scenarios. How else would I know what I could and couldn't get away with?'

'Behavioural responses? How long have you been doing this?'

'For seven years now. I refine them every day.'

Ryu was stunned and disturbed. He knew enough of his brother to know that there would be no limits to what he would test. Anything his particular mind could think of.

'I don't want to come across as a hypocrite, Ryu, but you need to get out of bed.'

'I just need time to absorb. I'll be okay.'

'I know you will, but you need to look okay faster. The Weave is watching.'

'How do I go on? This ...' He held up the screen. 'Nobody sees him. He could be standing in the corner right now, and we wouldn't know it.'

'Yeah, but probably not.'

'Probably? That's all you've got?'

'Statistically, he is very unlikely to be here. He seems to like crowds more.'

Ryu sighed. His brother was trying to make him laugh and on the inside he felt a desperate need to, but his shell was so crisp and fragile.

'Did you say you were deleting these sightings from the Weave? No one else will be able to find them?'

'Only if they can get through my wall. Do you want to hide it completely?'

'That is a good question. Does it help for the world to know he exists or not?'

'Not a question for me, Ryu. You have strategic advisors.'

'Then for now let's keep it hidden. What do I have next?'

'You have a queue to get through and your pet project is ready for your wisdom.'

'Yes. At least that will improve my mood.'

'That's what I thought.' Takashi patted him on the knee. 'Mind if I stay around for a while?'


The next morning while Peter was eating breakfast, the elevator slid open and out stepped the psi from yesterday's collection. File 378. Risom Cawthorne.

'You?' Pete leapt to his feet and triggered all the alarms.

Risom put his hands up. 'Don't be a stoob, I'm not going to hurt you.'

'How'd you get in here?'

'Nice to see you too, traitor. Why don't you just tap me and move this intro on?'

Pete's heart sank in his chest. It was a set-up. Risom was an agent, like Tamsin had been, but where Tamsin was the best tapper, this guy was the best kinetic. From origami flowers to squib juggling, Risom was as good as they came. Yesterday's scene was entirely staged, by Ryu Shima.

'Hi, I'm Risom. I'm your new partner.'

Pete took a long look at the boy. Lean, thin legs and an angular chest. Hair blond, overall quite preened, even after yesterday's battle, except for the rash of pubescent hair growing on his chin. Of course, he was botted with a symbiot lock, just like Pete was, and had been since he was four. Services sure did know their business.

'That was quite a show you put on. I didn't pick up anything from you yesterday.'

'Perhaps the excitement confused you.'

'Have you done that before?'

Risom didn't answer out loud, but Pete could see that he had.

'How does that feel, traitor? You fell right into their little trap.'

*And you led me into it. You're the traitor.*

Gock came out of his room and was startled to see Risom standing in the needle. 'You!?' He fled back into his room. Risom tripped his legs from under him and the proxy fell to the floor.

Risom didn't care. He found it rather amusing. He took a place on the long couch and put his feet up on the table. 'So what happens around here?' he asked, flicking the window to screen and browsing the Weave.

'Gock? May I speak with the Prime, please?'

Gock shook his head. 'We are in his queue.'

Drinks and food began floating from the kitchen bench to where Risom was relaxing. He did nothing with his hands except fold them into a cradle for his head. His drink floated to his lips and he lay back while his shoes undid themselves and dropped to the floor.

'Why would you do that?' Pete asked.

'They treat me well. They give me respect.'

'Who do? Services?'

'That's right. I live like a prince.'

'And you call me traitor.'

'Listen, tapper. Don't start thinking that we are the same kind. The only thing that makes the psis a group is the restrictions on them — which don't apply to me. So, Mister Peter Lazarus, sir, don't be thinking you and I will be friends. The only thing you and I have in common is the symb-lock. Brothers in chains.'

It struck Pete that he had heard these sentiments before. Tamsin had used almost the same wording. It made him wonder if this was an essential part of agent training, conditioned disassociation. He was beginning to see how it all came together. Services built and trained the people it needed, like Geof, like the marauders. Like Tamsin. Those it couldn't control were exiled or conditioned. That was how the system maintained itself.

'Okay, Risom. Not friends. Just tell me about your childhood.'

Gock let Peter know that they were waiting for a meeting to assemble. No training was planned for today.

'Has something happened? Has there been another manifestation?' Gock didn't know and the open Weave wasn't talking about anything like that.

The twinbots came out of the elevator doors and began prowling like cats around Risom.

'What are you doing here?'

'Didn't you get enough yesterday?'

Risom poked his tongue out at them and tried to ignore them.

'Nice to see you again, Risom. Great performance.'

'You could have hurt someone,' Aiko added.

'And one of you threw my squib to the ground. That wasn't in the script,' Risom answered.

'Don't try to wriggle out of it, bendy. You went too far.'

The entire ten squad joined them soon enough and one of the soldiers darkened the room and set all the windows to screen. Everyone was quiet.

It was Ten who spoke rather than Gock. Ryu must have been busy with something else. 'Now that the team is assembled there is some information the Prime would like shared with everyone. Please save your questions for now; put them in your nightlies.'

'What's a nightly?' Pete asked.

'I said no questions, Lazarus,' Ten growled. Pete realised the man who had been his conspiratorial trainer was now in command mode. In his mind everyone was a soldier. He got the answer he wanted though, from everyone in the room. Nightlies were the reports that every active Serviceman and conscript completed at the end of their day. No excuses. They were fed into the system for processing and collation. Another small practice that reinforced the system.

'Since the Dome incident, there has been an increase in collections, as you know. What you haven't been told is that someone has been hitting our squads. There have been three attacks so far, eleven casualties and nineteen concussions. Three psi agents are unaccounted for.'

Ten keyed the screen to play the surveillance from the ops, taken from ten multi-view points on the collection team's body

267

armour as they went about their missions. Half the squad positioned themselves for escape vectors while the other five crashed direct to the target and went for disablement.

'Notice that none of these teams have adopted the Ryu protocols. For the two telepaths they should have used remotes first. For the kinetic target they did send an agent, but behind two MUs. Look what happened.'

They watched as the black-clad agent followed the marauder units into the bedroom where the collection was happening. The MUs quickly froze in position, interference locks activated. The psi agent stepped into the room, followed by three more MUs. Then all the feeds disconnected in chain.

'And pause on the last frame of Four A,' Ten commanded the screen. Standing in the shadows with the target next to her was a light-skinned woman in the wrapped clothing of a denny. The image zoomed in. 'We don't know who this woman is yet or what she was doing on the scene. This partial isn't enough to run.'

Ten looked around the room at everyone. His ten squad had removed their helmets for the first time that Pete had seen since leaving the outpost. There was a range of faces, but all had the same haircut.

'Would anyone care to speculate?'

'Out of the three breakouts, they only took the benders with them. Why?' Six was a sharp one; he would rise fast.

'Good question. Answers?'

'They don't like telepaths,' Aiko suggested.

'Yeah, psi-man. Who would?'

'Keep grounded, twins, or I'll bust you down. Anyone with real answers?'

'They were only after the agents,' Risom suggested.

'But why not take the people you rescued with you? Or why take just the kinetics?'

Pete picked up something from Gock's mind. 'To see where Services takes the psis.'

Ten clicked his fingers. 'Good. That's what the ups think. The next thing I have to show you happened yesterday.'

The screen glowed up and showed a six-screen split of a small prefab building divided into cells, with a main corridor in between, along which an armed servitor tracked up and down, keeping a laser eye on the prisoners. The cells were barred and the corridor was blocked at one end by the main wall of the building and at the other by a laser grid.

Besides those in the cells, the facility was devoid of humans. Only a troop of remotes patrolled the outside. Their operators were likely stationed nearby but out of range.

Surveillance from the outside showed an open area that was designed to give a clear visual warning of any approach. It was a tessellated plain of prefab hexagons, creating a clear firing range of one hundred metres. Pete read from Gock's slithery mind that this area was known as the killing field, and likely booby-trapped — as per Services regular tactics, or perhaps it was just what Gock would do.

Without prompt or cue the remotes turned to each other and began firing their weapons. A full projectile release that disabled them in a coloured froth of smokes and sparks. They dropped to the ground in pieces.

From above a fat squib glided in and three figures dropped swiftly to the ground, with no apparent ropes or conduit, and began assaulting the building with splash-on explosives. A breach was quickly formed in the outer wall. The guard servitor cannoned out of the hole and crashed to the ground, where the figures destroyed it with the explosives already in their hands.

Ten directed the footage to closer shots of the attackers, but it revealed little of their identities. They were in the wrap-style clothing worn by dennies worldwide: versatile leggings and short cloak-jackets roped down with belts of weapons. Their faces were wrapped in polyplastic scarves that didn't show their eyes. It was impossible to guess even the gender of the attackers.

While two of them shepherded the prisoners out from their cells, one took the time to carve a marking into the wall.

'What are they writing?' Pete asked and the view changed to show a mark, like a fork or a 'y' with three prongs. His symbiot quickly trawled and recognised it as the ancient Greek symbol for psi.

'This symbol is beginning to appear around the world,' Ten reported. 'We presume it is the mark of the psi rebellion.'

The figure ended carving with a smooth pivot and joined its group as they levitated quickly skyward to the waiting transport. *Tamsin*, Pete knew.

'That. Was. Cooooool,' Endo summarised. 'Can you make us fly like that, Risom?'

'I'd be happy to try.'

'Aw, Gock, we need a bender like they have. Ask the Prime for a nicer one.'

'The Prime is busy right now.'

'I bet he is,' Aiko commented. She was only slightly more serious than her sister.

*  *  *

Ryu Shima was again only available after midnight and Gock was awoken to act as interface. They met in the crescent lounge, looking out on a clear black sky, made grey with the lights of the multitude below.

'Thank you for your patience. The demands on my time today were great.'

'I understand. Was there more than the breakout?'

'There is always more. You can have no comprehension.'

'I have seen the footage you transmitted to us.'

'Yes. I know. And what do you make of it?'

'I'm not sure what to make of it. It seems clear that Pierre Jnr was not involved.'

'How was that clear?' Gock asked.

'It was only a group of psi resistants. As professional as their attack was, if Pierre was involved I think it would have been more dramatic. Besides, I do not think that Pierre is any more interested in psis than he is in other humans.'

'If that was the case, why is it that only yourself and Tamsin Grey were left alive in the Paris attack?' Pete had no answer for that and waited for Ryu to continue. 'I would be interested to have that question answered, but I must get some rest tonight. You have seen what you are up against. Do you think Miz Grey is behind the upheaval?'

'I have no evidence.'

'But you suspect. Yes. I am in the same position. Now that we have two targets we must consider how to tackle each of them.'

271

'I've told you before. I'm only here to find Pierre Jnr.'

'Who is in league with, or controlling, Tamsin Grey and the psi rebels. They are one and the same if it helps to think that way.'

'And every psi in the world, I suppose?' Pete objected. 'Does it surprise you that there are people trying to stop you?'

'No. It is a natural reaction. It is abnormal for them to have such success though. Do you support them?'

Pete hesitated. 'Not as such.'

'For a moment there I thought I'd caught you.'

*Ah, the trial.* Pete had forgotten for a moment that every conversation with the Prime was just another opportunity for an interrogation. 'Why are you doing this? Ryu Shima? Prime? I am a telepath. You suspect me of colluding with Pierre Jnr. What more excuse do you need to put me away?'

Gock's face split into a wet smile, drooling with maliciousness.

'Gock, make him answer.'

'Gock does not make me do anything. He is a mouthpiece, nothing more.'

*How does that make you feel, Gock?*

The smile left Gock's eyes and hatred turned his expression to a sneer. 'Do not try to interfere with Gock, Mister Lazarus. No matter what you think about him, he serves his clients and his family loyally. Can you say the same for yourself?'

Pete gritted his teeth. 'What do you want with me?'

'I want you to confess. It's a bit of a coincidence, isn't it, Mister Lazarus? That you volunteered at precisely the moment that Pierre Jnr reveals himself for the first time in eight years?'

'It is a coincidence, yes. Or are you forgetting that it was perhaps our actions that pushed him to come out of hiding?'

'To then go straight back into hiding? Without a trace?'

'Just because we didn't succeed in stopping him doesn't mean we didn't try.'

'No, but perhaps your motivations were otherwise aligned. Either way, for me you are a curiosity. You are now my little experiment. My hypothesis is that you are working for Pierre either consciously or as his puppet, and if I push you around enough you will again reveal your master. And I shall be ready for him.'

'What will you do?'

'Is that you asking, or Pierre?'

'I am not part of that monster.'

'Please don't strain yourself, Peter. You will need your energies for the next few weeks. It is time to put you back to work.'

'Doing what?'

'Doing what I tell you to do.' Gock stood and moved to the doorway. 'Is there a problem, Mister Lazarus? Are you now reluctant to help us with this case?'

'I volunteered to help stop Pierre Jnr. That is all. I won't be turned into an agent like Tamsin was.'

'There is a psionic threat to the safety of the people of Earth. We both recognise that, but for now you are fixated on only one portion of that threat. Either way —'

'No, I won't betray my own kind.'

Gock raised his hand to stop him speaking. 'There it is. Your *own* kind. You admit that you identify with the psis and not with non-psis.'

273

Pete was silent under the accusation. It was, after all, true.

'I don't have any more time for you tonight, Mister Lazarus. For now you shall remain on the team, but if you do not prove yourself useful you shall be restricted to the islands. With the rest of "your kind". Are we clear?'

The lights in Peter's bedchamber flared up only two hours into his rest period. When he didn't rise instantly, a tapping buzz faded up, built and then crescendoed until he lifted his head.

'I'm up. What is it?'

Ryu: Your first mission begins in fifteen minutes. I will brief you through Gock.

Pete: Why not just send me the brief?

Ryu: Do not question the command.

Pete dressed as quickly as he could. Gock was ready and waiting for him at the table. He had been notified about the assignment while Pete was sleeping.

'There is a man on the list of institute patients, Arthur Grimaldi. He was not close to Pierre Jnr in any way, that we know of, but after the birth his mental state began deteriorating rapidly. He exhibits signs of high sensitivity and depression, as well as an inability to control his psionic output. A squad found him two weeks ago, but they failed to collect him.'

'What happened to them?' Pete asked.

'They did not come out intact.'

'Like the people at the midland farm?'

'Not quite. They are clinically paranoid, mildly schizophrenic, but their condition seems to be improving.'

'But you clearly think there is a connection between Arthur Grimaldi and Pierre Jnr?'

'There *is* a connection. They were in the institute at the same time. Let's move along. The collection manoeuvre did not follow the procedure I have since instigated globally.'

'The fools.'

'Was that humour, Mister Lazarus?'

'Only if you say it was.'

'You are beginning to understand. Good.' Gock took a lot of pleasure from being able to make other people squirm; something he lacked the power to do himself.

'Why did it take so long to find him?'

'Grimaldi has been found four times in the past eight years, but has avoided collection each time. Though I no longer allow the practice, some provinces have relied on cooperative telepaths to help find psis and he was painted three weeks ago.'

'An agent like Tamsin?'

'Yes. Tamsin Grey had an impeccable record, until her disappearance. Would you like to tell me more about your relationship with Miz Grey?'

'Not really.'

'There is an unaccounted hour you spent alone with her. Would you like to share what took place in that time?'

'No.'

'Were you romantically involved with Tamsin Grey?'

'No.'

'Any admission would be considered an act of good faith, Mister Lazarus.'

'I thought we had an assignment to complete.'

'There is no rush. We have plenty of time if you would like to make a new statement.'

Pete held his silence. Ryu Shima had waited until the middle of the night intentionally. He knew the Prime was trying to grind him down. He understood that. What he didn't like was that it was working. 'Let's just get on with this.'

'As you wish. Grimaldi is located nearby, in Reclaimed Hong Kong. The ten are waiting for you at the launching pad.'

'And are we interviewing him?'

'Mister Lazarus, I want you to bring this man in. By whatever means necessary.'

'So he can be taken to the islands?'

'Perhaps. Perhaps we may find other uses for him. It is not your concern.'

He forced himself not to respond to that point. 'Is the whole team coming?' Pete asked.

'Just you and your ten. The twins will be nearby.'

'Not Risom?'

'Do not question the command.' Of course, you wouldn't want to put a powerful and temperamental bender like Risom in the hands of a chronically depressed telepath.

When Pete saw Ten at the bottom of the elevator, he asked him, 'Just out of curiosity, how long have you known about this assignment?'

'Two days.'

'That's what I thought.'

Arthur Grimaldi had confined himself to a prison boarding house on Kowloon. Prisons in this area were different from the penal islands of other WU precincts, in that inmates were not completely cut off from the outside world. The prisons themselves were open to the flow of pedestrian traffic and only the prisoners themselves had to remain within the boundaries.

It was more of a boarding house than a jail. These places were stepping stones that could be used by people progressing up or down the path of life. Some inmates, like Arthur, took to living in the prisons by choice, to protect themselves from incurring deeper debts, from harm in general, or because they simply found living in the wider world too confronting. Anyone could request sanctuary.

There was only one portal in and out, an open footway, two metres wide and sensitive to the passing of its restricted members. If one of the prisoners tried to leave, their ankle-locks would cripple them with pain and a guard would have to drag them back inside the zone.

Tamsin had heard of Arthur from Okonta and she wanted to know more about how he did what he did. Services had had Okonta do a probe on a collection team that had failed a mission and come out scatty. Okonta had told her that Arthur seemed to have an ability to project emotions and thoughts onto others. He soaked in everything around him and then redirected it. This was what had happened to the previous team that tried to collect him.

It was easy for Tamsin, under the guise of Maria, to request entry and then explore the floors of the prison house. Lighting was clearly not a priority in these dark bamboo corridors.

When she knocked, he didn't answer. The door was unlocked and she stepped inside. She could feel his mind at the furthest end of the room.

He kept himself in the dark. He ate from the cans that were put by his door and left them where they fell. The room smelt of breathed air, food gone bad and human juices. Arthur lay in the corner, feeling everything around him.

'Arthur?' she called gently.

'Go away,' the rags and blankets replied.

'I've come to help you, Arthur. I'm a friend. I'm like you.'

'You have the curse. You have been touched by him! Don't come near me, or you'll regret it.'

'Don't be like that, Arthur. Come with me. It's time to get you out of this hovel.' She stepped toward him.

*No. You brought him here. Why did you bring him here?*

*Who are you talking about? I came alone.*

*No.* 'No. You have the taint.' *Like I do …*

She felt fear and pain, the echoes of suffering. The urge to cry was injected into her heart and made her hands shake. It was just as Okonta described.

'What are you doing, Arthur?'

'I said not to come near me.'

'I'm not going to harm you. I'm a friend.'

'Leave now or you'll hurt. I'll make you feel what I feel.'

*How do you do that?*

*It's just how I am.*

Though her breath stalled, she pushed further into Arthur's mind, bracing for the cold black fear. He didn't know how he was doing what he was doing, but Tamsin could see, and she could learn.

When she pulled out, she was on her knees, tears flowing from her, and her body shaking with irreconcilable tremors. She hadn't cried since she was a child.

'Are you happy now, Tamsin Grey? Now you think you can do what I do? It won't work for you. First you have to let the emotions inside you.'

'I can help you. Join us.'

Arthur pushed himself to his feet, laborious as an old horse. 'You don't want me. You've got what you came for, now go.' *I live in gloom. I don't want anyone else in here with me.*

She felt again the cold brush of his mind, soaked with every dark emotion he had ever come into contact with. 'I won't be the only one coming to you, Arthur. You've got about five minutes before Services come in through the roof and cart you off to the islands. I don't want that to happen to you. It shouldn't happen to any of us.'

'They've come before. They'll come again.'

'It will be different this time. They will have a man with them.'

'Peter Lazarus will succumb like the others.'

'I'm not so sure about that.'

'Then I shall make you sure.'

Wave after wave of tangled emotions slapped inside her, corroding her resolve. Tamsin had no choice but to raise her block and run from the room.

She hated herself for giving in so easily and thought about going back inside. One look at her shaking hands changed her mind. Arthur was too dangerous to control and he was right, she had gotten what she needed from him.

As she stepped onto the footway outside the prison house, she felt a familiar mind approaching and kept her block raised. He was close and there was nowhere to hide.

On the corner a group of rentals were displaying their flesh to the passing public. With the fakes so real, and the realsies so augmented, it didn't take much work from her symbskin to make her blend in with the clique of dolls. She stood amongst them and influenced one of the humans to lend her a burner to smoke. Tamsin tried not to inhale — the last thing she needed after meeting with Arthur was mesh making more of her emotions.

Peter Lazarus walked past, his eyes trailing over the prostitutes. Body willing, mind fraught. *Poor Peter*, Tamsin thought. He had changed, or been changed. He had lost a lot of weight since she'd last seen him upright, and with his head shaved he looked gaunt and slightly ... predatory. Was it desperation or determination that was driving him?

She felt the squad of shadows that circled him. She had once been assigned a shadow like that. Orbiting around her as she moved from place to place, only seen when needed.

So Peter was fully on their side now. Tamsin found it hard to believe. Then again, what choice did he have? *One day I will come for you.*

He stopped walking.

'What is it?' a short slippery-looking man asked him.

Pete raised his hand for silence.

*Tamsin?*

*The one and only. I like your hair like that.*

*What are you doing here?*

*The same as you, I imagine. Do take care with Arthur. He is extremely sensitive.*

*You tried to take him?*

*Something like that.*

*Is Pierre here?*

*No, Pete. He's gone.*

*Gone where?*

*Have you missed me, Pete?*

*I don't have time for this. Where is Pierre? And what is he planning?*

*I don't know, Pete. I wish I did.*

Pete looked around him; she must be close. His eyes scanned the group of flesh renters, focused for a moment on her and then made a show of looking elsewhere.

Ten to Pete: What's the hold-up, Lazarus?

*You look different too. We've seen your new face on some footage.*

*I bet you have. What do you think? You want to take me home with you? A special discount for my friends.*

*Come back.*

*Never.*

*I need you.*

*Maybe you do, but we don't want the same things.*

*You want war.*

*Freedom.*

*And Pierre? You admire him.*

*Of course.*

*He's killed innocent people.*

*Nobody is innocent in this world. None of us.*

*How can you say that?*

Pete: I think Tamsin Grey is close.

Ten: Understood. Can you be more specific?

Pete: Her block is up. I think she's in the building somewhere.

*Peter, we are on the same side. You just don't know it yet.*

*I can't let you go.*

*You can't stop me either. Don't be a puppet, Pete. I can see what they are doing to you. Don't let them control you.*

*I won't become like you.*

*You already have. If you go in there and help them collect Arthur, then you're exactly what I was.*

*They are helping me train. I'm stronger than I was before.*

*I can see that. Stronger and angrier, and twisted up inside. Look at what they are doing to you.*

*Enough!*

'I felt Tamsin Grey. She's gone,' he told Gock.

'Really? We must alert the team.'

'I already have.'

'Very good, Mister Lazarus. Your behaviour will please the Prime. Is she gone?'

'Gone or quiet.'

Peter and Gock stood for a moment longer while the squad checked every room before clearing them to go into the prison.

For cover, in case the surveillance was watching, Tamsin tempted a pedestrian to be her customer and together they wandered away.

*I will come back for you*, she promised.

*I'll be waiting.*

He didn't watch her go.

Pete walked up the two flights of stairs in silence, ignoring Gock's questions about what had transpired between him and Tamsin. The door to Arthur's room was unlocked.

Stepping across the threshold of Arthur's room felt akin to stepping from a humid summer day into a chilled room. The air was too sharp to breathe and the cold froze your soul. Pete commanded his symb to turn the lights on and one pathetic lamp flickered, casting the room in yellow and black.

A man in filthy rags was standing at the other end of the room, as if he had been waiting for them.

'She said you would come and you did.'

'Did she?' Pete turned to Gock. 'Tamsin was just here.'

'How did she know we were coming?' Gock whispered back. He felt the fear on him thickly and wouldn't take another step forward.

'I won't go with you either,' the rag man replied, presumably Arthur Grimaldi.

'Why didn't you go with her?'

'I'm not going anywhere. Why can't you people just leave me alone?'

'We just want to ask you some questions, Arthur. That's all.'

Arthur peered at him, as if he could only just see him in the gloamy darkness. 'You've got the taint on you too.'

'Taint?'

*Taint?* Gock frowned.

'So many of you now.' Arthur spoke so low Pete had to use his symb to amplify. 'All touched by him. All cursed.' A cold ripple lapped over Pete and Gock, both hunching over with the foreboding emanating from the rag man in the corner. Arthur was so used to it that he no longer noticed the emotion field that surrounded him.

Pete: His moods affect everyone around him. He can't control it.

Ten: We've got the command to grab him. Ask your questions quick.

'Arthur, what can you tell me about Pierre Jnr?'

The name triggered a storm of primal fear, which was redirected at his visitors. Pete was suddenly an infant without thought, defiled and awestruck with undefined fear. Inside him he saw those eyes, those eyes that always stared, never blinking, patient.

'When did you last see Pierre Jnr?' he asked, doing his best to ignore his own mind. *Arthur? We don't want to hurt you.*

*He is here. He is there. He is everywhere. He is here, he is there, he is everywhere ...*

Pete was filled with hate. It poured in from outside of him, but he couldn't deny it. *Arthur ... Stop this. Please.*

The flood didn't stop. Arthur felt and Arthur made others feel. Pete's teeth crushed each other, his tongue caught between, filling his mouth with blood taste. He was decomposing from the inside. Frothing, phlegmy loathing. He bit over his lip, top teeth digging deep into the skin. The pain was enough to break the spell and Pete shielded his mind.

He wasn't sure how, but the raging torrent was blocked out, the window closed so it could be seen and not heard. Inside, he floated and was able to see that there was only a dark figure standing at the far end of a dark cell. He grabbed Gock by the collar and dragged him from the room.

Pete: Do what you have to do. Gas first, Ten. You don't want to go in there with him awake.

The journey home was silent. Pete practised his new skill. On, off. Open, shut. How the block worked was hard to explain. It was like opening and closing your eyes, not so that you couldn't see out but so that no one could see in.

Now that he knew the difference it seemed only a small effort to raise and lower the drawbridge of his mind. He felt silly that it had taken him this long to discover it. All his life he had been like a talkative moron who could not close his mouth.

'Another excellent performance,' Gock repeated Ryu's words verbatim. Unfortunately Gock was still shaky from his exposure to Arthur's field and he did not manage to convey Ryu's message with the assurance intended.

Pete too couldn't get his mind off Arthur.

'Thank you, Prime. I didn't know what else to do. I've never seen a psi like him.'

'You followed procedure to the letter.'

'What will become of him now?'

'Well that, Peter, is up to you and Geof. If you think you can work with him, he may be of use to you.'

'How so?'

'His sensitivity is unprecedented. He could be useful as a sniffer.'

Pete nodded. Early psi detection.

'You said Geof and I. Does that mean we can have contact again?'

'Yes. I will inform him once we are done.'

'Is my trial over then?'

'No. But your performance today, with Arthur, and reporting your possible contact with Tamsin Grey, has been noted.'

*And now he is beginning to trust me? Did it really take so little?* Pete wondered. *Or was there more to this? Was this just preparation for something else?*

'How do you feel about Arthur Grimaldi?'

'I feel sorry for him.'

'Oh, and why is that?'

Peter struggled to formulate an answer. He felt bad for Arthur because he had felt the darkness he lived within. He was unable to control his powers and had to shut himself away. 'It just didn't seem like a good life.'

'No. And why do you think Tamsin Grey would have been there, at the same time as you?'

*Ah, so the trial continues. First he praises, then he questions.*

'I don't know about the timing, that is most likely coincidence, but I presume she was trying to win Arthur to her cause.'

'And he did not go. That is interesting, isn't it?'

'Not every psi wants to become a combatant.'

'Such as yourself, you mean?'

'Yes.' Pete articulated the word precisely.

'Did she offer to free you?'

'No.'

'But you had one of your conversations with her, did you not?'

'I was trying to locate her. I notified the squad as soon as I knew she was close.'

'So you say.' Gock felt better being able to inflict some discomfort on another after the day he had had. He was looking forward to double tranqs and sleeping this nightmare off. 'Tell me what took place in this conversation.'

'She said she liked my haircut.'

'Don't play games with me, Mister Lazarus.'

'She said that I had become like her and warned me not to let you break me.'

'And have we broken you yet?'

'No, sir.'

'We will have to try harder then.'

'Yes, sir.'

'If you disobey me, Lazarus, you will be shipped to the islands. It is as simple as that.'

'To live out my days in peace and harmony?'

Ryu saw Gock sneer. He had no need to answer.

'You have left me no choice but to obey.'

'I did not intend to. You could try to escape if you wanted. Tamsin Grey has proven it can be done.'

Ryu to Gock: Smile.

The Prime ordered Pete's symbiot to give him a loving squeeze. It tightened on his arm, the blood pressure rising toward the pain threshold and Peter's fingers mottling to purple.

'Okay.' He gave out. 'I'll do as you say.'

Ryu allowed the symbiot to relax and Pete flexed his hand to restore the feeling.

'What do you want me to do now?'

'Geof Ozenbach will make contact with you. I'll wait for his recommendation on what to do with Grimaldi. Prime out.'

Geof and Peter had their first direct connection while both were immersed in the surveillance streams of Grimaldi's lockup. Pete watched Arthur through symb-overlay. Geof was doing the same from wherever in the world he was. It was a strange way to remeet.

'Hello, Geof.'

'Hello, Pete.'

'How have you been?'

'Much the same. Working for the Will.'

'And the Colonel?' Pete asked.

'No contact for twenty-six days now.'

'Any parting message?'

'Not to me.'

'Nor to me.'

'He's on another team,' Geof added.

'Oh.'

Pete wished he could talk properly with Geof, without the interpretations of Services oversight. It felt like Geof was standoffish, but how else could he act? He switched to message mode, which was less personal anyway.

Pete: What do you think of this guy then?

They turned their attentions to Arthur Grimaldi. He had been cleaned up and dressed in a wrap shirt, drawstring pants and a thick pocketed obi; standard *accoutrements gratuits* that were available to any Citizen who needed them. He could blend into a crowd in any of the megapolises now.

Geof: He seems calmer. Perhaps the medications are working.

Pete: We won't know for sure until there is a live person in there.

Geof: True. Who should we send in?

Pete: Gock?

Geof: Larks. No, it has to be you.

Pete: Why me?

Geof: Because you've already been exposed and you seem to have found a way to resist the effect. Have you managed to develop the psychic block you were jealous of Grey for?

Pete: I think so. Are you really Geof? This is sounding a lot like how the Prime cross-examines.

Geof: I apologise. Since I have been put in charge of the investigation, I have been trying to make my decisions carefully. It all rests on me now.

Pete: I understand. But you can trust me.

Geof: I appreciate that. Now what about Arthur Grimaldi?

**Peter sighed. That Geof had changed his attitude to him couldn't be more obvious.**

Pete: He is unique. But his ability to leave an impression is the same as any other telepath.

Geof: How do you mean?

Pete: He affects the mind, but in a different way. It is more emotion than thought.

Geof: And I thought mind control was bad enough.

Pete: You admit then, that you have lost trust in me?

Geof: Not in the way you think.

Pete: You don't have to be a telepath to spread fear, or ideas. That has been happening for centuries.

Geof: We can debate this later. Is he of any use to us?

Arthur hadn't moved. He sat in his chair, one hand resting on the symbiot he had been fitted with.

Pete: If he can be kept under control, his sensitivity could help us find Pierre.

Geof: That is what I hoped. I have a lead on Sullivan St Clare. We could test him on a collection.

Pete: Do you still think delving into Pierre's origins will help us understand what he has become?

Geof: We follow the leads we have. We have a shortage of information so anything helps make a picture.

Geof had patterned a set of unconnected reports of a denizen who regularly appeared on the outskirts of Seaboard, driving a beat-up hover that was covered in mud and dust. Every year before winter he appeared in town, buying portable batteries, fertiliser and boxes of general dose. Each year the same reports were recorded of an untrimmed, unwashed denny with a bank of cash.

The hover was found five hundred kilometres toward the red centre, at the mouth of a narrow valley, covered over with sheets and leaves. The area was meant to be uninhabited.

Geof: It could just be a bushcracker, but the height and age match Sullivan's profile. I want you and your squad to go into the valley and find him.

Pete: Into the bush? On foot?

Geof: The squad knows its business. And you have passed enough tests for the Prime to trust you.

Pete: Can't we just do a fly-through?

Geof: It's too narrow and dense for squibs. Eyes have been through but not thoroughly enough.

Pete: Hasn't anyone looked for Sullivan before? Surely if he was there, Services would have found him by now.

Geof: You're misunderstanding the Will. Not enough people wanted to find him. Some attempt was made eight years ago, but after such a long time hidden, not causing anyone any trouble, most wanted to forget the PDP ever happened.

Pete: Like Pierre? The world just wanted to forget?

Geof: It wasn't a priority.

Pete: The Prime suggested I may have been controlled by Pierre. That he may have pushed me to volunteer for the hunt.

Geof: And?

Pete: There is still no evidence that I had a sister.

Geof: And?

Pete: I have doubts.

Geof: Ah.

'I wish you knew my mentor. If Shen doesn't already have a wise saying for every topic, he has the knack for coining new ones.' Geof had switched to audio. 'Do you know what you do when you have doubts?'

'No.'

'Keep going. A man with doubts is like a ship in a storm; the fastest way out is to keep sailing.'

'I'm not sure I know what you mean.'

'There's only one way to find the answers you seek, Peter.'

Pete nodded and thought about this for a moment. He took a long look at the projection of the prisoner. He hadn't realised before how old Arthur looked, how close to starvation. Liquids were being drip-fed into his body as he sat stroking the symbiot that was new to his arm.

Pete: How physically demanding is this trip you have planned for us?

Geof: You're right. If you want him, we should wait a couple days for him to stabilise.

Pete: You still think we should take him?

Geof: I haven't been exposed to his field, Pete. I think we need some sort of detector. Why don't you see how he is now?

Pete: Is that an order?

Geof: I don't like this belligerence you've developed. You and I both have the same goals.

Pete: You're right.

Pete entered the box Grimaldi was being held in and stood waiting.

Geof: Are you feeling anything?

Pete: Something. Not much. Not like before.

*Hello, Peter. I can hear everything you are saying to your friend.*

'Hello, Arthur. Do you remember me?'

'Peter Lazarus.'

'That's good. You seem much better than you were a few hours ago.' Arthur shrugged happily and continued stroking the back of the symbiot. 'You seem to like that thing,' Pete said.

'It tells me everything will be alright.'

Pete couldn't help thinking about the chemical control it was also distilling to keep Arthur calm. Arthur only smiled at the thought. 'I don't mind, Mister Lazarus. I haven't felt this happy in ... as long as I can remember.'

'How long is that?'

'I don't know. I guess I should know that kind of thing.'

*You spoke of a taint before. Can you tell me more about that?*

'Hmm? Oh, I did?' *He leaves his mark wherever he goes. Yes. I can tell when someone has had contact with him.*

*And I have it?*

*Yes. But it is okay. He did not bring the darkness upon you like he did for me. He likes you.*

Pete shuddered.

'Would you like to take a trip with us, Arthur? We are looking for a man.'

'Sully St Clare. I knew him well.'

'We think he is in the wilds.'

'We can go camping. I've never been camping.'

'Will you help us find him?' Pete asked.

'I am happy to try.'

*What is your reach?*

*Higher than I care to count. Perhaps four or five hundred paces.*

Pete looked hard at him. 'I need to know something.'

'You may ask.'

'How do you feel about what we are doing?'

'Trying to stop Pierre Jnr? It doesn't matter. It may be the narcotic combo in my veins, but I feel happy being here. This feeling will come with us, won't it?'

*You could feel that way on an island.*

*I'd like to go camping.*

* * *

Arthur, Pete, Risom, Gock and the ten had been ambling through the bush for eight days. The twins were left behind at the mouth of the valley, where Sullivan, presumably, had hidden the old hover. They waited ready to ambush, in case the fugitive tried to escape.

Ten had the search team maintain a strict pattern, making sure Arthur covered as much territory in one day as was possible while the rest of the team took their symbs and close-range camera flies with them to look for signs of habitation.

The ten were dressed in soft armour. This area was meant to be pristine and a squad of MUs would make a trail and a lot of noise. The men seemed happy out of their suits with nothing but the arms and shoulders sheathed.

Everyone's symbs were plugged with data and procedures to review. Topographic maps and recorded fly-throughs, including an index of the local plant and wildlife.

The trees were too tall for a squib flyover to get Arthur close enough to detect anything. So far he had detected nothing. They followed a clean creek, thinking that at least Sullivan must need water to survive.

Rations were air-dropped to them each day. They only had to carry water and equipment. Each night they camped out, finding a gap in the tree canopy for supplies to be dropped down and where the embers from the fire didn't rise into the branches.

The camp was organised with the psis in the centre by the campfire and the ten in a protective ring around them. There wasn't much chatter. Even the soldiers seemed content to watch the fire and the smoke rise up to the stars.

They were far enough from Seaboard, the megapolis of the east Australian coast, that the stars came out and put on a show every night. The Milky Way was spilt across the sky as though a child had been playing with glitter and meteors, and space trash scratched the sky often enough to keep them watching. The closer layer of dots that traced over the sky was the 'rocky road' of the satellite layer.

Since Arthur's capture, the Prime had had him worked over by a psychologist and was medicating him to keep him calm. Even so, being around him for more than five minutes allowed his mood to affect everyone in the group. It was a good thing he was enjoying the outdoors.

Peter wondered if this peace was the result of being near Arthur when he was in a good mood or from the nature-effect he had heard some of the soldiers thinking about: the sounds of the bush, the thick crick of insects, the carrying buzz of cicadas. Both Pete and Arthur found it unfamiliar, but only the latter was calmed by it.

*I am. Thank you. I didn't want to come, but you made me.*

*I am sorry we collected you so roughly.*

*I know, Peter. I know.*

*You're the most sensitive I've ever met.*

*I was touched by him. Like you were. He changed you too.*

Pete couldn't help reacting: his eyes widened and he looked at the back of Arthur's head. Arthur did not turn around — he was doped enough or smart enough. Gock would know they were communicating.

*Don't worry so much. You should presume they assume.*

*I can't trust them.*

*Nobody can trust anybody.*

*Can I trust you?*

*You can try.* Arthur was slightly amused. *I'm sorry. I haven't felt this good in years. Do you think they'll let me stay out here?*

*Not very likely.*

On their ninth day, as they were tracking further into the valley, Arthur's arm raised and pointed forward. He himself didn't look where his finger went, he kept his head down.

'What is it, Grimaldi?' Ten asked.

'There is something.'

The squad went active on Ten's signal. The insect sounds were interrupted by hums and chimes as they powered up their weapons. It was like an orchestra warming up, each member starting their instrument and ramping to check its sanctity, before they even began putting them on.

Following Arthur's pointed arm, they went another hundred metres before one of the team found a trash pile behind a small rise.

They circled around, surveying and recording the area. The small pile seemed to be compost. Food scraps were dotted inside a yard of turned earth. Up the hill a short way was a path of chipped shale that led to an overhang. A quick peek with a drone showed that the rock pile concealed a natural tunnel entrance. Arthur's finger was pointing directly at it.

'What have you got in there, Arthur?'

'There is a man.'

'Is it St Clare?' Ten asked.

'H-he may not be alone,' Arthur stammered.

*What is it, Arthur?*

*I don't know. His mind is —*

'Is it him?' Ten insisted.

'I can't be sure. Whoever it is, is odd.'

'Let's give it a wait. See what happens.'

An hour passed in which the team held their position and communicated through symb only. They discussed contingencies. It was 'a job for ups', but Ten let the team indulge themselves. How deep do the caves go? What if it isn't Sullivan? What if Pierre is in there?

The command came down on the last tick of the hour.

'Okay. Let's go in.' Ten picked the odds — Nine, Seven, Five, Three and One — and they prepared themselves to go in. From their packs they pulled out stick-on lumens and placed them on their foreheads, the undersides of their wrists and the sides of their boots.

'Drop a booster before you go too deep. We don't want to lose contact.' Ten read through a stream of orders that were duplicated in their symb mission overlays. 'You don't have dead man's handles so if you feel anything out of the ordinary, if you think anything out of the ordinary, if you sense anything that isn't there, or even if your imagination goes hyperactive, report it through your symb.'

Each order was met with a co-ordinated, 'Yes, sir.'

'Nine, ping me every two metres. Everyone go silent.'

In normal operation mode the marauders let off occasional compression sounds, mechanical ticks and the whirr and flex of their actuators. Now they flicked to a dampened stealth mode that made them perfectly silent.

'Alright, good luck.'

The odds saluted and went into the cave, Nine first.

Nine: We are just beyond the opening. No movement. Floor looks scuffed. There is a crevice at the east rear. We should be able to get through.

Outside, the rest of the squad waited. Arthur paced back and forth. Pete could feel his peace becoming unsettled.

Pete to Ten: Arthur's meds aren't coping with the stress.

Nine: We are through the crevice. It is a scrape, but it opens up after three metres. This room has signs of habitation. Boxes and crates, some farming tools. We are dropping the first booster.

Ten: Be alert. The canary has a bad feeling.

Nine: Received. There is a path leading deeper, on the southern end. Nothing moving. We'll take a look ... Getting pretty tight here ... I'm through. There is a big cavern. No movement. The lumens don't reach the far side. There are shelves of mushroom beds. I'm moving forward.

The link to Nine went static.

Ten: Seven, can you still pick up Nine? We've lost signal.

Seven: Sir, no —

Ten: Five, pull back. Pull back.

Five: One, reverse. Ten, I'm just through to the big cave. I can't see Nine or Seven —

The lines went dead one by one.

'Ten? What just happened?'

'I lost contact with half my team, telepath. That's what

happened,' Ten said harshly. He was busy sending messages to Nine and to the ups for emergency orders.

Ten: Nine? Report in, Nine. Odds, backtrack immediately. We have lost signal.

He cursed.

'What do we do now?' Pete asked.

They all felt the fear. It had begun to permeate them. Ten stared down at his shaking hands while the Command came in.

'Four, I want you to take Grimaldi back to this morning's camp. He's freaking me out.'

'Yes, sir.' Arthur was only too happy to go along. He didn't want to be anywhere near that cave.

*I don't know what's down there*, he warned Pete.

'I say we send Gock down with a rope around his waist. Use him as bait,' Risom suggested. Gock gulped and begged off.

'I'll go,' Pete volunteered. 'If it is a psi down there, I'm the best one to try dealing with it.' The Prime sent a message to his symb, reminding him he was watching.

Ten and Two were assigned to go with him. Pete raised his block and put on a helmet and mantle designed for caving, then stuck the lumens on as Ten instructed.

Their bright glow cut the dark of the tight tunnel, though the shadows managed to fight back from behind overhangs, stalactites and every sharp change of direction. They passed the outer room and went one by one through the crevice.

Ahead they could see the light from the transmission booster, its per-second red flashes bumping the walls as it ticked. In the second cavern they saw the boxes and tools the first team described. Higher up the cave were hanging pots of lichen and moss.

On the south wall was the dark crack the odds had gone through.

Ten: Odds. Report. Is there anyone receiving? Check in.

The big leader waved for Peter to come closer. 'Their symbs are ten metres in the direction of that opening. Are you picking up anything?'

'There is something there. I can't even be sure it is human.'

Ten: I'll go first. Two, you take the rear.

A few metres into the opening the tunnel stooped down and they crouched and duck-walked through. Ten saw the feet of one of his men lying before him and he scrambled quickly out.

Ten: I see Three. Man down —

His messaging was interrupted by his own screaming and Ten collapsed to the rock floor. Pete and Two rushed in, the soldier firing beams into the dark without aiming. Then he too was rolling on the floor, clutching at his helmet before he vomited inside it.

Pete grabbed some flash pellets from his belt and overdosed the room with bang and light. The screaming of the soldiers turned to whimpers and panting, and he wiped the room with his torch until he saw a thin nook on one side. Enough for a man to slip through.

He could feel him now. Whoever it was had been dazed by the light assault and the sound had deafened him. He lived in a cave after all; nothing but quiet and dark. Pete threw more flash into the gap, turning his head away to protect his vision, and then rushed forward, grabbing at the pale arms and ribby body.

Pete dragged him out of his hole, into the light of the big cave. The eyes were animal and pinched by the brightness. His symb confirmed that it was Sullivan St Clare and Pete didn't hesitate to pull a mask from his kit and slap it over the feverish visage.

The squad explored and recorded the caves while Sullivan was being transported to a secure facility that was quickly being stacked together in the red mudflats in the centre of the continent — what had once been desert was now slowly drowning with the relentless bombardment of rain.

Deep in the side of the mountain they found hydroponic chambers filled with mesh plants and mushrooms.

'Not exactly a balanced diet,' Geof commented, his voice transmitting directly to Pete's ears.

Pete found a desk which was stacked with papiers, in dire need of repair and recharging. He prodded through a few slides, charts, notated tables of data.

'I don't think it was food he was interested in.' He held up a diary with annotations about what he had taken and the effect it had on his abilities. 'Do you think there is anything in this?'

'Okay, everybody out once you've got the lights up. I want to keep the site as clean as possible.' Geof sent through the command.

Geof: Ten, there is a box of sylus being dropped. I want you to plant one in each cave. Only you.

Pete had to read from Ten what a sylus was. Something like a symbiot in composition and function but free-roaming and self-powered. Geof was using them to get a complete scan of the cave system.

'I think you're right, Peter. The quick screen shows hallucinogens in the fungi. We'll just let the sylus do a crawl and compile, then we'll know more.'

Pete: What should I do?

Geof: I want you to interview. Take the line coming down on the drop. The facility is nearly complete.

The compound they set up for Sullivan was similar to the one Pete had recuperated in, though smaller. It had only one capsule and a landing pad. Armed servitors made a laser fence fifty metres around.

Geof had the builders clear the area, leaving only bots on site, when Pete touched down and debarked. The squib immediately lifted off, leaving Pete and Sullivan the only mammals in the compound.

Pete: Is all this really necessary?

Geof: Unknowns have become a bit of a thorny issue. The Prime had to manage a lot of complaints from the Services personnel who held Arthur.

Hearing of the Prime's discomfort pleased Pete slightly. He hooked into the room surveillance watching St Clare.

Pete: Here we are again. Different room, different prisoner. Same sacrificial lamb.

Geof: That's enough complaining. You could also be flattered that you are considered the best man for the job.

Pete: I can't stand not knowing whether you say that with humour or not.

Geof: Copy.

Pete: What have you got him on?

Geof: Suppressants. If you're not getting any sense out of him, we can try a transfusion. At the moment his toxicity is still very high, which might make for interesting answers.

Pete: Okay. For the record, I'm starting to hate interviewing. When was the last time I got to speak to someone who hasn't been touched by Pierre?

Geof: Copy.

Pete: Where is he? I can't sense him.

Geof: Underground. Deep. We are controlling all contact with St Clare for now. You will question him through a simulator room.

Pete: Don't I lose my advantage if I can't tap him?

Geof: Let's see how it goes first before putting you near him again.

The doors opened automatically. The simulator was a capsule with a cube in the centre which represented the black box Sullivan was sitting in that was buried five hundred metres away. The box was wrapped with wall screens and Pete could circle the interview room and talk to Sullivan from all sides. He could choose to let the interviewee see him or not.

Sullivan sat patiently on a red-backed chair. From his perspective he saw only mirrors looking back in on him, and he heard a voice, encoded and mechanised to obscure the original. Pete stood before him and allowed St Clare to see him.

'Mister St Clare, do you know where you are?'

'Who is that?'

'You can call me Peter.'

'Oh. Hello, Peter. I have heard a lot about you.'

Pete: Geof? How could he have?

Geof: Ask him where he heard about you.

'I don't think we have met before. Can you tell me where you have heard of me?'

Sullivan cocked his head to one side, like a curious raven. 'From Pierre, of course.'

'You've seen Pierre Jnr? When was the last time you saw him?'

'Is this a test? This room reminds me of the testing rooms.'

'Do you mean from the psionic development facility? When you worked with Doctor Rhee?' Pete asked.

'Yes. Is this a test?'

'No, Sullivan. I'm just asking you some questions.'

'Okay. Who are you? I can't see you.'

'My name is Peter. I'm far away from you.'

'Peter Lazarus. I remember.'

'How do you know my name?'

'Pierre told me.'

Geof: He could have got it before you masked him, or from one of your ten. Don't overthink, Pete.

'Do you know how long you have been gone from the institute?'

'Eight years, one month and five days.'

'You have been keeping track?'

'We remember things like that.'

'Did you enjoy your time at the institute?'

'Yes.'

'You were close to Mary Kastonovich, weren't you?'

'Mary. Nobody could help loving Mary.' Sullivan drifted off. He muttered under his breath.

'Mister St Clare, I can't hear what you are saying. Was that about Mary?'

304

'No. I'm just — just — I haven't gone this long without a chew for a while.'

'Can you explain?'

'A chew? A fix? Man, the fungi in my home. You know?'

'Yes, tell me about that. We found that most of your garden was hallucinatory. Your notes seem to indicate you were studying the effects.'

'Yeah. Yeah.' He began holding himself. 'If I go ecky on you, just give me one of those pills you confiscated in my clothing. It's just withdrawal.'

'I'll look into returning them to you.'

'Oh, don't pretend, Lazarus.' His speech suddenly hardened. 'You've got no power. You're just a puppet.'

'Tell me more about your studies. What effects did you find?'

'Is that why you're here? It doesn't work, okay.'

'Then why do you still grow them?'

'I'm addicted. Is that so hard for you to get? I knew that years ago. But even once I knew they were doing nothing, I had no reason to stop. I've been high for seven years, man.'

'How did you know they weren't working? What were you expecting them to do?'

'Make me stronger, of course. It wasn't hard to see when it didn't work.'

'Why do you think it didn't work?'

'Because psionics isn't like that. Lazarus, you should know this. Every psi should know this. Strength ain't strength. It's the wrong word for what we do.'

Geof: Steer it back to Pierre. Find out what he knows.

Pete: One second.

'So what is the right word?'

'Fluency.'

'Like language?'

'Yeah, man. It's like a frequency, a wavelength, a vocabulary. It's all these things, and to get stronger you just have to get better.'

Geof: Pete. First and only warning.

Pete: Understood.

'May I call you by your first name?'

'I don't care. Call me Sully if you want.'

'Okay, Sully. We were talking about Pierre Jnr a moment ago. You said you had spoken with him.'

'I am talking with him all the time, Peter. We have a permanent connection.'

'Are you talking to him now?'

'I said always, didn't I?'

'What does Pierre say?' Pete asked.

'He doesn't speak directly. It's not like that. Are you sure you're a mindee? You are as ignorant as a norm.'

'Is he out to harm us?'

Geof: Pete, don't get caught up in his madness. The toxins are talking.

Sullivan paused for a moment. 'How could he harm us? We are him and he is us.'

'I don't understand.'

'He says you will.' Sullivan was so calm.

Geof: Pete. He is not sane. Nobody is in the room with him and there is no way he is communicating from underground. Look at the tox report. You'll see that anything he says is not coming from a place of sanity.

*But it does come from somewhere*, Pete thought to himself. He drew the medical information from his symb and saw a bunch of data of which he had no comprehension. The summary was clear though: Sullivan St Clare was not functioning on a normal chemical balance.

'Sullivan? What about the people in the Dome who were killed?' Pete asked.

'He didn't kill anyone.'

'Are you saying Pierre wasn't responsible?'

'He says no one was harmed.'

'Sullivan, I was there. Many people died.'

'He says he made sure they were not. Nobody was harmed.'

Pete: Geof, can you think of a question we can ask to test out if he is in contact?

Geof: No. We can't be sure of what he already knows.

Pete: And what if Pierre is transmitting to him?

Geof: Impossible.

Pete: Kinetically destroying a city block was also thought impossible a month ago. What if telepathy is just a language, like he says — brain code — that some can use and others can't?

Geof: It's a possibility, and we'll look into it. Nobody expects us to come up with all the answers today.

Pete: I want to know my mind is free. Isn't that what we are fighting for? We need to be able to test if psionic influence is limited to contact.

Geof: Then we must draw a line. If we keep him isolated, then we can test in a week to see if he has acquired new knowledge. Break off the interview.

*  *  *

Every day the Primacy council opened a chat circuit to report on recent developments and discuss future actions. It was a non-public discussion, though participation was notable.

Every day the weighting of the players shifted, though there had been no change in the Primacy since Ryu had risen. To his chagrin, Charlotte Betts had gained credibility. As the world was swept for psis, the imposition of security was pushing more people toward her way of thinking. Something would have to be done.

Charlotte Betts spoke more often now. 'If Sullivan is right and psionic ability is more like a language skill, perhaps Pierre Jnr can't hear us.'

'Are you defending him again? Why are you so intent on him being innocent?' Admiral Zim accused and the assembly rumbled in tones of agreement.

Demos's avatar leant conspiratorially toward hers. 'The Admiral has a point, Charlotte. The evidence points toward a certain malice.'

At least Demos had become more compliant. It had only taken a little attention to have his dominions fall in line with the security measures.

'But what if Pierre doesn't recognise non-telepaths as people? What if he doesn't see them? We could just be like ants to him and he doesn't know he is hurting anybody.'

'Is this idea supposed to reassure us?' asked Shreet.

'And even if that was true, he can still read minds and

therefore he is fully aware of his actions. You must begin to accept this, Representative Betts,' Ryu said.

'It is for that reason I find it hard to imagine that he acts with cruelty. Surely he suffers the pain of those he hurts?'

'Are you out of your mind, woman?' Admiral Zim shouted.

'Admiral, I must rebuke you there,' Ryu responded. 'These sessions are for discussing developments. There is no value in them if we degenerate to insult. Let us end for today. Representative Betts, while your opinions are not in line with the rest of the group, I think we should recognise what you have suggested: that the nature of the threat may not be as we assume.

'We shall reconvene tomorrow. Until then, watch the feeds and the Will.'


Takashi tapped Ryu on the shoulder as he demersed.

'Takashi, what are you doing in my rooms?' Ryu asked. No one was supposed to enter. No one was *allowed* to enter — though clearly his brother had found a way around that edict.

'Mother has sent me to force-feed you. She has alerts that tell her when you aren't eating enough.'

'I eat every meal.'

'Yes, but you aren't used to the permanent connection like I am. Please, Ryu. This is one area I know better than you.'

Ryu stared at him, his eyes dry and red-rimmed. 'Were you watching that last session?' he asked.

'Only out of the corner of my eye. It seemed the same as the others. The Will versus the kinder heart of Charlotte Betts.'

Ryu scoffed. 'I should have you disconnected for crossing the line.'

Takashi shrugged at that. 'Just because you are my brother, doesn't mean I have to heed level restrictions. What kind of weaver would I be if I only went where I was allowed?'

When the second Dark Age came, after the collapse, wealth shifted with every global mood swing. After the weather went neurotic, it was a lottery of sentiment and rainfall that determined which cities floundered or flourished.

War, following the dirt winds, made the entire American continent split east and west: populations driven to the coasts, where the cities were battling the aggravated oceans, but managing to feed themselves.

When the desert bowl stirred, and the midland towns evacuated, it was only a matter of chance that the survivors congregated on the eastern seaboard, creating an unintended and fragmented megapolis between Washington DC and New York.

Atlantic, as it became known — or the Cape — like many of the coastal mega-cities, hid behind gigantic seawalls and dykes that held back the sea swell and drew a lot of their energy from the ocean's fury with near-shore turbines and wave harnesses that, from above, looked like a dock line being gnawed by a school of eels.

It was one of the first cities to establish a raised floor in response to the rising seas — a layer of hard composite that became the new street level while the ground beneath was either drowned or drowning. This gave the city the capacity to establish reasonable sewerage, electricity and connectivity grids, and made a muddy basement for the subterraneans, who had their own reasons to stay underground.

Most of the Cape was stuck in the mode of the twenty-first century, pre-Dark Age and pre-World Union. The city was a subdivided chaos with each population striving for survival and dreaming of flourishing. Only the top five per cent were even classed as Citizens, most choosing, or ignoring, the civil games of the WU.

Here, Services was limited to two embassy compounds. The last of the megapolises to resist global governance, Atlantic was a plutocracy, which is to say: those who had power wielded it, primarily for their own interests.

Tamsin was not as polite as other telepaths when it came to gathering information. When she met someone, she pushed them to think what she wanted them to. People would stop what they were doing and suddenly be thinking of something else: a painful memory, their first love, kiss, or taste of cruelty. Seemingly unconnected to what they were doing, their memories would replay, jump about and abruptly change.

At first she was directionless, but after encouraging a few passers-by to think about the recent manifestation they inevitably connected their thoughts to the people they suspected of being psis, or having psi sympathies. Then she would move along, following the hint or suspicion she had picked up. The passers-by were left in momentary confusion until they managed to remember what they were meant to be doing.

Since waking up — her reawakening — Tamsin had a new understanding of her powers. She had always been strong, but never particularly deft. She could use her kinetics for everything now: dressing, undressing, washing, eating, pushing the curtains of her room aside to look out.

Her telepathy too was more refined. It was like someone had replaced her hammer with a suite of lock picks. With enough time alone there wasn't anything that could be kept hidden from her.

She stood to one side of the footpath, the people of the Cape passing in front of her like streams on the Weave. A man stopped to stand before her, face beaming with lecherous thoughts and hungry eyes. Tamsin-Maria smiled at him.

'Well, hello there, would you like to take me somewhere more interesting?' she asked him.

'How much for?'

*Whatever you can afford, big boy.*

He led her off the main street toward a motel, but as soon as they were out of sight of the thoroughfare she pulled him into a shaded alley. He leant in to lick at her lips and she broke his nose with the butt of her hand.

Grabbing his ears, she held down his head so he was forced to meet her eyes. 'Tell me everything you know about psionics in this town.' *Everything.*

Fortunately for him, he didn't know much. There were rumours of psis in the gaming parlours, rigging everything for the house, and that the basement was full of dennies who were telepathic and rode around on giant rats. She knocked him out, took his cash and moved on.

Tamsin had never lived amongst the public before. Not since she was very young, when life was a dash between classes and play and home. Services took away all that before she knew what was happening. She couldn't remember much.

As she walked around, she learnt a lot about where she was. Atlantic had two extremes and every step in between.

At the city's best, the causeways were tessellated poly-paving, beautified with elm trees and street chandeliers, plant walls and fountains. The people walked tall and dressed proud in well-cut clothing of natural fibre. All their mess was dispensed with by the miniature army of robo sweepers.

At its worst, the streets had built up a carpet of dirt and pressed litter and, in places, holes broke through to the level below. The walls were piled with garbage slopes, broken only by the homes people had made within them and dogs on chains to protect them while they slept. As she walked through these unlit alleys, she regularly saw robberies and molestations and lifelong drunks cackling away at nothing in particular. She didn't get involved; she just tried to watch where she stepped.

After dropping her customer, folded neatly into a corner, Tamsin once again planted the suggestion into the minds of the passers-by that they should go immediately toward anyone they suspected of being a psi, or someone they thought might know that kind of person. Then she would follow.

She went in circles chasing groundless suspicions until eventually the stories of the strangers coalesced and she found herself walking behind a short woman who had once been helped by a most miraculous surgeon.

The woman caught a rail car north, changing to a coach that stopped at old town, where she had to walk the rest of the way. This Doctor Alexi Salvator, in the woman's head, was either a psionic scalpel or worked closely with one. *A kinetic surgeon*, Tamsin thought. *How excruciating.*

The woman palmed the office door for her and said she needed to see the doctor right away. A middle-aged string of a man with silvering hair hurried into the waiting room.

'Stacy, is there something wrong?'

Tamsin dropped Stacy to the ground with a pulse of awe and exhaustion.

'Sorry to barge in like this, doctor, but I need to know something.'

Piri's mother watched with amusement as her daughter, all of six years old, stomped back and forth across the room, collecting all the things she would need on her adventure.

It was a one-room home, with a small en suite bathroom behind a plastic curtain. The pair of them slept in the same room, cots along the wall and a common table for the preparing and eating of meals. They had one door, and a small window that Piri wouldn't be able to look out of until she was fully grown.

'What about a blanket? You'll need to stay warm,' she suggested and Piri went to her bed and folded up her blanket.

'You should take some food too, Piri. It could be a long journey.'

'Won't you get hungry, Momi?'

'Not as much as you, dear. You should take it.'

'Okay, I'll take some. But I'll leave some for you.'

'And when will you come back to your loving mother?'

'I don't know, Momi. First I must find him, and I don't know how long it will take.'

'Who are you finding? Prince Charming?' she laughed.

'No, Momi. Pierre Jnr.'

'The boy in the news? Darling, he is make-believe.'

'No, he isn't. He's been seen.'

'No, my darling, that is just people talking. He's pretend, I promise you.'

'I know better, Momi. He has given us a sign and is calling us to him. I have to go. I just have to.'

'Piri, sweetie, who has been filling your head with this nonsense?' Piri did not answer. 'Who have you been talking to?' Her mother was worried. She had to spend a lot of time out of the unit to earn money and often had to leave Piri alone. Her daughter still didn't answer. 'If he was calling to us, why did I not hear about it? Hmm? It is just in your head, darling.'

Piri mumbled something, which her mother asked her to repeat. 'You are not one of us.'

'What? What are you saying?'

'Momi, please. Just let me go.'

'I'm not letting you out that door.'

'You can't keep me in here forever.'

'Piri, I have had enough. Put down that bag, wash your hands and go to sleep. Perhaps by morning this ridiculous notion will have disappeared.' Her mother pointed sharply at the foldout that was her bed. Piri didn't move. 'Put the bag down, now.'

'No. I have to go.'

She reached for the bag and tore it from her daughter's shoulders and began pushing her to the bed. 'Bedtime. To bed with you. Now.'

'No, Momi, please. Please! I have to go!' Piri screamed and screamed. Her mother had never seen her in such a state. She began flailing her arms about, not even watching where she was hitting. Her mother bent down and trapped her in a hug.

'Piri, please, calm down.' She felt her daughter's panting body shuddering, the tight arms ready to hit. She stroked her hair and found it sweaty and hot. 'Oh, darling, you have a fever. Let me get you a medicine.'

She pulled away and went to the bathroom, looking for something that would lower a fever. *Oh no*, she thought. *It could be anything. She's burning up.*

A drop of blood fell on the wet white of the porcelain. It spread through the sprinkle of leftover water. Another drop hit the white. Her nose was warm and, reaching up, her hand came away filmed in red. Her head wobbled with dizziness.

'Piri, darling. Go get a doctor. There's something wrong with us.' She tried to keep the panic from her voice as she lowered herself gently to the floor. Piri was standing in the doorway to the bathroom, bag on her back. 'Quickly, honey, go find Doctor Salvator. Tell him we're both sick.'

Piri shook her head. Her face was both red from perspiration and washed with tears now. 'I'm sorry, Momi. Not us. Only you. I'm okay.'

'Hurry, Piri, please. I need a doctor.'

Piri turned and ran from the room.

She ran all the way to Doctor Salvator's offices and didn't stop to knock. Inside she saw a blonde woman leaning over the prostrate form of the doctor, and another woman collapsed by the doorway.

'Hey, you get off of him!' Piri shouted and rammed the

316

woman with her shoulder. She blasted the stranger with all the emotions she was currently feeling and then knelt by Salvator.

'Doctor, wake up. Wake up. Wake up. My mother has been hurt.'

'Piri?' He blinked. 'What happened?'

'No time, Doctor Sal. My mother.'

'Okay, I'm coming. Just let me grab my —' He saw the woman who had attacked him. 'Who *are* you?'

She stood up and stared both of them down.

'You had no right to do that.'

'I did what I needed to.'

'Doctor Sal! Momi!' Piri pulled at his arm.

'Okay, Piri. Let's go. I'll deal with you later,' he said to Tamsin.

Tamsin followed the doctor and the child as they hurried through the streets. This old town area was filled with blind turns and streets that had been cut off for living spaces.

Piri led them to what looked like a kennel, but ducking inside and seeing the small frames that were their beds, Tamsin understood that this was her home. A woman was on the floor in the bathroom, a twitching foot scraping the floor.

Salvator went to her side and pulled equipment from his bags. 'What happened here, Piri? How long has she been like this?'

'I came as soon as it happened.'

'As soon as what happened?'

'I'm sorry, Doctor Sal. I didn't mean it.' The child was sniffling back tears. She tried peering around the doctor to see how her mother was. 'I just wanted her to let me go.'

He tried everything, checked her heart, pulse, temperature, pupils. He put a sylus on her to check for tox, but he knew there would be no explanation. Her body was functionally normal, but her brain showed no activity. Piri's mother had become a drool, another mind-mushed denny; they were common in Atlantic.

He turned to look at Tamsin gravely. 'What about you? Is there anything you can do?'

Tamsin approached the body on the floor. She looked downward, looking inward. After a moment, she bent down and placed her fingers around the mother's face. Tamsin shook her head.

'Piri, what did you do?' she asked.

'She was going to stop me.'

'It wasn't your fault, child,' the doctor insisted.

'Doctor,' Tamsin whispered to him, 'do you realise this child is psionic?'

'Oh, child ... no.' Salvator's heart was breaking. 'You didn't ... You can't ... just ...'

Piri backed away from him toward Tamsin. *You're like me.*

'She's just a child, doctor. She'll only understand later.'

*You think I will be sad*, Piri thought to Tamsin.

*Yes. One day you will realise what you have done.*

*But she was going to stop me.*

*She was still your mother.*

The three of them returned to the doctor's offices, waiting as the sanctuary that the doctor had contacted came to collect Piri's mother. They stood without talking, Tamsin watching the doctor and his thoughts while Sal watched her and tried not to think too much. Piri was quiet, on the outside. Underneath she was bubbling with questions for Tamsin. She ignored them.

'How are you feeling, Piri?' Salvator asked her gently. Tamsin sat on a stool in the corner.

'Okay, I guess.'

'I didn't realise you were gifted, Piri. I try to watch out for the signs in all my patients.'

'I know. I didn't want to have them take me.'

'Who? Services?' Tamsin asked.

'La Grêle.'

'You know of La Grêle?' he asked Piri.

'No, but you do. That's who you tell when you find ones like me. Isn't it?'

'Yes. But she is nothing to fear. She helps children like you.' Piri shook her head. 'Where were you trying to go?'

'I was going to look for Pierre Jnr. He has called for us to join him. Can you take me to him?' Her eyes were full of hope.

'No, Piri. I don't know where Pierre Jnr is.'

Piri looked over at Tamsin. *You know, don't you?*

*You and I can talk about that later, kid. Just talk to the doctor for now.*

*Okay.*

'Tell me, Piri. What can you do? Can you hear what I am thinking?'

'Sometimes. But you think things I don't understand. Who is La Grêle?'

'Never mind that for now. What else can you do? Can you move things without touching them?'

'Only very small things.'

'Oh, but still, that is a marvellous gift. And it is a very rare child indeed who can do either, let alone both.'

'Doctor Sal? Will Momi be okay? In the morning everything will be better, won't it?'

'Maybe …'

'You're lying. Did I hurt her bad?'

'Yes, Piri. Sometimes our gifts can be dangerous.'

'Will she die?'

'Only if we don't take care of her.' Tamsin could see what the doctor was thinking. The mother would join the wandering brainless, and eventually starve to death.

'Piri, why don't you go in the other room for a moment. I need to speak privately with the doctor.'

*I hurt Momi.*

*I know, child. But it was an accident. Now go watch some shows in the back room.*

*That is the doctor's house.*

*He won't mind. He wants you to make yourself at home. Go find something to eat.*

When they were alone, Salvator stood and stretched. 'I guess you must be Tamsin Grey.'

'How do you know that? You're not a tapper.'

'I was warned you might come. Where are the others?'

'What others?'

'The ones you have freed. We know about them.'

'It seems you know quite a bit. Services would not be pleased about that. My people are safe. Nearby.'

'And what are you doing in our fair city?'

'Doctor, I must insist I complete my delve. As you must understand, it is very hard to trust anyone these days.'

'And why should I trust you, Miz Grey?'

'Do or don't, but it will be easier on you if you don't fight me.'

'What are you —' Tamsin caught him before he fell and laid him down on the floor. She folded her legs beside him, tapped in and pushed his memory a long way back.

Salvator's parents always knew. Apparently he'd exhibited signs of telekinesis as a baby. Forty years ago Services was only just getting organised and the WU didn't span the globe like it did now so they managed not to be noticed. The town that they lived in, that was later overcome by the growth of Santiago, gave them enough room for him to go into the mountains and learn to control his powers. They said he needed to be able to control them so he didn't get caught.

It wasn't enough though. When the collections began after the institute fiasco, the marauders came to collect him. He was in the middle of surgery and a sharp vibration made him split a blood vessel as the patient's body was shaken.

Services failed to collect him. Salvator cut them to shreds as they came into the room and then he finished the procedure and stitched up his patient. After that he collected his family and ran to Atlantic.

He'd lived in this building for thirteen years, with a wife, two children and his elderly parents who slept on the second floor.

He was as pure as she could hope for: never a part of Services, his Citizenship renounced, finding and protecting emergent psis. Tamsin sat back and tickled through the minor memories since then. The people he had helped, as a doctor and as a part of the psi underground.

Salvator's eyes opened in alarm. 'How dare you!' he shouted and lashed out at her. She reached in and swerved his desire to dissect her toward a metal stand with surgical toys on it. 'I don't like to think back to those times.'

'I had to.' *Don't try anything or I'll mush you up.* 'That's better. I'm sorry for the invasion, but it's hard to know who you can trust these days.'

'You don't say,' he responded wryly. 'So, do you trust me enough now to tell me why you're here?'

'I'm here to help. I know there are psi groups in the Cape. And I now know you're in charge of one of them. I want you to get me in touch with the others. I want to meet this La Grêle.'

He shook his head. 'No, not without telling me what you want. La Grêle is very careful.'

'And she's who warned you about me?'

'As you can see, I don't know much. I can't even be sure the woman I know is La Grêle. She could just be a stand-in.'

Tamsin knew that Salvator didn't believe that. He was in thrall to the woman he knew as La Grêle, though his actual memories had little evidence to believe her to be more than just another telepath. Over the years he had taken children to her for help, and she had always been kind. He believed her to be the head of a vast network of psis that lived in the World Union undiscovered. Services had often speculated that such an organisation could exist, but no trace had ever been found; at least, not to Tamsin's knowledge.

'Please, Salvator. I need to speak with her. Don't make me force you.'

'Okay.' He gave in, as she knew he would. La Grêle had instructed him to keep Tamsin in town if he came across her. 'It may take some time to organise. Like I said, La Grêle is very careful. How can I find you?'

'I'll come back tomorrow, and the day after that and the day after that. Make sure they know I won't stop and that they *do* want to talk to me. It's in their best interests.'

'I understand.'

'And I'm taking Piri with me.'

'No. I can't allow that.'

'You can't stop me either.' Tamsin met his angry stare with a smirk.

'Is this how you get your way? Threats and force?'

Tamsin shrugged. 'If that's what it takes.'

'La Grêle isn't going to like you.'

The girl walked beside her and occasionally looked up at her.

*You have two skins.*

Tamsin paused. *How can you tell?*

*I can tell.*

*What else can you tell?*

*You've met Pierre.*

*Yes, I have.*

*Will you take me to him?*

*Yes. In time. I don't know where he is right now.*

Piri had been in the slums since she was young, living in the hovel with only her mother. She'd developed her abilities

323

quickly and knew that she had to keep her gift secret. She didn't want her mother getting in trouble.

*How did you know I was telepathic?* Tamsin asked her.

*What do you mean? I can just tell. Can't you?*

*Just by looking at someone? No.*

*I don't need to look with my eyes, I just feel it.*

*... This child could be very helpful,* Tamsin thought to herself.

*I'm happy to help. I don't think we should have to hide. I want to join Pierre Jnr.*

*So do I.*


Two days later Doctor Salvator arranged a meeting for that evening. He explained that even though gatherings were rare, they never met in the same place twice, in case Services was watching.

While everyone in the rebellion wanted to come along, Tamsin chose only to take Okonta for extra protection. Since she had freed him, Okonta had proven himself to be disciplined, perceptive and considered himself forever in her debt. If she fell, he would take her place to lead the revolution.

Their journey began with the doctor handing each of them a hand lamp and warning them to watch where they stepped. The location was to be kept secret, even from Salvator, until the very last minute.

'The basement is old and broken down. The ground can give way at any time.' They began their descent via a maintenance stairwell that let out on the old ground level. He pulled a paper map from his jacket, looked over it for a moment and then directed them forward.

The air was thick with moisture. In the areas where the old tarmac had given way, pools of dirty water made traps for unwary feet. In the distance, the lap of the tides licked and echoed. Tamsin could see small glimmers of fires and silhouettes warming themselves.

'Dennies. Watch out not to drift away. Not all psis are part of La Grêle's network.'

They followed Salvator through the muddy winding of the basement streets, with Piri holding onto her hand and Okonta behind. A century ago this was the street level, signs of which were still obvious: the gutters that followed the interstices of roads, telegraph poles and street signs. The original buildings had been torn open, decimated, now broken-down caves whose insides held collections of dark rubbish that not even the dennies cared about.

The second level was fifty metres above, held up by strong steel girders in a tight grid under the city. By pointing their lamps upward they could see the underside of the streets, the pipes and circuitry of sewerage and cabling; a base that kept this old world in permanent shadow.

Salvator approached a pair of men who were standing at the entrance of an old cinema. They whispered with Sal and looked suspiciously at the group he was leading.

*He's telling them they don't need to come down. That they can trust you,* Piri informed her. Tamsin could get that much for herself, but the girl had taken it upon herself to report everything her powers could detect.

'That's nice.'

'He doesn't trust you though.'

'I was mean to him.'

'You should learn to be more gentle.'

Tamsin turned to catch Okonta smiling.

The two men pointed to a spot on Salvator's map and he returned to the group. 'It's still a way yet.'

He led them through more of the same dark roads until they eventually came to a pair of large trapdoors that opened upward and exposed a staircase leading down.

'A bit excessive, isn't it, Salvator?'

'La Grêle likes to be cautious.'

'And she wanted to make sure we couldn't escape too easily, right?'

'We will stop now if you can't show respect.' The doctor twisted around to stare her down. 'If you go in there with that attitude, don't expect their help.'

'I'm sorry. It was only a little joke.'

'There is nothing to joke about. Don't think that just because I can't read your mind, I don't know why you've come here.'

The room at the bottom of the stairs was about fifteen paces across and had once been some sort of storage area. The walls were brick and mould. There was no furniture in the room and all the clutter and debris had been pushed to one corner.

Their group was the last to arrive. Piri let Tamsin know who was waiting for her as they got closer: three tappers and four benders, from the four corners of Atlantic. When they entered, the two groups stood separated from each other, indicating an uneasy alliance. The telepaths were forewarned of their arrival and showed nothing but impatience, but the benders turned as one when they came through the doorway, also impatient.

It was not a friendly room. The benders were aggressive and the telepaths had blocks up, shielding their minds.

'Who are they?' one of the benders asked Tamsin — Vincent Lang from the Phili side. He was the most powerful kinetic in the Cape, as recent competitions had proved. This was his first meeting as part of this ad hoc psionic council; apparently he didn't really know, or care to know, the older members.

'They are with me. This gentleman here is Okonta, who like me has recently been freed from Services employment, and this girl, Piri, is an orphan I have adopted.'

'Why are we meeting this woman, Sal? She used to be a collector,' said another bender. She was thickset, homespun and nicknamed Rocks. She had been sent by someone called Chiggy, who never let himself get close to tappers.

'She says she means no harm,' the doctor replied. 'Her background is enough to make her at least interesting for us to talk to.'

The woman known as La Grêle grunted. Tamsin turned her attentions toward her. She was tall for a woman and old enough for her hair to silver. Her body was slim, face noble and she wore layers of grey. She had a block up that Tamsin couldn't push through and from her crossed arms and tight lips it was clear she also wasn't happy to be called here.

'Let's get this over with. We know why you are here, Tamsin Grey,' La Grêle said.

'I am open to you as requested. My mind submits to your investigation.' She bowed. *While you are allowed to remain closed to me. I understand and forgive.*

*And we shall try to forgive your arrogance,* La Grêle projected in return.

It was agreed that Tamsin would be able to present her case and then the two group leaders would speak without interruption, Salvator for the benders and La Grêle for the telepaths. For the sake of the benders they would communicate vocally only. Silent conversations were forbidden.

'Miz Grey, please begin. Why is it that you have come here?' Salvator prompted.

Tamsin took a small step forward. Piri was telling her everything she was picking up from the group and Tamsin silently shushed her.

She panned around the room as she spoke, matching each of their hot glares with her own. 'I have come here for your help. My name is Tamsin Grey. At least, that is the name I was given by Services when they took me for training. I do not know if that is my original name.' She commanded her symbskin to roll back to reveal her underskin. It began a slow crawl down to her neck, a process that took a couple of minutes to complete. 'I was taught to hunt psis. To collect those who didn't volunteer themselves. I was one of their best agents.'

'And now you want us to listen to you? I think it is time we got our own back.'

'Just try, Vincent.' She smiled and pushed force on his chest. 'I can understand your anger toward me. I am not proud of what I have done, but I was just a little kid when they took me, like Piri here. I didn't understand what was happening, and by the time I did they didn't have to force me. Okonta and I, like many others, were trained. We were locked in. And you think you're angry? Where were any of you?'

By now her second skin was down to a roll around her neck and she ordered her hair to change back to its natural colour. They must see the real her, her true face.

'We do have one thing in common though. I too think it's time to get our own back. I cannot undo what I have done, but at least I am trying to reverse it. So far I have freed thirty psis who were collected and I will continue to free more. And when I have enough, I will free our cousins on the islands.'

'Wait a minute,' said one of the tappers who had been silent until now. Hiero Blish, according to Piri. To Tamsin, all the telepaths had blocks up that she couldn't see through, but Piri didn't seem impeded. Hiero worked as a monitor for a cartel of gaming arenas in the Washington precinct, security against psionic cheating. 'Isn't there an elephant in the room you seem to have bypassed? What about Pierre Jnr?'

'Tell me what you would like to know,' Tamsin replied, spreading her hands.

'What can you tell us about the Dome manifestation? Was it him or not?'

'It was him. I was part of a Services team that was tracking him so I was there that day.' Hiero at least seemed keen to hear more; it was hard to tell with the rest of the group. The benders were impressed by the force of the manifestation more than anything else. 'Pierre is the only reason I can stand before you today. He freed me.'

'Where is he now? Why has he not come to us instead of talking through a proxy?' Vincent asked.

329

'I am not a proxy. The truth — since you will undoubtedly delve it from me anyway — the truth is that I don't know where he is. Four weeks ago I woke up in Joberg with a cyberdoc putting a new skin on me.'

'So what does he want?'

'He didn't say. But he freed me and set me on this path, so I believe that this is what I am meant to be doing.'

'And what is that?'

'Fighting for a world where psis can live in peace without having to hide our abilities.'

'Yes, Miz Grey,' a redheaded man behind La Grêle interrupted. 'You are certainly not the first to have thought of this … it is an amusing pastime to speculate on. You cannot be thinking you are the first to attempt it? How do we win? Tell me that, Miz Grey, and I'll keep listening.'

'Together. We will win together. I know how Services hunts us. I've been leading them my entire adult life.'

'And you want us to trust you?' Vincent smirked.

'"Traitor", I hear you thinking. To who? To you? To psis everywhere? Where were you when they took me? Down here in the dark. It's them I'm betraying more than you. They took me in. They manipulated me. They locked me. But when the opportunity came, I broke free. And now I'm going to win a war against them. You're either with me, or you're a coward.'

'What about the marauders? You can deal with them?'

'Anyone with a little willpower can take out a marauder, Vincent. Each suit has a fail-safe to protect it against a psionic takeover. All you have to do is control them so that their

330

pattern changes enough to raise suspicion. Then they get frozen and can't move until a release code is uploaded.'

'It sounds too easy.'

'Don't forget fun. I think we're going to have a good time.'

'We haven't agreed yet.'

'You agreed when you started asking questions.' Tamsin grinned.

'Just what do you want us to do?'

'Resist. Fight back.'

'And then?'

'Then we can be free.'

'We can never be free,' La Grêle spoke. 'When would the fighting stop?'

'When they stop persecuting us.'

'Do you know so little about fear, Tamsin Grey? They will never stop, they will never be able to stop.'

'I want psi freedom now.' Tamsin clenched her teeth. She had presumed that they'd feel as she did, but they were in less of a rush to go up against Services.

'We have heard the slogan,' La Grêle answered, 'but what does it mean to you to be free? Have you asked what must change in the world for it to be possible for us all to coexist?'

'They must stop imprisoning our people, for one thing.'

'It is as simple as that?'

'It's a start.'

'I understand that. But what comes next?'

Tamsin didn't have an answer.

'You see, I know what you are fighting against. But I don't know what you are fighting for. We all want to be free. We all want our station in life to be improved, but there are billions of people who wish that.'

'This is different.'

'Somewhat. But you have come to us asking for, what exactly? Support to build an army to fight against the World Union?'

'The time has come when we can stand no more.'

'You mean when you can stand no more. Do you know how many people are in the World Union? Sixteen billion. What are you going to do with all of them?'

'Not all of them are locking us up,' Tamsin insisted.

'No, but all of them aren't stopping it either.'

'You're right that we cannot win an open fight. They are many and their technological superiority is formidable. So we don't fight. We strike, we hide. We must resist their incursions and rescue our people.'

'You talk about psis as if they were one. I have never met you before. We have nothing in common.' This, of course, from Vincent.

'We live under the same oppression. The same restrictions.'

'I don't know about you, Miz Grey, but I have not found these to be an impediment to my lifestyle.' The bender smiled coldly. Indeed, as Tamsin could see, most of those in this room lived in equal comfort.

'Here in the Cape you might. But if Services set up here like they have everywhere else —'

'Won't your boy keep them occupied for a while?'

'My …?' They meant Pierre! 'Boy? How dare you refer to him as a boy.'

'I told you, didn't I? Not five minutes in and the fanatic is revealed. I don't think there is anything more to discuss, except perhaps for whether you leave peacefully or as a mindless drool.'

*Fools!*

'Miz Grey, we agreed: spoken only.'

'I'm sorry, La Grêle. It was a moment of frustration caused by the small-mindedness of your peers.'

'I won't listen to any more of this!' Vincent shouted.

Loose bricks leapt from the wall toward Tamsin's head, only to be shattered after a few feet, shards spraying at the group of tappers who had to fling their arms up to protect their eyes.

'Perhaps it is true what they say about benders. If their brains were bigger, they might be dangerous.'

Vincent made to rush at her, but he was suddenly stopped in his tracks and pushed backward.

'Don't be an idiot, Vincent. I could drop you dead in an instant or get one of your friends to crush you slowly. So don't think there is anything you can do to hurt me. I came to talk. You will listen. Then, at the end, you can leave if you want.'

Vincent threw his arms up and turned away.

'We need a place of our own. You live here, down below, in a grey area. That is what the data men call it. A place where they do not have the surveillance that they do in the majority of the World Union. You hide here in the Cape, in places like this, blanket over your heads, but somehow Services keeps finding you, don't they? You hide. You all do. But you also know that if they wanted to, they could reach out and grab you at any time. I have hunted with them. I know they can bring any of us down. We need a place we can go and be safe.'

'You won't find it on this planet, psister.'

'You're right. We won't find one. We have to make one. Here. In Atlantic, Services is weak. There are only two bases.'

'Only two? How many times have you ever seen a Services base getting knocked down?'

'Never. But I've never tried before either. I've been with them for ten years — I know how they do things.'

'And Pierre?' Hiero asked.

'He is with us.' Tamsin nodded. 'He will aid us. I am sure of it.'

'You are, we can see that, but we don't share your confidence. Fanaticism does not impress me,' La Grêle chipped in.

'Will he repeat his manifestation here, Miz Grey? Destroying the city?' Salvator asked.

'He was attacked in Paris. He defended himself.'

'He certainly did,' La Grêle replied.

Sal cleared his throat. 'I believe it is my turn now. Obviously there are some innate emotions in play here. So, we should take into account, when thinking about Tamsin Grey's proposal, that there may already be an element of sympathy in our midst.

'I don't have much to say. If La Grêle tells me we can trust Grey, then that is good enough for me. But that is not the question. For me it still has to be determined if her plans are realistic, or even if the effects of them are desired. We all think a lot about being free, in the way that other humans are. It is the psi dream we all share. I have spoken of it many times with many different people. I was recently reminded of my own time in a Services area and how they came for me. I escaped, but so many do not. I cannot imagine what life is like for those who are taken.

'In the Cape, we are tolerated because they have found a use for us. We are lucky, relative to those on the islands. It is up to each of us as individuals to decide if we are happy with our circumstances.'

He stopped to take a deep breath.

'As much as I crave that dream, that life that all of us hope for, I do not believe in war. I do not believe that that will get us what we want.

'There are three actions open to us. Join Grey's rebellion and begin a life of fighting, killing and running until one side has defeated the other. Or we can abstain from taking part and simply watch to see how long the rebellion lasts. But if we want things to stay the same, then we must be prepared to stop Tamsin Grey now.'

'Doctor!' Tamsin leapt into a defensive stance and Okonta was instantly shielding her with his body. Then neither of them could move.

'No interruptions, Miz Grey,' La Grêle commanded. 'Everyone relax your attacks. We have them in hand.'

'Let me go,' Tamsin spat.

'Be quiet, Miz Grey, I just saved your life. Let us see how the rest of this conversation progresses. Alexi, did you have any more to say?'

'No. You can take your turn, La Grêle.'

The older woman stepped forward and spread her arms to include the group.

'Salvator has made excellent points, and as you know, open conflict has never been my approach. But ... change is coming. Change that I don't think we, or anyone, have the power to stop.

'I do not endorse Tamsin Grey's plan. I believe it will result in aggravating the World Union even further. Every act of psionic aggression leads to more restrictions and more hunts. I believe the Primacy will be more determined than ever to absorb Atlantic into their system. But it is your city and your lives, not mine.

'Another part of me wonders if Tamsin Grey is the only one of us seeing things clearly. Perhaps there is already a war taking place and she is the only one to recognise it. Maybe being on the other side of that war gives her a perspective we don't have. I know that outside the Cape, Services have been coming down hard on any suspects they have. Many of my people have disappeared; I must presume they have been taken. There is nowhere for a psi to hide now. Once the World Union has secured everywhere else, what is to stop them coming to Atlantic and imposing control?

'I don't think they will ever stop. So long as the system perceives a threat, be it Pierre Jnr or us, I don't think it can stop itself. And that is why I am willing to listen.

'If none of you have any objections, I will commune with Tamsin Grey. If she is withholding anything, I will find it out. I will discover her true motivations so we can know if we can trust her.'

None objected. Tamsin got the impression that no one ever did. 'It will be okay,' she said to Piri and Okonta. 'I don't believe she intends me any harm.'

'She is correct,' La Grêle said from close behind her. 'Your care for her is admirable, Okonta Bora, but in this instance misplaced. Your leader will come back to you safely.'

They cleared the room. Leaving just the two of them alone.

'Make yourself comfortable,' La Grêle said, gracefully assuming a cross-legged position on the floor. Tamsin mirrored her pose.

'Where do you come from, Miz Grey?'

'I do not know where I was born.'

'Would you like to?'

'Not really.'

La Grêle nodded. 'And your parents? Would you like to know who they were?'

'I have wondered in the past, but not any more.'

'I find that interesting.'

'Do you? What is so interesting about it? I've told you I was raised by Services.'

'Yes. But to not have an origin must have an interesting effect on the psyche. I'm not sure I understand that sort of mind.'

'Is this the communing?'

'No. I am building myself up for that. Communing involves getting closer to someone than you ever have before. So with you I am naturally hesitant.'

'I guess I should thank you for your honesty,' Tamsin replied.

'Have you known many telepaths in your time?'

'I've met hundreds.'

'Do you mean collected?'

'Look, can't we just lower our blocks and have a real conversation?'

'Not yet,' La Grêle replied. 'And this is real conversation. The items you prefer not to discuss, the topics you skip across, it all communicates.'

'Well, you're not communicating very much. So that makes this a one-way conversation,' Tamsin objected and stood up.

La Grêle looked at her with pale eyes. 'I am communicating in questions, Tamsin. I am asking you about your past, your experience. Obviously I ask to test your level of exposure, your knowledge. I have learnt much about you already.'

'If you're so against me, why are we bothering with this charade?'

'I shall forgive you, for I know you have lived a sheltered life. It is often hard for people who have never had friendships to know how to begin them.' She sighed and straightened her back. 'Please, sit back down. Just a few more questions before we open ourselves up.'

Tamsin relented and sat, folding her legs beneath her.

'What has Salvator told you about me?' La Grêle asked.

'Nothing at all. Only that he would take your opinion over his own.'

'That is a very high compliment. What have you deduced so far?'

'You are obviously a very competent telepath with a lot of influence in the psi underground.'

'Obviously. The reason I asked about your past, Grey, is that I wanted to know if you had had much exposure to telepaths. If you had any teachers.'

'None.'

'My mother and father were telepaths. They taught me everything they knew.' La Grêle closed her eyes and pushed herself out, washing Tamsin with the experience she had of her parents.

Tamsin had no response to that. The possibility had never occurred to her. A lump rose in her throat and her chest felt like it couldn't move to breathe. All her memories swirled into one single word.

'Saudade,' she whispered.

'I don't know what that means,' La Grêle said.

She repeated it, not knowing herself. 'I just remember this,' she said, touching her hand to the empty place she felt on her chest where her heartbeat was strongest. 'Saudade.'

'Take my hands,' La Grêle said. 'This is a good place to start.'

Tamsin put out shaky hands and let the older woman take them.

'Now lower your block.'

'What have you done to me? I'm not like this.' This was similar to what Arthur had done to her. She began to raise her block.

'Please, Tamsin. Just this one time, trust a stranger. Let your mind flow to me.'

She did as she was asked.

*I talk. You listen*, La Grêle explained firmly. *One of the saddest things about the oppression of our kind, Tamsin, is that we are born with these abilities and have to discover how to use them without any help. What could we do if we had a teacher to show us the way? I am one of the lucky ones. My parents had the ability and they taught me what they could. Together we discovered even more.*

La Grêle kept her thoughts calm. She dropped Tamsin's hands, stood and began walking in a circle around Tamsin as she communicated. *Let my mind swim around yours.* Tamsin saw La Grêle's parents, the long afternoons spent together. Traversing the southern continent, hiding, but always in contact with each other.

*You might have to do this someday, so be aware. It can be very dangerous if we both slip away and neither of us can manage to detach. While we are connected this way, we will be like two drops of ink in water. At first we have different colours, but the longer we swim together, the more time passes, the more mixed we will become.*

Together they slipped into a shallow coma, their bodies stilling. Their minds, however, became one pool. They knew everything there was to know about the other. Everything that had ever happened to one, had happened to the other.

*I try to pass on as much as I can so it is not lost should anything happen to me.*

*How selfless of you.*

*You are strong. I can sense that. You have proven that. You do not need to keep proving it. Not tonight.*

*What are you doing?* Tamsin demanded.

*Shhh. You will have to trust me, Tamsin Grey. Or you will get no help from me.*

*But what are you doing?*

*I'm showing you what you should be fighting for.*

Tamsin didn't remember being so young, or so short. She had no control of what her body was doing. She just stood there, twisting back and forth restlessly.

'Saudade,' a man's voice said to her. She couldn't repeat the word. She was only small.

The man was now before her. He had one big hand on her shoulder and the other touching the place where his heart beat. She had learnt that. The heart beats in the chest, not in the centre, a little to the left.

'Saudade,' he said again.

*That is a Portuguese word*, La Grêle explained.

*How do you know?*

*Because you knew. This man is your father.*

*Why can't I see him properly?*

*Because you were young. A lot has happened to you since then.*

*What is he saying to me? Why is he saying nothing but that one word?*

*I think he was upset. This is the day they came for you.*

*I don't remember that. Did they hurt him?*

*I don't know. I only know what you know.*

*What does it mean?*

*I can't be sure. Memory is not perfect. Your father is trying to project an emotion upon you, but you are just getting sadder and sadder.*

*It sounds like 'sad'.*

*No, it is more complicated than that. It is like a sadness over something that can never be, or never was. It is the feeling of loss when nothing has been lost.*

*And my mother? Where is she? Can I see her?*

*You don't have any memories of her. I'm sorry.*

*It's okay. Just take me away. I can't bear it.*

'Saudade,' her father said, tapping at his chest.

The memory faded away to be replaced by another.

They stood at a window in a stone wall. They were one body with two minds peeking out.

*It's about to happen.*

Tamsin watched as the nose of a black limousine floated into her line of sight. She regulated her breath. Slowly the limo came forward, a languorous pace. It seemed to linger more than it progressed. The wait was unbearable.

*Pierre ...?*

She didn't mean to. She wished she could take it back, but she needed to know what was inside.

In shock, she punched at the car, knocking it in from both sides, but it was already too late. A ravine opened between her and the target, fountains of dust shooting in every direction. The cloud came straight at her, tore the window in two and darkness took over ...

*You warned him?*

*I didn't know if it was him or not. I wasn't even sure he existed.*

*But now you put your faith in him?*

*Yes.*

*And what does he intend?*

*I don't know ... Can you help me remember my time with him?*

*No. There seem to be no memories of your days together. Only this moment ...*

Tamsin was walking down a linoleum corridor, black and white tiles, black white, black white. She had just left Peter Lazarus, telling him that she was going to escape. She felt annoyed and upset and then there was a small hand holding hers.

*That is where it ends.*

*Pierre ...*

*He is real.*

*You weren't sure?*

*How can one be sure of that? My network has reported nothing.*

Their thoughts seemed more distinguishable now.

*You can feel us separating?*

*Yes.*

*Good. We'll go slow. I want you to know how to end a commune. It's important. Imagine a rope's threads, bound and entwined. The threads unfurling, spreading apart.*

*I can't believe you have been able to hide from Services for so long.*

*Right under their noses.*

*Will you help me?*

*I won't risk everything, but I will help.*

*Thank you ... Thank you for showing me my father.*

Tamsin woke calm.

La Grêle was standing beside her, adjusting her drapery back into position. 'Now you and I are not so different.'

343

Yes. Tamsin had absorbed some of her colour. She knew La Grêle's past, but it wasn't just a sharing of knowledge; she had felt her emotions and experienced how she thought. She was changed. 'I never knew about that.'

'We have never had the chance to grow our own culture. It makes me very angry,' La Grêle said.

'Angry enough?'

'I took some of yours.' La Grêle smiled and stroked Tamsin's cheek gently. 'It's good to know you are human.'

'Don't feel sorry for me. You haven't had it so easy yourself.'

'But at least I was able to be myself. Now you must do that. Your life cannot just be about the fight.'

'It will have to be for now.'

Tamsin reached up to let her finger touch the soft and downy skin of the older woman. They had been one.

*We know what we must do.*

*We know what we must do.*

That night Tamsin couldn't sleep. She was excited. The adrenalin of the day hadn't worn off and her visions of what was to come filled her with trepidation and bliss. A place for psis to exist and learn. It hadn't occurred to her until it had been said.

In the dark she held her hand out. *Are you there, Pierre?* She could picture him. She could. But then she couldn't. Was he there and hiding from her? Or had he left her? *Why are you doing this? Why are you silent? Am I doing what you want?*

Then she thought of Pete. Why was she thinking of a man she'd only known for a few days … she really didn't want to know. She had enjoyed taunting him, that much she could admit.

*What is he thinking of me now?* she wondered. Probably trying to decide if she was a traitor or a puppet. She didn't feel like a puppet. And how could she be betraying something she hated? Or was he right about Pierre?

*Please, Pierre. Just let me know.*

The Sullivan expedition and the interviews left Pete exhausted and disturbed.

He rewound the conversations in his head. Everything Sullivan had said was touched with unreality, probably from long-term drug use, but his insights into how psionics worked presented Pete with a new framework. He'd never previously questioned how his abilities worked; he had them, he used them. He understood now why Tamsin's trick was so hard to comprehend at first and then so easy after.

'Just a puppet.' Sullivan didn't even know him and he'd managed to pinpoint Pete's worry. Tamsin had warned him of the same thing. 'Don't be a puppet, Pete.' He had been so determined not to come under Pierre's control that he had put himself in the hands of others. *I walked right in off the street. Services just used me as a decoy and I let myself be used.*

He remembered his last day. A motel room. A restaurant and an empty chair. The sand of the beach under his toes. A last swim. Nothing before that.

*Peter Lazarus, the puppet.* Next to him in the squib was Gock. The proxy and the puppet. Not so different after all.

There was no exit from his thought spiral. Everything twisted back in on itself. Was he a real person or not? Had Pierre reprogrammed him? How could a man go through thirty-five years and not develop any relationships? He closed his eyes and saw those staring eyes. Tranquillity in the midst of a huge scarred head. *What have you done to me?*

Pete felt every metre of the tower as they ascended rapidly in the elevator, his stomach dropping further into his feet and the pain of his weary muscles pulsing.

He knew someone was in the needle before the doors opened, and then he found her standing at the window in the crescent lounge. She was besotted with the view and he had a moment to admire her before she noticed him. He had never seen her with her hair loose. It ended in the small of her back, tips curling in.

*Anchali?*

*Peter?*

'Nurse Anchali, what are you doing here?' he asked out loud.

'I've come to —' She collapsed into his arms and started shaking.

'What's wrong? It's okay.' He held her close. He sent soothing messages to her through the bond.

It came out in drips how she was removed from the outpost when he'd left. After he and the others were gone, they put the compound back into storage. Anchali thought she was being transported to her next assignment but found herself in a black box and the next thing she knew there was a voice offering her a choice between going to the islands or doing what they wanted.

*Which kind of island did they mean?*

'They know, Pete. Oh, the gods, they know.' She sobbed, barely getting her words out.

He hushed her and sat with her on the couch, ordering water from the kitchen.

*Did you get word out?*

*I never had a chance.*

*What about the friends you told me about? Are they safe?*

*I haven't told Services anything, I swear.*

*Of course you didn't, but can they help you escape?*

*Maybe, but they wouldn't expose themselves just for me. It would be too risky. They don't even know where I am.*

'It's okay. It will be alright,' he repeated. *Why have they brought you here? What do they want from you?*

*They haven't told me. I was just told that you would be here.*

*I think you might be a reward for good behaviour.*

*What do you mean?*

*It's part of their process, Anchali. This reorientation is just behavioural conditioning. That's what they've been doing since I left the hospital, teaching me to follow orders. If I do wrong, I get punished. If I do well, I get rewarded.*

She pulled away from him and retreated back to the window. *What do they think I am?*

*I think they just know how I feel about you.*

Pete tried to take her hand, but she pulled it away. *Did you tell them about me?*

*Anchali, no. I would never. Look inside me, you can see I haven't betrayed you.*

She looked directly into his eyes and took both of his hands in her small fingers. *Did you tell Services about me?*

'No,' Pete answered.

Her eyes were still wet, and she blinked to clear them. *My life is over*, she realised and collapsed into deeper misery. Pete steadied her wavering balance until she managed to take hold of herself again.

*Who is that man?*

Gock had been standing behind them the whole time. Greasy smile and fondling eyes sliding over Anchali's backside.

'Let's go to my room.' *That one is always near me. He is the Prime's proxy.*

*I don't like him.*

*I'm not sure it is possible to like him.*

'How long will you be here?' he asked when they were alone, though aware that he was still watched in his room.

'I don't know. I know that you're leaving again tomorrow.'

'Tomorrow?' He needed rest. *He is wearing me down, Anchali. Since you saw me …* 'It seems you know more than I.' *I'm not sure how much longer I can do this.*

*You must be strong, Peter. Don't let them break you.*

*It may be too late for that.*

*No. I can see you have changed since I saw you last. But you are still strong. Still you.*

*I have done things that I regret. I've turned against my own kind, just to earn the trust of the Prime. I do everything he asks me to and he only becomes more suspicious.*

*Peter, you don't gain trust by doing what people say. It is only when you put your trust in them that they may start trusting you. If you want his trust, you have to give him something.*

*You mean, something that gives him more power over me?*

*That is how it works.*

*It doesn't matter now.*

*What do you mean?*

*He's done it already. I am full of doubt now. What if he is right? What if Pierre Jnr is not the only threat? What if this psi rebellion is just as bad? Whose side will you be on?*

*You have to ask?*

They had lain down next to each other for their silent conversation. Her eyes were so close to his, soft as butter, her mouth near enough to feel her exhales on his lips.

'You are beautiful.'

'Shhh, Peter.' *Don't let them see you weak.*

'Oh, why not? He knows my weaknesses. Don't you, Prime?' Pete snarled at the ceiling. 'He's got me all figured out. That's why you're here.'

'Please stop.' *At least I am happy to see you.*

*But he knows now. He knows you are a psi and he'll never let you go.*

*Who knows how long they have known?*

*And what does he expect of you?*

*Does it matter? Forget the Prime. Forget everything. It may not be the best circumstance, but we are together. I care for you. And I know you care for me.*

*Of course I do. I wish I didn't. I wish he didn't know how much I needed someone.*

*Peter. The reasons why don't matter. You don't have to be alone.*

*You were an excellent nurse.*

She kissed him softly and then deeply. Peter didn't resist. He was so hungry for contact.

It was the final morning of Peter Lazarus's scheduled reorientation, the day after he had accepted his reward so readily. Ryu did not watch the ménage, leaving that for Takashi to peruse.

Ryu had Gock waiting for him to wake. Gock was a loyal and accurate messenger and watched his subject like a toad.

Whenever he spoke to Peter Lazarus, he put the surveillance feeds from the needle and his proxy's eyes up on the wall screen of his command room. A spread of six cameras and microphones that gave the discussions a near-sensorium experience. It was much more visceral than talking face to face with somebody. The close-up shots revealed so much more than was possible in person; so much more intimate, but still objective and perfectly one-sided.

Ryu studied Peter as he waited for Gock to speak. Gock was waiting for Ryu to tell him what to say. Everyone waited for the Prime to speak first. He started brushing his hair for washing.

*Divide each problem into two steps: definition and solution. Which for the psi problem meant: identification then pacification.*

These were the principles that had got him through thus far. *Confine the problem*, Ryu told himself. *The first step in complex problem solving is to clarify and identify all components.*

But he knew that that wasn't the only way of understanding. And it wasn't the right way to understand a systemic problem that required a holistic approach; holism didn't allow such separation of factors. The psionic situation had certainly gone beyond reducible components.

A grave fear was creeping up on Ryu. The testimonies and abilities of Sullivan St Clare and Arthur Grimaldi had given this situation a new worst-case scenario. The Will was under threat of being artificially manipulated. Although the Will was the Will and it was always manipulated, this was different.

Geof's contagion theory, the infection model, was on his mind and Ryu couldn't help now being suspicious of anyone who came near him. Any of them could be a psi, or could have come into contact with Pierre Jnr. He wondered if he could reduce his human contact even further, for security.

It had been six weeks since he had taken the psi under his control. That was the standard reorientation period for a normal Citizen who had fallen into antisocial behaviour. He had taught him to respond to his orders, he had engaged his abilities in self-defence and he had him aid in the collection of two fugitive psis. Ryu did not, and would never, trust him. But as long as Pete was under control, he would use him.

'I would like you to tell me about your nightmares. Do you dream of him?'

'Is that you asking, Gock? Or your master?' Peter replied, still resistant.

'Gock does not ask, Mister Lazarus. You must know that by now. Please answer.'

Pete, still dressed in his bed clothes, sat across the island bench, looking the bald man in the eyes. This was the masterful stroke that Ryu Shima had made by acting through a proxy. No telepath could get a read on what the other person would say next, and they would be distracted by the thoughts of the person reciting. He felt sorry for Gock in some ways, but he knew he was being handsomely rewarded.

'Yes,' Peter answered, pausing to order a biscuit, caf and juice; the symbiot was second nature to him now. 'I dream of him.'

'I am glad you have not denied it.'

'I know you've got sensors on me all the time, so you must know when I'm dreaming something. For all I know, you might have another spy like Tamsin Grey hidden in the walls, reading my every thought.'

'Please, there is no cause for paranoia. Tell me what happens in your dreams.'

'To be honest, there isn't a lot to tell. He just holds me there, in front of him. His eyes burn into mine. That's all. At least, that's all I ever remember.'

'And you have been having these dreams since the manifestation?'

'Yes. Most nights I have the same dream.'

'And how do they make you feel? Please, answer honestly.'

'Scared. Helpless.'

'And do you know about the movement following Pierre Jnr?'

'No. My access to the Weave is limited.'

'Let me show you.' He fed Pete's symbiot with images and footage that the psi then overlaid on his vision. He showed him the offerings that were being placed at the site of the manifestation, and people praying to images of Pierre Jnr. He shared a poster image that was being swapped around: a photo of Pierre Jnr as a newborn that must have escaped the walls of the PDP archive. It had been reconstituted with the heart-warming glow and symbols of religious iconography.

'How much of this is taking place?' Pete asked.

'It is only a small sect. Only a few hundred people.'

'Can't you stop it?'

'That is not the way of the World Union, Mister Lazarus. People are allowed to express how they feel. You are one of the few who have met him. Do you think he is a god?'

'No. He is powerful. But he is no god.'

'He has followers, and his followers are building an army.'

'For what purpose?' Pete asked.

'There is only one purpose I know of for an army.'

'I mean, what will they do? Who will they attack? You?'

'That would be logical. Me and anyone who is actively opposing them.'

'But where does it stop?'

'I'm sorry, Peter. But I cannot see into the future. I presume you cannot either.' Lazarus shook his head. 'Do you see now why I have been paying such close attention to you?'

'To fight fire with fire?'

'Not exactly. I need more from you than that. I need you to help me stop this war before it can begin.'

'How?' Pete asked.

'In conflict, if you react to your opponent's actions, it means they are in control. They strike, you strike back. If they

353

strike and you retaliate, then they have provoked your action. Countering is not the same as reacting. Respond. Never react. Only choose the action that will achieve the result you desire.'

'Meaning we do what?'

'It means we will take the battle to them. We know where the fugitives are hiding.'

'And you want me to help capture them?'

'The word we use is "collect", Peter. We collect them and put them in a nicer place.'

'A place they can never leave.'

'As is the Will. There are worse solutions.'

'And what about Pierre?'

'Until we find out where he is hiding, our best course of action is to prepare.'

Pete pondered this for a time. In his rooms Ryu finished his brushing and began rubbing dry shampoo into his hair, rolling the long strands between his palms until the powder disappeared. The script Takashi had generated for this conversation was hardly deviating at all.

'You're right. I hate that you're right,' Pete said. 'If there is an army of psis ready to fight alongside Pierre, then we need to be ready to fight back.'

'Are you telling me this to please me?' Ryu asked.

'I know I will never earn your trust, but I have to pick a side, and the side I am on, and have always been on, is that one person shall not have dominion over another.'

'I couldn't have put it better myself.'

'May I ask you a question?'

'Certainly,' Ryu granted.

'How could I ever be ready for Pierre Jnr? He is much more powerful than I. You must realise this, so you must have a plan.'

'Of course. You are just one of many contingencies being co-ordinated. I hope that comforts you.' He told Gock to smile.

Lazarus nodded almost imperceptibly, though it was huge on Ryu's screens.

'Can you help me learn?'

The Prime watched him. Made him wait for the next words. He was in control here.

'I can only challenge you and prompt you to become more fluent.'

'But you hate psis. Why help train one?'

'I do what needs to be done. You are the lesser of two evils.'

'I guess that is the best I can hope for.'

'For the record, I do not hate psionics. I am merely an agent of the Will. Our society is not capable of coping with such a drastic change to the status quo.' Ryu watched his toy for a moment. 'I would like you to consider something for me.' He paused for Peter to become curious enough to listen closely. 'There is a fear I have that once people have been in contact with Pierre Jnr, that even after contact is broken, his influence remains. Have you considered this?'

'I've seen it. We saw it at the farm a few weeks ago, and I saw it in my sister.'

'Again, we have no record of a second child born to your parents.'

'What are you suggesting?'

Ryu ignored the question and moved on. 'I am also of the understanding that even before you confronted Pierre Jnr under the Dome, you reported some memory loss. Or rather, it was reported about you. Do you feel that to be true?'

'Is this really you, Ryu Shima? These questions do not sound like you.'

'How do they sound?'

'Almost gentle.'

'There is something I want from you, and I have determined that this approach is the best way to get it.' He didn't say that it was thanks to one of Takashi's simulations that he had found the best strategy.

'Your kindness is appreciated.'

'Have you ever thought that the manifestation was not your first contact with Pierre Jnr? That perhaps you encountered him some time ago?'

'No.'

'No? It is not possible? Or, no, you have not considered it?' Gock resisted an urge to smile at Pete's discomfort. 'Perhaps you had no sister and it was you that sought out Pierre Jnr, as many escaped psis do. Looking for their saviour. Perhaps you found him and he did to you what you believe he did to her.'

'What? And then sent me to Services to volunteer to hunt him down?'

'Perhaps.'

'Why?'

'If only I knew. But the possibility worries me.'

The elevator doors opened and the entire ten squad entered the main room, followed by Risom, Arthur and the twinbots. With Pete, their count was fifteen. With Gock, fifteen and a half.

'Where are we going that we'll need an entourage like this?' Pete asked, the answer flashing into the minds of everyone in the room at once. Of course, the answer was so obvious he should have guessed.

'You should say goodbye to Nurse Anchali. You leave for the Cape within the hour.'

When he clicked off, he watched Pete's reaction and didn't notice his brother waiting for him at the doorway.

'That was curious, Ryu san. Why'd you do that to him?' Takashi asked.

'I merely discussed with him a possibility he might not have thought of.'

'But why give the information away?'

'Why shouldn't I?' Ryu exploded with frustration. 'Takashi, do you realise that it has been over a month since the manifestation and we still don't know who or what caused it?'

'In my defence, I did know that,' Takashi replied, but Ryu was talking over him already.

'You ask me why I contributed to Peter Lazarus's paranoid condition? I did it because I need to know where it ends.'

'Where what ends?'

'Pierre's influence. We have to assume that Lazarus's contact with Pierre has left him reprogrammed, but the question is: does it spread? Is it contagious?'

'Brother, you've gone insane.'

'Have I? If we acknowledge the existence of psionic powers, mind control, then we have to acknowledge the next logical step. It would be like a more potent form of brainwashing, and if it was done to one person with telepathy, why wouldn't it

357

spread? You have to acknowledge the possibility, despite the improbability.'

'Are you suggesting a sort of mental contagion rather than a cultural virus?'

'It may be unlikely. Ozenbach's analysis implies it would have either happened already, or it wasn't going to.'

'But why did you want Lazarus to fear it?'

'For two reasons: one is that, if it is possible, he might be able to help prove it. But, more to the point, Takashi, if you want to train an animal, first you must break its spirit.'

'And then what will you do?'

'Then you train the animal to react how you want it to. Apply stimuli, apply reward or punishment. It is basic conditioning.'

'Ryu san, I am glad you have never put your attentions upon me.'

Ryu laughed out loud. Takashi always had a knack for making him laugh. 'Tell me, Takashi, the simulation you have of me. How good is it?'

A small boy sat patiently in a chair before a glowing terminal. He was facing into the aisle of cubicles where men and women of all ages had their backs turned, hunching and leaning forward, intent behind their goggles.

This café boasted the most comfortable set-up for long uninterrupted immersions. People sat in their chairs for hours, completely indrawn. Servitors worked their way around the room, delivering drinks, nibbles and the occasional hot towel wash.

The most serious divers in the room wore ganzfeld

suits, thick hoods and bodysuits that shielded their senses from outside stimulation, so as not to distract them in their immersions. They moved the least of all the weavers in the room, neither scratching nor sucking on straws, just held upright with seat belts across their chests, drip tubes into their necks and servitors keeping the corners of their mouths dry.

The thoughts in this room were like a waterfall. Thousands of drops a second, making up the stream they created in the virtual space. Pierre had no need to plug in himself. He was connected to a roomful of people who were.

Pete woke in the air. The jet would only take an hour longer to arrive and he used the time to sieve information from the squad's minds. As always, he used conversation to focus their minds to what he was interested in learning.

'Ten?'

'Yes, Peter Lazarus?'

'Have you been to the Cape before?'

He was surprised by the memories the question triggered amongst the soldiers. Atlantic was where muscle like these went to play. The town had no law, not like in the WU. Every now and then, when on leave, they stayed together in their pack and went spoiling for an opportunity to inflict justice. They went to serve and protect the denizens of the Cape, like avenging angels who then enjoyed reaping rewards for their deeds.

Pete remembered spending time there too, though only fragments, mostly empty hotel rooms … Shima was right. If he didn't remember the years before the hunt began, what could he trust of what he did recall?

As far as the Weave went, Atlantic was one of the most consolidated areas of grey patches. It was the obvious place to hide if you were a psi. The lack of Services monitoring made it an attractive part of the world and he had spent much time there.

He found himself muttering out loud, 'As they say in the Cape, no one cares if you scream.'

'Ha!' Ten barked in amusement. 'Except when Services is in town.'

Atlantic really was a city of brights and darks. Many areas were unlit at night, creating dark patches between streets that were a tumble of colour, each trying to outshine the others with light projections, multi-hued paving, hanging lights and fire.

The WU had two identical embassies in the Cape, one in the south, the other in the north where the team was heading. Services had established a square kilometre of order. Regular white street lighting lined up over grey poly-paved streets. The compound itself was a sand-coloured fort with a fifty-metre killing field on all sides. Peter wished the soldiers didn't think of every open space as a killing field.

The embassy was of military design: an external wall with the main building running along the inside and a large internal courtyard for protected landing and takeoff. Geometrically it was a perfect cube, though a third of it was unseen below the ground level.

The transport landed and Pete, the ten, Gock, Arthur and Risom had enough time to drop their kits before their first appointment. Pete and Arthur were able to maintain a link even though their rooms were on opposite sides of the compound, but Risom was just out of his reach.

*Arthur, have you been here before?*

*Many times.*

*What do you think?*

*I prefer the forest.*

*Why do you think we are here?*

*The same reason you do. This is the obvious place to hide. Here is where the Prime has determined the front line to be.*

*Risom seems happy.*

*His ego looks forward to proving itself.*

*I'm sorry I got you into this.*

*Don't be. I understand the coercion that controls you. And, to be honest, even though this euphoria of mine is artificial, it is still much nicer than before.*

*Betraying one's own has its rewards.*

*Now you're thinking like Risom.*

They gathered back in the courtyard. The only team members missing were the twins, whose real bodies were stationed in the southern embassy, to keep them away from the psis. Their bots would join the ten as shadow for the agents.

'What's the command, Ten?' Pete asked.

'Peter Lazarus, we are on field protocols now. You will speak when told to do so. Is that clear?'

'Clear, sir.'

'That goes for everyone, including you, Gock. If any of you fall out of line, I am authorised to take disciplinary action. Is that clear?'

'Yes, sir,' they answered.

'I am aware that none of you, barring Risom here, has had a Services upbringing, but that will not be considered an excuse. The Cape area is not like other parts of the world. There is no WU and the only Services to help you are here, and one hundred klicks south and west. Your symbs have been loaded up with situational strategies should the team become separated or attacked. You will be on constant ping so Services know where you are at all times. If you need help, they will respond.

'You may have heard that the Cape is a wild and uncivilised society, and that there is no law. But that is not true. Here we work by the law of the jungle. Our best defence is to make sure that your shadow is seen and your bark is heard. The squad and the twins will be in plain sight. Make sure there is a squad member in front of you and one behind at all times. Do not proceed without an escort. Is that clear?'

'Yes, sir.'

'Okay then. Squad, power up. We are heading east. The command will be delivered en route.'

They piled into two open-topped hovers and eased out into the killing field, laser portcullis flashing on and off to let them through.

It was past midnight. Pete wondered who they could be going to see.

*Atlantic is more active at night, Pete.*

As they were leaving the Services zone, one of the streetlights overhead exploded. They didn't stop, but Pete and Arthur turned to look back at the second car. Risom was grinning.

*Just practising my aim.*

* * *

Nothing could prepare Pete for the sights and sounds of Atlantic street life. The first lit street they went through was almost blinding after the dark of its surrounds. Every building had attempted to be unique with its light show, using colour, movement, pulsation and saturation as originally as they could. Many people in the Cape lived in garish hotels rather than keeping their own homes, and spent their leisure time gaming or exploring their mind state.

The other thing that was easily observed about the Cape was that people were more obviously cybernetic. With the casual attitude to violence, it was common to see a replaced finger, or patent skin graft. They were open to it. Many of the locals couldn't afford perfect cosmetic installations, so alteration had become accepted and even a little fashionable.

Adolescents confused the streets, standing in chittering blocks, dressed in the latest fashions of pragnancz patterns and geometric hats. Freaking and cyberism were popular, each trying to be weirder than the next. Many were ready for violence with taloned nails, or fangs, or, for the cybers, blades and saws that rose from their arms and hands. It was also an opportunity for toughs to rig their add-ons with snitch blades and barbs. Pete could tell that many of them had found an excuse to use them.

From what Pete could detect, and from Arthur's observations, a great proportion of the people on the streets were Citizens. Visiting.

*That's where the money comes from*, Arthur explained.

*Is it all money here?*

*Without civics there is only money. Unless you're a gamer.*

Few lived in the border area between the zones. Apartment buildings were broken down and even the floors were cracked open, making dark holes to fall through. Pete realised that even on these streets the inhabitants were considered wealthy.

In the eyes of the WU, any non-Citizen was a denizen, a person who wasn't a part of any society. To the people of the Cape, dennies were the ones who made their beds on the streets, or in the basement underneath. They took what they could, however they could get it. They were the ones to be avoided. They were the ones you didn't want to touch you.

Soon enough they were in another bright street behind some impassable traffic. Ahead of them a crowd of people was jumping up and down, screaming ecstatically as other people were arriving at a big gaming arena called the TigerPark, which distinguished itself with twenty-foot holographic tigers that stalked the entrance.

'Permission to speak, sir?'

'What is it, Lazarus?'

'I wondered if you knew what was happening ahead.'

'Just one of the big gamers. SmithGo, he calls himself. It's a scheduled show match. We should be able to get past in a minute.'

Behind the crowd Pete saw what he thought was a denny. A middle-aged woman whose rags were barely able to hold themselves together. She shuffled toward the lights and noise. Pete could detect nothing from her mind.

*Is she blocked?*

*She's a drool. They have them around here*, Risom replied.

Pete accessed the files in his symb. 'Drools' was a term the locals of the Cape used to describe the brain-dead denizens who had started appearing on the streets. Mostly they fell asleep and died unnoticed, or stumbled about with only a handful of words and almost total loss of bodily control. Services' hypothesis was that they were people who had run afoul of the local psis and had had their minds so brutally tampered with they no longer functioned on a conscious level.

*Or Pierre?* Pete thought.

*You wish*, Risom answered.

*He could be here …*

*I do not think the drool was made by him. It feels different,* Arthur interjected.

*We should get you to visit the people from the farm we found to see if it is the same.*

*As you wish.*

As the drool got closer to the crowd, two men in tiger-striped uniforms closed in on her from either side and lifted her by the arms. They carried her down an alley to dump her further away.

The complex they arrived at was huge. Bigger than the Services compound and the TigerPark. The welcoming plaza held a large circular pool that caught the co-ordinated downpour of four waterfalls and a lively central fountain. Water and light jumped to the music that emanated from within.

Ten let the squad roam and put Seven as front guard and took the rear position himself. The Jackpot! was ten levels of music, gambling machines and gaming mats; layer upon layer of people trying out their luck or just losing themselves in the hedonism.

'Welcome to the Jackpot! What pleasure do you seek?'

'None, thank you. We're here to see Boris Arkady,' Pete answered the glittering girl who came to greet them.

She blinked and ran a message through the management system. Pete noticed something odd about her eyes. He couldn't help but stare into them to see. She had been freaked with false irises with light and dark spirals that slowly spun the longer he looked. All the hosts at the Jackpot! had them. It was part of the uniform, like the e-ttoos on her skin and the extensions in her hair.

She went wide-eyed as the request was instantly processed. Almost nobody got through to see Mister Arkady. She herself had never met the man who owned the Jackpot! and was one of the most powerful people in Atlantic.

'Of course you are, Mister Lazarus. Did you want me to take you to him right away?'

Pete motioned for the girl to lead them forward through the throng. Gock leered at the amount of flesh that was displayed, as nubiles of both genders wandered the parlours, sharing drinks and gentle touches with the players. They were employed by the house, a mix of flesh and fleshbots; in the frenzied lighting it was impossible to tell. He couldn't break his gaze from a dwarfish blonde girl who knew he was looking and shuffled her bosom to the music.

Peter wasn't familiar with any of the games that were being run. Frenzy, Mark, Jesuo; Warball he'd heard of from the squad, though he picked up Seven's cynicism that it wasn't the same game in immersion.

'The Jackpot! has every kind of game on offer. Immersive, physical, overlay and any combo you can imagine,' the girl explained habitually as she led them to an elevator deep in the building. Each time they passed through different lighting her skin would change, as if she had fluorescent glitter scattered over her.

'Is it always this busy?'

'Busy, yes, but not always this rowdy. It's nearly tournament season, so the players are showing off, trying to get picked for teams. It's a good time to have a good time.' She winked at them both.

'I'm not sure that is what my keepers have in mind for me,' Pete answered.

'You mean this one? I'm sure we can keep him distracted for you if you want to play for a while.'

'I wish I could.'

'No problem. I'll be here when you come back down. Don't forget to say hi.' She indicated the elevator slit that irised open in the carpeted wall.

Gock let out a pleased sigh as the elevator led them through the building, up and across, until it once again opened, this time in a large room that was simultaneously plush and austere. The flooring was black polished marble, broken up with white fur rugs and ivory stands that held oversized candles.

A man was sitting with his back to them. He wore white to match the lounges, stools and tables.

'Come in, come in.' He beckoned casually, obviously not wanting to rise from his newly acquired seating. 'Come join me over here,' he said without turning to face them.

The soldiers stayed by the entrance even though with the aperture closed the exit was non-existent. Peter and Gock moved to sit with their host.

The owner of Jackpot! waited, making no rush to interact. He regarded them and sipped at a glass of bubbly water. Peter, in turn, took the time to study this new entrant in his life. He was getting more information now than he ever had from Services.

Sometime in the past, Arkady had had his arms replaced with two elegant cybernetic prosthetics. His suit was cut tight and sleeveless so they were always on show. When he smiled, he revealed a convex wall of mirrored dentures.

They sat this way for a full two minutes, each waiting for the other to speak first. Arkady's furniture had a strange smell to it, which was quickly explained by his host's thoughts. *The cretin doesn't appreciate real leather when he sits on it.*

'Real leather, really? How much does something like this cost?' Peter asked.

'Cost? You don't pay for goods like these. Only influence can acquire something of this rarity ... Was that you reading my thoughts?'

'Am I the cretin?' Pete smiled.

Arkady mirrored his smile. It was cold and professional. As calculated as an emoticon in a message. 'Can I get you a glass of water?'

'Please.'

A servitor brought a ridiculously tall glass of iced water for each of them.

'I don't really believe in telepaths, do you know that? Can you prove it to me?' Arkady asked.

'I know already that you have employed telepaths in the past to clear your casinos. How can you not believe?' Pete asked.

Boris smiled, mirrors bouncing the candle flames back at Pete. 'I employ people who say they are telepaths. Whether they are or not ... The numbers don't lie. Profits are always higher after a tapper has been through.'

'And that is not evidence enough?'

'Evidence — not proof.' Arkady closed his mirror smile. 'The truth is, I don't care if they are psionic or not, so long as the end result is in my favour.'

'So why did you want to talk to me?' Pete asked.

'Can't you pluck it from my mind? Really, what is the point of being able to read someone's mind if you don't make use of it?'

'If that is your wish. Most people like to keep their thoughts private.'

Boris snorted. 'Get on with it.'

'I will ask you some questions, just to lead your mind where I want it. It will speed things up if you cooperate.'

'As you can see,' he leant back on his couch, arms out on either side, 'I am nothing if not cooperative.'

'You are a Citizen of the WU?'

'Yes.'

'You have been in contact with the Prime?'

'Yes.'

369

'Through a man called Zim?'

'General Zim to you, but yes, I only think of him as Zim. He is on the Primacy council.'

Now that Arkady was thinking of more than intimidating his guest with silence, Pete could skim his thoughts easily enough. 'You have something to show me?'

'Yes, but I wanted to meet you first. It is not a part of your investigation, but the Prime and I came to an agreement.'

'You leant on Shima and the Prime was obliged,' Pete clarified.

'Something like that. I own a piece of this town, we have much to offer each other.'

'So what do you want with me?'

'You are the only eyewitness. I want to hear it from you.' Arkady tapped his glass with an anxious finger.

'Have you not heard my statements?' He had, but Boris was the kind of person who needed to get information first-hand. 'What is your interest?'

'It is the most significant event in our lifetime. Why wouldn't I be interested?'

'I really don't have any more to add.'

'You saw him?'

'Yes.'

'What did he look like?'

Pete saw those eyes, that boy, the tranquillity of death … 'Just a nasty boy with a big head. I don't like discussing it.'

Boris Arkady sat still for a moment, toying with his glass. He was tempted to ask more questions, just for the fun of it. He was fascinated with the manifestation, and had even acquired a small collection of debris from the site. He was going to have a cabinet made for them.

'My apologies. I was just curious. Let me show you why you're here.' He tapped the table and it switched to screen mode. With a gesture, a show of images appeared before them.

'We have been seeing this symbol appearing throughout the Cape. Do you recognise it?' Arkady slid through image after image of graffiti markings: the three-pronged Y they'd seen in the psi breakout. 'It's an ancient Greek letter: psi.'

'We've seen it,' Ryu-Gock answered before Pete could respond.

'Someone is trying to make a symbol out of it. We presume it indicates a psionic area, or acts as a territorial marker.'

'Services is presuming the same. We can confirm that it is a mark used by some psi rebels we have had contact with,' Pete advised.

'Outside of the Cape?'

'Yes. How long have you been seeing it for?'

'A couple weeks now,' Boris answered.

'And how widespread is it?'

'From what we've gathered, and remember this isn't like the WU, we think it started in the north. That's where it has been spotted the most. But we have seen it all the way to the waterline.'

'What are the locals making of it? Have they noticed it?'

'They think it's a campaign for a new game. I've begun work on making that our cover story.'

'Our cover ...' Now Pete could see it. The Prime, Admiral Zim, Boris Arkady and now his team. There was an alliance being built to penetrate Atlantic, to make it compliant with the anti-psi laws of the rest of the world. 'You want to clear Atlantic of psis?'

Arkady shrugged and tilted his head. 'Like I said. I don't even believe in psis. But there is a group on the rise and I'm just protecting what is mine. You cannot begrudge me that.'

'Has this group done anything harmful?'

'Not that I am aware of, but who can say what they are forcing people to do? Doing something against your will becomes a murky point when your will can be changed.'

'What do you know about the psi population of Atlantic?' Gock asked.

'I don't know anything. They are not seen and not heard. I presume most of them are in the basement. Down below where the dennies go. Scuttling around with the crabs. I wouldn't go there if I was you, even though it probably has what you're looking for.'

'And what exactly is it you want me to do?' Pete asked.

'Do what you people do. Catch psis. You can go now. I'll contact Zim if I have anything more I want from you.'

Pete and Gock stood and rejoined the soldiers as the portal opened.

'Ten?' Pete asked after the elevator iris closed them in. 'Why are we here?'

'I know as much as you do, Peter Lazarus. They can't tell me more without risk that you would find out.'

'Why do you think we are here then?'

'Just as Mister Arkady said. To do what we do. Catch psis.'

\* \* \*

'You seem tense,' Gock said. They had been sitting in a black box in the Services compound all evening, waiting for Ryu to come online.

'Shouldn't I be? What are you planning here, Prime?'

'I wouldn't be too inquisitive if I was you, Peter. I could have you disciplined.' From his remote command room the Prime ordered Pete's symb to tighten. Always the reminder. 'Tell me, how was Boris Arkady? I've never met him in person.'

'He is a little strange.'

'On the inside or the outside?'

'Overall. He is obsessed with the manifestation.'

'Did he show you the chairs I sent him?'

'He did.'

'Was he pleased with them?'

'He seemed very happy. He was intending to show them off to a lot of people after we left. May I ask what is the connection between the two of you?'

'Common interests is all.'

Pete to Geof: What have you gotten me into here?

'Mister Lazarus, if you would like to bring Geof into the conversation, you need only say. I consider passing messages as petty.'

Geof: I'm coming, just let me dress.

Soon the viewscreen in the briefing room glowed on and showed a close-up of Geof's hairy face.

'Morning, Pete.'

'Morning, Geof.'

'Morning, Prime,' Geof added. 'What's this all about?'

'That's what I asked you. What am I doing here? Why am I not getting any information?'

Geof scrubbed his face. 'What information do you want? What the next operation is? The importance of Atlantic? The overall global strategy?'

'I just want to know what I'm doing. What are we trying to achieve?'

'I'm sorry, Pete. We can't divulge any strategic information to field operatives. It's not just you. We can't risk our plans getting out into the open.'

'Well, at least I know there is a plan now.'

'Are we working together or not?' Geof asked. 'I can't be sure which side you are on any more.'

'Please don't tell me the Prime's theory has gotten to you too? Pierre does not control me.'

'It was my theory. I was simulating meme carrier diffusion. Every possibility has to be considered, Pete. It was nothing personal.'

'Nothing personal? You're suggesting my mind isn't my own. How much more personal could it be?'

'Now you know how us norms feel —'

'Ozenbach, Lazarus. Stop,' Gock ordered. 'We have to keep this civil. For what it is worth, I believe we are on the same side. Peter has done nothing during the reorientation period to suggest otherwise. If it helps you, Peter, I can remind you that you both work for me, so the direction Geof is taking is under my orders. Understood?'

'Yes, Prime,' Peter muttered.

'I suggest we take a five-minute break to cool off. Ozenbach, your joules are low; get yourself something to eat. I would like to come back to the topic of transmission on our return.'

Pete stood and paced the short length of the room. How had the Prime gotten him into this so easily? He'd resisted, but still, here he was in the Cape, leading the charge for Services.

Gock began the second session. 'I think we can all agree that Geof's theory of something akin to a mental virus is troubling. We are monitoring for any signs of a pattern change. Mister Lazarus, can you acknowledge for me that you understand why we must take this threat seriously?'

'Yes. I understand. If there was any foundation for it, I'd be very worried.'

'But can you prove it to be true or false? As a telepath you must have more insight than us?' Geof asked.

'Only that I have never had such a lasting effect on people. My ... manipulations ... last only as long as I maintain them.'

'But what Pierre does is different, isn't it? Remember the midlanders? They had been changed, altered permanently.'

'Yes, but ...' Pete struggled. 'That was very noticeable. We wouldn't be in any doubt if it was so obvious.'

'Pete, I consider you a friend. I hope you think of me that way too. Isn't it possible that Pierre might have gotten better at it?'

'Are you talking about me?'

'I'm just asking you to consider that it's possible.'

'Of course it's possible,' he answered. 'The whole reason I turned myself in was to prove to myself that I wasn't in his control ...' Pete's heart sank as he realised the truth of what he'd just said. He'd never put it into words before.

*It's okay, Peter. It's okay.*

*Arthur?*

*Yes. It's me. I know how you feel. Remember I knew him long before you did.*

*How do I go on?*

*I think you just do, though I wouldn't be the man to ask.*

Gock cleared his throat. 'Would you like to stop for this evening?'

Pete shook his head. 'No. No, thank you.'

'Alright then. We can pause any time. There is no rush to resolve all our problems in one night.'

Pete wondered again if this was the same Ryu Shima he knew originally. There had been a new level of compassion in recent discussions. *Gock, how do you know it is him?* he asked, but received no reaction.

'Geof, Peter would like to know why we have brought him and his squad to Atlantic. I don't think it would hurt to provide him with the reasoning.'

'As you wish, Prime. It is simple enough. The Cape area is one of the largest grey zones on the planet. The monitoring we have is scattered and the majority of it comes indirectly through private surveillance. It is essentially the best place in the world to hide, and we suspect a great many psis may be here and possibly even Pierre Jnr.'

'And you intend to collect them all?'

'If that is the Will,' Gock answered.

'How will we draw them out?'

'One at a time, Pete. Yours is the first ready team, so we don't want you to overdo it. Get to know the territory, learn what you can. That knowledge will come in handy when the other teams arrive.'

'How long will the operation last?'

'This isn't one operation. This is a campaign. We'll be here as long as it takes.'

'And Arkady is cooperating. He is going to help you?'

'He is helping himself, but through common interests our goals will align,' Gock supplied. 'Is that enough? Do you feel you can proceed as directed now?'

'Yes, thank you.'

'Okay, we'll call this session closed. The next period will be trying for us, especially our squads. While we may have personal doubts, we cannot afford to forget the greater mission ...' Gock trailed off. The voice of Ryu Shima had stopped transmitting.

The screen with Geof on it changed to static before defaulting to a bouncing moire pattern. 'Gock? What is happening?'

*Arthur?*

*My arm isn't talking to me.*

Pete rubbed his symb. It responded, but its connection to the Weave was gone.

Pete: Geof? Can you read me?

Nothing.

The room shook as if nudged from outside. The lighting faded from normal to the uncanny red of alarm. The building was under attack.

It was a co-ordinated assault. Two blasts detonated close to the walls, forming gaping rents that led to the subterranean level. One on the east side, the other at the west.

Dark figures in the bound-up rag uniform of the psi resistance leapt from the holes and scattered like jumping insects. They zipped from position to position, using kinetics to accelerate their every movement. Each time they paused they launched projectiles that stuck to the walls and exploded as they zipped away.

There seemed to be no aim other than to breach the walls. Services were quick to respond: marauders poured out to meet the attacks from the corner towers and from the gate, and squibs leapt into the air to drop a rain of lasers on the attackers.

Expecting the counterattack, half the psis jumped and flew straight at the squibs like bullets, splattering their hulls with their sticky explosives. They dropped back to Earth lightly while the squibs burst into flames and crashed to the ground.

The marauders fared no better. As they entered firing range, their interference switches activated as telepaths wrestled control from the controllers, leaving them as useless as statues in the defence of the building.

This left only bots and droids to engage, pumping the vicinity with beam weapons. They were fast, but the rebels moved erratically and the kinetics amongst them crushed the machines' shells until sparks burst from their insides.

Services North was defeated within five minutes. A humiliating defeat for the World Union.

*Arthur — are you alright? What's happening?* Pete sent out.

*They're outside. They're moving so fast.*

*We are cut off from the above. Just like last time.*

*It's not him, Peter*, Arthur reassured him. *Pierre is not out there.*

*Who is it then?*

*There are over a dozen of them.*

Ten burst in through the door. Two of his squad were at his heels, panning their weapons around the room.

'Asset secured,' Ten reported.

'You have a connection? Who are you talking to?' Peter asked.

'Negative. Just recording. The entire embassy has gone into grey. We don't know what's happening.'

'Arthur says there are about a dozen psis outside.'

'How many tappers and benders?'

Pete relayed the question to Arthur.

'He says eight benders, two crossovers and two straight tappers.'

'Looks like they have brought the fight to us after all.' Ten grimaced and flicked hand signals to his men. They covered the entrance and swarmed the room.

'The rebellion is attacking a Services compound?'

'We have to assume they are coming for you and your team. I need to know if you are with us, Pete. Man to man.'

He felt their targeters locking onto his body. 'I'm with you, Ten.'

'Good.' The squad kept him programmed, but turned their attentions elsewhere. 'I would have hoped we'd do better against a dozen.'

'So what do we do?' Pete asked.

'We try to hold out and get to a launch point. Where's Arthur?'

'On the other side of the building.'

'And Risom?'

'I don't know … Give me a moment.'

Pete pushed his mind out. *Arthur, we're looking for Risom. He's out of my range.*

*I'll find him.*

Ten gathered his men together. 'Okay, squad, here's the sitch. There are approximately twelve psi targets who have broken through the walls. They are armed with explosives and acting as a co-ordinated group. We have trained for this. Let's stay tight, pick up who we can and fall back.'

*I've got him.*

'Arthur's found Risom,' Pete reported. 'They are on the south side.'

'Okay. Let's get somewhere we can see what's happening. For now you and Arthur are our eyes. Do it just like we practised in Yantz, Lazarus. Understood?'

'Let me go first,' Pete said.

'We will be one step behind.'

Pete tuned in around him, pinpointing the ten and Gock in his mind before letting himself range out. Just like in Yantz, but with the floor vibrating from explosions and the ground cracking around him.

'Where to, Ten?'

'Where does Arthur say they are?'

*Arthur, where are the attackers?*

*They came from two sides, east and west. They're inside the building now.*

*Is Risom with you?*

*No, but he's close.*

*Get to him. Let him know we're coming.*

380

'Arthur says they came from east and west and are through the defences.'

'The psis have never attacked such a large target before. What are they up to? Nine, any ideas?' Ten asked.

'They might be after the assets, but this doesn't seem like the best approach.'

'What if they're just escalating?' Seven suggested.

Pete caught a slither of something from Gock's mind. 'What was that? Say it out loud, Gock.'

Gock was surprised and fearful of his mind being read like that, but answered without waiting, 'They will want to destroy it completely. If they clear Services out of Atlantic, then they establish a psi territory.'

'He's right,' Nine whispered.

'We need to know what's happening at Services South,' Seven said. 'I bet you anything the same thing is happening there.'

'Right now we concentrate on keeping our assets secure,' Ten took over. 'Lazarus, tell Arthur to go toward the courtyard. We'll rendezvous there and buzz out at the first opportunity. If South has been hit, the twins will be on their way to protect Lazarus. Until then he, Arthur and Risom must be secured. Get those suits to full power, men.'

They prowled forward, weapons scanning back and forth, across and around in steady figure eights. The ground shook again and again, each blast halting the team as they fought to keep their balance.

'They're bombing their way to the sublevels.'

'The reactor!' Nine slapped his palm against his helmet.

'Tell Arthur to hurry it up,' Ten said.

'What happens if they get to the reactor?' Pete asked.

'If they blast it open, then this whole site will become toxic.'

*Hello, Peter.* He heard her greet him just as the wall broke into pieces and exploded toward them. Pete was knocked flat by the blast and his ears rang. He breathed in a lungful of dirty air and began coughing hysterically.

*Oops.*

*Tamsin …*

*Time to pick a side, Peter.*

Pete looked around him. Gock was down, Ten was floored and the rest of the squad seemed to be locked up by their suit fail-safes. He found their frustrated minds and tried to calm them: *Stay down.*

*Peter, where are you? We are down near the courtyard, but we're not alone.*

*Arthur?* Pete answered. *I can feel Risom now. Risom, can you hear me?*

*I'm here, Lazarus. What's the plan?*

*Keep hidden. Tamsin Grey is —*

'The choice is yours, Pete.' Tamsin's voice echoed around them, amplified to maximum. 'Join us or die.'

*Ignore them. You don't want to join them.*

*Don't I?* Risom thought back.

Pete crept toward the hole in the wall and watched as Tamsin welcomed Risom. 'That's the spirit. What about you, Arthur?'

Arthur didn't respond. He was rocking back and forth, his symbiot fighting to control the fear that was building.

*That just leaves you, Pete. Don't you want to come and play with us?*

*This is not the way.*

*I think it is.* She smiled up at him and he stood to look straight at her. She knew where he was; there was no point hiding.

*Tamsin, I'm begging you. You are under Pierre's control. You have to fight him.*

*I really don't, Pete.*

Behind her the rebels gathered, looking up to where Pete stood. Some of them trained their weapons on his position.

'It is done, Grey,' a young man rushed up to her to report.

*Time's up,* she projected to Pete.

'Let's shake it to the ground and get running!' Tamsin shouted to her group. Those with their weapons raised pressed the triggers. Pete swore and dived out of the way. The corridor was rocked by multiple hits. Daylight streamed in through new holes in the walls.

*Arthur?* ... No response.

Pete's symb told him the only way left to go was up and he had no choice but to trust it. There was less damage above and lots of holes to get out from.

He sprinted up the stairwell, making himself breathless. The building rattled and cracked a little bit more with each explosion. His symb stretched to cover his ears and protect him somewhat from the sound while feeding tactical information of the scene, looking for an opening in the offensive line.

An alert blazed into his symbiot in flashing red across his visual overlay. The chemical reactor below the embassy had been ruptured and was out of control. If everyone didn't get out of there soon, they could look forward to a purifying shower of acids.

The explosions stopped. Pete crept to one of the holes in the wall to look out. Ammunition spent, the psis left as they came; with movements like a blink they retreated into the holes in the street.

For the first time in a long time Pete had a decision to make. *Tamsin.* He pushed out. She was still waiting.

*Don't follow me, Pete.*

*You've started a war.*

*I didn't start it. Can't you see that?*

*I'll stop you.*

*You try it. I'm pointing six rounds at your position that will blow your house down.*

*He's controlling you, Tamsin. This isn't the way.*

*No, Pete. This is me. And we're the same, you just haven't decided whose team you are on.*

She raised her block and Pete lost her.

Without warning, communications came back online. A message queue came up before he could respond.

Geof: Pete? What's happening?

Prime: Report in.

Geof: Report. We are sending in backup.

Geof: Tick?

Pete: Tock.

'Pete, you're okay?' Geof's voice came in through his ears, quickly followed by the Prime's demanding him to report.

'Only just. The reactor has been destroyed. You have to get us out of here.'

'Evac is already underway. Are you all that's left?' Ryu asked.

'Arthur is here, but he's catatonic. The ten have been tripped, but they are unharmed. I don't know about the rest of the compound. They were pretty thorough.'

'I'll get the suits cleared, but there's a command log to get through. What happened?' Geof asked.

'Tamsin.'

Geof cursed.

'Did they attack the South?' Pete asked.

'Confirmed. South too.'

Pete looked down at the hole to the basement, a gaping mouth. His sense of the rebels was fading and Pete waited. He had a hunch Tamsin would lower her block once she thought she was out of his range. He waited and waited, feeling nothing. Then at a hundred paces she dropped her guard and he sprung from his position. He would have to be fast to keep her in his field, and he would have to hold his block the whole time to avoid detection.

'Where are you going, Lazarus?' the Prime asked.

'I'm going after them.'

'Not by yourself you're not.'

'Don't, Pete. You can't fight that many,' Geof added.

'I said, no,' Ryu's voice came in slow and cold. Pete felt his symb shrink into his arm and he gasped.

'Please, Prime. Just let me go after her.' He stopped running and dropped to his knees, holding his arm close to his chest as if it would lessen the pain. 'Let me go after them. I won't betray you.' He felt like the symb had grown teeth, tiny spikes that were pushing through toward his bone.

'If you do, this is how you will die.' The pain disappeared; his symb once again became a friendly second skin. 'Go hunt,' Ryu commanded and switched off.

'The twins are en route. They will be right behind you,' Geof said.

Pete rose to his feet and shook his head clear before running into the void.

*Tamsin, this time I am coming for you.*

The way to the basement floor was a scramble down the rubble ramp of the explosion. The light from the hole above came down in a shaft and spilt only a little way inside. Pete could feel the psis faintly, and disappearing east toward the coast.

He ran as fast and quietly as he could. His symb boosted his eyes and the scene was washed with heavy colour and total black shadows. As he made it past the Services zone, the ancient city streets began to distinguish themselves.

The basement was patchy darkness that stank of stale ocean, with a mud floor and crabs that rushed from his steps. Dennies camped around barrel fires and looked over at the sound of him running past, chasing the footsteps in the mud.

Out of nowhere a blow struck him across his chest, knocking him flat on his back. He probed outward. He was sure he hadn't run into anything … Then he was lifted from the ground and held upside-down by his feet.

'What are you doing down here, tapper? This is bender territory,' a voice scraped out from the darkness. Pete couldn't sense where the mind was that was holding him up.

'I'm after the group that just ran through here. It's no business of yours.'

'It's all my business down here, tapper. And you don't have a pass.'

'Oh yes he does,' a cheerful voice called out. There was the sound of something hard hitting something soft. Pete dropped back to the ground. 'One point, Endo.'

Aiko's bot came and lifted Peter up. 'Are you okay?'

'I'm okay. Just a bit winded.'

'Which way are we chasing?'

'You're with me?'

'Just following the command, psi-man.'

'East. But they're splitting up.'

'Then we better run. Jump on my back.'

The twins moved at pace. Their long strides covered tens of metres at a time, small jets on their feet flaring to add lift to each stride. 'Which way, psi-man?'

Pete held his arm forward, pointing with each change of direction that Tamsin took. Now they were gaining fast.

'She's close.'

'Flash it up, Endo.'

'Boomboom.' Her bot levelled a spray of flash and the basement lit up and thunder rocked the underworld.

'Well, that might get their attention.'

'I see five on my sensors. Endo?'

'Concur.'

'No time for a plan, glue and goo until they take us out. Jump off, Pete. Do what you can.'

They fired off another barrage of flash and Pete covered his ears and twisted away. When he turned back, he could see the twinbots moving faster than his eyes could follow, round after round of glowing goo launching at the fleeing figures.

'Bappity bap bap, that's three for me.'

'You have to mask them for full points. Wah?'

'What?'

'I'm being pushed. Psi-man, help me out here.'

He turned to where Aiko was sliding toward the deep water. She'd locked her legs in position, but there was a kinetic standing a few metres away, forcing her backward.

*You don't want to do that, my friend.*

The man looked at Pete and stopped. He just stood limply and blinked. Aiko dove in and masked him, then leapt away before he dropped to the ground.

'Umm, Aiko? I'm in trouble,' Endo patched.

'They got you?'

'Yeah. They're trying to drown my poor bot.'

'Can't help you, Endo. I got my own problems. Pete, where are they?'

'I see them. Give me a sec —'

A block of wood swung across the back of his head and he collapsed into the mud of the shallow water.

'I told you not to follow me,' he heard and passed out.

Tamsin knelt down beside Peter Lazarus, placing her fingers to his wrist. Her makeshift club had opened a jagged wound on the side of his head, blood making half of his face black in this dismal light. She unwrapped her headscarf and pressed it against his skull.

The two robots that had come with him were drowning in the silt, held down by Okonta and his kinetics while they pummelled them into the mud with invisible punches. She could feel La Grêle sliding closer as she arrived with skiffs for them to escape.

*You succeeded.*

*Yes, but my fool chased us down here.*

*Leave him. We must go.*

Tamsin lifted his symbiot arm and used its weight to hold the scarf in place. It was active still and should keep his vitals steady until help could arrive. She met La Grêle at the tide line as the boats ploughed into the shore.

'Let's go.'

'I'll catch up with you.'

'Tamsin,' she admonished.

'Just to make sure he wakes up. I don't want the dennies to tear him apart for supper.'

'You're too soft, Grey.' La Grêle stroked the other woman's face and Tamsin returned the gesture. *You know what you have to do.*

*We both do.*

The psis loaded onto the boats and pulled away. Okonta and Piri waited to one side for Tamsin.

She was worried for Pete. She took off another of her wrappings, wet it in the water and began cleaning off his face.

'Anchali?' he whispered. Tamsin saw another woman in Pete's memory, a beautiful dark-skinned nurse.

'Pete,' she cooed. 'Wake up.'

He blinked his eyes open and was alarmed to discover it was Tamsin hovering above him. 'What are you doing here?'

'I just wanted to make sure you were going to make it.'

He tried to sit up but woozed back down to lie flat. His symbiot told him the ten squad was approaching. She tapped her nail on its shell.

*I can get this off you if you want.*

*I thought it couldn't be done.*

*Easy when you know how.*

*Did Pierre teach you that?*

*Don't be jealous, Pete. You could join us.*

*Join your killing spree? You murdered innocent people back there.*

*Innocent.* She slapped him across the face. *We are the innocent ones.*

The slap wasn't hard, but his head felt fractured already and he entered another swoon. Through Pete, she could feel the squad approaching, the symb's signal directing them to him.

'Don't chase me,' she said, trying to stand up but finding her limbs couldn't move. She felt too heavy to budge. The weight was pushing her knees into the ground and her muscles were paper-thin.

'Stop it.'

*Tamsin.*

*Let go of me.*

*No.*

*I knew you were getting stronger, Pete, but this really is impressive. You're actually exercising control over my mind. I thought you weren't into that kind of thing.*

*I can't let you go.*

*From what I see, you already have.*

*It's not as simple as that.*

*Nothing is. Now let me go.*

*Where is Pierre?*

*I don't know.*

*Tell me.*

*I wouldn't, even if I knew. For your sake.*

*How can you follow him?*

*Because he is strong, Pete, and that is enough. There will be a second manifestation and he will decide who survives. He will free us.*

*He is not a god.*

*He is a god. If only you knew.*

*Tamsin, no. He's a monster. He's out of control.*

*I believe he will free us all. Just like he has freed me. Don't you want to be free, Pete? ... Together?*

*He's controlling you.*

They're *controlling you.*

*They know your disguise now. They'll find you.*

*No, they won't. I'm very good at hiding.*

By now they could both hear the pounding of marauder footsteps.

*Please let me go.* Pete dropped the hold he had on her mind. She kissed him quickly on the lips. *Take care of yourself.*

Peter Lazarus lay very still in the slime, the cool tide pushing the water slowly up to his ears and then retreating again. The mud sucking at his clothes, drawing him deeper with every lap. He felt Tamsin and her psis pulling further away, pushing

391

through the low water until it was deep enough for motors. He closed his eyes and felt the cool of the water as he slipped into unconsciousness, slipped into the pinpricks of pain and looked once more into the eyes of the child.

# Pierre Jnr will save us

The moon was only a half, and cut again horizontally by a single thin cloud. It was set in faded orange tonight, but glowing enough that only the brightest of stars could be seen. Centauri stood out clearest, its promise still potent after all this time and all this failure. The stars of the Chameleon constellation were just beginning to show.

He went through them one by one. By the time Ryu had named the visible stars the vapour of the clouds had diffused and the moon was an almost imperceptible smudge. Then it was gone.

The skyline was a line of lights stretching along the low horizon. Homes, turrets, cranes and hoists. Squibs paced the resting skyways, fluorescent.

*The organism never sleeps,* he thought.

His mother was right. The family needed separation from the Prime. For just such reasons as this. On the other side of the world, clean-up squads were ferrying in Servicemen and ferrying out Citizens needing safe passage home. Negotiations with Atlantic had broken down.

From his needle Ryu could see Shima Palace and felt the pull of it upon his soul. He was glad that Takashi had agreed to join him in this artificial exile. So long as Ryu never demanded any changes in his behaviour or mode of living, he would be happy to stay and more than happy to get away from the guilt-inducing eyes of their parents. He was taking his time to arrive though. Insisting that none but he could touch his dolls; not even a surgical bot with rubberised hands would be gentle enough. He had spent the day carefully wrapping and boxing them.

Today was a catastrophe. A calamity that nearly equalled the manifestation. Services had been deliberately and openly attacked. Atlantic, that cesspool of atavistic fetishists, no longer had even a token presence of the WU. The Weave was livid.

There was no hiding the psi rebellion now. Not that he would want to. Their symbol was appearing in cities worldwide. Psi spotting and reporting was becoming an everyday activity that even children could play. The attack had escalated the fear amongst the general population. The manifestation was now assumed to be the work of the rebellion and the actions Services were taking to make the rest of the world safe were considered fair and justified.

All had played out as Pinter had predicted, which was only cold comfort under the heat of inquisition.

At least Ryu now had a small inner circle who knew his plans and could reassure the rest of the group in their own way. A small group but better than working alone. More of his mother's advice he was following.

There would be fresh tumult in the civics balance, but his position seemed secure and the Prime had dedicated the entirety of the next cycle to making personal calls to new and current members of the Primacy to build rapport and spread the word that while this attack was 'unprovoked' and 'violent', it was not unexpected. Above all he needed them to know that he was prepared.

There was one call he was not looking forward to. He put her on the screens and paced slowly around the room.

'Good evening, Prime.'

'Representative Betts.' For every action there is an equal and opposite reaction. While the fear of the psi rebellion had increased the influence of Ryu and his immediates, so too had Charlotte Betts and her partner Max Angelo been reinforced. At the next count both the tolerants might be included in the Primacy council. 'Congratulations on your rise.'

'Thank you, Prime. I wish only that it was not a tragedy that contributed to it.'

'It is the nature of the Will. Fear and crisis are key motivators.'

'As are hope and opportunity — as I believe my constituency understands.' The younger Betts was proving she had her mother's tongue.

'The reason for my contacting you is to pass on that while this violent attack was unprovoked, we have been preparing for such an event for a long time now.'

'Unprovoked? Do you not consider the hunting and capture of every psionic you can detect to be provocation?'

'We provide peaceful accommodations for those who are collected. Their lifestyle is maintained at an exceptionally high grade.'

'An easy claim to make when access to the islands is so heavily restricted.'

'It is for the people's own safety. Both peoples.'

'But you are breaking families apart. Taking children from parents. And then you don't allow any access? I should be thankful your lack of basic decency is aiding our cause.'

'I take it that this is the essence of your next campaign against our directives.'

'You can be sure it will be.'

'Then I thank you for the advance warning. I will make use of it. Now if you don't mind, Representative Betts, I have many more calls to make.'

'One more question if I may, Prime. When you have collected all the psis in the world, what will you do with them? Where will you put them?'

'On the islands.'

'And as more and more are born. You'll put them on the islands too?'

'Is this a question of capacity?'

'This is about the long-term problem. If the world confines a continually growing population, then at some point the cost to resources will outweigh the benefits.'

'I think that is a question that can wait.'

'Is it? You and I may not be in power by then, but aren't you creating the enemy you are now claiming to fight?'

'Claim? Did you not see the damage that your friendly psionics did to two Services compounds? People died there, Representative Betts, and I'd expect someone in your position to be a bit more respectful of their sacrifice.'

'That is not what I said.'

'There are real threats at work here and you will forgive me if I work to defeat them. You may choose to create artificial problems to boost your standing, but don't forget that by doing so you are also using fear as a tactic. That is all.'

Ryu cut the connection before she could say anything more. That woman and her strange way of thinking was infuriating. No, it was the way the Will was supporting her that was infuriating. At least when Takashi arrived they could start trialling the simulator he had programmed. Then he might never have to talk directly with her again.

Takashi took great care with his girls. He led them by the hand to flat boxes that were the length and width of a single bed, lined with satin, with horseshoe pillows for their heads and feet.

He kissed each of them in turn and wished them goodnight. 'Go to sleep, Jasmin. Wake only when you hear me calling your name.'

'Goodnight, Belle … Poco … Tiffani.' The experience was too erotic for him and the packing was interrupted when he came to Sanchal, but went smoothly after that until all eighteen were stowed and the cases sealed so only he could open them.

The only thing left to do was christen the new doll he had ordered. He always acquired a new doll for landmark times in his life, as rewards. Mostly they had been for breaking down a wall that blocked his data mining, or when he had succeeded in blocking his parents from entering his level of the palace.

He was moving out from the family home and needed the distraction, or a motivator. And this one was special. It looked just like his sister Sato. He planned that she would walk with him all the way to his new home. Arm in arm they would stroll to Ryu's needle and she would enter with him, never to leave.

It would drive the real Sato crazy. The Weave would figure it out quickly and forever remind her that her fat little brother kept a sexual surrogate in her form doing who knows what, who knew how often. But first things first.

Takashi had a ceremony for new dolls. A mesh tea ceremony. He took a long time brewing his mix. Turning the pot, adding ingredients, greedily breathing in the waft of the steam. He sweetened it with cardamom and lime. Then he sipped, sipped, sipped.

From the box stepped a woman that wasn't what he ordered. She was tall and her hair was fair. *There must be a mistake*, he thought — then thought again. She had a fierce body and surprise was a rare arousal for him to come by.

The doll pointed her finger at him, cocked like a pistol.

*Don't move, Takashi. I'm going to probe your mind.*

Within five minutes Tamsin had everything she needed. It was more than she'd hoped for. Takashi had monitored the Prime's communications, everything, including the hunt's investigations. She had suspected the brothers were close, but the bounty of data was beyond her imagining. Of particular interest was the contagion projection from her former colleague Geof.

*Ozenbach, you beautiful hairy man.*

She stood and looked over the spread of the megapolis with a new feeling inside her. Through the bedroom window she saw everything. She saw the data that Geof had collected, the viral spread they were so afraid of. The difference for Tamsin was that she knew what they didn't. She knew how many psis it would take to turn the Will.

All she had to do was get this information to La Grêle as soon as she could. Her network could use it. She took his now cold cup of tea and poured the contents over Takashi's face. A man with mesh-induced memories was always an unreliable witness, even to himself.

Tamsin walked calmly to the elevators and headed down to the market level. There was never any trouble at the Shima market, only times when the throng became so thick they had to push the crowd back to keep the elevator clear. The area around the gate was kept restricted by a barrier and a line of armed men and women in armour, wearing the chameleon sigil. When she had come in, she kept their attention elsewhere. This time she let them see her and their weapons located her instantly.

The flies in the room gathered to watch what would happen next and Tamsin rolled back her second skin and changed her hair to the colour the records knew. When everyone was watching, she began kinetically carving her symbol into the doors behind her, deep gouges cutting through the filigree of family decoration. It didn't take long to complete, but before she was finished the crowd had begun to babble and gasp.

Look at me, she said with her fighting stance. Camera flies buzzed above the heads of the crowd. The guards tried to turn to face her, but she collapsed them where they stood, bringing another gasp from the crowd.

'Know this symbol,' she spoke. 'We will leave it wherever we pass. If you see it, it means we have been there. It means: Psi Freedom Now.

'If you wear it, it means you support us and we will know you mean us no harm. Put it up in your workplaces. Put it on

401

the windows of your homes. Tell the World Union that you don't want this war.

'We don't want it either. The psionic people are just like you. We are human. We wish you no harm. But as humans, if the choice is put to us, then we will respond.'

There was too much noise from the crowd. Most seemed confused by what was happening, but so long as the cameras were getting her message then it didn't matter. The Weave had to capture her declaration.

Services were coming closer, she knew. She didn't have much time. The chatter she picked up from the connected crowd was that they were sending every squad they had against her.

'To my fellow psis. We did not choose this division. Like you, I have tried to exist peacefully and in harmony with all around us. But we have been hunted and confined, like criminals. Like animals. Though we have done no wrong.

'What you have seen in the Cape is the beginning. We have created a zone free of the Services dictatorship. The Cape is now rid of permanent Services interference. We do not know how long this will last.

'If the Primacy allows us to remain in peace, then there will be no more need for conflict. But if they come to imprison any more of our people, then we will fight back.

'Brothers and sisters. Those who have spent their lives pretending not to be special, to not have the gifts you have and to those who are still to discover them: you must take great care. Greater care than ever, for the Prime will not stop. He will not rest until every one of us is disabled.

'If you can hide, then hide. If you can run, run. But if you can hide no longer, and you are tired of running, then join us. We'll be waiting.'

Even before her final words she was reaching out and nudging the minds of the nearby spectators. You didn't need to put a thought in someone's head. It was nearly impossible to craft a clear thought with compatible reasoning. People had stray thoughts all the time that they dismissed. Overheard lyrics, news items, a glanced conversation on the Weave. Rejected from the mind as alien.

Emotions on the other hand were rarely questioned. If someone felt happy, they rarely asked why. And when someone feels fear they don't stop to wonder, they just look for what is causing it. Emotions are primal. She didn't know why she hadn't tried this before. It was so simple. As La Grêle had shown her and just as Arthur did it. Feel the emotions around and then push it back upon them.

Tamsin stepped down from the Shima gate and spread fear in pulses. They feared the psi before them and she created a feedback loop to turn their fear into panic. Tamsin pulsed again, stirring the pot until they started to move. Like spooked cattle, like the frightened herd they were, they began a stampede and she raised her cowl and disappeared into the maddened crowd.

# Epilogue

Shen Li sat at his workbench, continuing to fuss with the metal sphere he had constructed. He was using a hot pin to seal in the fluid he had just injected. It was a delicate and repetitive process as each time he raised the temperature even slightly, the liquid expanded, forcing itself through holes he hadn't completely sealed. He had been at it for hours.

'Nearly done,' he said to himself.

'I'll wait,' somebody responded.

When he next looked up, the sensors told him that someone was in the room, but looking around he could see no one. It was impossible that anything could make it down here without him noticing, without him allowing access through the cage. He didn't think he remembered doing that.

'Who goes there?' he ventured.

'I am Pierre.'

A chill ran through him. 'Are you the one they are looking for?' No answer. 'Can I see you, please?'

Shen blinked and in a chair beside him sat a boy. His head looked painfully large, but his eyes were placid.

'Hello,' Shen said.

'Are you not afraid of me?' the boy asked.

'Are you as terrible as I've been told?'

'I don't think so.'

'I suppose I should be honoured that you have come to visit me.'

'I heard a lot about you. You have an interesting mind.'

'Thank you.'

'You don't think like others do.'

'I try not to.'

'Do you like it here? By yourself?'

'Enough. I can't think around the distractions of others.'

'What are you working on?'

Shen sighed. 'A toy.'

'May I see it?' The boy's small hand reached toward him and Shen uncomplainingly placed the metal ball in his palm. 'What does it do?'

'It is meant to react to your thoughts. I'm not sure it works yet.'

'Oh, I see now.' The boy laughed, making Shen laugh too. 'It is a good toy.'

'I didn't want to tell anyone.'

'I understand. Is there anything else you want to tell me?'

'Yes.' Tears began flowing from Shen's eyes.

'It's okay.' The boy patted him. 'You don't have to say. I know already.'

'Can you make it stop?'

'Yes. I can do that for you.'

Shen wondered why he had been crying. He felt more buoyant than he had in a long time. He took a screwdriver to the far end of the room, to the reinforced door that ticked as if someone was on the other side. He tapped back to it with the tip of the screwdriver and the ticking stopped.

'Why did you call him Kronos?' a voice behind him asked. He turned to find a young boy standing near him. He seemed a boy of seven or eight, young at least, and dressed in fitted linen. Shen couldn't remember where he had come from.

'He was my eleventh experiment: K. I didn't mean to name it; the word just sprang to mind.'

'Why do you keep it?'

'He was alive … he is of my mind. It would be like killing myself and I couldn't do it.' He tapped again at the door. 'Hello, me.'

'Does it hurt you?'

Shen nodded. 'He is going mad in there.'

'Would you like me to make it better?'

Shen nodded again. There was such a pain in his heart for what he had done, birthing an innocent monster.

He didn't know why he was leaning with his head pressed against the cool metal of the vault. He didn't quite know where he was. Everything in the room looked familiar, it looked like he had been here before. He knew the tools, the scraps, where he was up to with each project. He knew this door.

'Where does it go?' he asked. No one answered. He seemed to be alone. Wasn't there someone with him?

The door was secured with a code lock and a thick pin. It opened easily.

'Kronos?'

409

# Acknowledgements

The world of Pierre Jnr has been in development for years and many people have supported and encouraged me along the way. From my earliest writing teachers, David Gray and Kerrie Grundy, to those who have actively goaded both my creative and professional pursuits, Franscois McHardy, Matt Hoy, Rod Morrison. To my family for their forbearance and my lifelong friends and collaborators Jon MacDonald and Matthew Venables, who constantly challenge and inspire in equal measure.

To those who made this thing bigger than I dreamt, Kevin O'Brien, Steph Smith, Deonie Fiford and the HarperVoyager team: thank you for helping birth a bouncing melon-headed boy. Pierre Jnr controls you all.

Lastly I'd like to thank writers and creators past and present, your ideas have filled my mind all my life. I only hope I can do the same for others as you have for me.